ROBYN CARR

PROMISE CANYON

MIRA®

MIRA®

ISBN-13: 978-1-61129-005-9

Recycling programs
for this product may
not exist in your area.

PROMISE CANYON

MIRA and the Star Colophon are trademarks used under license and registered
in Australia, New Zealand, Philippines, United States Patent and Trademark
Office and in other countries.

Printed in U.S.A.

One

Clay Tahoma headed into the mountains of Humboldt County, Northern California, along Highway 36, a narrow road that had lots of sharp turns along the way. According to his GPS the next left would lead him to a town called Virgin River. It appeared to be the nearest town to his destination, the Jensen Veterinary Clinic and Stables, and he wanted to check it out. He was nearing the turnoff when he noticed something up ahead—some pickups parked at the side of the road.

He slowed down and pulled over, curious to see what was going on. He got out of his truck and walked past a number of vehicles toward a large flatbed truck. There were men standing around watching as a forklift with a large cable attached pulled away from the edge of the road. Clay approached one of the men. He was as tall as Clay and wore a plaid shirt, jeans, boots and ball cap. "Whatcha got, friend?" Clay asked.

"One of our town slipped off the road and got stuck— luckily came up against a big tree not too far down the hill. That's how he managed to get out and climb back up."

"Who's pulling him out?" Clay asked.

"Aw, one of our boys has a lot of construction equipment. He's a contractor up this way." The man put out his big hand. "Jack Sheridan. You from around here?"

"Name's Clay Tahoma, originally from Flagstaff and the Navajo Nation. Lately from L.A. I'm up here to work with an old friend, Nathaniel Jensen."

Jack's face took light at that. "Nate's a friend of mine, too! Pleasure to meet you."

Jack introduced Clay to some other men who were standing around—a guy named John, who they called Preacher; Paul, who owned the flatbed and forklift; Dan Brady, who was Paul's foreman; and Noah, the minister whose truck slipped off the road. Noah smiled sheepishly as he shook Clay's hand. No one seemed to react to the sight of a Native American with a ponytail that reached past his waist and an eagle feather in his hat. And right at that moment Noah's old blue Ford truck began to clear the edge of the road.

"Don't you guys have a Highway Department or Fire Department you could call to do this?" Clay asked.

"If we had all day," Jack said. "We tend to take care of ourselves out here. But the big problem is that weak shoulder. Highway Department reinforces it every time we have a slide, but what we really need is something more permanent. A wider road and a guardrail. A long and strong guardrail. We've requested it, but this road doesn't see a lot of travel so our request just gets ignored or denied." He nodded toward the stretch of road he was talking about. "We had a school bus slide down that hill a couple of years ago. Minor injuries, but it could'a been horrible. Now I hold my breath every time there's ice on the road."

"What's the holdup on the guardrail?"

He shrugged. "Real small population in an unincorporated town in a county in recession that has bigger challenges. Like I said, we get used to taking care of things the best we can."

"There's no ice in August," Clay said. "What happened to the pastor?"

"Deer," Noah said. "I came around the curve and there she was. I hardly swerved, but all you have to do is get a little too close to the edge and you're toast. Ohhhh, my poor truck," he said as the vehicle made it to the road.

"Doesn't look any worse than it did, Noah," Jack said.

"Seriously," Preacher said, hands on his hips.

"What are you talking about?" Noah returned indignantly. "It's got several new dents!"

"How can you tell?" Jack asked. "That old truck is one big dent!" Then he turned to Clay and said, "Go easy around these curves and tell Doc Jensen I said hello."

Clay Tahoma drove his diesel truck up to the Jensen Veterinary Clinic and Stables. His truck pulled a large horse trailer that he'd filled with his personal belongings. Shutting off the engine, Clay jumped out of the truck and looked around. The clinic consisted of the veterinary office attached to a big barn, a nice-sized covered round pen for exams, several large pastures for the horses to exercise, the horses' turnout and a couple of small paddocks for controlled, individual turnout. Horses can't be turned out together unless they're acquainted; they can get aggressive with each other.

Opposite the clinic, across what functioned as a

parking area large enough for trucks and trailers, was a house built for a big family. The whole lot was surrounded by trees, full with their summer green, barely swaying in the early-August breeze.

He sniffed the air; he smelled hay, horses, dirt, flowers, contentment. There was honeysuckle nearby; his nose caught it. He got close to the ground, sitting on one boot heel, touching the dirt with his long, tan fingers. He was filled with a feeling of inner peace. This was a good place. A place with promise.

"Is that some old Navajo thing you're doing there?"

Before he could rise Dr. Nathaniel Jensen was walking out of his veterinary office door, wiping his hands on a small blue towel.

Clay laughed and stood up. "Listening for cavalry," he said.

"How was the drive?" Nate asked Clay, stuffing the towel in his pocket and stretching out a hand.

Clay took Nate's hand in a hearty shake. "Long. Boring until I got closer—some guys from Virgin River were hauling a truck up a hill. The town minister slid off the road avoiding a deer. No injuries, just a lot of grumbling. How's the building coming?"

"Excellent. I'll get you something to drink, then take you on a tour." Still shaking Clay's hand, Nate clapped his other hand on his friend's shoulder and said, "I'm really sorry about Isabel, Clay."

Clay smiled with melancholy. "If we hadn't divorced, I wouldn't be here. Besides, not much has really changed between us, except that I moved out of L.A."

"A divorce that hasn't changed much?" Nate asked, tilting his head in question. "Never mind," he said, shaking his head. "Don't tell me. It might be more than I want to know."

Clay laughed in good humor, though he wasn't sure it was funny. He and Isabel weren't right for each other, but that hadn't stopped them from falling in love. They were nothing alike and had little in common beyond the equine industry—and even then they were on completely opposite ends of it. She was a rich horsewoman, a breeder and equestrienne of Swedish descent—a ravishing, delicious blonde who had grown up privileged— while he was a Navajo farrier and veterinary technician who had been raised on a reservation. They had been impossibly attracted to each other, had gotten married, and then encountered predictable problems with communication and lifestyle choices. There was also the resistance from her family, who probably thought he was marrying her money. When Isabel had suggested they divorce, Clay had known it was coming and didn't argue. Divorce was for the best and he'd agreed to her terms, but they hadn't stopped caring about each other. They hadn't stopped sleeping together, either. But Isabel's father probably slept better at night knowing his beautiful, wealthy daughter was no longer legally attached to a Navajo of simple means and some old tribal notions. And he hadn't exactly been thrilled that Clay had a son prior to marrying Isabel. Gabe lived back on Navajo Nation with Clay's parents and extended family, but he was still very much a part of Clay's life and he knew Isabel's family wasn't too happy about that history.

Nate Jensen worked with Clay years ago in Los Angeles, long before Nate took over his father's veterinary practice near Virgin River. It made sense that Nate would have called Clay to ask if he could recommend a good vet tech; Nate's tech had retired after working first for Nate's father and then himself.

"I can think of a number of excellent people," Clay had replied. "But I'm looking for a change and I have family up that way. Any chance you'd consider me?"

Nate jumped on that; Clay was a much-sought-after tech and could function as a farrier, as well. And so here they were.

"I have tea and lemonade in the house," Nate said. "Can I help you unload anything?"

"I think I'll leave everything in the trailer for now," Clay said. "You're sure you don't mind if I just use the tech's overnight quarters?"

"It's yours for as long as you want it. There are other options, of course. You're welcome to share the house with me and Annie—it's just the two of us and there's lots of room. If you want something larger for yourself, we can help you find a house. It's all up to you, my friend. I'm just so damn glad you're here."

Clay smiled warmly. "Thank you, Nathaniel. The tech's quarters will be fine. Let's test that lemonade and look around."

"Dinner with us tonight, Clay?" he asked.

"It would be a privilege. I can't imagine a woman who would be willing to marry you—I look forward to meeting her."

"Annie will blow you away. She's amazing."

Clay was thirty-four and had been reared by Navajo men of legend; there was a long history of chiefs, elders, World War II Code Talkers, mystics and warriors. They were naturalists and spiritualists. His father and uncles had been a lot to take with all their tales and teachings while he was growing up, but eventually he came to appreciate the value of some of their lessons. More than once they'd come to his rescue, banding together to help him turn his life around, and for that alone Clay owed them his respect and gratitude.

He grew up in the mountains and canyons around Flagstaff, on a large family ranch on the Navajo Nation. There was plenty of poverty around the reservation, but some families did well. The Navajos didn't erect casinos but they were rich in magnificent land. The Tahoma family was well-off by comparison to most. They lived simply, then saved, invested, expanded, built and increased the value of what they had. They were not considered wealthy but Clay and his sister grew up in a fine, comfortable home in a family compound that included aunts, uncles and cousins.

When Clay was sixteen, he had a girlfriend. She was a young girl he met at a football game and they fell in love, but under pressure from her parents, she broke up with him. He made a desperate attempt to get her back some months later and found her pregnant. Though she denied it, he knew he was the father, and he was nothing but a boy.

He had no choice but to go to his parents and uncles with the embarrassing news. They, of course, went to the girl's family. The family claimed Clay had nothing to do with their daughter's situation; they had arranged an adoption to a very comfortable Arizona family who had no ties to the Native community.

Legal help was readily available to the Tahoma family through the tribe, and there was no tribe on earth that easily lets go of one of their own. When it became clear how far the Tahomas would go to keep this baby if it proved to be Clay's, the girl's family simply gave up. There were laws protecting Native Americans from being adopted away from their families against the family's will. Clay's son, Gabe, who looked too much like him for anyone to deny their relationship, was brought home to the family.

Clay had raised Gabe while living on the Navajo Nation, and even when he moved to L.A. to try and build his career, he visited his son as often as possible and still talked to him almost every day. But what he really wanted was to have his son with him, close by. Now that he was divorced from Isabel and her intolerant family no longer played a role in his life, maybe he could think about moving Gabe out here with him. Clay's sister, Ursula, had long ago offered to take Gabe in, but Clay's dad insisted she focus on her own children, saying Gabe was fine out in Flagstaff with the Tahoma family. But perhaps Clay could bring him out here now…maybe they could finally be a real father and son. Gabe could benefit from being around horses here at the stables, just as Clay had been around horses when he was growing up.

Clay had bonded with horses at an early age—he seemed to understand them and they understood him. It made sense that he would end up in the horse industry, but he didn't start there. Clay began his education at Northern Arizona University studying business. Classmates who weren't Navajo asked him why he wasn't enrolled in Native American Studies. He said, "You're kidding me, right? I'm a Tahoma—I grew up in Native American Studies." After a couple of years of college, he started working as a farrier, with the skills he'd learned from his father and uncles. He worked rodeos, stables, farms, eventually being formally trained as a farrier and vet tech and doing out-of-town jobs here and there. There were some real rough patches along the way, but by the time he was twenty-eight he was offered a good position with a Southern California breeder of race-horses. He would manage the stable and several hands would work under his supervision. It was hard to leave Gabe and his family behind, but the opportunity was such a good one, and he thought he'd be there for a long time and could eventually move his son out there with him.

But then he fell in love with the breeder's daughter, Isabel. And the rest was history.

The call from Nathaniel, looking for a vet tech and assistant for his relatively small operation, came as a surprise, but it shouldn't have. Nathaniel Jensen had always aspired to own and operate a large equine clinic, breeding horses for competition and racing. His father's large animal practice had been built to provide care for the local livestock, including horses, and the practice became Nathaniel's when his father retired. With the right help, he could do both—breeding and veterinary services. He was expanding, building a second barn that would be complete within weeks. Nate's fiancée, Annie, was an accomplished equestrienne who could teach riding, and Nate was a talented vet. The location might be a bit off the beaten track and served mainly farmers and ranchers who made their living off the land, but there was no reason Nathaniel couldn't make a significant impact on the racing and show industries.

Clay got calls *all* the time. Offers of employment and requests for help. Owners, breeders and vets all wanted him and he'd been quoted salaries that would put what Nate was paying him to shame. Besides his technical skills, there was a rumor he took care not to exploit— that he communicated with the thousand-pound beasts. That he read their minds and they read his. That he was a *horse whisperer.*

Maybe he was, maybe he wasn't. He had luck with horses, but then he never hurried them or took them for granted and they appreciated that. There were three reasons he'd taken Nathaniel's offer without hesitation. Clay's sister lived in the area—Ursula Toopeek was married to the police chief in Grace Valley, a nearby town. Clay was close to Ursula, Tom and their five children. Reason two—Clay respected Nathaniel's skill and ethics and thought the veterinarian would be successful in this expanded endeavor. Plus Nate wasn't hooking his potential success to any mystical ability Clay might have.

And three—it was time to make a break from Isabel.

Clay had known Nate for years but had never before been to his Northern California stable and practice. He was somewhat familiar with the area, having visited his sister in Grace Valley many times. Carrying glasses of lemonade, Nate and Clay toured the compound. Clay was impressed; the new stable under construction was going to be awesome. The vet tech's quarters in the original stable were small but sufficient and had been built for that occasional night there was a sick animal on the premises and someone had to sleep in the stable to be on hand. It was one room with a small bathroom and shower, a bar-sized refrigerator and a couple of kitchenette cupboards. The bed was built into a wall unit with closets, drawers and shelves, much like a Murphy bed. Opposite that, under the only window, was an additional bureau. Virginia, the tech who had recently retired, had added a microwave and hot plate so she could heat her tea or pop her popcorn and had generously left both behind.

There was an industrial-size washer and dryer set in the stable, but Clay was invited to use the set in the house so he wouldn't be mixing up his laundry with animal excretions and blood. Clay laughed. "Like I won't have plenty of that on my clothes in any case."

"Still," Nate said. "Maybe it's psychological. Clay, I'm afraid you won't be happy in the stable quarters for long."

"How do you know?" he asked, lifting a black brow.

"It's too small. There are no amenities. No TV or DVD player. Nothing for the long term. And I don't want you resigning because you're cramped. We have options," Nate said. "If you won't bunk with us in the house, we can always bring in a mobile home. Lots of property here to park it. Or when the new stable is finished in just a few weeks, we could knock out a wall and enlarge the quarters."

Clay chuckled. "Before I hand in my resignation because my digs aren't fancy enough, I'll think about that." He laughed some more, remembering. "You have no idea how I lived when I followed the rodeo around, and in some ways I was happier than I'd ever been."

"That was then. This is now."

Right, Clay thought. Because at a point a man has to have stability if not roots. He'd lived in Isabel's big house, the cooking and cleaning done on a daily basis by a woman named Juanita and her daughter. It was a beautiful home, but he'd never been comfortable there. It was too much house and designed more for entertaining than for daily living. Isabel had many wealthy and influential acquaintances in the horse business and beyond.

It had been six years since they first met. He moved in with her five years ago, married her four years ago, agreed to the divorce two years ago and when it was final, a year and a half ago, he rented a small cabin on the other side of her family's property. But he was frequently invited back to Isabel's big house, back to her bed. She even braved his cabin sometimes. There seemed to be too many complications for them to make a marriage work, but there was undeniable chemistry between them. The only way Clay could stop that was by moving hundreds of miles north.

They exited the new construction and walked into the corral. "The stable quarters will be fine, Nathaniel," Clay said. "Just let me get acclimated and then maybe I'll look around. By the way, I brought a flat screen and I have my iPod. There's also the guitar and flute...."

"Just let me know how I can help," he said. "Hey, there's Annie." He strode across the corral toward a tall woman near the original stable. She was brushing down a handsome Thoroughbred.

Clay followed. He smiled appreciatively, maybe enviously, as Nathaniel slipped an arm around her waist and gave her a brief kiss on the cheek. All the while she was looking over Nathaniel's shoulder at Clay, her smile instant and her eyes sparkling. She transferred the brush to her left hand and stuck out her right. The kiss was barely finished as she said, "You must be Clay. At last! I'm so happy to meet you."

She's so pretty, he thought. She had earthy beauty; she was long-legged and slim, tall in her boots, and she had shiny dark red hair, bright green eyes and a rosy, freckled complexion. Her smile was strong, as was her hand when she grasped Clay's. "Nice to meet you," Clay said. "How'd he get you to agree to marry him?"

She didn't bite at the joke, but rather chuckled and said, "We've been so excited for you to get here. Nate's been telling me stories about some of the experiences you've had together. I understand you have a special relationship with the horses and I have a couple who could use some lessons in manners if you'd just have a word with them."

Clay tipped his head back slightly, smiling, silent and tolerant.

"Don't worry," she said. "I've been told you'd rather not advertise that ability."

"If I could count on it, I might. Some animals are more private than others. I'd hate to crush expectations. I have other skills."

"As I've also been told. Best farrier in the business, complete with digital diagnostic equipment to use in examining gaits, alignment and sports performance. I can't wait for a demonstration."

His grin widened at that. "It's the ONTRACK-EQUINE software. I can't wait to show you."

"But I want to hear about the other skill." She lowered her voice when she said, "The *whispering*."

He tilted his head. "Do you garden?" he asked her.

"She's a farmer's daughter. She can grow anything," Nathaniel answered for her.

Clay focused on Annie. "Do you talk to plants?" When she nodded he asked, "And do they respond by becoming tall and healthy? Robust?"

"Sometimes. I've heard it's the oxygen you breathe on them," she said.

He shook his head. "You emit more carbon dioxide than oxygen. Perhaps it's the sound of your voice or your intention or it could be hypnosis," he said with a shrug. "Whatever that is, it's been working since the sun first warmed the ground. Sometimes it's better not to question but just accept. And also accept that there are no guarantees on anything."

She edged closer. "But if I promise not to advertise this magical thing that works sometimes, will you tell me a little about it? Some of your experiences? Friend to friend?"

"Yes, Annie. I'll tell you training stories as long as you promise to remember no one knows if the horse and I communicated or if the horse just decided to stop screwing around and get with the program."

"Promise," she said with a laugh. "I'd better get in the shower," Annie said. "I'll have dinner ready in an hour and a half. Is there anything you need in the meantime?"

He shook his head. "I'll grab my duffel. Nathaniel will show me where to park the truck and trailer and maybe I'll get my own shower before dinner."

So, Nathaniel was worried about the lack of amenities in the tech's quarters, Clay mused. The biggest problem he could tell from checking the place out was the bed. He was a long-legged man for a regular-size double bed. And the showerhead was a little low. But there'd been times he'd slept in his truck or trailer, camped, borrowed cots or couches, made a nest in a stall, whatever worked. The best thing about Isabel's big house was her extra-long king-size platform bed, good even when she wasn't in it.

There had been no settlement in the divorce; he hadn't wanted anything of hers and she couldn't get away with asking a farrier for money when she had so much personal wealth. It was interesting that they hadn't put together a prenup, that she trusted him in marriage *and* in divorce. He briefly wondered if he'd remembered to thank her for that. Trust was more valuable to Clay than money. But he regretted that he hadn't asked for the bed. That was a good bed. Firm like the ground, not hard like asphalt, but with a little give like the earth. Spacious. Generous. *Long.*

Clay pulled clean jeans out of his duffel and a fresh denim shirt. He brushed off his boots and combed his long, damp hair back into its ponytail. With his bronze skin, high cheekbones and long, silky black ponytail, there was no need for him to drive the point home with Native American affectations, but his cowboy hat sported an eagle feather. Even when his hats got worn to death and he got new ones, he transferred the feather. Finding an eagle feather was good mojo.

He heard the grinding of an engine and distant barking of a dog. Of course his immediate thought was that it was a patient. He put the hat on his head and exited the stable in time to see an old Ford pickup back up to the barn's double doors. It was full of hay and feed. As he watched, a young woman with black hair and tan skin jumped energetically out of the cab, ran around to the back, donned heavy work gloves, dropped the tailgate on the pickup and grabbed a fifty-pound bale. She was short and trim, maybe five foot four and a hundred and fifteen pounds, but she pulled that bale out of the truck, hefted it and carried it into the stable.

Clay backtracked into his new quarters and grabbed a pair of work gloves from his duffel. He joined her at the back of her truck when she returned.

She stopped in her tracks when she saw him. She looked more than surprised, her blue eyes wide with shock. It was almost as if she'd seen a ghost. "Nate didn't mention he had a new hand," she said, eyeing the work gloves.

"I'm Clay," he said, introducing himself. "Let me give you a hand here."

"I have it," she said, moving past him to the truck. She jumped up on the tailgate and pulled another bale toward her.

Clay ignored her dismissal, but he smiled at the sight of her hefting that heavy bale and marching into the stable. She was wearing a denim jacket and he would bet that underneath it she had some shoulders and guns on her that other women would kill for. And that tight round butt in a pair of jeans was pretty sweet, too. But the kid didn't make five and a half feet even in her cowboy boots. Tiny. Firm. *Young.*

He grabbed two bales and followed her into the stable. She actually jumped in surprise when she turned around and found him standing there behind her with a fifty-pound bale in each hand. She seemed to struggle for words for a second and finally settled on, "Thanks, but I can handle it just fine."

"Me, too," he said. "You do the feed delivery all the time?"

"Mondays and Thursdays," she said, lowering her gaze and quickly walking around him, back to the truck. She reached in after another bale, leaving only a couple of feed bags in the back.

He followed her. "Do you have a name?" he bluntly asked.

"Lilly," she said, pulling that bale toward her out of the truck bed. "Yazhi," she added with a grunt.

"You're Hopi?" he asked. His eyebrows rose. "A blue-eyed Hopi?"

She hesitated before answering. You had to have blue-eyed DNA on both sides to get more blue eyes. Lilly's father was unknown to her, but she'd always been told her mother had always believed herself to be one hundred percent Native. "About half, yes," she finally said, hefting the bale. "Where are you from?"

"Flagstaff," he answered.

"Navajo?" she asked.

He smiled lazily. "Yes, ma'am."

"We're historic enemies."

He smiled enthusiastically. "I've gotten over it," he said. "You still mad?"

She rolled her eyes and turned away, carrying her bale. Little Indian girl didn't want to play. Once again he couldn't help but notice the strain in her shoulders, the firm muscles under those jeans. "I don't pay attention to all that stuff," she said as she went into the barn.

Clay chuckled. He grabbed the last two bags of feed, stacked one on top of the other and threw them up on a shoulder, following her. When he caught up with her he asked, "Where do you want the feed?"

"Feed room, with the hay. When did you start here?"

"Actually, today. Have you been delivering feed long?"

"Part-time, a few years. I do it for my grandfather. He owns the feed business. He's an old Hopi man and doesn't like his business out of the family. Trouble is, there's not that much family."

Clay understood all of that, the thing about her people and family. First off, most people preferred their tribal designation when referred to, and family was everything; they were slow to trust anyone outside the race, the tribe, the family.

"Couple of old grandfathers in my family, also," he said by way of understanding. "You're good to help him."

"If I didn't, I'd never hear the end of it."

He began to notice pleasant things about her face. She wore her hair in a sleek, modern cut, short in the back and longer along her jaw. Her brows were beautifully shaped. Her blue eyes sparkled and her lips were glossy. She wasn't wearing makeup and her skin looked like tan butter. Soft and tender. She was beautiful. He guessed she was in her early twenties at most.

"And when you're not delivering feed on Tuesdays and Fridays?" he asked. "What do you do then?"

"Mondays and Thursdays," she corrected. "Pay attention. I work in the feed store."

"Bagging feed?" he asked, his eyebrows lifted curiously.

She put her hands on her hips. "I do the books. Accounts payable and receivable."

"Ah. Married?"

"Listen—"

"Lilly! How's it going?" Nate yelled out, approaching

from the house, followed by three trotting border collies. "I didn't hear you pull up. I see you met Clay, my new assistant."

"Assistant?" she asked.

"Tech, farrier, jack of all horse trades," Nate clarified. "While we're getting business up, Clay can function in a lot of roles."

"Has Virginia actually cleared out? Gone?" Lilly asked.

"Once Clay was en route, she made good on her threats and retired. She's spending more time with her husband and the grandkids. I'll be adding too many new requirements to the equine operation and she really wasn't up for that. I've known Clay for a long time. He has a good reputation in the horse industry. We worked together years ago in Los Angeles County."

"I just saw her a few days ago. I didn't realize she was that close to her last day. Actually, I thought it would be months," Lilly said.

"So did we, Virginia and I. But I was lucky enough to get Clay up here from L.A. in a matter of days. As soon as he said yes to the job, Virginia said, 'Thank God,' and headed for home. She offered to come back to help or do some job training if Clay needed it, but she's ready for a little time on her own. She's been talking retirement for at least a couple of years now but until I found Annie, she wouldn't leave me alone on the property. She thought I'd mess up the practice." Nate shook his head in silent laughter.

"You'll miss her," Lilly said.

"I know where to find her if I miss her, and so do you! Drop in on her sometime. She promises regular cookies for the clinic."

"I'll do that. I'll make it a point. Let me get your vitamin supplements," she said, turning to pull a very large plastic jar out of the truck bed. She handed it off to Nate and then fetched her clipboard from the cab so he could sign off on the feed.

"I'm taking delivery on a horse in a couple of days, Lilly. An Arabian. He's coming for boarding and training, though I think the owner is going to need more training than the horse. Increase the feed for my next order, please. And tell your grandfather I said hello."

"Absolutely. See you later," she said, jumping in her truck to head out.

When the truck had cleared the drive, Clay asked, "Is she always in and out of here that fast?"

"She's pretty efficient. She's always on schedule. Her grandpa Yaz counts on her. I don't know if there's other family. As far as I know, Lilly is the only other Yahzi who works in the business."

"There's a new horse coming?" Clay asked. "What's that about?"

"Last-minute deal," Nathaniel said. "A woman who doesn't know much about horses but has an unfortunate excess of money bought herself an expensive Arabian from a good line, learned about enough to keep him alive but can't get near him. Her stable hand can barely get a halter on him and saddling him is out of the question. If they can get him in the trailer, the hand is going to bring him over here to board so we can work with him. The owner wants to ride him, but if that doesn't work out she's thinking of selling him to replace him with a gentler horse. She thinks the horse is defective."

Clay lifted a brow. "Gelding?"

"Oh, no," Nate said with a laugh. "Two-year-old stud

colt from the national champion Magnum Psyche blood-lines. I had a look at him—he'd be too much horse for a lot of people."

"She bought herself a young *stallion?*" Clay asked, then whistled.

Nate slapped a hand on Clay's shoulder. "Did I mention I'm glad you're here?"

"I haven't unpacked and you have a special project for me," he said, trying to disguise his pleasure.

Nathaniel grinned. "You don't fool me. You were a little afraid of being bored and now you're relieved that there's a difficult horse coming. It's written all over your face. Come on—Annie made pot roast. You'll think you've died and gone to heaven."

Two

Lilly was a bit shaken as she drove away from the Jensen stable. The new assistant was drop-dead gorgeous and totally flirting with her. He didn't have to carry two fifty-pound sacks of feed at a time into the feed room! A show-off, trying to impress her with his strength, his bulging arms, as if that would make her life worth living.

Well, he was in for a few surprises if he wanted to get a rise out of her. First of all, she'd grown up around a lot of Native males and had them all figured out. Many of them developed self-esteem issues in adolescence, stemming from the discrimination they faced, and it seemed one of the best ways they could feel better about themselves was by reeling in a girl. That pumped 'em right up, got their testosterone flowing, kicked their confidence into gear. Well, she'd been reeled in, cruelly dumped and survived it; she wasn't going there again!

And most of them, at least the ones she had known, had old-fashioned ideas about calling all the shots. From the time they glanced down and noticed they were males, they assumed the dominant role. Well, Lilly had enough on her plate with a grandfather who liked running things. That was one of many reasons she stayed away from other Native men. She was capable of taking care of herself and not at all afraid of being a woman on her own. In fact, she rather liked it.

Then there was that whole Hopi/Navajo thing; their tribal traditions and customs. Tons of it was ingrained in her as her grandfather never let it go. She never tried to deny her connection to the Native community, but she'd been trying to get some distance from all of that for a long time. She felt she could be a proud Hopi woman without being constantly steeped in all the old tribal stuff. After all she was also French, German, Polish and Irish—or so her mother had told her grandfather. She never did give Lilly's father's name, but she knew his heritage.

Lilly's mother, only a teenager herself when Lilly was born, had left her to be raised by her grandparents. She ran off, no one knew where. Friends from the Hopi reservation had heard that Lilly's mother died, but had no proof or details. But Lilly and her grandparents had never heard from her again, and neither of them had bothered trying to find any more information about her.

Her grandfather was a strong, formidable man. When her grandmother was alive, he'd treated her as if she were made of solid gold, but Grandma still let him make all the decisions. Lilly was not looking for one of those old-world tribal relationships either—one of the reasons that when she did date, which was rare, she stuck to the beige race and avoided those too-hot-to-handle Native men.

She'd been in love with a Navajo once. She had been

a mere child of thirteen and he'd been eighteen. He'd pressed every button she had—he was a temptation so powerful she had defied her grandfather to be with him. But she'd gotten much more than she could handle. And when their relationship had met its tragic end, she swore she'd never be tempted by another like him. Never.

No doubt that was why the sudden appearance of Clay shook her. He was at least equal in handsomeness to that long-ago boy who had devastated her. No, not equal. Clay might have been the most beautiful man she'd ever seen. Huge. Powerful. Exotic.

Lilly drove the pickup around yet another curve en route back to the feed warehouse when she came upon something that caught her attention—a black mound in the grass on the other side of a poorly maintained barbed wire fence. A horse, lying on the ground. It was not an altogether unusual sight, but Lilly slowed. As she neared, she kept sensing that something was not right about this. Then she saw the horse thrashing on the ground.

When Lilly and her grandparents had lived back on the Hopi reservation, she'd been around her neighbor's horses a great deal, and had done a lot of riding as a young girl. But since Lilly and her grandfather had moved to California when Lilly was thirteen she'd been around feed more often than the animals that ate it. Her grandfather had bought the feed and grain business, but he didn't keep any livestock. She rode rarely now, and only in the last couple of years, but she still remembered a lot about horses.

She pulled onto the shoulder and watched the horse. The mare jolted suddenly, rolled a bit, then stood and attempted to stretch out, curling her lip and pawing at the ground with her front hooves and kicking with her hind. Then down she went again.

Shit, Lilly thought. That horse was sick. *Very* sick. The only house in sight was on the wrong side of the road, but maybe someone there could direct her to the owners of this pasture, this horse. She went to the house, and an unshaven man in a T-shirt answered the door. He didn't know the name of the horse's owner, but he knew where it came from. He gave her directions up the road to the next turnoff and another quarter mile to an old farmhouse and barn. She went quickly, and what she found there stunned and confused her.

She called Dr. Jensen's cell phone at once. "Nathaniel, I found a sick mare by the side of the road and the owner's property is deserted. It looks abandoned. No one in the house, all the furniture's gone, a couple of real skinny dogs are hanging out around the barn, the feed bin's half-full of grain and trough's empty. The horse is rolling, kicking, curling, sweating…"

"Where are you, Lilly?"

"Off 36 and Bell Road at a crossroad called Mercury Pass, but there's no road sign. A neighbor directed me to this old farmhouse. The horse is rolling around just off Bell near 36."

"I know the property," Nathaniel said. "That's the Jeromes'. As far as I know, they just had the one horse—a twelve-year-old black mare. But I haven't been out there in about a year…maybe longer."

She was, in fact, a very pretty black mare with back stockings and a diamond on her forehead. "That's her. She's a beauty. And she's in a *bad* way."

"I'll be there soon as I can," he said, clicking off.

Lilly wanted to get back to the horse, but she couldn't

resist a quick check of the barn and around the outside to be sure there weren't any other casualties—horses, goats, cows or chickens. The small corral was neglected and full of manure, the barn was a filthy mess, manure and trash littering the place. There was no gear for the horse in the barn that she could see, no bridle, saddle or grooming gear. Behind the barn she found a chicken coop, the door left open, a few broken shells on the ground and a lot of scattered feathers. Had the chickens been left as food for the pumas, coyotes and wild dogs?

She'd seen enough. She jumped in the truck and sped back to the roadside. The horse was up again, stretching out her legs and curling her lip. She was in abdominal pain—that was clear. She kicked at her midsection a little, unsuccessfully, and then she was on the ground again, rolling around before lying listless and sweating. Lilly jumped the fence and kneeled at the horse's head, stroking her snout and murmuring that everything would be all right, though she wasn't the least confident about that.

It seemed an eternity before she saw a truck pulling a horse trailer come into view. When it came closer she saw that Nathaniel had brought his new assistant with him. Just as they were getting out of the truck the horse was struggling to her feet again, going through all the same motions.

"What's going on here, Lilly?" Nathaniel asked. He braced both hands on a fence post and leaped over the barbed wire while Clay went to the back of the horse trailer and opened it up, lowering the ramp.

"She's acting like colic, Doc. And like she's had it awhile."

"You find anyone around the Jeromes'?"

"No. It's like they ran off. There was a chicken coop behind the barn, door standing open, broken eggs and a lot of feathers. You don't suppose…?"

"That they left the horse in the pasture, the henhouse door open, the dogs to fend for themselves?" Nathaniel pulled back the horse's lips to look at her gums. He listened to her stomach for gut sounds and felt her tight belly, an action that made her prance a little. "This sort of thing hasn't happened in such numbers since the Depression, or so my dad tells me. With unemployment so high and money so tight, folks are faced with hard choices. Sometimes they have to decide between feeding their kids or their animals. Some abandon their property, mortgages and animals and just look for shelter."

"They took their furniture," she said. "The house is empty. So is the grain bin and trough. Think it's possible they put out the last of the feed and left some water for this horse and she gorged herself?"

"Anything is possible. A few weeks ago some folks from downriver found a dead seven-year-old gelding by the road, starved. I didn't know the horse. Someone who couldn't afford to keep it might've taken it to an empty pasture and left him, hoping it would be rescued."

"They couldn't've sold him?"

"In this economy? It's tough."

Clay joined them, a halter and lead rope in his hand. Nate took them from him and said, "You mind fetching my bag, Clay? And please, draw up 10cc of Banamine."

"Got it," he said.

"What can you do, Nate?" she asked him.

"I'll get her temperature, make sure she's not diseased.

They could've poisoned her to put her down before leaving her, but I'd be surprised by that. Most folks who run into situations that force them to leave their animals behind hope for the best. If we have advanced colic, I'll give her some Banamine for the pain, run a stomach tube into her and administer some mineral oil, see if that moves things along. If it's an intestinal twist and she needs surgery…well, let's hope it's a blockage…"

Lilly bit her lip; she understood. Nathaniel couldn't do surgery, hospitalize the equine patient and care for her while she was at great risk of expiring. She was an orphan. No vet could afford a lot of expensive charity cases.

When Clay returned with the bag and drug, Lilly stepped back out of their way and marveled at the way they worked together. Clay wasn't flirting now; he was focused on the horse and assisting his vet. Over the course of about thirty minutes, the animal was agitated, stretching and kicking. Clay had the halter on her and held the lead rope so he could control her movements somewhat, keeping her upright so she wouldn't twist her intestines, but he mainly stroked her and held her as motionless as possible while Nathaniel first completed his exam and then injected her with Banamine. That seemed to almost immediately quiet the animal. But she wasn't real crazy about the stomach tube that was run down her throat.

It was amazing the way Clay and Nathaniel worked together, as if they'd been in this situation a hundred times before. When the mare was resisting the tubing, Lilly stepped forward to help in some way, but Clay's hand came up, palm toward her. "No, Lilly. She's in pain and when she's thrashing, she could kick you. Stay back, please," he said quietly, calmly.

After the mineral oil was infused and the tubing removed, the horse moved as though she'd go down again, but Nathaniel instructed Clay to try to keep her up, walking her slowly and quietly. If she continued rolling around on the ground, she increased the chances of twisting her intestines into a knot.

"Will you take her to your stable?" Lilly asked Nate.

"Not anytime soon," he said. "Maybe later, if the oil works on loosening up a blockage. The truth? This horse is lucky if it's a blockage and there's a little movement because putting her in the trailer in her condition isn't going to be good for me or her—she's bound to kick it into tin cans or hurt herself as she struggles to ease the pain in her belly."

"You'll leave her here?"

"Probably have to, Lilly. But with any luck, the treatment will work and we'll find a relieved horse by morning. You can go, Lilly. Clay and I will take it from here."

"But… But will you leave her alone out here?" she asked.

"We're not going to leave her in this condition. I'll stay until I see which way it's going. And if it gets worse…"

She stiffened immediately. "What?" she said.

"She has no owner that we can find and she's in pain," Nathaniel said. "If it gets worse, I'll put her down."

"No—"

"She'll get every chance and every possible treatment, Lilly," Clay said, his low voice soft and gentle.

Reassuring. "We won't let go of a horse that has a chance."

"You promise?" she asked.

"Promise," he said, giving her a firm nod. "Go on home. You've done enough. And thank you."

She backed away almost fearfully. "No. Thank *you*," she said. "Please take care of her."

"Of course," Clay said. "Try not to worry."

As Lilly backed away, she muttered, "How could someone just leave her like that? Abandon her...?" But Clay and Nathaniel didn't hear her; they were busy working with the horse.

When Lilly delivered feed for her grandfather, who everyone called Yaz, she used one of the company trucks. Her personal vehicle was a little red Jeep, which she'd park in the rear of the store. She spent the majority of her time managing invoices, ordering supplies and cutting payroll checks. Two afternoons a week she'd take out one of Yaz's company trucks, and one of the guys who worked for him would load up the back each time she returned empty after deliveries. She made several runs to smaller stables and horse properties. The larger orders to big ranches and farms were handled by Yaz and a couple of his employees on the flatbed truck. Yaz was sixty-nine and still strong as a bull. Some farmers and ranchers grew their own feed; some picked up their feed and saved a little money.

Lilly took the pickup keys and clipboard to Yaz's desk at the back of the store. "Got it done, Grandpa," she said, handing off the paperwork and keys. "Need anything more from me today?"

"Thank you, Lilly. Any problems I should know about?"

"The delivery went just fine. Dr. Jensen is taking on another horse tomorrow so I'll increase his delivery for the next time."

"Does he need a special run?"

"He didn't ask for an extra delivery, just an increase. I looked in the feed room and he's well stocked. And he has a new guy working for him." Her grandfather didn't even look up from the signed delivery receipts she had handed him. "Virginia went ahead and retired the second the new guy was on his way," she said. He nodded at his paperwork. "He hired himself an assistant. Big guy. A Navajo."

Yaz looked up then and connected eyes with his granddaughter. He smiled just slightly. "Is that a fact? Why'd he come here?"

Lilly almost blushed; she had no idea because she didn't ask him about himself at all. He had asked her questions, general flirting and being friendly she supposed, but all she knew of him was that he was Navajo and could carry two bales at a time. "I didn't really talk to him. Just to say hello, that's all."

"Is he good with horses?"

"Yes, he… Grandpa, on my way home I found a sick horse by the road. Probably colic. I called Nathaniel and he came out with Clay—that's the new guy's name, Clay. They came right away but what we found out, the people who owned that pasture where the mare was and the house and barn that went with it, they cleared out and left their animals to starve. Nathaniel says they're seeing more of that sort of thing all the time because of the economy and unemployment."

"People who were having a hard time before are having a harder time now," Yaz said.

"He said sometimes they have to choose between feeding their children and their animals. But there are rescue groups! Why wouldn't they call a rescue group?"

Yaz looked up at her, his dark eyes gathering a little moisture, the flesh below and at the corners crepey and wrinkled. "Even the rescue groups are stretched to the limit. Then there's pride and shame," he said. He leaned back in his old desk chair. "When a man is running out on his debts, he doesn't usually say goodbye."

"You'd think whoever did that could've swallowed enough pride to let someone know the animals were left behind," she said.

"You'd think," he agreed. "The horse going to be all right?"

She shrugged. "Nathaniel was treating her with pain medication and mineral oil when I left, even though there's no one to pay him."

Yaz looked down at the clipboard again, paging through her collection of deliveries. "Well, at least she got the best, and at a bargain."

"True," Lilly agreed softly. "You'll want to meet the new man—he grew up around Flagstaff."

A smile hinted at the corners of Yaz's mouth. "It will be good to see a neighbor, even an inferior neighbor." The Hopi and Navajo had long lived side by side, alternately getting along and squabbling. "I look forward to knowing him. See you on Sunday." That was the day they set aside to eat together at his house. It was a traditional house—Lilly cooked. She also made sure her grandfather's house was clean and his laundry done.

So much for her nontraditional ways....

"Sunday," she echoed, leaving the warehouse.

Her heart was still heavy, however. It was likely Lilly had an issue with this business about the horse for more than one reason. Lilly's mother had abandoned her when she was an infant, leaving her with her grandparents on the reservation in Arizona. Lilly's grandma had passed when Lilly was nine and while Yaz was grief-stricken, he was not intimidated by the prospect of raising her alone, without the help of a woman. In fact, it was possible he'd risen to the occasion. He seemed to relish his parenting duties. And at thirteen, the boy she'd loved had run out on her, leaving her high and dry, and with bigger problems than she knew how to deal with. Abandonment was an issue for her and she knew it.

It was that same year that Yaz brought her to California. He heard about the sale of the feed store from a friend of a friend, and for his entire life on the reservation he'd been saving and investing for just such an opportunity. That had been fourteen years ago. She hadn't moved out of her grandfather's house until she was twenty-five and that had been a difficult transition; he clearly wanted her to stay with him forever or at least until she was married.

While Lilly was on her way to her little rented house at the edge of Fortuna, she realized she'd have to go back to that pasture. She needed to know if the horse was there alone, if she was hurting, if she was sick, if she was... Her mind couldn't form the word *dead*. She needed closure. And if Nathaniel and Clay had left her alone, Lilly would be the one to stay with her until she

was either recovered or… Again, she couldn't allow
certain potential outcomes to enter her mind.

But when she did allow her mind to go that far, she
knew that if the horse had to be put down, Lilly would
stroke her head and send her off with loving words.

By the time she got home, fixed herself a portobello,
cheese, pepper and tomato sandwich and wrapped it, a
couple of hours had passed since she'd first found the
horse. She grabbed a bag of soy nuts and almonds, a
bottle of apple juice and one of water. Then she dug
through the detached garage for an old sleeping bag that
smelled vaguely of storage. If the horse didn't have serious digestion problems, she'd have taken a few carrots
and a couple of apples, but the mare would be off food
for the time being.

It was almost seven by the time she was back on the
road, seven-thirty by the time she approached the place
she'd found the mare. It was August; the sun was just
lowering in the west. Because of the tall trees it dark-
ened a bit earlier here than on the Pacific Coast. She was
shocked to see that not only were the truck and trailer
still there, but surrounded by reflective, triangular col-
lapsible cones to notify any other vehicles that might
come along after dark.

Lilly pulled up in front of the pickup and got out,
leaving her food behind. It was already dusk, but she
could see Clay walking the horse in a wide circle around
the pasture. She remembered from her horse days in
childhood that was one of the treatments for colic, a little
walking. Not too much; a safe and moderate amount.
She didn't see Dr. Jensen.

She jumped the fence to get in the pasture. Soon

enough he came toward her, leading the mare. "You're back," he said. "Need something?"

"Yes," Lilly answered, "I need to know if she's going to be all right."

"She's hanging in there. She needs a little time."

"She's not getting worse, is she?"

"Nope, she's doing fine. But she's pumped full of Banamine and it's a waiting game to see if the treatment worked for her. She's still stressed. She's still pawing and stretching out. This is an unhappy lady here. Is that the only reason you're here?"

Lilly shrugged and put her hands in the back pockets of her jeans. "I was afraid you'd leave her and she'd be... I didn't want her to be alone. In case... Well, in case she got a lot worse."

"Lilly," he said, bending a little until their eyes connected. "I wouldn't leave a sick animal unless I had to. I'll see it through. You don't have to worry." He straightened. "Those blue eyes really freak me out."

She grinned at him. "Freaked out my grandfather, too."

"I'll bet the old Hopi just about passed out."

"Well, since you have to have the blue DNA on both sides and he thinks both himself and my grandma are a hundred percent Native, it means there was a bad pilgrim back there somewhere." She smiled brightly. "Have you eaten?"

"Not yet," he said.

"Would you like half a sandwich?"

He lifted one expressive brow. "Whatcha got?"

"Mushroom, tomato, peppers and cheese. On wheat."

He grimaced. "I was promised a welcome dinner of pot roast," he informed her.

She smiled lazily. "Do they deliver?"

"I sincerely hope so, but it's more likely there will be leftovers. Annie came to fetch Nathaniel home and I offered to stay on, but I think I'm going to be able to take the horse back to the clinic before too much—"

Right then the horse decided to stretch out again to ease her abdominal pain.

"You're going to take her to Nathaniel's?"

"Lilly, it's for the convenience of dealing with her condition, not to give her a new home. Nate didn't want to transport her until she was more stable and I think we're just about there, but that doesn't guarantee her recovery. If she doesn't improve, he won't let her go on like this, in pain."

"I understand."

"What were you going to do out here at night?"

"I don't know. Eat my sandwich. Be with her, I guess."

He tilted his head. "Do you have horses?"

She shook her head. "Never have, but when I was real young I rode some. Well, it's been a long time, but when I was a kid, I was surrounded by them. Back on the reservation. I've ridden with Annie a few times, but I'm not around horses much, just when I deliver their feed. Finding her like this, it kind of made me responsible in a way. At least for making sure she wasn't alone."

"It could be midnight before she's either better, worse, ready to transport or..." He didn't finish.

"I brought a jacket and a—" She felt silly about the sleeping bag. Did she really plan to lie on the ground next to a twisting, kicking horse through the night? Even in August, in the mountains or surrounded by them, it was cold after dark. "I'd be willing to share the sandwich," she said. "Who knows, you might not get pot roast delivery for a long time."

"I don't know. I feel like I'm taking a chance on a mushroom sandwich."

"You might actually like it. Hey, you aren't planning on leaving this horse in the pasture, are you? Because, if I remember, she can't be grazing. Isn't she off food?"

"I'm on top of it, Lilly. The barn and corral where she was kept—Nathaniel looked at it and it's out of the question. It's filthy, cluttered, the fence in poor condition. Once she takes a turn for the better, I'm going to take her to Nathaniel's clinic. And until she's feeling a lot better, believe me, I won't let her graze. She's miserable."

"Yeah," Lilly said, connecting with the mare's eyes. "Be right back," she said. She jogged toward her Jeep. With her hands on a fence post, she put one booted foot on the top barbed wire, pressed down and jumped over. Getting back over the fence was slightly more difficult— her hands were full of food and drink. "Bottled water or apple juice?" she asked him.

"You first," he said. "I have a couple of warm colas in the truck."

She smirked and handed him the apple juice. "This is much better for you. And hold these, please."

"Nuts?" he asked.

"Also good for you, as is the half sandwich."

"I don't know.…"

"Be a big boy," she said, and then thought, he is really such a big boy! But she kept her eyes cast down and opened the wrapping of her sandwich. She'd already cut it in half, thankfully. She put her water on the ground and traded with him—sandwich for bags of nuts. "Think she'll let us sit down?" she asked.

Clay dropped the rope and backed away. "Better give her space. She isn't thinking about her human friends right now. She could drop on you and grind you right into the pasture."

Lilly followed him about ten feet away from the mare, then carefully sat. "I probably have a...a blanket or sleeping bag in the Jeep...." She still couldn't admit to planning to sleep beside a sick horse she had no real connection to.

"Yeah, me, too," he said. "But the ground is dry enough." Down he went, crossing his legs. "And so. We have a *mushroom* sandwich."

"One of my favorites," she said. "What brought you to Nate's practice?" With the question, she bit into hers.

"I have family nearby. A married sister with a family in Grace Valley. And if you come from the mountains, the cold mountains at about seven thousand feet, Los Angeles County is a little low, hot and smoggy. Even out in the hills."

"Why don't you just go back to Flagstaff?"

"Because there's no opportunity in Flagstaff. Do you know how many Northern Arizona U PhDs are waiting tables there because they just can't make themselves leave? And God knows there aren't any rich horse breeders looking for help on the reservation. Nah, this is pretty, around here, and close to family, and Nathaniel is good people and he's offering me a terrific opportunity to help grow his business. How'd you end up here?" he asked. And then he bit into his sandwich. He chewed a bit, then winced and made a face.

She couldn't help it—she laughed and covered her mouth with her hand.

"How do you *eat* this?" he asked.

"I like it," she said, still laughing. "Give it to me. Eat nuts, that'll hold you awhile."

"So?" he asked, passing the sandwich back.

"So my grandma died and a few years later my grandpa heard through a friend that the feed company was for sale and he thought he could make it work. He'd always wanted his own business. And it was just him and me, so..."

"Where are your parents?" he asked.

"Anyone's guess," she answered, filling her mouth again.

He let her chew. He piled nuts in his mouth while she worked on her mouthful. When she had finally swallowed, he asked, "So, are you...?"

"Grandpa and I moved here when I was thirteen and I think it was the right move," she said, cutting off his next question. "Because I did well in school, made new friends, and although Yaz will never admit it, he's making money on silage and hay." She laughed and shook her head. "Don't try to trick an old Hopi into telling you what he's got in his pocket. He's crafty."

Clay studied her for a moment, really wanting to know a lot more about her and fully aware she was keeping her answers impersonal. "I think maybe you're crafty, too."

She smiled as though she had a secret. "I have been trained by the best."

She bit into her sandwich and the mare farted.

"Well, that was nice," Lilly said. "Very ladylike."

Clay laughed at her. "Music to my ears," he said.

He stood up. "I think she'll be going in the trailer real soon. I think what you call that in veterinary medicine is *progress*."

Lilly hated the idea of ending the conversation even if it was getting a little close for comfort for her. "Shouldn't you wait until you're sure that blockage clears?"

"As long as she's not in pain and there's progress, I'll be more than happy to hose out the trailer when I'm back at the clinic." He stood and went to the mare, took the lead rope and led her to the fence. He pulled a small wire cutter out of his back pocket and made fast work of the barbed-wire fence. Once cut, the wire sprang away and gave them an exit. Why worry about the pasture's security now? The owners had clearly fled.

But he turned toward Lilly. She cradled all her picnic stuff in her arms—nuts, remaining sandwich, bottles.... "That was so nice, Lilly," he said. "So nice that you'd worry about the horse and come to be with her. And so nice that you'd share your meal with me."

"Even though it was a mushroom sandwich?" she asked.

When he looked at her, his brows relaxed and his eyes seemed to darken. "Even though," he said.

Then he made clicking noises and said, "Come on, precious. Let's get you outta here...." And he led her to the trailer.

Three

Colic, a term that covered a litany of equine intestinal disorders from a bowel obstruction to twisted intestines, was one of the most common and dangerous illnesses in horses. If diagnosed early, treated quickly and if it wasn't the critical variety that required surgery, the prognosis was typically good.

Clay delivered the mare to the Jensen stable and reported improved gut sounds and even a little excrement in the trailer, evidence that there was some digestive action and the blockage might clear. Luckily for him, he was able to wash up, sit down to some of Annie's fantastic pot roast and visit with his friends before the worst of the horse's recovery happened in the stall. When he returned to the stable, he could have sworn the mare was smiling.

"Well," he said. "Feeling better?" She saw him and whinnied. "Tender belly, I'll bet. And Nathaniel's records of his single visit to the Jerome house indicate your name is Blue Rhapsody. You're a beauty. Must've half killed them to leave you behind." Then he shook his head and muttered, "Things must've gotten real bad around the old homestead."

One anonymous phone call to Nathaniel Jensen's answering machine stating that the horse was being abandoned might have seen a brighter immediate future for the mare. Nathaniel might not be in the rescue business, but he'd have tried his best to make arrangements.

At 6:00 a.m. Clay turned her out in one of the small paddocks where she could see the Jensen horses. Then he went about the business of cleaning stalls. When he'd finished that, he went back to check on the mare. It shouldn't have surprised him at all to find that Hopi girl leaning on the fence at the crack of dawn, watching her. He got rid of the rake and leaned on the rail beside her. "They call her Blue Rhapsody."

"Blue," she said in a breath, keeping her eyes on the horse. "Perfect." Then she turned toward him. "And she's going to be all right?"

"Unless there's a chronic condition that hasn't revealed itself," he said with a shrug. "My instincts say you probably had it right—the owners left out feed, thinking they'd give her a better chance to survive and be found, and it did more harm than good."

"What will happen to her now?" Lilly asked.

"If she proves healthy and sound, which I assume she will, we'll make some calls and see if we can place her. She's actually a valuable horse. They shouldn't have left her. A black Arabian with those markings, gentle, bred a few times which means a proven uterus and she's a good potential surrogate, twelve isn't too old..."

"I can't imagine why they didn't look for at least a few hundred dollars for her," Lilly said.

"Maybe they did," Clay said. "Or maybe they came

by the horse some other way—took her to help some-one out, or she was a gift for the kids, or something like that—and they weren't really aware of her poten-tial value. They weren't horse people. They just had Blue."

"Blue," she repeated. "It suits her."

"She's twelve and yet Nathaniel only made one visit to that farm a year ago. He didn't know her. That means she's not from around here. She has a story we don't know."

They stood quietly and watched her in the paddock. She seemed peaceful and relaxed. "I should talk to Na-thaniel about her," Lilly said.

"Oh?"

"Will he want to sell her? Blue?"

Clay frowned and shook his head. "He doesn't own her, Lilly."

"I wonder if he'd give it a few days to see if I know anyone responsible who might want to take her.…"

"Oh?" Clay asked again.

"I have friends. My grandpa has customers. People post animal sales on his bulletin board sometimes, so… I'd feel so much better if I knew she'd found a good home. Where she'd be appreciated—she's such a nice horse. Didn't you get a sense from her that she's sweet-natured but has a wicked sense of humor, too?"

Actually, he had gotten that from her, but since that sort of thing happened to him all the time he tended to take it for granted. Lilly's blue eyes twinkled in an-ticipation, so Clay just said, "You have your few days, Lilly. Call your friends or customers. Consider the favor granted and I'll talk to Nathaniel for you. He won't be hard to convince."

"He won't?"

"He likes it when things work out for the best." He felt an urge to lift her chin with one finger and look into those deep blue eyes for a long time. Maybe whisper to her; maybe even... "I'd better get back to work, Lilly. Stay as long as you like. I'll be in the barn if you need anything."

Getting acclimated to Nathaniel's practice was more than a full-time job for Clay, and as they didn't have any hands at the moment, the daily stable chores were handled by Clay, Nathaniel and Annie. Since Clay's main function would be assisting the practice and managing the barn, he'd have to bring on a hand or two right away, probably two hands for now—one full-time and one part-time. He'd have to talk over some ideas with Nathaniel later.

With the troubled economy, it was a good time to grow the equine business; Nathaniel's farm practice would keep them afloat. While some stables were struggling, some even closing, Jensen's could grow slowly because it was not solely dependent on the horse business. Nathaniel said that he'd eventually bring on another vet to assist in the livestock practice and more hands to free up his time so he could concentrate on horses. But all that was in the future.

Their new customer arrived the first afternoon Clay was on the job and they were all on hand to greet Magnum's Winning Streak, known as Streak for short. He came from the National champion Magnum Psyche line; he was young, unproven, unbroke and undisciplined, but magnificent to look at. He was powerful and impressive, but there was something about him Clay just couldn't put his finger on. The original owner had decided to let him go, sell him, rather than invest more money in him, which was how Ginny Norton came to own him. He was truly beautiful; definitely irresistible.

Ginny's hired hand, Will Burry, expertly backed him out of the trailer and once he was free he immediately began to snort, dig at the ground and pull away with his tail propped in the air. Will tried to coo, soothe and move the horse to the round pen to turn him loose, but he was a handful and it took Will a while. Then he faced his gathering, pulled the hat off his head and wiped a sleeve across his brow. "I told Miss Norton, there's more to this horse. I've seen plenty of unbroke animals, but he acts downright dangerous. Young fella doesn't trust anyone or anything, and he's got a lousy temper besides."

When Nathaniel had seen the horse a couple of days earlier in Ginny's small backyard stable, he had asked her to let Will bring him over alone, give them a few days with the animal before any assessment was made. So Ginny was not here as they first observed him in his new surroundings. Inside the round pen, Streak ran in circles as if he had months' worth of pent-up energy to burn off.

While Nate and Annie spoke with Will, Clay leaned his forearms on the fence and watched the two-year-old work off some steam. People had many and varied reasons for selling a horse. Could be they took stock of their stable and decided to thin it out to make room for better investments; they could have decided putting more into this particular animal was throwing good money after bad and chose to cut their losses. Only time would tell with Streak, but he was too young to write off. As Clay watched him run, throw his head, snort, rear and dig at the ground, he found himself hoping it was something a little experience and intuition could resolve because the horse was so damn beautiful.

He was chestnut in color, had four white stockings and a white blaze that ran down the bridge of his nose. He was big for a young Arabian—sixteen and a half hands at least, maybe thirteen hundred pounds. Willful, energetic, maybe a little crazy. For about the millionth time Clay was asking himself why some of God's most amazing creatures were so difficult to harness. So much trouble to befriend. He just shook his head and laughed. The horse shook his head and snorted at Clay, then ran another lap.

That horse needed to be let loose in the round pen for a few hours. He had a bad case of stable fever.

Clay heard Will's pickup depart and then Nathaniel and Annie were flanking him. With all eyes on Streak, Nathaniel said, "Some days are better than others with this horse, Will says, but even brushing him is dangerous. When Will can get a harness on him, he's fitful. When Ginny attempts to touch him, he shies. She's afraid that even if they eventually saddle him, she'll be thrown."

"She should be afraid," Clay said. "Look at him. He has some serious trust issues." Clay turned to Nate. "I'll try to catch him, put him in the stallion stall and feed him."

"Want help?"

"Nah," Clay said, smiling. "But I'm going to let him get good and tired before I try to catch him."

Nate gave him a slap on the back and went back to his office.

By the time Clay got around to the horse, he was

still skittish, but Clay had seen far worse. Streak had worked up a lather, but Clay wasn't going to attempt any grooming; getting him acclimated was enough for today. Besides, just catching him was a huge accomplishment. They communed in silence, but all Clay was picking up was a nervous colt. He decided to work with him in the morning.

Once Streak was fed, settled in his stall and alone for the night, Clay's mind moved on to other things. He hadn't yet had a chance to get acquainted with Nate's computerized records and if he was going to contribute to animal care and stable management, he'd have to be up to speed on that. Annie had offered him dinner again but Clay declined. He didn't want to set a precedent of spending all his time off with them. Although he considered Nathaniel a friend, he was also a boss. So Clay made himself a couple of sandwiches in his room and worked on a list of things he'd like to accomplish his first week.

He eventually pulled a book out of his duffel. Clay liked to read about earth sciences—geography, geology, meteorology, ecology. He also liked astronomy and still packed in that horse trailer, due to the lack of room afforded by his current living quarters, was a state-of-the-art telescope. But when the book dropped into his lap and he lay reclined on his bed, his sleepy thoughts drifted toward the long-legged blonde he had been married to and he wondered if she was all right, if her loneliness and anxiety plagued her now that he was no longer there for her.

And then, inexplicably, he began to think about that little Hopi girl who was certainly in love with a horse....

He hadn't been asleep long when his pleasant man-dreams shifted to oppressive darkness. He didn't know whether he moved in his sleep, but in the dream he was thrashing around. He was looking up at a black, starless sky from a deep hole and his entire being was suffused with panic, his heart racing with fear. There was no way out; he used his hands to claw at the sides of the hole, but without success. He tried to yell for help, but no sound came out. And it seemed to go on for an intolerably long time.

When Clay's eyes finally burst open, he was panting and drenched in sweat. His reading lamp was still on, of course. The darkness was all contained in the dream, not his surroundings. He had to work to slow his pulse and control his breathing. His immediate thought was, *What the hell was that?* He hadn't had a nightmare in so long, he couldn't remember the last time. He thought it might've been more than a dozen years ago, in his early twenties, when his life had been very unstable and his future impossible to envision.

Clay meditated briefly. It took only moments for him to calm his body and mind. He took a deep, cleansing breath. And then he heard a thump from the stable.

He rose from his bed, pulled on his boots and went to check things out. He walked down the aisle between the stalls and all seemed under control. Then he heard another thump, this time accompanied by a soft whinny.

Streak. Anxious in his new surroundings? He went to the stall and looked in. Streak was facing a corner, whinnying in his sleep and pawing the wall of the stall with one foreleg. The second Clay was near the colt, he felt his fear. He sensed the deep, dark, muddy hole; entrapment. It was dark and cold in the horse's dream.

Not a good time to enter the stall, so he reached a hand in. "Hey, hey, hey," he said very softly. "Easy now." The horse's head came up, turned and his large brown eyes took in Clay. He snorted and shook his head. In a few moments the horse calmed enough to wander over to the half door, close enough for Clay to stroke him. Alone and frightened, Streak was willing to take a chance and trust Clay. This was a huge bonding moment. Clay stroked him gently. "There now, young man," he said. "Those weren't sweet dreams, were they, boy?"

Clay only enjoyed the bonding for a short time, then closed the horse in and quietly walked away, leaving Streak feeling the trust and wanting more. Clay realized he'd been caught in the colt's dream. He'd been trapped in a hole, afraid, left too long, traumatized. There had been many times he felt he'd picked up an animal's thoughts, but he'd never had this kind of channeling experience before.

"That's a first," he said to himself.

He leaned against the wall out of Streak's sight and waited for any more uproars in the stable. But it remained quiet for a long time, so Clay went to bed, this time turning off the lights. He rested comfortably through what remained of the night.

Clay tended all six horses in the early morning, turning out Nathaniel and Annie's four horses into the big pasture and Blue into her own paddock. He kept Streak in the round pen for now; he wasn't going to integrate the horses until he had time to observe and manage them. He wouldn't be surprised if Streak caused trouble.

It wasn't yet seven when he went to Nate and Annie's back kitchen door. It was almost time for the practice to open for business; Nathaniel might have house calls to make first thing for all he knew. Clay needed to talk to him before he got too busy.

"Good morning," Nate said, opening the door. "Coffee?"

"Sure. I want to talk to you about Streak before start of business."

"Come in. Grab a cup. Hungry?"

In honesty, he was. He was going to have to steal a couple of hours later, run into Fortuna and buy a few things for his quarters so he could take care of the majority of his meals without imposing on Nathaniel and Annie. Not only didn't he want them to feel obliged to watch over him all the time, feeding him at every turn, but they were a relatively new couple with a wedding in the plans. They didn't need some third wheel in their space all the time. So he said, "No thanks, I'm fine. About the horse—he appears sound, but I think there's something emotional going on with the guy. Here's what I recommend. First, I need to talk to the previous owner or trainer. I know he or she wasn't obligated to give a complete disclosure besides bloodlines to the buyer, but maybe they'll talk to me. If I know what went on with the horse, I might have some ideas. Second, tell Miss Norton not to visit the horse for at least a week, then we'll reappraise. I think Streak is developing trust and I want him to focus on me. And, we're going to need a night-light…"

"A night-light?" Nate echoed. "What went on last night?"

"Night anxiety," Clay said with a shrug. "I think the horse had an accident of some kind. Obviously, if he'd been physically hurt there would be evidence on the exam or X-rays, but I think he has nightmares."

A short burst of laughter escaped Nathaniel, but Clay didn't even crack a smile. "Nightmares?"

"He's fitful in his sleep."

"In his awake, too," Nathaniel joked.

"He'll need a lot of reassurance, but thankfully the equine practice isn't overflowing yet and we have time for him." He lifted a black brow. "If his behavior is accountable to a trauma, once he's fit, he'll be an excellent stud candidate. His breeding is excellent. Damn, but that's a fine-looking horse." Clay sighed appreciatively, almost reverently. "Get me the owner's phone number, Nathaniel. Since Miss Norton can't return him, there's no reason for the previous owner to keep secrets."

"Ahhh, how about the lawsuit reason? What if something happened to render the animal unfit and the owner didn't come clean before the sale?"

"I'm not worried about that," Clay said. "I have an old tried-and-true Navajo method of getting to the truth."

"Is that a fact? And what would that be?"

He took a leisurely sip of his coffee. "Listening like a horse," he said with a sly grin. "Nathaniel," he said, once again serious, leaning toward his friend, "will you leave the colt to me? It will require patience."

Nate just smiled and said, "He's all yours."

Lilly made it a point to drive to the Jensen clinic before work started at the feed store on the days she wouldn't be delivering. She liked to check up on Blue; in just days it was clear she was thriving. Before a week was out she'd been integrated with the Jensen horses in the big pasture. No surprise, she fit in. Lilly had known from the first time she touched her, she was an amiable mare who could get along with anyone.

It was a bonus to watch what Clay was doing with the stud colt in the round pen. It looked like the two of them were taking it real, real slow. Clay haltered him and after the colt had time to work off some steam from being pent up in the stallion pen, Clay worked him out on the lead rope, taking turns running him in larger then smaller circles. At intervals, he'd pull the colt in and talk to him a bit, touch him. Sometimes Streak seemed to go along with that idea; sometimes he resisted.

But what was fascinating was the way Clay managed the horse—his focus was amazing. Lilly was sure he had never once noticed she watched.

"How's it going, girlfriend?"

Lilly turned and found Annie boosted up on a rail beside her, watching Streak with her.

"Never better, Annie. How about you?"

"Busy and happy. I see you know our newest guest.…" Lilly simply nodded, unsure whether Annie meant Streak or Clay. "He's coming along. You should've seen him the first day."

"The horse or the new assistant?" Lilly asked with a laugh.

"They're both acclimating well, I think."

"I noticed you put Blue in the big pasture with your horses. They seem to be getting along."

"Very well. She's a good horse."

"I've been meaning to talk to Nate about her.…"

"Talk to me," Annie said.

"I called some people and put up a notice on Yaz's bulletin board, but there hasn't been any response yet. I think if anyone saw her, they'd jump on a chance to adopt her. And if they met her… By the way, what does it cost to board here?"

"Without training, feed, grooming, et cetera? Three hundred a month," Annie said. "Listen, you're not kidding me—you like her. A lot."

Lilly shook her head. "But three hundred is out of my range."

Annie turned toward her. "Still, the two of you are good together. And I bet owning your own horse would be perfect for you. And this one—you wouldn't have to buy her—just run some ads saying you found her and if she has an owner, give them a chance to claim her. If no one responds to the ads, she's yours."

"I've never even imagined I could own a horse," she said. "When I was a kid I was surrounded by horses, took some instruction from the neighbor—I think Yaz worked out a barter or something. Since moving here, I've only ridden a few times. I have a lot going on between my job, my house and my grandpa's place."

"I know," Annie said. "We could put a saddle on her for you," she offered.

"No, let's not do that," Lilly said. "I'm on a tight budget. Not a good time to fall in love." She smiled at Annie. "I better get to the feed store. Yaz will be looking for me."

"See you later, then. And if you change your mind…"

"Thanks," Lilly said, her mind changing even as she walked away.

When Clay went to the clinic office, Annie was at the computer. She looked up, smiled and asked, "How are things going with Streak?"

"Slowly, but he's doing a little better every day. I noticed I have an audience every day, also. Is that typical of Lilly? Observing the animals?"

"We've been seeing a lot of her since she rescued Blue and since you started working with the colt. I think all of the above has caught her interest."

"Have you known her a long time?" Clay asked.

Annie pushed away from the desk on her roller chair. "Longer than I've known Nathaniel," she said. "In fact, Nathaniel has known Lilly longer than he's known me. She's been delivering his feed since he took over the practice from his father. And I cut her hair."

"Huh?"

Annie laughed. "I grew up on a farm, had horses, had a prize-winning bull, in fact. But when I met Nate I was a hairdresser. I have my own little shop in Fortuna, although it's being completely run by my manager and I spend all my time here now."

Clay leaned one hip against the other desk in the office. "No kidding? Hairdresser?"

"Not something you have a need for, I take it?" she asked with a laugh. "I plan to sell the franchise eventually, but I'm kind of waiting for my manager to work up to buying it, and she doesn't have the cash yet. Tough economy, you know. As for Lilly—I think she has a major crush on a horse." Annie leaned back in her chair and rocked slightly. "I have a feeling we're going to keep seeing her as long as Blue is here. I suggested we put a saddle on her, but Lilly declined. She said it wasn't a good time to fall in love. I take that to mean it's already too late."

"Maybe she'll take Blue," Clay said.

"She asked what we charge to board and said it was out of her reach."

"But there's Grandpa," Clay said.

"And I think Yaz would move heaven and earth for the girl's happiness—it's just the two of them, you know. But as you get to know Lilly better you'll see—she's very proud of her independence. She works hard to maintain it. We've been friends for years and she won't even take a free haircut from me."

That caused Clay to smile. "I recognize the tendency to be proud...."

"Oh?" Annie asked, lifting her eyebrows. "Spoken as a man who won't accept dinner with his friends more than once a week at most."

"Poor Annie," Clay said. "Have you and Nathaniel been together long enough that you have already run out of things to say to each other when you eat alone?"

"Oh, get out!" she said with a laugh.

Lilly discovered yoga her second year of college; it kept her flexible, fit and serene. After college she found some yoga and Pilates classes offered at a community center not too far from her little rented house and managed to take them at least three days a week. Then she discovered a funky little coffee shop nearby, in an old storefront that had been painted turquoise and stuck out like a sore thumb. When she could make that late-morning yoga class, she stopped at the Loving Cup for lunch afterward, where she had green tea and a croissant sandwich of avocado, tomato, sprouts and sliced zucchini, or some similar vegetarian treat. Over lunch she'd visit with one of the owners, Dane, who had become her closest friend.

She looked forward as much to seeing Dane as to the tea and sandwich. In the few years she'd been dropping in, they occasionally met for dinner or a movie or even a hike along the coast. Dane was the closest thing to a boyfriend Lilly had. Although he'd never really qualify as a boyfriend, he made an amazing best friend. Even though Lilly had had the occasional date with other guys over the past several years, none of them at all serious, she vastly preferred spending time with Dane.

She couldn't wait to tell him about finding the horse, about watching her get better and about the new crazy colt they'd taken on. Dane was not a horse person. "Never been on one, thank you, and never tempted," he said. "I'm more of a cat person."

"You should let me take you for a ride sometime," Lilly said. "I go so seldom myself, but I know enough to pick out a very gentle horse for you. And I'd be there to protect you the whole time." Then she grinned at him.

"We shouldn't waste our time—I'm not interested. I love hearing you talk about your horse stuff, though. Your eyes sparkle."

"You should see the new guy at the clinic—Navajo with hair down to his butt. High cheekbones, kind of grim-faced. When he gets alone with that stallion in the round pen, it's like a kind of hypnotism is going on, he's so focused on the horse. And when the colt rears or pulls away—"

"Okay, stallion or colt?" Dane asked.

"A very grown-up unbroken colt. A big two-year-old male, a stallion, which means a male that hasn't been gelded, over a thousand pounds of horse with very long, very strong legs and a lot of attitude."

Dane whistled. "See now, when I think of a colt, I think of a cute little thing about the size of a rocking horse. This doesn't sound like a youngster."

She laughed. "If this guy didn't like your face, he could stomp you to death in a second and feel no regret. But Clay, the new vet tech, he gets up close and personal, and when the colt resists him, they look into each other's eyes for a second, the colt calms again and they start over. The colt only gets touched or talked to when he does a good job of minding his manners. It's very cool to watch. The guy has phenomenal control and insight into the animal. They're communicating."

Dane tilted his head. "You sure it's the horses that interest you? Sounds like the man has some mystical savage thing going on...."

"Native men do not appreciate being referred to as *savage*," she informed him.

"I bet there are times they're not totally insulted," Dane said with a smile. "I think you like him."

"A Navajo man? Ah—that brings back some very unpleasant memories. I stay far away from Native men."

Dane held her hand across the counter. "That was all a long time ago, Lilly. Ever consider moving past that?"

"I don't want to move past it."

"Did I mention you could use counseling?"

"About a thousand times," she said.

"Okay then. Want to catch a movie Friday night?" he asked.

"That would be cool," she said. "Yeah, let's do that."

Four

Clay Tahoma was honest to a fault and hated to mislead anyone, but when the future of a fine horse was at stake, he was willing to go there. If something wasn't done about Streak, he could wind up being put out to pasture, gelded, maybe even put down. Unless he could compete, race, breed or function as a family pet, his future wouldn't be too bright.

Once Clay had the name of the previous owner's trainer, he realized he knew him. They hadn't been close, but Clay had met Joshua Bledsoe on several occasions. He called him at once and was direct; he explained they were boarding and training the colt for the new owner. "I'm hoping you'll tell me the rehab or training techniques you used on Streak following the accident," Clay said.

"Accident?" Josh answered.

"Yes. Before we got him. There doesn't seem to be any physical problem—it's all emotional. But if I know what you did, I won't cover the same ground. I think he's salvageable. In fact, I'm sure of it. While we're on the subject, I could use more details about the accident."

"Details about the accident?" Joshua repeated.

"Just get me up to speed—how deep was the pit or hole, how long was he trapped and how'd he end up in it—I can't imagine someone rode him into it. Then tell me what you did after the rescue to get him back in shape. I don't want to plow the same field twice, if you get my drift."

In fact, the accident had been no one's fault—turned out it was a barn fire. Streak had been very young, and when the owners released the animals from the burning barn, a few of them, including Streak's mother, wouldn't come out and died before the blaze was under control. Streak got out of the pasture he'd escaped to and in the dark he ran down a nearby road that was under construction, slid on loose gravel and into a pit. He couldn't get out. By the time stable hands rescued him, using a lift, he was half out of his mind.

As Clay already knew, there was no evidence the horse was physically injured from his mishap, but the fall, the isolation, the separation from his mother, the frustration with trying to find a way out, the lift rescue—or the combination of all these events—had traumatized him.

Clay told the colt, "We'll start at the beginning, young man—just a little walking around with the harness and lead rope until you get more comfortable."

And the horse said to Clay, *I can't forget!*

As he stroked the horse, Clay thought, *Good. Don't forget. Remembering will keep you sharp and safe.*

This was the part that made sense only to Clay—he didn't hear the voice of the horse, he felt it. When he was sending a mental message to the animal, sometimes the horse seemed to receive it and they were both on the same page. How do you explain something like that? How do you explain getting drawn into an animal's dream?

In just a week, they had come a long way.

The next time Lilly came by with her delivery, Clay wanted to go help her haul the hay and feed, but the horse felt it and pulled him back. *Sorry,* Clay thought. *I don't usually get distracted. Let's just do our job.* And he focused again. He pushed the pretty Hopi out of his mind as he slowly led Streak around, creating comforting images in his mind and murmuring soothing sounds and words.

When they were finished, he removed the lead and set the horse free for a little exercise. When he turned he was pleased to see Lilly was still there. She leaned her forearms on the rail and watched him, her booted foot resting on the bottom rail.

Clay walked over to her, detached lead in hand, while the horse romped behind him. "I'm sorry I couldn't help you unload today," he said as he neared.

She shrugged. "I told you before, I can handle it. It's my job." She jutted her chin toward Streak. "He's amazing."

"Beautiful, isn't he?" A thought emerged in his mind—how wonderful she would look astride a large chestnut creature like Streak—but he stopped the thought at once. The downside to letting a young horse into your head—you could accidentally send a message you didn't intend.

"He seems to have calmed down a lot in a week, but he's still…wild and crazy. But he likes you."

"He comes from a champion line, but he was

traumatized by an accident when he was young. Anxiousness in combination with strength can be lethal. So we're going back in time, returning to his early training. And going slow."

"Does he get that? That you're starting from the beginning?" she asked.

"I don't know," Clay said. "He's cooperating for the moment. If I could, I'd regress him to the womb." Then he smiled and said, "You hung around again."

"I saw you working the horse and just wanted to look at him. And I like to check on Blue. That's all."

"She's in fine shape. How long since you've ridden?"

She shrugged. "I bet it's been six months. I rode almost every day as a young girl."

He grinned at her. "You're still a young girl," he said.

"Really, I'm not that into riding. Just occasionally. If Annie wants someone to ride with." And then she thought about what a huge lie that was. She'd revised her budget a hundred times to see how she could squeeze three hundred a month out of it. It didn't look possible and she was just saving face. Oh, her pride! How it plagued her.

Clay glanced over his shoulder at Streak. "I have to work things out with that horse. He's too damn valuable and good-looking to lose."

"How would you lose him?" she asked.

"Well, if he can't be ridden, if he can't compete, he can't work. If he can't be ridden, no rider will want him, and if he's got a personality disorder and can't be trained, he shouldn't be bred. A breeder with half a brain wouldn't buy his sperm. Can't breed him just for his good looks."

"The animal kingdom is so civilized that way," she said under her breath.

He shot her a look and laughed outright. "Completely." He put a booted foot on the lowest rung of the fence and hoisted himself over to her side, facing the pen. "I shouldn't take a chance like that, showing him my back." He leaned on the fence along with her and watched Streak run back and forth. "Just because he's cutting me some slack doesn't mean he can be trusted. He's got a short fuse and it doesn't take much to ignite it."

"Why is he like that? All high-strung and cranky."

"Could be many things," Clay said with a shrug. "I do know he had that accident—fell in a ditch and wasn't rescued for a long time. Hours. I think he almost drove himself crazy trying to find a way out, and then had to be pulled out mechanically. You can't hoist a colt up in the air in the dark of night and not expect repercussions. He's screwed up, that's all. So how's that make him so different from the rest of us? He just needs understanding."

"That's all it takes? Understanding?"

"A little experience with horses doesn't hurt. It's horses like him that make me want to do my best. He's big, smart enough to learn, to bond with and work through his fears. Right now he's hard to handle, but if he ever gets under control, he's got unimaginable power and grace. Sixteen and a half hands at two years— tall for an Arabian. Not mellow. But there are lots of things an edgy stallion can get done that a mellow horse just isn't good for. Just like the rest of us, they come prepackaged with their very individual DNA."

She didn't respond to that. Eventually he turned toward her. "Who taught you to ride?" he asked.

"My grandfather and neighbors on the reservation. We were right next door to a big ranch and were friends with the owners till I was thirteen, when we moved away."

Streak stopped running back and forth and began making wide, slow circles inside the corral. As he edged closer to the fence, Lilly made a clicking and humming sound, reaching a hand into the corral. Clay just watched curiously. Streak was looking at him expectantly, something he'd just begun to do in the past couple of days. It wasn't quick, but on the fourth or fifth wide circle, the horse slowed dramatically. He tossed his head, dug at the ground a couple of times, then walked right up to Lilly.

Very softly, under his breath, Clay whispered, "No way…"

"Just a baby under all that temper and fuss," she said gently, stroking his face, his neck. "Someone knows he's pretty, that's what. Never a good thing for a man—you'll learn that. The women take to you at first, but they figure you out fast and then you're on your own again. Shhhh, too handsome for your own good. A bit too strong. Go slowly, little man."

Clay momentarily wondered, *Who is she talking to? Him or me?*

"There's nothing much wrong with this horse except he isn't comfortable with his own strength. He needs the right hand—gentle control. He needs a mommy who can handle him."

"I thought he needed a good trainer...."

"Well, yeah," she said, stroking the white blaze that ran down the bridge of his nose. "But like most pretty boys, he's full of himself and he's going to need a well-trained rider. He'd prefer to run free and not be handled. He is filled with the spirit of youth."

He stared at her in some wonder. "How do you know this, Lilly?"

She turned back to the horse's eyes. "Who says I know? It's my opinion and I could be totally off. He's a toddler. A thousand pounds of terrible two. He needs a good mother, that's all. A strong mother with lots of love and an iron will. Is there any chance he was removed from his mother too soon?"

Clay was stunned and couldn't answer for a moment. "There's a chance of that, yes," he finally said.

"Ah. See, we never allowed that on the reservation." She flashed Clay a smile that transformed her whole face. He was struck by how truly beautiful she was. "But you will do fine. You'll do it *ta-bilh*." Together.

Surprise widened his eyes. "*Niik'eh*," he agreed in his Native language. Sure enough.

"I have to go now," she told him. She gave the horse one more stroke. "Behave," she warned him.

"Wait a minute," Clay said as she turned. "I think we should do something. Break bread, get to know each other. We can find out if we have any friends in common." The Hopi Reservation was completely surrounded by the Navajo Nation and she had just spoken in Navajo.

She shook her head. She was not getting any more entangled with him; he scared her to death! "Thank you, but no, I couldn't do that. I have a boyfriend."

"Yeah, but how much of a boyfriend?"

She laughed out loud, her face lighting up. "Enough of a boyfriend," she said.

She had almost made it to the truck when he called to her back, "So bring him. I'd like to meet him."

She turned back and her laughter was amused. "I don't think so, but it's very nice of you to include him," she said with a twinkle in her eye.

"Well, maybe he won't last. He probably doesn't deserve you anyway. Besides, I just want to hear you talk about horses—the one who's a little boy, the one with the wicked sense of humor. You know what I mean. I won't get in the way."

"Yes, you will," she said, smiling and getting into the truck. *You already are,* she thought.

She drove away from the stable and he watched until she was nothing but a faint cloud of dust. Then he turned back to Streak. He gave the horse a gentle stroke. "I have a feeling you just let another person into your head. You cheated on me, you mangy beast." The horse tossed his head arrogantly. "Thousand-pound terrible two—she's right. Were you talking to her? Were you?" The horse turned his head away, looking in the other direction. "Yeah, you were. Totally cheated on me. Well, if you've got some influence there, why don't you make yourself useful for once and tell her she should go out with me?"

The horse looked back at him and they locked eyes, holding for a minute. Then the horse backed away, snorted and resumed trotting in wide circles around the round pen, expecting Clay to catch him if he wanted to bring him in.

* * *

After a week at the stable, Clay drove over to Grace
Valley to have dinner with his sister and her family.
Ursula was six years older than Clay and despite the
fact she'd often been tasked with minding him when
they were growing up, and he was admittedly a handful,
they'd remained close. Clay wholly approved of the mate
she'd chosen—Tom Toopeek, the Grace Valley police
chief. Tom was Cherokee, and Clay had no trouble accepting him as a brother.

Ursula was living a life similar to the one in which
they grew up. It was a busy life, full of work and family,
and Clay could see it brought her great satisfaction. Tom
and Ursula built their house on the land homesteaded
by Tom's parents, Lincoln and Philana, who still lived
there, their original cabin attached to the end of Tom and
Ursula's newer, larger construction. With five children
and Tom's parents, Ursula's was always a full house even
with their oldest away at college. They had their meals
at a roughly hewn oak dining table that could easily
seat twelve; the evening meal came after homework
was cleared away from that same table. Ursula was a
schoolteacher. She paid very close attention to the kids'
studies.

Clay and Ursula didn't have any other siblings, but
they grew up in a family compound with their aunts,
uncles and cousins. Even though there were only the
four of them in the immediate Tahoma family, their
dinner table, like Ursula's, had been large enough to seat
many more. Whether there were big family dinners at
Clay's house or at one of his extended family's homes,
they were always surrounded by good food, good smells

and people—babies, children, teens and young adults as well as parents and grandparents.

Yet for all the people around the Toopeek house, there was hardly ever mess or chaos, which also resembled the old Tahoma home. The Cherokee and the Navajo had similar expectations of their offspring, and Tom's parents were also enforcers on Tom and Ursula's kids. Not that the kids were unreasonably subdued—there was lots of time for running wild in the forests and valleys; there was plentiful laughter and normal arguing.

And when their uncle Clay arrived, there were fits of excitement.

He couldn't explain why they received him with such enthusiasm. Besides putting them on a horse when they visited him or when they all visited their Tahoma grandparents, he didn't feel that he did enough to charm them. But they ran to him when he arrived. He could still lift his ten-year-old niece, Shannon. He hated to even think about the day, which was fast approaching, that he wouldn't be allowed to do that. She was the baby and Ursula said the last one. Clay had fully enjoyed Ursula and Tom's children.

A surprise awaited Clay at this visit—his brother-in-law had cut off his long, traditional ponytail, which had been pretty much identical to Clay's. Tom had short black hair now, cut in a buzz.

"You look like a marine," Clay said, grabbing his hand and pulling him into a brief man-hug.

"You'll get used to it," Tom said. "My wife isn't happy about it yet, but she'll adjust."

And then Ursula was there, reaching to pull him into a hug of her own. "I'm still so happy you're here, I can't quite believe it's true." She kissed his cheek. "I hope this works out for you the way you want it to, Clay. Because having you near is perfect for my family. I want to make it perfect for you, too."

"You do that every time you welcome me to dinner."

He was dragged outside by the younger boys to assess the progress they'd made on a tree fort, then he was pulled into Shannon's room to look at all the As she'd gotten on her papers. Only his oldest niece, Tanya, was missing from the family. She was on a full-ride scholarship at Northern Arizona University in Flagstaff, near her maternal grandparents and the rest of the extended Tahoma family, while eighteen-year-old Johnny attended a local college and lived at home. Tanya went to school year-round—a difficult three-year premed program that didn't appear to give her much difficulty. Tanya was beautiful and brilliant and, if you could trust a twenty-year-old's ambitions, wanted a future in medical research. "She's in love with the microscope," Tom said. "Which suits me fine—exactly where I want her passion to be focused."

"Tom has a very good memory about when we met and fell in love," Ursula said with a laugh. "It scares him to death."

There were many hands to serve the table—Ursula had help from her mother-in-law and the children. Lincoln Toopeek reminded Clay of his father—quiet and stoic, but that stern silence shouldn't be taken for granted. Clay knew that Lincoln could make himself heard, make his presence known, just like the elder Tahoma. And then he noticed that when Lincoln Toopeek sat beside his youngest granddaughter, Shannon, and helped her serve her plate, all the harsh lines on his face smoothed and there was such an expression of peace there. Peace and love.

The food at Ursula's table was so abundant and delicious, Clay was surprised that nobody at the table was fat. There was a thick vegetable soup, then roasted chickens rubbed in some oils and herbs that almost made him drool. A potato-and-cheese casserole with crumbled bacon on top, roasted vegetables—seasoned peppers, onions, asparagus, sliced baby yellow squash. Fresh, sweet bread.

"Ah! If you all keep feeding me this way, I'm going to have to start exercising all the time!"

"Didn't you eat well in Los Angeles County?" Ursula asked.

"On my own, it was only what I could throw together quickly, and I'm very lazy. When Isabel invited me to dinner, her cook served tiny bites of funny-looking food because Isabel worried constantly about her weight. So the answer is no—I did not eat well!"

There was a moment of silence before Ursula said, "How is Isabel, Clay?"

He trained his voice to sincerity. "She's just fine, Ursula. Her life has hardly changed. She was the one who needed a divorce. The marriage wasn't working for her. I understood perfectly."

Another moment of silence. "This is a better place for you, I think," Ursula said.

He grinned at his sister. "I agree. I'm very excited about Nathaniel's plans. And it's good to be near family." He took a breath. "I have a favor to ask. Would you like to discuss it in private?"

"Is it obscene?" she countered.

He swallowed. "I want to bring Gabe out here. I wish

I could have him live with me, but that's not possible where I'm living right now. So I'm wondering if he could live with you. That way at least I could see him every day. I'd like him to do his last year of high school at your kids' school. I want to start training him as a farrier, if he's interested, but more important, I want him to live with two professionals, two college graduates who encouraged his cousins to go to college." He looked away just briefly, then back at his sister and brother-in-law. "It's time. It's past time. I hope I haven't waited too long."

Ursula reached across the table and covered Clay's hand with her own. "You know nothing could make me happier."

Then Lincoln's voice, loud and stern, boomed across the table. "The boy will thrive here, even though he's Navajo."

The entire family laughed softly, respectfully. There was no bad blood between Cherokee and Navajo, but they each thought themselves a bit more evolved, wiser, stronger.

"I agree, sir. Thank you for that welcoming remark. I know my parents, aunts and uncles have done a fine job raising him while I've been trying to set up a life, but I'm planning to be here for the long haul, and I'd love to finally have a normal father-son relationship with Gabe. I haven't been with him enough."

"You were young, Clay. And you did very well as a father. Gabe hasn't suffered. He had good role models and he was raised with love and every advantage."

Clay looked at his sister and whispered, "Thank you, Ursula."

"No," she said, "thank *you!* I love that boy."

Much later, after coffee and some of the best pie imaginable, Ursula walked Clay out to his truck. "I meant what I said, you know. I'm so glad you're here and I hope this works for you. I want you close and happy. And I want you to have the life you want with your son, finally."

"I think that will be the case," he said. But what he thought was, *The life I really want is yours. The life I thought I'd have, filled with family and intimacy and friendship and trust. It happens around your table and I always dreamed my table would be the same.*

He pushed the self-pitying thoughts from his mind. "I'm very glad to be near you and your family again," he said. "But I don't like your husband's haircut."

"I don't know what possessed him," she said, looking over her shoulder as if Tom might be there, listening. "He said he's tired of it. Lincoln gave him a lot of shit."

Clay lifted his dark brows. "Nice talk for the police chief's wife."

"Aw, cut me some slack—I'm not around the elders or children and I bet you've heard that word before." Then she grinned. "Clay, you know I've wanted Gabe here with me since he was little. I know Father was right, that I should concentrate on my own children and I know Gabe did well with the Tahomas, but I want you to know, this is as happy a day for me as for you."

"If he'll come," Clay said. "I won't force him. He's been on the reservation a long time and it's a safe place for him."

"He'll come," she said, giving him a reassuring smile. "He might be comfortable where he is, but when he's with you he comes alive. He wants to be with his father. This is a very good thing—for all of us."

Clay smiled. "I'm glad you're happy about it, Ursula. Because I've heard Tom say that when you're happy, everyone is happy."

"It's true," she said, not embarrassed in the least by that comment. "How soon can he be here?"

"Let me call him tomorrow and let you know."

"Thank you, Clay. Thank you for trusting me with your son."

He felt a small surge in his breast; he was so proud of his sister. She was a good woman, a good wife, a good mother. He grabbed her to him, held her tight and said, "Thank you, Ursula. I love you like a sister."

She laughed and hugged him. Hard.

Except for visiting his father out in L.A. a few times, Gabe's home since his birth had been with his grandparents. Clay had hoped for this day for a very long time, the day he could offer his son a home at least close enough that they could see each other every day. It was tempting to head for the reservation, gather up his boy and bring him back to California. But Gabe was a young man now—a seventeen-year-old; it would be selfish of Clay to insist on this change if it wasn't in his son's best interest, if it wouldn't make him happy. So rather than traveling out there, he called.

Out of respect, Clay spoke first to his father about bringing Gabe to California. He then spoke to his mother. Their response was as expected—Gabe was past the age of having such decisions made for him and if he chose to leave their house to be closer to his father and aunt, they would respect his decision. Likewise,

Clay would have to respect Gabe's decision if he chose to stay with his grandparents.

It was only after introducing the idea to the elder Tahomas that Clay talked about it with Gabe.

"But I have friends here," was Gabe's response. "And my cousins…"

"I'm not going to force the issue, son," Clay said. "If you'd rather stay with your grandparents, that's what you should do. Just keep a couple of things in mind before you make a final decision—I would have brought you with me a long time ago if I'd been in a position to do it, but my life was unstable in too many ways until now, until I moved to your aunt Ursula's part of the world. You're getting to that age where you have to make some future plans, and I'd like those plans to include more education. And before you strike out on your own, I want a little time with you."

"You could come home," Gabe said. "There's room for you here. There's work here, too."

Although they'd been over this before, Clay answered patiently, "As the family grows, the potential for success is spread over more and more people. The company you'll keep is excellent, but opportunity is limited. And if everything goes as planned here, I may be able to settle in permanently. And you have cousins here, as well. We could work together. Nathaniel has asked me to do some hiring, and I'm going to need a part-timer. It could be ideal if you want to go to school out here, too. But this is up to you. You might try it, son. Give it six months and see how it goes."

There was only silence on the phone.

"Take some time to think it over, Gabe," Clay said. "I don't want you to have regrets."

"I need to be with my father," the boy finally said. "Grandfather says you need looking after."

Clay let out a bark of laughter. "Does he, now? I'll have to thank him for the confidence he shows in me. School starts out here very soon, Gabe. I'll come and get you...."

"No, let me come on my own. I'm not a kid. I want you to show some confidence in *me*."

It was settled that Gabe would drive himself from Flagstaff; he was adamant. He owned a little green truck that Clay had helped him buy last year and he saw himself as a man capable of traveling alone. He wanted a couple of weeks to say his goodbyes, then he would be on his way.

Clay wanted to make the trip with him, but he had to remind himself that when he was Gabe's age, he was already a father. They may have lived with the family, but that didn't mean Clay wasn't up through the night when Gabe was hungry, teething, sick or just asserting himself. Clay hadn't left the boy to seek a better life for them until Gabe was eleven, and even then he was back home often to be sure he was not forgotten.

"I've hoped for this day to come for a very long time, Gabe," Clay said.

Clay wasted no time in speaking with Nathaniel about Gabe. "He won't be staying with me, though I wouldn't be surprised if he camped the occasional night. He's going to stay with my sister and her family in Grace Valley. It's close so I'll be able to see him all the time, but the most important reason is that Ursula is a gifted teacher and her children have all been great students. She gets very involved in their homework, she knows all the teachers, and she's devoted to Gabe, who is far smarter than he realizes. She'll coach him in the SATs—he needs to retake the tests for college. But I want to bring him on as a hand, Nathaniel. Given that my father and uncles have raised him, he knows about horses and—"

"Whoa, whoa, whoa," Nate said, holding up a hand. "Wait a minute here. Isn't he just a little kid?"

"He's seventeen. Ready for his last year of high school."

Nathaniel rubbed the top of his head. "When you mentioned that you had a son, I assumed... Clay, you're not that old yourself."

Clay grinned. "I was seventeen when he was born. His mother was a teenager, also, and wanted to give him up, but I couldn't. I brought him home to the family."

"How is it I've known you so long and didn't know the details about your son?"

Clay chuckled with some embarrassment. "I didn't throw that around a lot, but one of the reasons I traveled back to the reservation so often was more because of Gabe than other family. Since I was never married to the boy's mother, it was important that I be there for him. With your permission, if he proves competent— which he will—I'll give him some work around the barn after school and on weekends. It's important he work, earn a little money. And frankly, we need good help."

"Sure, I don't have a problem with that," Nate said.

Clay grinned and stood a little taller. "I'll see if I can refine the boy's farrier skills and train him on our digital equipment so he has a trade, but I want my son to go further in his life than I have."

"Shew," Nate said. "Didn't he live with you and Isabel?"

"It was complicated. Her family wasn't exactly into my bringing a kid along into our marriage. And besides, I was raised a certain way, a traditional way, surrounded by family who all took a role. In our community it really does take a village. Despite the fact that I grew up to make some stupid mistakes, I know it wasn't really the fault of my teachers. Gabe visited me in Los Angeles, but for all kinds of reasons it wasn't the right place for him to stay. The only person invested in him was me and I had too much responsibility. It prevented me from keeping a close hand on him. And Isabel's father...he never seemed to warm up to Gabe. For that matter, he never really warmed up to me. And Isabel had trouble, as well—she's not very maternal." He shook his head. "Gabe had fun there on visits, but it wasn't a good place for a young boy. Gabe was at that age. He needed a lot of positive reinforcement and a firm hand."

"Bring him on," Nate said. "I can't wait to meet him. Why did I think your life was uncomplicated?"

"I have no idea, Nathaniel."

Five

Clay had stocked his small refrigerator and a cupboard with a few items for quick, easy meals, and he'd had dinner with Nate and Annie a couple of times, but by far the best tip he'd gotten since arriving in the area was about Jack's Bar. Nathaniel mentioned that he and Annie met at Jack's in Virgin River and enjoyed some of the most delectable dinners they'd ever had while taking care of a boxful of puppies…and falling in love. Since Clay had met Jack on his way into town, watching that group of men as they pulled the old pickup up the hill, he was anxious to give the bar a try. Clay wasted no time in getting over there to see what was on the menu.

The first revelation—there was no menu. Preacher served up one dinner item daily and decided what it would be based on whatever suited him that day. It was whispered to Clay that there were sometimes leftovers from previous nights, and nobody would take offense if he preferred those to the special of the day. But Clay was more than satisfied with any of Preacher's dinners—the man knew what to do with a piece of meat. Jack proved a pleasant dinner companion, making introductions as people wandered into the bar, then standing on the other side of the bar with his coffee while Clay ate.

By his third visit to Jack's bar, Clay knew all the regulars. The local constable and Jack's brother-in-law, Mike Valenzuela, dropped by frequently. Jack's wife, the local midwife, Mel, would take a swing through before heading home from work. If she had a house call, she'd drop off their small children for Jack to tend, or she'd drop them at Preacher's house to be tended by a sitter or Preacher's wife, Paige. He saw the town minister again; Noah Kincaid made it a point to drop by and visit with folks. And there was Hope McCrea, town busybody, who stopped by almost daily for her shot of Jack Daniel's.

"Do anything special?" Hope asked him right off.

"Special?" he asked, picking up his coffee. "I shoe horses. And do some other stable chores."

She snorted, held up a finger to order her drink and shook a cigarette out of her pack. "Haven't got any use for that," she informed him.

"Lucky for me, Nathaniel Jensen does."

"That who brought you to town? The vet?"

"Yes, ma'am. We go way back. And I have a sister in Grace Valley—Ursula Toopeek."

"Is that a fact? I don't know Mrs. Toopeek, but I've had a little traffic with the police chief."

"Have a little trouble with the law?" he asked, the corners of his mouth twitching.

She grinned at him and pushed her heavy black-framed glasses up the bridge of her nose. "You should fit in around here. Just another smart-ass."

Clay liked the cranky old woman. But theirs was not to be a lengthy relationship, it turned out. On his fourth visit to Jack's for dinner, Jack's wife came into the bar. She jumped up on a bar stool without saying hello to anyone and, looking grimly serious, she said, "I have some sad news, Jack. Bruce was delivering mail to Hope McCrea and noticed some had piled up in her box. He walked around the house to see if anything seemed out of order.... He found her on the back porch." A tear slid down Mel's cheek. "She's dead, Jack."

He looked thunderstruck. "I wondered if she was okay—she hasn't come by for a couple of days. Not that it's totally unusual—sometimes days go by before we see her—especially when she's got some project going on. But, man... Natural causes?"

"I guess you could say so," Mel said with a sniff. She pulled a tissue out of her pocket. "It wasn't a homicide, but she was sitting in her porch chair, her cigarette burned down to her fingertips. She was eighty, Jack. Bruce called the county coroner to pick her up, but I can't think of any reason there would be an investigation."

"Damn," Clay said. "I liked her. She reminded me of some of my family." They turned and looked at him. He shrugged. "I'd have taken her for at least ninety-five." He turned to Mel and touched her arm gently. "You gonna be all right?"

"She brought me to Virgin River," Mel informed him. "Well, she tricked me, but she got me here and for that I owe her a lot. If it wasn't for Hope, I wouldn't know my husband, wouldn't have had my children." She looked back at Jack. "I have even worse news. You're going to have to go in that house. You're probably the closest thing to family she's got and someone has to go in, look around, figure out what's to be done next. Hope would spin in her grave if that house was taken by the bank or state for unpaid taxes. There must be a bankbook or will or something in there somewhere. If you can't find anything, we should keep up the bills until we can figure something out."

"Awww, Mel…" he said.

Clay shot him a look. "Did you just *whine?*"

"You gotta understand, Clay. I'm pretty sure that house is something out of a nightmare. I don't think Hope threw anything away in at least fifty years."

"When I got here and asked her if there was a better place to stay than the falling-down, leaky cabin she had arranged for me," Mel said, "she said it would take her all night to clear a space on her couch for me. Jack's right—it can't be good. But she looked after this town. Likely she had some kind of plan. Maybe Jack can unearth a deed or strongbox or something. Or, like with old Doc Mullins when he went, at least a scrawled-out note of intentions."

"Can't the police go in there?" Jack asked.

"I think you should take the police, by all means. Your brother-in-law, Mike—local police. Take Preacher, too. I think Clay here might like to go along—Hope reminds him of family members."

"Not enough for that," Clay said.

"Gather your troops, Jack," Mel said. "Go tell Preacher. Call Mike and Paul Haggerty. It wouldn't hurt to have a minister along—give Noah a call—he'll go with you. The house will keep till morning. It might scare the liver out of you at night."

"Are you coming with me?"

She shook her head. "Not a chance. That place is bound to give us all bad dreams."

* * *

Five men stood in the doorway of Hope's house, which had not been locked. Mike Valenzuela, Paul Haggerty, Noah Kincaid, Preacher and Jack.

"Holy Mother of God," Preacher said. "She really *didn't* throw anything away."

"I bet she could have been on that TV show," Noah said. "You know the one—about the hoarders. Ellie loves that show."

It turned out to be the predictable truth that Hope was a pack rat, but although her house—every single room of it—was stacked with things she'd saved, she had somehow never crossed the line into saving newspapers or empty cans and bottles. She might have saved a lot of useless stuff but at first glance it didn't appear she'd saved garbage. And, to Hope's credit, may she rest in peace, the house could be navigated easily enough. She'd made definite paths through the clutter.

"I'm just trying to figure out when she had the time to buy any of this stuff," Jack said. "She was always working on a project, getting in people's business or gardening. Anyone have any idea how many rooms we got here?"

"We're gonna find out," Paul said. "First thing to do, just take a visual inventory, get the lay of the land, and look for a place she might've stored vital papers—like a will. We'll decide how to handle this mess later. I don't think we can legally start sorting and pitching anyway. Thank God."

Noah broke away from the group and walked through the living room, past junk stacked on both sides of the room, down a path in the dining room, toward the back of the house. The remaining four men very slowly began to enter the room, gingerly lifting items to look underneath—a stray lamp shade, a few lamps without shades, a couple of unopened boxes shipped from Craft World, not one but two disconnected fax machines and a couple of outdated computer printers. There were stacks of mismatched dishes, paperbacks tossed everywhere, and—just as Mel said—underneath an enormous mound of sheets, towels and clothes was an old, purple velvet sofa.

Jack cautiously opened a tied-off garbage bag and peeked inside. "Anyone remember Hope ever wearing a ball cap?" he asked.

Heads were shaking—no.

He pulled one out of the bag. It was for the Denver Broncos. "There must be a hundred of 'em in here. But why?"

"Do you suppose this could be what we're looking for?" Noah said from the dining room. He held a square metal strongbox. Written in marker on it, Vital Papers.

"Be damned," Jack muttered. "How'd you go right to it?"

"I just tried to think about where she might spend the majority of her time," Noah said with a shrug. "It sure wasn't on the sofa. There's a big kitchen back there— with a table, desk, computer and TV. Also a fantastic fireplace and big recliner—I think she worked in it, ate in it, slept in it. It was her office, bedroom and living room, I presume."

"All right, gentlemen," Mike said, heading for the dining table. "Let's clear a space and see if we can find any pertinent information in that box."

"You guys mind if I poke around a little?" Paul asked.

"I'd like to see how many rooms in this old house. How many stairwells, water closets, that sort of thing."

"Why?" Jack asked, lifting a pile of cookie sheets and pots off the table and transferring them to another pile.

"Because I'm a builder, and a little curious," Paul said. "This place is a wreck, no doubt, but have you noticed it doesn't smell or anything? No cracks, no walls caved in. There aren't any stains from mysterious leaks, no obvious mold in one of the dampest places on the planet, the paint is chipped and peeling here and there, the floor is scratched and scarred, but it's quality wood and it's level, not warped. I think maybe under all the junk there might be a good, solid old house. When was it built?"

"Not sure," Jack said, moving a pile of towels and gardening books in one heap. He took a stack of coffee table books off a dining-room chair, placing them on the floor. "In fact, I'm not sure of anything. I didn't know much about Hope, and to tell the truth I don't know who did. I never heard her say anything about who her oldest friends were. She knew Doc Mullins a long time, I know that, but they mostly squabbled. And Doc said she'd been in this house forever, widowed for over thirty years." He took a breath. "That's not a lot to know about a person."

"Did you ever ask?" Noah inquired.

"Sure, but she was stingy with personal information. She said she married young, never had children, that once there had been a lot of land under the house but she'd sold it off to neighbors who needed grazing and planting land. I'm a bartender, man. We lend an ear, but try not to pry."

"You might want to practice up on that not prying part," Preacher mumbled.

Jack glowered at him. "Hope just wanted her one drink and a little conversation. She wanted a little peace," Jack said. Looking around the room, he added, "And who could blame her?"

"And she wanted to fix up the town," Preacher put in, moving a badly tarnished silver tea service all the way into the kitchen. He came back directly. "I think she did that because she was bored, and because she thought she was about the oldest resident of this town and had a stake in it. You know—leaving it better than she found it."

As Paul wandered off to check out the house, the men settled in at a now-cleared, round dining table. Noah pushed the strongbox toward Jack. He opened it as if expecting a bunch of coiled snakes to jump out. Then he flipped the lid all the way back. "Wow. Appears she had one area of neatness in her life. Files. Labels." He pulled out one that clearly said Birth Certificate. Then he pulled out one that said Marriage License. He couldn't resist—he opened the file. "Whoa. She was married in 1941. Either Hope was lying about her age or she was about ten years old." Under the papers lay an old black-and-white photo, which he pulled out. "Jeez, she was a looker," he said, passing it around. She was a beautiful young blonde wearing an elaborate satin gown and gauzy veil and she stood next to a *much* older man.

"Grab a look at that birth certificate, Jack," Preacher said.

Jack did so and nearly blanched. "Good God, she

was older than she let on, born in 1925. She was…
what…?"

"Eighty-six. Sixteen when she married," Noah said,
studying the photo. "And this guy, for a guy in '41, I bet
he's at least fifty, which back then wasn't considered
young like it is now."

"Fifty is considered young now?" Jack asked. "That's
encouraging…. Well, here's a death certificate for the
old boy. He died in…in… Here it is. He died in '61. Fifty
years ago. Hope was only…only…"

"Thirty-six," Noah said.

"Are you going to keep doing that?" Jack asked
irritably.

"At least until you can add and subtract faster," the
minister replied good-naturedly. He smiled at Jack.

Jack went through the files some more. One was labeled Deeds, one labeled Police Officer, one said Midwife. Jack peeked in that file—Hope's contract with
Mel, the position that brought his wife to Virgin River.
Finally he passed a file that was labeled Will. "Oh, boy,
here we go." He pulled the folder and it was suspiciously
thick. "This is a mess of papers."

"Good," Noah said. "She wouldn't have any use for a
lot of paperwork unless she had an idea what she wanted
done with her remains and property."

Jack didn't feel like wasting time. He pushed the
folder toward Noah. "Knock yourself out." He passed
the file labeled Deeds to Preacher. "Have a look in here.
It's probably records of property she sold off, that kind
of thing."

Noah chuckled at him and began leafing through the
papers. "Interesting," he muttered. Upstairs came the
sound of a few thumps; Paul was pounding on walls to

locate studs. "Amazing," Noah said. Paul knocked on more walls. "Well, I'll be…" More knocking sounded from upstairs.

"Care to share anytime soon, Your Worship?" Jack asked.

Noah smiled. "Mrs. McCrea had an attorney—Jacob Stanley of Eureka—and set up a Virgin River Trust so that whatever she left behind wouldn't be eaten up in taxes but could benefit the town."

Preacher was stacking up papers and spreading out a map that had been neatly folded in the file.

"Anything else?" Jack asked. "Any idea what she wants done with her possessions? Or her remains, for that matter?"

"I have to read a minute," Noah said, flipping through documents.

Preacher appeared to be comparing deeds to the old map, moving them from one side of the map to the other as if checking them off. Noah was passing the pages he perused to Mike Valenzuela, Paul was upstairs banging on walls and Jack was starting to twitch.

"Oh, boy," Preacher said finally. "Okay, near as I can tell from this, old Percival McCrea had a lot of money and bought himself just about all the land under what's called Virgin River. Have no idea where he got his money, but it seems it was a long time ago and construction started on this house when he was a young man. Took three years to build and was finished in 1921. Whew. It looks like Hope started selling off the land in parcels right after he died. How old is this town anyway?"

"Was all of it his?" Jack asked, pulling the map closer. It had been divvied up in different colors and some of the names printed on the map he recognized. Bristol, Anderson, Givens, Fishburn. "Holy cow," he said.

"Looks like there were some homesteaders back a long time ago," Preacher said. "But whatever wasn't homesteaded, old Percival bought up. Then he shared it with his sixteen-year-old bride. Then she disposed of it. I'll have to research a little, see what the land values were when she did these deed transfers, but it kinda looks like she let 'em go cheap. Hope built a town. Cool."

"Jack?" Noah said. "Here it is, Jack. She's left *everything* to the town. Her husband left her everything he had, and she left it all to the town." He passed the document to Mike, who passed it to Preacher.

"No surprise there," Jack said. "According to Hope, she didn't have anyone else."

"And you're in charge of it. You were named the executor."

"Me? Why me?" he asked.

"You probably seemed the obvious choice." Noah flipped through the pages a bit. "Looks like it was Doc Mullins until you came to town. So, how about that? We don't have to start calling you *sir* or anything, do we?"

"When you say *everything*..." Jack said hesitantly.

Preacher was the one to answer. "House, contents, land... I wonder if there's something like a bank account. Knowing Hope, I wouldn't be surprised if the mattresses and cubbyholes were stuffed with bills."

"No," Noah said. "Remember, this is the woman who was auctioning the church on eBay. She's computer savvy. I bet half the stuff she bought she got off the Internet. I bet she has accounts on the computer. It's in the kitchen. We might have a challenge figuring out passwords, that sort of thing."

Jack leafed through her files. "Could it be filed under *Passwords?*" he asked, pulling out a file. He took on a decidedly superior air.

"Nicely done," Noah said with a grin.

"This is making me very uncomfortable," Jack said with a shudder. "I don't want to be in charge of Hope's stuff. I don't want to be the town manager, either."

"Take it easy. You start by going to see her lawyer. If there's any money—like after land sales and such—you're probably empowered to get a little help. You know—hire people."

"Really, I don't have time for this," he grumbled. "I don't want to be responsible for how it's used...."

The sound of Paul's heavy footfalls coming down three flights of stairs caused all the men to turn toward the staircase. He stopped at the bottom and smiled at them. "This is a great old house," he said. "Studs every twelve inches, fire walls, top-quality oak, marble and granite, tongue-and-groove hardwood floors… I couldn't build this house today for three million. It's old and it's *awesome.* I hope whoever gets it wants some help putting it right."

"And there is my first potential employee," Jack said.

Delivering feed to smaller ranches and stables was a job that Lilly had volunteered to do—she considered it as adding weight lifting to her exercise regimen. That, combined with yoga, kept her in shape. Plus, it was very important to Yaz that his only family stay involved in

She felt an instant rush of emotion, suspense, though she wasn't precisely sure what caused it. The prospect of watching him mount that surly two-year-old? Watching Streak throw him? Or was it the deep timbre of his voice when he said, *Stay a little while...*

"Just for a couple of minutes," she said. "I hope he's in the mood. I don't have much time today and I want to check on Blue."

"It won't take long. I'll know right away if he's going to cooperate. Any interest in Blue from your notice on the bulletin board?"

"Not yet, but it hasn't been up *that* long..."

"Longer than you asked for," Clay reminded her. "Lots more than a few days. We'll have to do something with her soon. This isn't Club Med."

"I'm bringing her feed free," Lilly said. "Have you noticed that?"

"I have," he said with a smile. "It's appreciated. Thank you."

And then he took off with the feed bags, depositing them and heading for the tack room to get ready for his horse.

Stay a little while... Oh, boy. Lilly hadn't realized she'd been longing to hear a man breathe that in her ear. That was *nice*.

"Your girlfriend is here," Clay said to the horse as he slipped the bit in his mouth and bridle over his head. "Would be nice if you showed her you're somewhat domesticated. She could be proud of you. How about that?"

She's so young, he thought. It wasn't like him to be attracted to a mere girl, a girl who looked more suited to his son, but he couldn't help how he felt. He thought about her when she wasn't around, and when she was around his heart picked up speed and he felt warm all over. She was just so damn cute in her torn jeans and denim jacket. She had herself some fine-looking boots— eel skin, if he wasn't mistaken. She pretended not to care all that much about riding, but she was clearly attached to the horses and those boots were too nice for just delivering feed.

And when he wasn't thinking about how cute she was, he was breathing heavy at how *hot* she was. Tiny, fit, sexy. That silky black hair, cut along her jawline and swinging with each movement, he could almost feel it against his fingers, against his bare chest. Her eyes were so large and blue and he had an overwhelming urge to cause them to roll back in her head.

But the last thing he needed right now was trouble from some ancient Hopi grandfather. The old man would probably not relish the idea of his very young granddaughter messing with a thirty-four-year-old Navajo. Not that he really stood a chance…there was a boyfriend in the picture. Some young buck? he wondered. Someone the grandfather would prefer? Someone the grandfather *chose?*

He tried to force all this from his mind as he led Streak from his stall. There was a blanket already draped over the gate rail. He led the horse to the far side of the corral, draped the blanket over his back and one last thought slipped through, directed at Streak. *Maybe you could try to not make me look like a fool.*

He put a right foot on the middle rung of the fence, threw the left leg over and sat on Streak's back. Clay stroked his neck and murmured in Navajo that all was well. And the horse seemed fine. Still. He didn't even prance. Clay was impressed and leaned down to his ear. "Yeah, not so bad. You're plenty strong enough for a big guy like me." Then he let up on the reins, gave the horse a gentle nudge with his heel and moved him forward. He pulled left on the bit and the horse followed. Then right. Then slowed him to a stop. "You're showing off," he whispered to the horse. "You get an A."

Clay took the horse around the pen again, nice and easy, pleased as much with himself as with Streak because timing was everything. He brought him up to an easy canter and took a couple of laps, then slowed him down.

Lilly had moved from her position behind the fence to a seat on top of the uppermost rail. She lifted her hand, beckoned, kissed the air and hummed, and damned if Streak didn't turn toward her. Clay relaxed his control of the reins; he wanted to see what the horse would do. Streak moved toward her. When he was near enough, he let Lilly touch him without pulling him away.

"Be careful, Lilly," Clay warned. "This guy is unpredictable."

"So you say," she said softly. "Let me have a turn. Come on."

"You're not serious.… I haven't even seen you on a horse yet."

"You're about to. Off," she demanded. "He'd rather have me anyway."

"I can't take that kind of chance. I—"

"I've been on unbroke colts before," she said. "It's been a long time, but I know what I'm doing."

"You could land on your ass, break your back."

"I'm not going to let him do that," she said. "Can't you see he doesn't want to do that to me?"

"Bad idea," he muttered to himself. "Bad, bad, bad idea," he said while he dismounted.

He had barely cleared the horse's back, his feet hardly on the ground a second when the heel of Lilly's boot boosted her from the top rung up onto the horse. She grabbed the reins and seated herself securely on the blanket. She clicked, barely moved the reins, gave a gentle nudge with her thighs and Streak was in motion. He was trotting around the pen in a neat circle. His cadence was perfect. He was balanced, level, his gait *stunning!*

Clay perched himself on the top rail and watched. She didn't pull on the reins, barely touched them; her boot heels didn't even nudge the horse, but he could see the hard muscles of her thighs and the pressure from her knees working to direct him. She shifted her weight to guide him in a flawless dressage. She was brilliant. There was one perfect tear in each knee of her jeans and something about that turned him on. Her lips were moving, but he couldn't hear anything. Streak moved in a perfect, obedient trot around the pen, commanded by this small woman's sheer will.

Clay jumped off the fence and into the pen, but Streak didn't even seem to notice. The horse was completely under Lilly's spell. Clay moved stealthily toward horse and rider, let them pass and finally stood in the center of the pen. He let her go around a couple more times, then held up his hand.

Lilly brought the horse up easily, stopping him on a dime. For someone not into riding, she was an expert.

Gifted. He wondered if Annie was even aware of her skills.

She stroked the horse's mane. "You're the best," she told Streak. "The best."

The *horse?* Clay thought. *She* was magnificent. No relationship or training with this troubled animal and she worked him like he was her lapdog! The damn horse would walk off a cliff for her! She had chemistry with him, an intimacy that Clay had only seen in special relationships between horse and rider.

Lilly threw her left leg over just as Clay reached up to help her down. She didn't need his assistance, but he wanted to touch her, however briefly. He had his hands on her waist as she slid off the horse, but he held her in place. Then he slid her very, very slowly down the length of his body. When her face was even with his, he stopped her descent for a moment, just long enough to look deeply into those blue eyes. Their faces were close and he wanted to kiss her, but he didn't dare. He had no idea how she'd react.

He let her down the rest of the way. "All right," he said. "Either you're lying and you've been on a horse every day for the past ten years or you've made a terrible mistake in being away from it."

"I used to ride every day," she said with a shrug. "Then everything changed and we moved and… I think this horse and I have a thing going on."

"Is that the true meaning of Winning Streak?" he asked hoarsely.

"It is what it is," she whispered. "I sure didn't plan it."

He couldn't help himself. "You and I should have a thing going on and you know it. Tomorrow night,

Lilly. You and me. Dinner. Or something…anything.
We really have to talk about horses and other things."

She shook her head. "Sorry," she said, wriggling free
of his hands. "I have plans." Then she pulled the blanket off Streak's back, handed it to Clay and walked the
horse into the barn.

This restlessness was not good, Lilly thought as she
led Streak back into the stable. She'd been so content
with her life, with her friends and her grandpa and no
confusion about the opposite sex. Dane had so often
warned her that someone would come along to shake
her up eventually, but Lilly hadn't been worried. She
frankly never believed it for a second.

Being lifted off the horse by Clay had weakened her,
left her all wobbly, and she honestly couldn't remember
feeling like that since… Oh, God, since her first love, so
long ago—arrogant, sexy, Native boy who'd made her
crazy, made her hurt, took her virginity and dumped
her. She had been so young, and she'd vowed to never
again be involved with his kind—young Navajo men
full of hormones trying to prove how virile they were.

Clay made her feel unsafe. Vulnerable. Something
she hadn't allowed herself to feel since she was thirteen!
And even though she was older and supposedly wiser,
feelings like that still had the power to overcome her.

She secured the horse and grabbed a brush; when
you ride, you take care of your horse. He hadn't been
worked hard; he didn't need much. But Clay had said
he was getting used to the brush and…

"You don't have to do that, Lilly," Clay said. "You
said you didn't have a lot of time today."

Well, of course he followed her into the stable. Where

else was he going to go? She was the one a bit out of place; this was where he belonged. She began brushing the horse. "How old are you?" she asked him.

"Thirty-four," he said, staying on the other side of the horse. "And you?"

Rather than answering the question, she asked, "Is there a woman somewhere? Women?"

"Why would you ask that?"

She put the brush aside and walked around the horse, ducking under his secured lead, until she was on the same side as Clay. "Because you flirt and try to make a date with me in spite of the fact you've been told I'm committed elsewhere. So, who are you cheating on? Because you Navajo men have a sense of entitlement that I experienced growing up and I really don't feel like playing these games with you. I like the horse. I know your kind and I—"

He had a patient smile on his lips as he gripped her upper arm with one large hand. He lifted her chin with a finger and planted a quick kiss on her mouth. She didn't fight him. He knew he was supposed to be insulted by her little tirade, but he also sensed it was all an act, meant to keep him at a distance. "We might have grown up around all the same canyons, Lilly, and you might have known your share of Navajos, but I think you're talking about boys, not men. The idiocy of boys supersedes all tribe and race connections. I know this from experience, believe me. Boys of all races are universally stupid about women. And you obviously didn't know any Tahoma men. We don't treat women that way. My mother would come out here and beat me if she caught wind of me using or disrespecting a woman. Now, are you over twenty-one?"

Shock settled over her face for a moment, then she burst into laughter. "Over twenty-one? For God's sake," she said, shaking her head. "I have a degree! I'm twenty-seven."

He lifted one black brow and peered at her. Then he pulled her hands toward his chest, placed them there and lowered his lips to hers a second time. But this time it was not a little peck; this time he had a much more serious kiss in mind. He put his arms around her waist, pulled her closer and leaned way down—she was so small—and moved over her lips.

She tasted like berries. Or her lip gloss tasted like berries. Her hair smelled like Ivory soap, a clean, pure smell. And even after moving hay and feed all day, her skin smelled like fresh, sweet grass. He tightened his arms around her and could have stayed that way all day. But she pushed him away and Streak began to get restless. He let her go and smiled at her. "Twenty-seven is good," he said.

"Get a grip," she snapped. "Not gonna happen!"

"Oh, I hope you're wrong," he said, unable to hide a little laughter from his voice.

"I might have to tell my grandfather to have one of the guys from the store deliver here."

"And not check on the horses?" he asked.

"It's a sacrifice I'd be willing to make."

But she hadn't pushed him away immediately. She'd given it some thought and indulged for a while. He'd definitely felt her kissing him back. So he said, "That would be a tragedy."

"Never do that again," she warned. She picked up the brush and put it in his hand. "I mean it."

"If that's what you want," he said with a nod.

"It is."

"Are you sure?" he asked.

It seemed as though she thought through her words before speaking. "Listen to me carefully. We have some things in common. A culture, for one thing. A couple of horses, for another. Nathaniel wouldn't be going to all this trouble if Streak was an ordinary horse. If you do things like this—grabbing and kissing me—we can't even be friends. Do you hear me?"

He gave his head a tilt. "Can we be friends?"

"If I can trust you."

He put his hands up, palms toward her. "You can trust me. And I want to be friends. I want you to come back, mix it up with the horses. I think you have something important to offer. I want to watch and learn."

A silent huff of laughter escaped her. She put her hands on her hips. "Learn from *me?* You're the one with all the experience."

"I'm not so sure about that," he said. "So—I'm very sorry. It won't happen again. And you can trust me. Come back as soon as you can."

"I'll think about it." And with that, she left the stable. But she was immediately back. "Tell Nathaniel I'm going to pay for Blue's board until I can find someone for her. Tell him not to move her out of Club Med. I'll bring a check." Then she disappeared again.

Clay began to brush Streak and very soon he heard her truck engine start and leave the area.

"Well," he said to the horse, "I certainly can't blame you for making me look like a fool."

Six

Jack Sheridan used stencils to create a couple of signs announcing a town meeting. He'd hang one on the bar door, the other on the church door. The meeting was set to take place in the church in a few days. He had the pages laid out on the bar and lettered with colored markers. Mel sat across from him, leaning her chin on her palm, watching.

"You don't have to do it this way," Mel said.

"I know it," he replied. "But I'm not much of an autocrat."

Preacher stood beside Jack, leaning one hand on the bar, watching as he stenciled. "He was a helluva autocrat when we were in the Marines," Preacher pointed out.

"A different situation entirely," Jack said. "Hope left everything she had to the town. I'm just the custodian. I owe it to her to find out what the town wants and needs."

"You're going to get six hundred opinions," Mel said. "Besides, Hope never asked anyone. I doubt she expected you to."

"It doesn't matter," Jack said, filling in letters with

colorful markers. "That was her money. Now it's the town's money. Shouldn't the town have a say in how it's used?"

"No," Mel and Preacher said together. Then they looked at each other in surprise.

"You know the saying—too many cooks in the kitchen," Mel said. "And also, there's nothing in her will saying it has to be dealt with right away, or used at all. It can be invested, saved for a real emergency."

"I'll suggest that option at the meeting," Jack said.

Jack had gone to visit the lawyer who had drawn up the will and trust; it turned out there was a lot of money invested in long-term stocks and bonds, in addition to the house, its contents and land—several million. Now, to a man like Jack, that was a fortune. But as the lawyer quickly pointed out, the budget to run a town, even a very small town, was usually considerably higher. This would at least partially explain why Hope had always kept a firm hand on the bottom line, invested cautiously and conservatively, and when she did spend money—like on hiring Mel as the town midwife or Mike Valenzuela as the town cop—the salaries she offered were not exactly impressive. Of course, also important to remember, Hope had done this out of the goodness of her bank account and no one in town held a meeting or contributed to those salaries. Doc Mullins had worked Mel into his practice then bequeathed the practice to her, relieving Hope of the expense. But as far as Jack could tell, Mike's modest salary was still being paid out of the Virgin River Trust.

"I hope I'm not spoiling a surprise," Mel said, "but Noah's going to make you an offer on behalf of the Presbyterian Women. If you can see your way clear to cut us in on some of the profits, the women's group could volunteer to get in that old house and sort, clean, pitch and restore items. We could hold an estate sale, and the town and the Presbyterian Women would both benefit. And since our women's group serves both the church and the town, it probably works into your plan."

He looked up from his work. He tilted his head and his eyes were large. "That's a very good idea," Jack said. "But, Melinda, it's a monumental job. How soon do you think the women can get to it?"

"Right away, I imagine."

"It could take forever," Jack pointed out.

"Nah," Mel said, shaking her head. "Not only are we a highly motivated group we expect some help from the Presbyterian Husbands." Then she grinned at him.

"I don't recall signing up for that group," Jack said.

"Comes with the territory, sweetheart. The Presbyterian Women are kinda busy with the Presbyterian Children and various jobs. Plus, it's bound to be heavy work and we'll be in need of some muscle." She reached across the bar and gave his biceps a pinch. "We'll be needing our big, strong, handsome partners."

"Why don't you ever flirt with me like that when you don't want something?"

"I'm monitoring the size of your head," she explained patiently. "This town meeting thing, Jack, I don't know…"

"What's the alternative? Just sit on the house, land and bankbook like some king, doling it out as I like? What's to prevent me from just giving Valenzuela a big raise and adding on to the bar and calling it a town hall?"

"Well, besides your ethics, nothing. But Hope was

very realistic in choosing you for this job—she knew you wouldn't do anything like that unless it was in the best interest of the town. And a good option would be a small board of directors to assist—one member who's good with finances, one with legal experience, one who knows town management, et cetera. It doesn't have to be a voting board, but more of a planning committee to assist you, because she really did give you a big job."

"Hope and everyone else. I used to be a bartender. Now I'm a church deacon who practically never went to church, an unelected mayor who never had an interest in running for office, a banker and soon-to-be renovator and real estate mogul. This town needs to delegate responsibility a little better."

She laughed at him, knowing he loved all the attention. "Yes, Your Majesty."

"But see, I don't want to be king of the town purse."

"Well, you will. As soon as you're faced with six hundred wannabe kings and queens trying to jump on your throne with some far-out ideas of how to spend that money. Speaking of money, Hope very cleverly never told anyone how much there was. I'm sure it was so that she wasn't overwhelmed with requests. Are you planning to tell?"

"Don't I have to? If it's the town's money?"

"I'd talk to a lawyer with estate experience about that. Hey—Erin Foley! She's an estate attorney and the family has that renovated cabin now. Plus she's hooked up to Aiden Riordan, who has family nearby, so they'll be spending enough time here to have a vested interest!" She leaned toward him. "Jack, don't tell what the bottom line is before you know whether you absolutely have to. People get very strange when they think they have money burning a hole in their pockets."

"But it's not their money!" Jack insisted.

"That's not going to matter," said Preacher, who had been pretty quiet until now. "Haven't you ever read about those Lotto winners whose lives are destroyed by their windfall?"

"You really think that could happen here?" Jack asked. "This is a good little town!"

"Goodness and opportunity don't always meet on level ground," Mel said.

Both Jack and Preacher straightened suddenly. "Whoa," Jack said. "Is that like from the Dalai Lama or something?"

"No, that's an original Melinda Sheridan. Or, you could try this one on for size, since I bet it fits you to a T. No good deed shall go unpunished." She took a last sip of her diet cola. "I gotta go. We have patients this afternoon. Good luck with this." She whirled off her stool and headed out the door.

Jack stared after her. "Why didn't Hope make her the custodian?"

"Executor and administrator," Preacher corrected. "Personally, I think Hope's watching and getting a big laugh out of it." And with that, Preacher went back to the kitchen and Jack was left alone.

Alone with one final thought: *We still haven't decided what to do with Hope's ashes. Don't we have to scatter her ashes before we start spending her money?*

He thought he heard a distant, gravelly laugh.

Jack struggled with his dilemma for a few days. He tried not to talk about it too much, but if the bar was quiet and someone he knew to be a trusted friend happened upon his path, he was susceptible to spilling his guts. But the last person he expected walked in the door—Luke Riordan.

"Hey, there!" Jack said. "I've hardly seen you since Brett was born!"

Luke stuck out his hand across the bar. "Shelby sprung me loose for a beer break. Since she started back to school, I have so much quality time with Brett I guess I'm getting a little cranky."

"That a fact?" Jack asked with a laugh. "I can relate to that." He served him up a cold beer. In addition to managing six rental cabins on the river, Luke was taking care of their two-month-old son while Shelby went to college. "Cabins busy right now?" Jack asked.

"About half-full. The summer people have pretty much stopped coming through, but fishing is picking up and come next month when hunting season opens, we're booked solid. When it's groups of men making the reservations I assume fishing or hunting."

"How can you handle all that? With the baby?"

"For right now, Shelby's uncle Walt sticks pretty close. Art's a great help," Luke said. Art was a man in his early thirties with Down syndrome who lived on their property and worked under their supervision. "But there are a lot of things that are just beyond him—anything up a ladder, paperwork or accounting, driving for supplies, you know. But so far, we're managing just fine." He took a drink of his beer and said, "Ahhhh. Not like I don't have cold beer at home, but I needed to get out. I feel like a nanny."

"How are your brothers getting along?" Jack asked.

"Let's see—the youngest, Patrick, is sitting alert on

an aircraft carrier, but it's a short three-month mission. Aiden and Erin are planning a small wedding for the spring. Sean is up to his eyeballs in Air Command and Staff College—boy's probably going to be an Air Force general. Now doesn't that make you laugh? Sean, the biggest screw-off I know. I guess he can get serious where the Air Force is concerned. And the only one we don't hear that much from is Colin, but that's always been the case. He's a loner."

"What's Colin doing these days?"

Luke took another swig of beer. "Black Hawk helicopters out of Fort Benning, Georgia."

"Shouldn't he be about ready to retire?" Jack asked. "Isn't he about forty?"

"About right, and already over twenty years in the Army—but they're going to have to throw him out. He'll never go quietly. He loves that helicopter and it loves him."

Jack poured himself a cup of coffee. "I never understood you flyboys. I never even liked riding in choppers."

Luke laughed at him. "All the boys fly except Aiden, and look what Aiden ended up doing—ob-gyn? Come on, that's weird if you ask me."

Jack took a sip. "Now, I think that makes sense. More sense than going up in the air in some kind of strange whirly machine. So, Luke, you and Shelby coming to the town meeting?"

Luke thought a moment before answering. He took a small taste of his beer for courage. "Hey, I'm real sorry, Jack, but that sounds like about the most boring thing I can think of and my fun meter is already way, way down."

"Mel thinks I shouldn't do it at all. She thinks every-one will have diverging ideas."

"No offense, Jack, but if you get ten people with enough time on their hands for a boring town meeting, you'll be lucky."

"Think so? You should come, Luke. Maybe you'll have some ideas for the town."

"Want to know what my best idea is? Sleeping through the night, that's the best idea I can come up with. I want that baby in his own room and me and Shelby sleeping straight through."

"It'll come," Jack said. "He's only a couple of months old."

"Yeah, a couple of months with a tapeworm. Kid eats nonstop. And he has the biggest feet I've ever seen. If babies grow into their feet like German shepherds, he's gonna be eight feet tall." He finished his beer slowly. "I'd like to stay longer, but I'm afraid if I do, you'll talk me into that meeting by calling in some marker or something."

"If you don't participate," Jack said solemnly, "no one will ever elect you mayor."

Luke stood up, tossed a couple of bills on the bar and said, "That works for me. You take care now." And he got out of there before it went any further.

While walking across the parking lot from the bar to the church for the town meeting, Jack asked Mel if she'd mind taking notes, just to have something to ref-erence if he wanted to review the suggestions of what to do with their inheritance from Hope. "Notes? Like minutes?" she asked.

"Totally unofficial—but I'd like some kind of record

of what was said. I don't know why or how I'll use it, but... You know—just jot down a name and a suggestion. That kind of thing."

"I guess so. Um, Jack—please play your cards close to your chest on this. Don't tell too much too fast. People never knew what Hope had and she was a cagey old broad—I suspect there was a reason for it. No one knew her town better than she did."

"I think you're selling this little town short, Melinda. I've always found most everyone to be responsible. Cautious, even. And certainly generous."

"Uh-huh," she said.

"Look, there are already cars and trucks parked outside." Jack smiled. "We're going to get a good turnout!"

"Uh-huh."

"Um, Jack?" a man's voice said.

Jack turned to find himself face-to-face with Hugh Givens, local apple orchard owner. He stuck out his hand. "Hey, Hugh, how's it going, man?"

"Good. Excellent. Listen, could I just have a quick word with you before the meeting starts?"

"You have ideas, Hugh? Because I'd prefer it if you'd—"

"No, sir, a question. If I could have a second... Alone?"

Mel's eyebrows lifted in surprise that anyone would ever question her discretion. She was probably the best secret keeper in the town. But she took the hint. Jack handed her the little notebook he'd been carrying and watched her go inside.

"What's up?" he said to Hugh.

"Well, I'm assuming Hope had her money mostly

invested, and tied up in that big old house and stuff. And I'm wondering—you planning to invest? Make sure that money for the town keeps making money?"

"I guess," Jack said with a shrug. "Why?"

"Well, I have a proposition. Could work out for both of us. Remember I built that room on the house? Well, rooms. One downstairs, one up, and a freestanding garage—more for farm equipment than trucks, really. Things were real skippy when I built on, you know? But I kinda got caught in the economic downturn with an adjustable second mortgage so I was just wondering—how do you feel about making a loan out of that money? I'd pay decent interest, of course. Just not insane interest, if you get my meaning. Could make the town money go a little further and save my butt."

"Aw, Hugh, I'm not a banker. Just an executor, that's all."

"Yeah, that means you can do pretty much whatever you want as long as you don't abuse the money, right? This ain't abuse! It's a good investment! No matter how bad things get, people still make apple cider and apple pie. And things are gonna swing back up. But that adjustable rate second could really kill me in the meantime."

"Hugh, I don't think Hope intended personal loans—"

"It's not exactly a loan. An investment! By the way, how much did she leave you?"

Jack was starting to doubt his wisdom on this matter. He put a strong hand on Hugh's shoulder. "She didn't leave me anything, Hugh. She left it to the town and put me in charge of making sure it's used responsibly.

I'm obligated to look at the past use of her funds to get a clue about how she thinks that should be done. Now let's go inside and have a meeting with the town."

"Is that a no?" he asked.

"That is a no," Jack said. "I'm sorry you got stuck with a bad loan, but Hope's money wasn't meant for any one person. I'm sure of that."

"Don't know why not, if the return is good," he said in a pout. "The others might not agree with you, you know."

"Well, let's hear what they have to say." But he was already starting to regret this idea of a town meeting. And it pissed him off that Mel and Preacher were onto this ahead of him.

Jack left Hugh to find himself a seat and strode down the center aisle of the church. He got a prickly sensation up his spine when he noted there were more people packed into the church to divvy up the money than attended Sunday morning service.

"Evening," he said when he faced the crowd. "If it wasn't clear in the notice, let me explain why we're all gathering here tonight. Hope McCrea, who did so many generous things for Virgin River, left the town a trust in her will. And because she was a little daft and short-sighted, she decided to put me in charge. So, I thought it made sense to listen to your suggestions and ideas and—"

"How much did she leave you?" a man's voice rang out from the back.

"Okay, let's be clear, here—she didn't leave *me* anything. I have no intention of ever using or borrowing from her funds. But I have been given a responsibility that I take very seriously—to use what she left in a way that she would approve of. Now, if you knew Hope you knew she was pretty well fixed, but she didn't throw money around. Hell, I don't know if I ever saw her in a coat with all its buttons and God knows that old Suburban of hers had a couple hundred thousand miles on it. I take that as a clue about how careful she was with—"

"How much is it?" a different male voice shouted from the back.

"I'm not telling you. Don't you get that? I invited you here to give you a chance to make suggestions, since Hope died with the intention that what she left behind would serve the town! Do I hear a suggestion?" he asked a little hotly.

"We need a sign!" a woman's voice rang out. An elderly lady stood up. "We really need a sign! People don't know where they are when they get off 36. We need a sign that says, Welcome to Virgin River, Population 623, et cetera."

"Okay, there's an idea. That's what I'm talking about," Jack said approvingly. He nodded at Mel to make sure she'd jotted it down, which she did right after rolling her eyes.

"It should have lights on it," the woman went on. "With a big blinking arrow. I'm talking about a *big* sign. Billboard size. Like they have for casinos."

"Whoa," Jack said. "Do we really need—"

"We need to bail out our friends and neighbors," Hugh Givens said, standing up. "I suggested this to Jack already but he could care less about an idea like this. We need to use that money to make some loans to folks who have been hit by this recession. I mean, with fair interest, it's a good investment for the town. Right? And some of us got caught in the crunch and could use a little help from someone who's not a bank."

"I could use some of that kind of help," one of the Andersons said. The Andersons were sheep ranchers.

"Hey, I could use a break on interest," said a man from the other side of the room.

"Bull, Lou, you're just broke 'cause you bought a new Dually and you don't even need no Dually—you just go back and forth to work, that's all."

"So my truck is less important than that rumpus room you built on the house?" the offended owner of the truck with dual back wheels asked hotly.

"Best thing we could do is double the size of that corner store so people would have a place to shop in this town," said Ron, who just happened to own the Corner Store. "Can't do that without a little help. And it would serve the town."

"How about a lottery?" a man said, standing. "'Course it would help to know how much money there is before we actually do it, but we could have a lottery and divide it up. Then a bunch of people could be winners."

"Listen to yourselves," Jo Ellen Fitch said. "We need a school! We've been bussing our children to other towns for years and even survived a bus accident! What could be a more responsible use for Hope's money than a school?"

"I got my kids through school!" someone shouted. "I put 'em on the bus or drove 'em myself. I don't want my one chance at some cash to go to some school when I don't have any need of one anymore!"

"Seriously—a lottery! Let's take care of it, here and now. It's town money and we're the town, right? So Jack, spit it out—how much is there?"

"Will you listen to yourselves?" Jack said angrily. "What are you going to do if there's an epidemic? A wildfire? If some kid goes missing in the forest? Don't you have any interest in saving up some money for emergencies? What if we have to rebuild the town someday? What if we need an ambulance or fire truck or—"

"I guess we'll do what we've always done," someone answered. "You ever know us to fail to pitch in?"

"You can't wait to get your greedy hands on this money!" he nearly shouted. "I'm totally shocked! I thought you'd come up with good ideas for the town! But no, you want to clear loans and win a lottery!"

"A school, at least for the little ones," Jo Fitch repeated. "It could be one room, grades one through six or something."

"What the hell for?" someone shouted. "The rest of us got our kids through school riding that bus! Paid for by the county, by the way!"

"I ain't giving up my share for someone else's elementary schoolers!" someone else shouted.

Jack's face grew red. He listened to people shouting back and forth and just went from red to purple. He glanced at his wife and saw her gently close her notebook. Finally, with no feedback from him, the din subsided. He cleared his throat. "Ahem. Hope did not leave her money to the people of the town, but the town. And she put me in charge of figuring out how to serve the town. So, you all sound like a bunch of selfish bastards who can't wait to get your paws on her money— excuse me, the school idea was not selfish, no offense intended...."

"What about my sign?" a woman asked.

"Also unselfish. But totally unnecessary. This was a bad idea. This meeting is over."

He walked back down the center aisle and out of the church.

The Loving Cup was Dane's brainchild. It was also a way for him to help his sister, Darlene, get on her feet after a rough divorce. They had started on a shoe-string, but Dane had catering experience and Darlene was a dream in the kitchen. They had decorated with an eclectic collection of comfy chairs from wing chairs to cushiony armchairs complete with mismatched side and coffee tables. Although they sold food ranging from cookies and slices of pie to breakfast and lunch sand-wiches, the front of the store was set up with a series of small sitting areas. And it was almost always full. People dropped in for as little as a cup of coffee or as much as a lunch meeting.

There were only two stools at the end of the long counter, and Lilly had claimed one of them as her fa-vorite perch.

Dane worked the front of the store, which was one of the reasons Lilly had formed a closer bond with him than with Darlene. Darlene was stuck in the kitchen, creating her masterpieces. And there was also the fact that five years postdivorce and four years post–Loving Cup opening, Darlene, a single mother of two teenag-ers, was in a very nice, comfortable relationship with the owner of a small hardware store. And Dane, like Lilly, was unattached. That allowed for their occasional nights out together.

There was undoubtedly more to it—Lilly and Dane had taken to each other. What began as a few friendly chats over tea and buns turned into deep conversations in which some confidences were exchanged. And because neither of them was romantically involved, it was a simple matter to arrange outings like trips to the wildlife sanctuary or movies or even shopping trips.

Most importantly she relied on his friendship because she'd told him things about herself that she hadn't even told any of her few girlfriends. And he had responded with both kindness and wisdom.

Dane and Darlene closed the coffee shop at six-thirty every evening. They had discovered that evening crowds were thin—people seemed to prefer dinner at real restaurants or bars, even if their drink of choice was a frothy coffee. Knowing it was closing time, Lilly popped into the shop after finishing work at the feed store. And knowing this was very rare for Lilly when they didn't have plans together, Dane walked around the counter, flipped the sign to Closed and locked the door.

He walked back around the counter, faced her and said, "I already washed the teapot. And you've been wearing that strange look for a couple of weeks at least, except tonight it just got stranger."

"Can I just have something from the case? Like a Snapple or something?"

"And then you'll talk?" he asked.

"I always talk," she said.

"Well, that's debatable," he said, getting her a cold drink. He twisted off the top and handed it across the counter. "You always talk *eventually*. Sometimes you lead up to it for *months*. I'm getting less patient with that."

She took a pull of a cold raspberry drink. "Got a date?"

"Hah. My Friday-night girl is sitting right here, and unless I missed something, we don't have plans. What has you so screwed up?"

She smirked before she said, "The vet tech."

"Ah-*hah!*" he said, victorious. "I knew it! Didn't I know it? I told you and you said it was the horses!"

"It's the vet tech *and* the horses," she corrected. "If I hadn't let myself get all hooked on the horses, I could have probably stayed away from the vet tech! Now going to see the horses means running into him and I have to figure out how to deal because I want to keep Blue and I'm trying to find a way." She leaned toward him. "The director at the community center would love to have me teach some yoga and if I did it three nights a week, I could pay her board."

"And never have time to ride her," Dane said. "Tell me about the guy."

She sat back. "He reminds me of He-Who-Shall-Not-Be-Named."

"The teenage werewolf?" Dane asked, speaking of the heartbreaker of her childhood. "How does he remind you? In looks? In personality? His voice? His mannerisms?"

"In general," she said. "He's very tall, like the teenage werewolf, and very Native—high cheekbones, long black hair, almost black eyes. He's incredibly sexy—to me, anyway—and that's the scariest part."

"Is he nice?" Dane asked.

She sucked in her breath. "Everyone is nice at first," she said. "Yes, he's nice. And maybe the most powerful man I've ever known—that's what's so scary. That's what makes me feel like running for my life. He has a

huge presence. His confidence and mastery is just…
Whew!"

Dane held one of her hands. "Honey, you were a
thirteen-year-old baby in a woman's body when an ir-
responsible but hot guy came after you. All your hormones were firing off rockets. You were too young to
be smart, and you got hurt so bad that you spent the
next fourteen years putting up your defenses so you'd
never be tempted by a good-looking guy again." He
grinned at her. "There are handsome, powerful men in
this world who are also good. You should be sure about
what you're dealing with before you run."

Dane was one of very few living people who knew
the whole traumatic story. Want of that eighteen-year-
old boy from a neighboring reservation turned Lilly
into a maniac who was willing to risk anything to be
with him. She sneaked out at night, didn't come home
by curfew or even all night, took money from and lied
to her grandpa… She was horrid; she dared anything
that boy asked. She gave him her virginity. And then
suddenly—and shamefully—she was pregnant. The
drama of it was shattering. Grandpa went after the boy,
his family, he even once loaded a rifle. In the end the
boy ran, leaving the Navajo Nation for parts unknown
to escape being tied to Lilly. She lost the baby before the
third month. Grandpa packed up the house and moved
them to California. She remembered him saying, "It's
not too late for you to turn your life around, Lilly. Not
too late for you to be different than your poor, wasted
mother."

And by God, she had!

"You are not that little girl anymore, Lilly," Dane said

to her now. "You're an educated adult and if he isn't a good man, you'll kick him to the curb."

"What if I give him a chance and it gets me really hurt, like the last time?"

"Annie McKenzie will shoot him."

That made Lilly smile. Annie probably would. "He asked me out."

"And you said?"

"That I had a boyfriend…"

"Aw, God," Dane said, rolling his eyes. "I feel dirty, I feel used.…"

"And he actually kissed me. Grabbed me and kissed me. And I *liked* it. And then I told him if he ever did that again, we couldn't even be friends. So the jerk forced me to agree to friendship, that's how sneaky he is. And how dense I am!"

"I have suggested counseling for this reason," Dane reminded her. "It's time to move on, Lilly. Time to leave the teenage misery in the past and get on with life. I know you think you want to be an old spinster with a feed store, but that'll never work for you. It's the coward's way out and when you're fifty you'll hate yourself for not giving a relationship and family a chance."

She gave him a weak smile. "I could make a life with you," she told him. "I love everything about you. Why can't you just marry me?"

"We would have fun, wouldn't we?" he asked, grinning at her. "But in the long run we probably wouldn't have sex."

She put her elbow on the counter and leaned her head into her hand. "Why do you have to be gay?"

He shrugged. "I was looking for a challenge."

Seven

Clay was standing in the aisle of the stable between the stalls, broom in one hand and cup of coffee in the other, when Annie and Nathaniel walked into the barn arm in arm.

"Good morning," he said to them. "You two going to be around today?"

"I am," Annie said.

"I probably will," Nate said. "Unless I get called out. Why?"

"I don't want us to act as if we've discussed or planned this, but if you're around here today there's something I think you should see. Something pretty remarkable. Yesterday Lilly rode Streak. Just a few laps around the round pen, but I was surprised he let her on him at all. She was brilliant."

"I've ridden with Lilly a few times," Annie said. "We shouldn't be surprised. She's very good on a horse. What surprises me is Streak. He must be coming along very well if he took a rider."

"That's just it, Annie—Streak shouldn't have been so willing. No one has worked him but me. Lilly has watched him almost every day. She's flirted with him, but no one has worked him but me. And there's no question in my mind, if it were anyone else, he wouldn't have let them mount him," Clay insisted. "He's come to respect me, but he loves her."

"Come on." Annie laughed.

"When Lilly comes by with the feed later on, take a break and watch her with the colt."

After Annie and Nathaniel agreed, he put his cup down on the bench outside the tack room and swept out the barn. He spent the rest of the day hoping that Lilly wouldn't make good on her promise and have someone else deliver for her. The truth was, Clay had been hoping to impress Lilly with his skill, but she'd turned the tables on him. Whatever mystical thing he had going on with animals, she had it twofold. There was no doubt in his mind—Lilly would never have mounted that colt had she gotten the message he didn't welcome her. Somehow she knew.

It was a little after three before she came. He helped her unload the hay and feed, then she brushed her hands on her jeans and asked, "Have you ridden Streak today?"

"No," he said. "I'm going to pass. Let's see if he feels like letting you on. I'll halter him, attach the lead and—"

"He did fine with the bit," she said. "I think it's all a question of how easy I go. He's so responsive."

"I'll find you a helmet...."

She shrugged. "Whatever," she said. "Will you let me get him ready?"

He loomed over her. "He's still edgy and unpredictable. I know you're somehow reading him, but the second you pick up any signals that he's not feeling docile toward you, I want you out of his way."

"Oh, don't worry," she said with a laugh, "if he's in a mood, he's all yours. But this horse isn't typical—he just wants a mommy. Well, apparently he's not opposed to a mommy and a trainer since he's willing to take you on. Let's see how difficult he makes taking the bit. Hmm?"

Clay just shook his head. "If you say so. Approach slowly, please."

She tilted her head. "Clay, I didn't just drop from the sky. I grew up around wild mares and stud colts. I learned how to finish a colt from some of the best, though when I was little I never got the job. But I wanted it. I wanted to beguile the horse, bond with it, bring it around, be its first..."

"Did you compete?"

"You grew up on a reservation so you know—competition is expensive. Besides, we moved when I was thirteen. My experience, such as it is, came when I was just a little kid. Now, are we almost ready?"

Clay handed her the bridle and went back to the tack room for a helmet, trying to judge the size of her head when really it was the contours of her small, muscular body that were burned into his mind.

She was the one to bring Streak into the round pen. Clay gave her a leg up and there she sat, composed. Streak was easy; he danced with his fores a couple of steps, but his ears were propped and his tail down. He was in a good mood and he liked having Lilly close. Maybe she was right about him—he just wanted someone to mother him a little bit.

The horse connected eyes with Clay, let Clay stroke

his powerful jaw, and then let Lilly move him away from his trainer and urge him around the pen in a wide circle. This had never, in Clay's long experience, happened before. The colt was bonded with two masters. He would take his instruction from Clay; he trusted Clay. But he was also bonded with Lilly and believed in her somehow. Young, unbroke colts didn't bond with two people!

Clay noticed that first Annie and then Nathaniel were watching from the far side of the pen. They would be seeing something neither of them had ever seen before despite the fact that Annie had ridden with Lilly. Taking a saddled horse out on the trail for a pleasure ride just wouldn't reveal the depth of skill Lilly possessed, evident now as she maneuvered the horse with only her knees, legs, body position and a very, very light control on the reins. And Lilly was oblivious to her audience; all she seemed to be aware of was her connection to the horse. Although she wasn't attempting anything too complicated with Streak, it was obvious how well she managed him, and with very little strain. Her lips moved, but no sound could be heard; Streak threw his head and stepped back a few times, but she brought him under control with a whisper and a firm but kind movement of the reins and her legs.

No question, she was a natural.

Clay was well trained, but he was not a natural. To do something like this when you'd had minimal contact with horses for years was astonishing.

Clay leaned back against the wall and just watched her with the colt. She had him trotting, walking, cantering.... That horse was ready for a saddle and by God he was going to wear one and behave himself. Then Clay felt a chuckle rise to his throat; he was feeling competitive. He was fine with Streak feeling affection for Lilly, but he was going to be the one to train the horse or break his legs trying.

At length, Lilly brought the horse around to him. "Thank you," he said softly to her. "Well done. Enough for today."

"You aren't going to ride him?"

"Not today," he said. He lifted his hands to her and she fell into them to be helped down.

When her feet were on the ground she said, "I don't know what's up with him, why he goes along with me the way he does. But it's working, right?"

Clay smiled at her. "Let's see how he likes the brush today. Will you join me?"

"Sure. For a little while..."

When they were in the stable together and Clay groomed the horse, Lilly sat on a bench. "Listen, you're not upset that he lets me near him, are you?"

Clay looked over his shoulder and smiled at Lilly. "I'm proud of you. You're exceptional. But tomorrow or the day after I'm going to take him out early and alone, to make sure he understands he's not just dating a pretty girl but actually training."

She laughed. "I understand. I won't get in your way." Then she sighed longingly. "I wish he was ready for me to saddle up Blue and ride alongside. That could be good."

"Soon, Lilly." There was the sound of a vehicle pulling up to the stable and clinic and Clay lifted his head with the grace of a buck sniffing the air. He recognized the sound of that engine. "Gabe," he said under his breath. "Excuse me, Lilly." Then he maneuvered Streak into the stallion pen without finishing his grooming and walked out of the barn.

Lilly watched Clay's long, powerful strides lead him outside; she listened to the sound of his boot heels hitting the ground, watched that long, silky black ponytail swing across his back. "You were almost done, anyway," she said to the horse.

Lilly followed Clay; she was wiping her hands on a rag, standing in the barn's double doors in time to see a young man jump from the driver's side of a small green truck, walk briskly to Clay and embrace him with power. Their fists banged on each other's backs. The young man looked like he could be Clay's younger brother—as tall, almost as broad, an identical black ponytail down his back. Jeans, denim shirt, boots, hat. Then Clay grasped the young man's upper arms, held him away, looked him up and down and murmured something that made the younger man laugh. Then he looked over Clay's shoulder curiously. And Clay turned.

"Lilly. Come here a second. Meet my son, Gabe."

Shock was evident on her face, but she moved toward them. Son? How was that possible? Clay was only thirty-four and this young man was too old.

"Gabe, meet Lilly. She delivers feed from her grandfather's feed store twice a week, and lately she's been helping me with a difficult horse. Lilly, this is Gabe." Clay put an arm around Gabe's shoulders and pulled him close. "He's going to stay with my sister in Grace Valley and finish high school here so we can spend a little more time together. He'll work here part-time."

Lilly stuck out her hand. She smiled a bit tremulously. "Nice to meet you. Wow. I'd have taken you for a younger brother."

Gabe laughed and grasped her hand. "Dad was barely seventeen when I was born. He got an early start, but probably not on purpose."

"Not on purpose, but with no regrets," Clay said. "Gabe grew up with the Tahoma family—my parents, aunts and uncles, many cousins. Regrettably, I wasn't always there, but I think he had a good upbringing."

"I did," he confirmed with a smile. "And you were there as often as you could be."

Lilly was quiet for a moment. Then she said, "There's a lot more to you than meets the eye."

"There's more to everyone than meets the eye," Clay said. "I hope you'll forgive me—I'm going to introduce Gabe to Nathaniel and Annie, then follow him to my sister's house. Is there anything else you need today?"

"I'll feed Streak and you can turn him out before you leave," she said.

"Thank you."

"Nice to meet you, Gabe. Welcome." As she walked away from them she thought, *Wow, he has more in common with the teenage werewolf than I thought. He found out a baby was coming when he was only a teenager, too...but the difference is, he didn't walk away.*

Lilly stayed away from the clinic for a couple of days, giving Clay, his son and the horse a little space. Then she ventured back. There was no need to deliver feed but Lilly was driven to explore Clay and whatever it was that compelled him to become an involved father at such a young age. In fact, if she was honest, there was much about Clay she wanted to learn.

The round pen and small pasture were both empty and she went into the barn. No one was around. There was only the sound of some faint swishing and soft whistling. Streak's stall was empty. She found Gabe in another stall with one of the Jensen Thoroughbreds, mucking it out. She tapped lightly on the wood.

Gabe's head came up and he smiled. "Hey, Miss Yazhi," he said. "Dr. Jensen has gone out to a farm to take a look at an old bull."

She glanced into Streak's stall. "Someone seems to be missing," she said.

"Oh, him. Dad took him out on the trail."

"Really?" she asked, eyes wide. "Saddled?"

Gabe nodded. "Didn't like it much, either. Yesterday he took him just around the pen with the saddle and even that was iffy. I hope Dad gets to ride back." And then he chuckled.

"He might be walking," she suggested.

"It wouldn't be the first time. He's had himself a tough horse or two before this."

"Tougher than Streak?"

"Streak's a pussycat. Back home, we brought 'em in from the open range sometimes. Had some stallions that had killed. Thousand-pound felons." And again, the boyish grin. He was such a handsome kid. He'd braided that long ponytail, probably to keep his hair out of his face while he did chores.

"Must have been an interesting life, back home."

He shrugged at first. Then he leaned his rake against the wall, smoothed back his black hair and said, "I probably took it for granted, since I didn't know much else. We worked hard, played hard, learned hard. My grandfather is a demanding man. He expects a lot."

"What about your parents?" she asked. "Did they expect a lot?"

Clear-eyed, steady, he said, "There was only my dad. I didn't meet my mom till I was twelve and that was mostly because my stepfather wanted me to know my younger brothers. They live in Scottsdale. He's a foot doctor. My dad calls him a corn shaver."

"So your mother didn't raise you?" she asked before she could stop herself. She might've colored a little; she knew she was asking too many questions. Personal questions.

Gabe didn't seem to mind. He grabbed the rake, exited the stall and closed the Thoroughbred inside. He talked while he put the rake away. "Not my mom, no," he said. "My parents were boyfriend and girlfriend till her parents broke them up. They didn't like their little girl mixed up with some Navajo from the Nation. Then it turned out my mom was pregnant. Her parents had control of the situation, wouldn't let her call him and had an adoption all lined up for me, but then my dad found out and he wasn't giving up that easy. He got his dad and his uncles, legal aid from the reservation, practically a warrior tribe. They paid a visit and geared up for a fight. Grandpa said they didn't expect to get their legal hands on me till I was two or three, but my maternal grandparents gave up. They knew they were gonna lose." He shrugged. "So two days after I was born, my dad took me home to the Tahoma ranch, where I lived till last week. Now I'm living with my aunt and uncle and their family, going to school and working with my dad."

Her mouth nearly stood open. She was thunderstruck. "That must have been… It must have been hard on you."

"On *me?*" he asked with a smile. "With a grandma,

grandpa, dad, aunts, uncles, cousins? I think I had it great."

"I thought your dad said he wasn't with you that much...."

"Oh, he says that out of guilt, but he doesn't have to. He left when I was about eleven years old. He had to."

"Had to?"

"He was a farrier trained by his father and uncles, but a farrier on the reservation doesn't make much of a living. He wanted to make his mark, to earn real money. He'd made a name for himself—going out on the road here and there—doing good work for ranches, and got offered a gig in L.A., managing stables for a rich breeder. He sent my grandparents money while he was away. And he came home whenever he could—didn't faze him to thumb a ride back to Arizona as long as he could be home at least a few days. I wasn't ever away from him that long."

She got sentimental at the thought of a young man who'd thumb hundreds of miles to see his little son. "I guess you two are real close."

"I'd say so, but if my grandfather was tough, my dad was usually tougher. And if you think the Tahoma men are a handful, you should meet the women. God," he said, giving his head a shake and absently running a hand over his ear. "I think I'm growing a tumor from where my grandma grabbed my ear and twisted. Man."

She laughed in spite of herself. "Looks like you survived it pretty well."

"No one's more surprised than me!"

"So, are you glad to be here?"

"Time will tell," he said. He stuck his hands in the

pockets of his jeans. "I wasn't real excited about the idea. I mean, it's my senior year. I have friends at home."

Home, she thought. "I was raised by my grandparents, too," she told him. "My grandma passed when I was little and when I was thirteen my grandpa decided it was time to make a change, get us off the reservation, where he said my opportunities were too limited. I know what it's like to make that change."

"Well, there are positives. I like my aunt and uncle and my Grace Valley cousins. I'm going to play some dangerous, integrated football instead of on a reservation team. Dad says we're going to hunt—I'm good with that. And…" He shrugged. "And my dad needs me."

"Oh?"

"Well, he needs me around. He's always talked about that, about the two of us finally living in the same county, at least. It's real important to him. And he's always done everything he could for—" He stopped abruptly and leaned one hand against the wall, peering out the rear stable doors. "Uh-oh," he said. He shifted his gaze to Lilly. "It would probably be best not to laugh."

Lilly stood from the bench and looked out the doors, across the corral and down the trail. Clay was leading Streak home. And he seemed to have a slight limp. "Uh-oh," she said.

"Yeah, he's going to be a little cranky.…"

"Your dad or Streak?" she asked.

"Looks to me like Streak probably won. But if I know my dad, that's his absolute last win."

As Clay drew closer, it was obvious there was more than the limp at issue. He was covered with dirt and dust, for one thing. He had some road rash on his cheek, and the knuckles and back of his hand that held the horse's lead were scraped and bleeding. And, once he got very close she could see a nice purple bruise was rising on the injured cheek.

He was wearing a very dark frown. He didn't look angry so much as deeply contemplative. He stopped briefly when he saw Lilly was there; he gave her a short, curt nod then lowered his gaze and proceeded into the stable.

Lilly decided to see how Gabe handled it, both out of curiosity and because she wasn't sure what to say.

Gabe put out a hand. "Want me to take care of him, Dad?"

"No," Clay said. "He's going to wait till I'm fucking ready." His eyes darted briefly to Lilly. "Pardon," he said for the profanity, leading the horse—still trapped in the despised saddle—to his stall.

Despite her best efforts, Lilly couldn't remain quiet. "What did you hurt? Ankle, knee, hip, back?"

"All of the above," he grumbled, moving the horse into his stall. "I might leave the saddle on all night, you ungrateful beast."

The horse lifted his head and shook it. It almost appeared as if Streak smiled, and Lilly thought, *My, my, doesn't he have the biggest teeth?* She covered her own smile with her hand.

"Excuse me," Clay said. "I'll be back." And he walked out of the barn.

When he was gone Gabe said, "If you'll excuse me, I'm going to find him some ice. He's going to clean up, put ice on something for a little while, then take the saddle off Streak and make up. But Streak will have to show some remorse."

"Remorse?"

"Uh-huh. Which he will do after about a half hour of itching because he's cooled down with no brush. Leaving the saddle on will annoy him."

"How will he show that remorse?" Lilly asked.

"With subtlety. But my dad can hear him think. And Streak can hear my dad think. And I can guarantee, Streak's been hearing my dad think all the way from whatever place he dumped him. Just makes me glad every day of my life that I can only hear him when he *talks*. I'll be—"

"I'll get the ice for him," she said, interrupting him. "Where will I find ice?"

"In Doc's surgery, in the freezer. Um, you'd better holler in. Dad could be...you know...not dressed."

"I'll holler," she said. Then she went quickly before Gabe could talk her out of it.

So—he hears the horses! She had thought so. Not because he'd wowed her with this ability, but because he'd questioned whether she had it, too. She didn't hear them, but she did often get a sense of what was going on with them, in their minds or with their emotional instability. She thought she felt them sometimes. But she was never sure she was right.

She found the ice, went to Clay's quarters and knocked on the door, but there was no answer. She opened the door and, looking down and covering her eyes with her hand like a visor, she called, "Clay?" Again, no answer. "Coming in," she announced to the sound of the shower. There was no response. She tapped on the door frame outside the bathroom. "Clay?"

"What?" he yelled unhappily.

"I have ice. Wrap a towel around yourself and I'll

keep my eyes closed until you find something to cover up with."

"Leave the ice and go away!" he called out of the shower.

She laughed. A bounce off the back of a little boy stallion didn't do much to ease his disposition. "I'm staying so try not to embarrass either of us. Just let me look at your hand and cheek. You must have been totally unprepared." And she tried to keep another laugh under her hand.

"Go *away!*"

"Nah, I'm staying."

The shower finally turned off. She trained her eyes on the floor. She heard the partially closed bathroom door squeak, then the sound of a drawer, followed by the words, "You can open your eyes."

He hadn't sounded real pleasant, so she lifted her eyes slowly, carefully. She connected with a safe place—his eyes. "So, Gabe told me—you talk to the horses. They talk to you."

"Not always. 'I'm going to buck you off' would've been nice to hear," he said.

She laughed. She let her eyes lower and almost breathed a sigh of relief at the sight of his sweatpants. But the sigh caught in her throat when she realized he was still shirtless—and as amazing as a statue. Tall, buff, his shoulders wide and hard, tattoos on both biceps, his wet hair falling long and unbound, curling in tendrils to his waist. It was enough to make her wet her pants. Gabe was pretty, but Clay was a breathtaking mountain of a man. Like nothing she had ever seen in her life. She looked down again.

"What hurts?" she asked.

"Hip, knee, face, hand."

"Back?"

"No more than usual."

"I better get more ice."

"Forget the ice," he said irritably. "I'll ice later. I have to take care of that blasted horse."

"Why don't Gabe and I take care of that while you…"

"It has to be me," he said. "If it's not me, the horse will think he's in control and has gotten away with something. Why are you here?"

"Honestly? To see you. I wanted to learn more about your family. I wondered if you were married or something."

"Didn't we go over that?" he asked, his brows drawing together.

"Man, are you in a mood! We talked about it briefly, very briefly, before your seventeen-year-old son suddenly appeared. But never mind, he's told me a lot about the whole…situation. I hope you don't mind."

"It's not a secret, for God's sake. And it's more Gabe's story to tell than mine." He rubbed his hand down his face and took a deep breath. "I'm sorry. The horse pissed me off. He was doing fine till he decided he wanted a little power struggle. The mangy beast."

"Sure you don't want to rethink the ice? And maybe a bandage for your hand? You're kind of scuffed up there."

"What I want is to find a pair of dry boots, clean jeans, a shirt, and to go take care of that horse. I'm going to send Gabe home to my sister's and when I have things under control here, I'll go over there for their family meal."

"Of course," she said.

He looked at her for a long moment, at the ice in her hand, then tilted his head. "May I?"

"Oh! Of course!" She tossed the ice at him and turned to flee.

"Lilly," he called. "Please don't cozy up to that horse. Don't tend him, pet him or feed him. Don't talk to him. Leave him to me."

"If that's what you want," she said, pulling the door closed behind her. Then she leaned against it and let out her breath in a long, slow whoosh. Here's where she could really run into trouble, harboring a clear memory of that gorgeous naked chest. And she couldn't help her ingrained admiration for the long, thick hair. A Native man's hair was part heritage and a whole lot of personal pride.

All that was definitely going to cost her sleep.

When Lilly got back to the stable, Gabe was sweeping up. She glanced at her watch and saw it was getting late. Yaz was going to wonder what had happened to her. She sat heavily on the bench.

"Is Dad icing his aches and pains?"

"Not exactly," she said. "He said he wants to deal with Streak first and ordered me not to get friendly with him, take care of him or feed him."

Gabe just laughed. "I guess they're pretty well matched as far as stubborn goes."

Streak was in a stall with a half door—there were no other horses in the barn, so he was no threat. He hung his head out of the stall and looked at Lilly beseechingly. She shrugged at him. "So, Clay Tahoma is stubborn, is he?"

"Oh, boy," Gabe answered. "He calls it steadfast.

When you get to know him better, let me know what you call it."

I don't have to know him better, she thought. He was pretty transparent—he might indeed be steadfast, but he was also stubborn.

She heard the sound of his heels hitting the ground as he came back to the barn. It was a slightly uneven gait; the knee and hip of his left side were sore.

"You finishing up, Gabe?" he asked.

"Unless you thought of something else for me?" Gabe answered.

"You can go ahead home when you're ready. I'm going to take care of this horse, then I'll be along for dinner. Well done, thank you."

"Sure," he said, sweeping the last of the dirt and hay out of the stable's double doors. "See you in a little while, then." Gabe grabbed his hat off the hook by the door, put it on his head and touched the brim. "Nice seeing you, Miss Yazhi."

"Please, call me Lilly. Good seeing you, too. Nice, um…nice talking to you."

"Likewise. You take care now."

And that fast, he was gone, followed by the sound of his little green truck.

Lilly pulled her feet up onto the bench and circled her knees with her arms, curiously and silently watching as Clay went about his business. He brought Streak out of the pen, secured him, removed the saddle and blanket and began to brush him without talking. It should be apparent to Streak that Clay was angry. It was certainly apparent to Lilly. She'd been around for the grooming of the horse before and Clay usually spoke in soft, reassuring tones, pausing now and then to give an affectionate stroke, rewarding the horse for bearing the brush. This was a very solemn procedure.

Lilly said nothing, nor did she ask any questions, though she wanted to. How did he know the horse was picking up on these subtle signals, for one thing? And how did he expect it to have a lasting effect? But she simply watched the routine that lasted more than a half hour. When Clay was done he looked into Streak's big, beautiful brown eyes and said, "You ever do that to me again and you'll be dog food." Then he fed him. He stroked him sparingly.

He forgave him.

Then he turned and limped out of the stable.

Of course Lilly knew he'd be back; he had to remove Streak's feed bucket, water him, turn him out for a while. It was only a moment before he came back with his ice pack. He found a spot directly opposite her and sat on the floor, leaning against the wall, the ice pack atop his left knee.

Only then did he look toward Lilly. As though nothing else had gone on today, he pleasantly asked, "So, you had a nice conversation with Gabe?"

She was almost startled. Hadn't they already covered that? She released a huff of laughter. "You were a little scary there for a while. I'll admit I was a little wary— do you often treat women that way?"

"Good God, no," he said. "I've found the most effective way to deal with a woman is to listen to her carefully and follow her instructions very closely. This," he said, jutting his chin toward Streak, "is one stubborn horse."

"Says the pot of the kettle."

"You had a nice talk with Gabe?" he asked again.

"I told you I did. He told me about how you rescued him from being adopted, how he was raised by his grandparents and other family."

"Yes, I apologize. You did tell me." He shook his head. "I wasn't paying attention—I was furious and my leg hurt. Sometimes I can be a little too focused. Or is that *un*focused? I won't do it again."

"Can I ask you something? You're under no obligation to—"

"Ask," he said.

"What was it like to find your girlfriend pregnant at seventeen?"

"Sixteen," he said. "She'd broken things off with me, and since things had been so good between us, I didn't understand. But a boy never does, I guess. Guys have so many confidence issues at that age. Months went by and I couldn't get past it, couldn't take the suspense any longer and I went to ask her, to demand she tell me what was wrong with me. I found her about six months pregnant. And she was not well. She looked thin and sick, not rosy cheeked and plump the way a pregnant woman should look. It was apparent the whole thing was harder on her than me. Of course I was terrified, but I tried to convince her I could take care of her. She rejected that idea at once. She wasn't strong enough to go up against her family. And I knew my family wouldn't just let one of our own go."

"Were you punished?" she asked.

"With disapproval and shame, and they took their pound of flesh over time—no one got up in the middle of the night to tend to Gabe but me. We shared a bedroom and although I worked and went to school, his 2:00 a.m. and 5:00 a.m. feedings were all mine. When he was sick, throwing up and crying and shitting all over, I was on duty. And when he was teething…man, I own every tooth in his head, I swear to God. My mother wore a superior smile while I suffered lack of sleep and frustration. It was as if she was saying, *Welcome to my world*." He chuckled. "It was very hard. But worth every minute. Look at him. He amazes me."

She was quiet for a moment. "That's very unusual," she finally said. "For a young boy to take on a massive responsibility like that."

"There were times I felt I had the weight of the world on my shoulders, alone, but let's be honest—my mother was always right on the other side of the door. She trained me. I took care of the feedings and changings, but she was up for each one, watching, being sure Gabe always came first in our household. An infant is always first."

"I asked him if it was hard on him, but he said he had it easy," she told Clay.

He let a small, proud smile touch his lips. After a moment of silence he said, "He's more than I ever deserved."

"I don't know about that. Sounds like you were completely devoted to him. That deserves gratitude, which he seems to have in abundance. I was an only child, as well."

"No doubt you were an excellent one."

"Also raised by my grandparents. Then my grandfather alone after my grandmother died—"

"And your parents?"

"Father unknown and my mother's been missing for a long time. She left me with my grandparents when I was a baby. She was an alcoholic and eventually just ran off."

"Alcoholic," he said solemnly. "Our people have an issue with that."

A strange thing happened to Lilly in that moment. In all the years her grandfather had tried in vain to pull her closer to her roots, her foundation, she'd pulled away. She pushed herself more into the opposite world, trading Native studies for accounting, Native spiritualism for the eastern pursuit of yoga. And yet when Clay made that simple statement—*Our people* have an issue with that—she felt an instant bond.

"Does your family have an issue?" she asked.

"A cousin or two have tested the evils, to their peril." He shook his head. "My family stripped the mystery from that a long time ago. Since I was a small child it was stressed that there's no escape—you drink alcohol, you become a drunk and die young. We're not like the French or English in that regard. Our bodies are simply more susceptible to alcohol's damages."

"Did you test it?" she wanted to know.

He shook his head. "Not a drop. I like being in control of my mind and body. I have a hard enough time with that sober. You?"

She shook her head. Then she laughed. "We have that in common—I struggle with control enough as it is."

Their conversation moved on to the more upbeat aspects of their race, tribes, families. Lilly hadn't lived on a ranch as Clay had, but she'd lived in a rural community where there was great freedom to run, play, ride. She just recently realized that sometimes she missed it desperately. And while Clay had been back to the Navajo Nation numerous times over the years, Lilly had never been back. And there was more—they had each attended college, though only Lilly had a degree. Clay had studied business because he wanted to learn how to turn his equine talents into a viable and successful business, which he had done.

"Are you well-known and rich then?" she asked.

"I'm known in the horse industry for various small things and I am rich in purpose and experience."

She laughed at him. "That was a dodge!"

"Want to see my bankbook?" he asked with a snicker. "I plan to take care of my son and my parents. I'm not comfortable that I'm prepared for that yet."

They talked about this part of Northern California and its most desirable aspects, the almost intimidating beauty, the pristine wilderness, the wildlife and clean air. Clay said he missed the mountains and canyons around Flagstaff and this was a good substitute. He told her what he'd already discovered in some of the small mountain towns and she told him what there was to enjoy on the coast.

While he finished with Streak—putting him up for the night—they continued their conversation. Finally, chores done and Clay's bag of ice warmed and reduced to water, he said, "My sister sets a big table every night—there's lots of family and sometimes friends. You can follow me there, join us for dinner. You would be welcome, and you'd like them—they're salt of the earth. Ursula is a teacher, one of the reasons I want Gabe living with them. He's a good student, but she'll make him better. And my brother-in-law is a police chief in a small town. There are kids—four besides Gabe still at home—and Tom's parents live with them."

She didn't have to look at her watch to know it was

dinnertime and she would spend it alone. She'd probably stop for a bean-and-cheese burrito to go, though really, she wanted nothing more than to sit down with Clay and his family; she'd like to know more about them. But she just wasn't ready yet.

"I'm sorry," she said. "I'm tied up."

"I'm sorry to hear that. Maybe another time?"

"Maybe," she said. "I'd better get going. And you should get to dinner."

"One of these days, Lilly, you'll take a chance on me."

She laughed and gave him a dismissive wave as she headed for the truck, but inside she was thinking, *I am taking a pretty big chance right now. For me...*

Eight

At Annie's request, Lilly saddled up Blue Rhapsody and joined her in the round pen for a little dressage instruction. Blue was wonderful; she could almost anticipate Lilly's next move.

"How much dressage training have you had?" Annie asked her.

"None. Right before leaving the reservation, I'd started barrel racing. My grandpa said it took twenty years off his life."

"You ride like you've done it forever," Annie said.

Lilly was shaking her head. "I think it's Blue," she said. "Whatever life she had before, I bet anything she went to show. By the way, I think I've come up with a plan—if I help teach three yoga classes a week, I can afford her board. And I can get a deal on feed." She grinned.

"What if I had a better idea?" Annie said. "Our training program is still small, but growing bit by bit. I could use someone like you to help me. If you're interested."

"Really?" Lilly asked. "I mean, really?"

"You'd be perfect," Annie insisted. "How flexible are your work hours?"

"Except for the feed delivery, Grandpa's easy to work with. I keep the books, Annie—the bills don't go away at 5:00 p.m."

"Kind of the way I ran the beauty shop," Annie said. "I cut, colored and permed all day, kept the books at night. Let me see what it'll take to bring you into the program and get your help. And maybe Blue's help—I think she has a lot of talent and training."

They talked a little bit about the many things they could accomplish with a riding academy, helping girls who wanted to compete, teaching them confidence and self-reliance. Annie and Lilly got to remembering what an important role riding had played in their early lives. Then Annie smiled lazily and said, "It'll mean spending more time around here. Not that you haven't been doing more of that lately."

So, that hadn't slipped anyone's notice at all. That was the only trepidation she had, putting herself in Clay's company more often. But hadn't she been here every day, edging closer all the time? If he turned out to be the kind of man she feared, why couldn't she kick him in the shins and avoid him forever? Or, she could tattle on him, tell Annie he was a louse and a jackass—and as Dane had said, Annie would shoot him or make Nathaniel fire him.

But if she was honest with herself, she wanted to be near Clay. When she was around him she felt good, she felt safe.

She stepped into the ring of fire. "It sounds wonderful," she told Annie. "You see what you can do. I'll see what I can do."

"Fantastic," Annie said. "In the meantime a friend of mine is coming over for a ride on Saturday. We'll go out on the trail for a couple of hours. Join us?"

"Oh…I don't want to intrude…"

"Don't be ridiculous! Shelby is a new mom who just got cleared to ride. She's been off a horse for quite a while and can't wait. She'd love the company."

So even though it was her day for chores and errands, Lilly cut a few hours out of her schedule to ride with Annie and Shelby. She shouldn't have been at all surprised that not only the riding energized her, but the company she kept with these women. Lilly had girlfriends, but none of them shared her passion for horses, which meant she tamped it down, herself. And while Dane was a perfect best friend in every way, he was not interested in riding.

Out on the trail, away from the men and the barn, they traded girl talk and confidences. Shelby said that now that the baby was a couple of months old and Luke was invited to make love again, he was driving her crazy. "I think he was counting the seconds until he was cleared for sex."

"Is that all they think about?" Annie asked.

"Not all," Shelby said. "Just *most* of what they think about." Then she grinned and said, "I have to admit, I was pretty anxious, too. Luke is hard for me to resist. Especially when I don't feel like a pole that swallowed a watermelon. We had a long dry spell while I was horribly pregnant and then when I'd just given birth. You know what I mean."

"I don't know anything about that," Annie said. "But I just found my Nathaniel last Christmas and I'm not tired of him yet. Not a bit!" Then she smiled. "You know what I mean, Lilly," she said.

"I have no idea what you mean! It's been so long since I had hot sex I'm not sure I remember how!"

"Well, there's always Clay…" Annie teased. "I know you're attracted to him."

"Clay? The new vet tech?" Shelby asked. "How could you not be? Have you been seeing him?"

"As in *dating* him? No," Lilly said. "He might be more than I can handle."

"Chicken!" Annie said.

"Luke was more than I could handle," Shelby admitted with a sigh. "But, boy, am I glad I took on the challenge! Lilly, Clay is so exotic, so beautiful. You must be tempted."

It was fun to blush, to tell dark jokes about wild sex with one of those hot, irresistible, Native men. "Seriously, it's really been a long, long time," Lilly declared, and it was the understatement of the century.

"Bet it comes right back to you," Annie said. "Just like the riding has."

Then Shelby was asking her about her riding history.

"My grandfather had me on a horse when I was barely walking. I could master a thousand-pound animal by the time I was ten, and when I was twelve, there wasn't a horse on the reservation I couldn't ride. Our neighbors took all the little girls on trail rides into the mountains and canyons. We slept on the ground, under an endless black sky sprinkled with a million stars and it made me feel connected to the entire earth. By the time I started junior high, my confidence was at a peak. Once we moved here, moved away from the horses and riding, I struggled to find anything that made me feel passionate. I didn't realize how much it would have helped to keep up with the riding. I didn't know until very recently that I need that in my life.

"Annie's invited me to work part-time at the stable. I'll make a little money if there are plenty of riding students, but mostly I'll get to keep Blue and board her at a discount. Annie and I were talking about doing trail rides for groups of girls—nothing gives a young girl a sense of power like taming a beast, like proving she's capable of doing it on her own, without a parent's guiding hand. You can't imagine, their grades in school even go up when they've mastered certain equestrian accomplishments, when they've camped in the wilds with just their horses and wits. I can't wait to do it again! I can't wait to take care of my own horse and have her depend on me while I depend on her. I can't wait to teach it to girls—even very little girls!

"Of course, this will put me in very close company with the very Navajo man I've been trying to avoid...."

Annie and Shelby were quiet for a very long moment before they both burst out laughing. Then Annie said, "Give it up! You're a goner." And all three of them laughed some more.

Lilly accepted an invitation to the Toopeek household for dinner with Clay's family just a few days later. It was a very big step for her. Since moving to California she'd been distancing herself from the whole Native community. But curiosity drove her because she'd grown so fond of Clay. She couldn't help wondering what his people were like.

She hadn't been at their table for fifteen minutes before she knew, as if she hadn't known before, that her future was irrevocably changed. Or changed back.

"You'll starve, eating that way," old Lincoln Toopeek had said.

"Let her eat what she likes," Ursula counseled. "She doesn't look like she's starving by any means. In fact, I might ask her about her diet. But not until after pie."

"You should taste the pork loin," Clay said. "It's out of this world."

"I'm a vegetarian," she explained under her breath.

"Well, that explains the mushroom sandwich. Okay, if it works for you," Clay said, putting a very large, juicy slab of meat on his plate.

"Those Hopi," Lincoln Toopeek said. "They have strange eating habits."

"My grandfather is a well established carnivore!" Lilly told him. "He sells feed to ranchers for cattle and sheep!"

The entire family—adults and children—laughed as the stone-faced, serious Lincoln was taken aback. He didn't appear offended, just surprised. After all, he clearly believed he was *right*.

"Please, Lincoln, don't start on her," Ursula said. Then, turning to Lilly, she said, "He's equally critical of the Navajo. He's Cherokee and God knows only the Cherokee know anything!"

"I hope pie is on your diet," Clay leaned over and said in a stage whisper. "You wouldn't want to miss it."

Family. Community. Camaraderie. Her grandfather had not been able to draw her back to the Native community the way this family had in fifteen minutes. She realized immediately, she had to risk letting them in. Letting *him* in.

She needed to be a part of something again, a community that understood her and whom she understood— tradition tugged at her.

By mid-September, Dr. Nathaniel Jensen's new clinic and barn had opened for business. Lilly and Yaz were both there for the opening celebration, as were a number of folks from the nearby towns. The Jensen Stables were located down the mountain from Virgin River and somewhere between there and Grace Valley. Horse owners from all over who relied on Nate's skills were all present, as were the owners of other livestock from near and far. Lilly helped Annie put plentiful food and drink out on a long trestle table that had been set up between the house and barn and watched with interest as Clay approached almost everyone who arrived, either greeting them or introducing himself to them. She spent some time helping Clay and Gabe saddle the Jensen horses for those who'd like a ride—something especially the children present took advantage of. Blue was exceptionally good with a young rider and it gave Lilly such pleasure to be the one leading her around.

To her surprise, Clay had invited the entire Toopeek family. Late in the afternoon he sidled close to her and pointed with his glass of lemonade at Yaz and Lincoln Toopeek, locked in a conversation that seemed to involve few words, bonding. Or arguing.

"See that?" Clay said. "That's pretty much how my father and your grandfather will look when they meet— standing nose to nose and yet a hundred miles apart."

"Do you think they'll meet?" she asked.

"I'm counting on it," he said.

Her world was going to get larger and she knew it.

When Lilly delivered feed on Thursday afternoon, she found Clay waiting for her. "I'm planning to watch my son play football tonight," he said. "Would you like to come with me?"

"I wish I could," she said sincerely. She was crazy about Gabe. "I have a commitment."

"That boyfriend?" he asked with a smile.

"No," she said, laughing. "I promised to help with a yoga class—it's a little extra money, which I need for Blue."

"Well, tomorrow night Gabe has plans with his friends and, you and I, we should spend an evening to- gether. Not with the Toopeek family, but just the two of us, so we can talk. And not just about horses. Let me take you to dinner or something," he said.

"I can't," she answered. "I have plans."

"The boyfriend?" he asked.

"With a very close friend, and these plans were made a while ago. Sorry."

"Cancel," he urged.

"I can't this time. Maybe another time."

Friday was an extremely busy day for Lilly and for that she was grateful. She did in fact have plans with Dane—they were going out for a movie and a bite to eat. Of course, not only would Dane be completely fine with a cancellation, he'd probably cheer. He had been urging her to take the dating game seriously for years. But the fact was, a man who made that very idea tempting had just barely come along and she was moving as quickly as she could. She just wasn't quite ready for the intimacy she knew was coming; she was serious when she'd told Annie and Shelby it had been a very long time.

She was getting closer to taking that step, however. Much closer. Thinking about it caused her to tremble.

Sometimes, if she could ignore the trembling, if she closed her eyes and was honest with herself, she could admit that since Clay had entered her life she'd hungered for the intensity of a night alone with him. She needed to be held, to be kissed, to be loved. And while his very power intimidated her, she didn't want anything less.

Dane finally knocked on her front door on Friday evening and she was so glad to see him. He was so good for her; he propped her up when she was down, laughed with her when she needed to laugh, never failed to be there for her. And as always, seeing him filled her with a feeling of affection. She smiled brightly.

But her smile quickly faded. He looked awful. "My gosh, what's wrong?"

Dane put up a hand as if to ward her off. "Don't get too close, Lilly," he said. "I thought I could ignore this, but I'm coming down with something. I feel terrible."

She took a couple of steps toward him, frowning. His handsome face was in a grimace, his eyebrows furrowed. "What in the world is the matter?"

"It started out as a headache and a tickle in my throat. I thought a couple of aspirin and a good gargle would do the trick, but on the way over here it got way worse. Hit me like a ton of bricks. The tickle turned into razor blades, my head is clogged and pounding, I have a cough, my body aches. I think I have a fever."

"Oh, Dane, lie down on the sofa. Take your shoes

off. I'll make you a strong broth, some green tea, dose you up with an anti—"

"I need to go home, honey," he said. "I need my bed and I don't want to give it to you. It could be the flu."

"I'll take my chances, Dane. I have a strong constitution—I never get sick. Let me do something to make you feel better."

"You better knock on wood. This could be that ugly virus going around. I'll call you tomorrow."

"Oh, Dane, I really needed to—" To what? Talk more about her crush on Clay? The crush Dane kept telling her to make a move on? Oh, he must be so sick of her by now.

"We'll do something later this week or next weekend. Ugh. I gotta go to bed...."

"I'm so sorry, Dane," she said.

He nodded, blew her a kiss and left her little house, the screen door shutting behind him as she stood at the open interior door.

"Crap," she said aloud, watching him go.

She'd dressed up for her evening with Dane; she wore a cinnamon-colored silk blouse, beige dress pants, gold belt, low heels...but the evening was off. She went to her bedroom to change. She tossed her clothes in the chair that sat in the corner and found herself some comfy yoga togs.

Back in the living room, she sat on the floor to pick through her CDs. The early fall weather was so beautiful; she enjoyed an early evening breeze coming in the screen door. She put on some music, cranked it up real loud, and went to the kitchen to forage for food. She pulled out some vegetables and cheese; she'd make herself a big, fluffy salad and a whole wheat macaroni and cheese dish topped with a little tomato puree and black olives. She had the water for the noodles on the fire, some of the veggies sliced and was starting to feel like herself again when suddenly the volume of the music went down.

She whirled around. There, in her very small living room, stood Clay. He put up his hands and said, "I'm sorry, I didn't mean to frighten you. You obviously couldn't hear me knock or ring the bell. If the door had been closed, I wouldn't have walked in, but it was only the screen door, unlocked."

She leaned against the sink, her heart hammering from the surprise. He was looking a bit different tonight; he wore navy blue slacks, low leather boots and a white long-sleeved shirt, sleeves rolled up and neck open. He held a sack in the crook of one arm. "What are you doing here?"

He looked around, then looked her up and down. "You don't look like you're going out. You said you had plans and I thought—"

"I'm staying in tonight."

Clay craned his neck. "Where's the boyfriend? What's his name?"

She couldn't help but smile at him. He was at least as much a brat as Streak. "He's sick. Coming down with something so he canceled. Now, why are you here?"

He took a step toward the kitchen. He smiled. "I wanted to meet him. At least get a look at him, see what I'm up against." He shrugged. "Maybe we could be friends, me and the boyfriend."

She laughed at him in spite of herself. "Well, that takes balls," she said. "Why don't we do this—when I feel like introducing the two of you, I'll let you know. And since you aren't going to get a look at him..."

"I brought something. Root beer." He tilted his head at her. "Was I out of line? Dropping in this way?"

"Absolutely!" she said, her blue eyes widening. "How'd you know where I lived?"

"Annie. And by the way, she'd never heard about this boyfriend, which I find curious."

"Maybe I don't tell everyone about him," she said. "But—your apology is accepted."

"I'm not sure if I'm sorry yet—since I ended up saving you from what appears to be a very boring night."

"You should have called ahead, though. You walked right in my house! Now, would I walk right in your house?"

"I believe you have—and I was naked. Besides, I did knock," he said with another shrug.

She couldn't argue that—she'd gone into his quarters at the stable without being invited. He looked huge standing there in her small living room—so big, so bronze, his eyes so penetrating, his teeth so white. He looked more like a monument in her little house than he did at the stable with a great big stallion as a backdrop.

"What's with this music?" he asked. "What are you listening to?"

She sighed and just shook her head. "Don't you like music?"

"Of course. I like Country."

"Well, this is a slightly more sophisticated version of 'my girl left me and my dog died.' It's called opera. And I like it."

"Do you understand it?" he asked.

"The language? No, I don't speak Italian. But I get what it's about." She put down her knife and walked the few steps into the living room. "This is Bocelli singing Puccini. *La bohème*. I like it loud. Would you like some of my salad and noodles and cheese? Since you've so rudely made yourself available?"

That widened his smile. "Yes. Yes I would. There's probably no meat, is there?"

"No meat, and I'm sure you'll live. Sit here on this couch, listen to the music while I finish cooking and see if you can absorb a little culture." She pulled a bottle out of his bagged six-pack and handed it to him. "I'll be in the kitchen awhile." She took the rest of the six-pack from him to put in the refrigerator.

"Why do you listen to it?"

"This one in particular? Because I love Bocelli's voice and the story is tragic and the music is powerful. I love opera. It moves me. This one ends in the woman's death. Come to think of it, a lot of them end in death, but the power of the music… Just listen. Let it seep into your veins and muscles and… Well, I'll finish up in the kitchen."

She pushed him onto the sofa, turned up the volume on her stereo and went back into the kitchen. He could still see her from where he sat, and the view was exquisite. She was standing at the counter beside the sink, her back to him. He twisted the top off his root beer and took a slug. It was hard to imagine a more intoxicating sight than her astride a big horse, but this was it. He was mesmerized. She wore a sleeveless, snug knit crop top that fit like a soft second skin and pants that hugged her hips and fell only to her calf. He'd been right about her arms and shoulders—she was ripped. Even the muscles of her back, visible under the shirt she wore, were defined. And that round, firm, muscled butt? He wiped a hand down the full length of his face. Zow. She said she was into yoga. Could you get muscles like that from yoga? Yes, if you topped it with hauling bales of hay....

She was right about the music. He wasn't sure he liked it, but he could feel it to the marrow of his bones. At times it was melodious and beautiful, then it would rise with the kind of force that suggested going to war or taking a ravishing woman to bed, then become subdued and seductive again.

He smiled. Little Hopi girl was a nerd. She leaned toward the classical. Sitting on her futon, which had a lot of growing to do to become a couch, he felt a long way from home.

Maybe *she* was a long way from home.

He hoisted his tall frame off the futon. It was only about ten steps to the kitchen. The music was so loud she wouldn't have been able to hear him, so he put his bottle of root beer down on the counter before he touched her. But she neither jumped nor stiffened; she had either felt, heard or sensed his approach. He had an instinct about her, that she had highly developed extrasensory skills.

He put his hand on her hip. His hand was so large on her small frame that his fingers splayed around to her flat belly. He gave her a second to protest or shove him away and when she didn't, he put his lips on the side of her neck, kissing, inhaling the scent of her. Sucking gently. Then his other hand found her other hip and he massaged with his palms and fingers, kissing both sides of her neck.

She turned her head so he would hear her. "You shouldn't..."

"I should..."

"Do *not* leave a mark on me," she warned.

"I would die before I would mark a beauty like yours."

And with that she was undone; she turned in his arms and tilted her face up. "You have to know something. I'm very afraid of you."

He stiffened and frowned. "Of me? Why?"

"I'm afraid you're going to hurt me."

He shook his head gently, still frowning. "Lilly, I'm not going to hurt you. I swear, I'm going to be good to you."

She inhaled, exhaled with a slow sigh and gently let her eyes drift closed in submission.

He didn't need any more invitation than that; he lowered his lips onto hers and when she parted her lips slightly, he took full advantage. His tongue entered the soft, slick velvet of her mouth and he moaned. He ran his tongue around her lips, tasting and pulling slightly, then welcomed her tongue into his mouth. He let his eyes open a slit, just enough to see that hers were still closed, her sooty lashes lying on her cheeks. "You're so beautiful," he whispered into her opened mouth. His large hands pressed against her firm butt, pulling her hard against him, and he devoured her mouth, entering, receding, entering....

Her hands moved from his shoulders to his neck, to his head. Her fingers threaded into his hair, moving to the tie that held it back, loosening it. He growled softly; he was already hard. "I could do this right here, right now," he whispered. "But I don't want to. I want to go slow with you."

Her answer was to hum softly and take his mouth again. And again.

He pulled back a tiny bit, enough to look down at her and see her hard nipples pressing against the soft fabric of her top. He slowly moved one of his hands from her butt to a breast, covering it, teasing the nipple gently with his thumb. He chuckled sensually against her lips. "Some things men and women can't really hide from each other." His thumb gave her hard nipple another soft tweak. He hated to let go of that breast, but he momentarily removed his hand to reach over and turn off the flame under the boiling water before he returned to it again. The loud music had picked up a drumming beat that he could feel in his veins. He put his lips against her ear and said, "I want to go slow with you, but I don't know if I can. I'll try, I promise."

He felt her small hand slide down his back to his butt, pulling him even harder against her. He let himself enjoy that for a moment, then he whisked her up in his arms. "You're light as a feather. I'm going to carry you to bed, sweetheart."

"I haven't said yes yet," she whispered in his ear.

He rested her on the counter, put a hand on her breast, ran a thumb over her erect nipple. "I thought you had."

"That's just nature."

"I worship nature. And I'm going to worship you...."
He grabbed her in his arms again and carried her through the small house. He passed by the front door as he went, kicking it closed and throwing the dead bolt, and headed to the bedroom. This was just a cracker box,

this tiny house, but it was a house that made sense. It was like her—efficient, compact, suited to her. This was a house made for her, not made for others who might visit it. He silently cursed himself—he had nearly let the memory of Isabel in and that was the last thing he intended. Right now his mind and his body were full of Lilly. Deliciously full.

He set her on her feet beside the bed and pulled her shirt up over her head. It was barely tossed aside when his mouth found that nipple and drew on it. "God," he said. "God."

Her hands were opening his shirt as she thought, *This is going to happen, ready or not.* She had spent about two seconds thinking about how long she had waited to bring a man into her life, her body; she remembered how afraid she'd been. But when Clay touched her she was done with that. Her body responded instantly with hard nipples and a wetness between her legs. And she thought, *oh, hell,* as she unbuttoned his last button.

"Do you have a condom?" she asked.

"Exactly one," he said, unlatching his belt. "Believe it or not, I didn't plan this. But when I'm close to you, Lilly, I don't want a breath of air as much as I want you. I don't know if this has ever happened to me before."

"Bull," she said, slipping her small hands along his hips to lower his pants. And then she had a look at him, hard and erect, and said, "Oh, my God."

He put his hands on her hips, his fingers slipping under the soft fabric of her pants, and gently slid them down. He looked down at her as he did so. She was bare. Not just bare, but *bare.* No pubic hair at all. A Brazilian wax, it was called, and it almost brought him to his knees. He wanted to kneel before her and put his mouth right on her, but he promised *slow.* If he could.

He reached for her hand, holding it while she kicked off those soft, lightweight trousers and climbed onto the bed. He had to sit down to remove his boots, the pants that had gathered around his ankles, and fetch that condom that went with him everywhere. He put it on the dresser beside the bed, one square little package. Then he reclined beside her and pulled her into his arms. "Problem is," he said, his hand lowering to her soft, hairless center, a finger slipping in to find her already wet and ready, "I think I might come right now. The good news is, I'll be ready again before you know it, and I can keep you busy until that happens...." He applied that finger to her clitoris, making her gasp and squirm.

"Do you have to talk?" she asked him, reaching her lips to his.

He laughed softly. "I have to talk about what's happening with us. It's like magic." Then his lips were on her breast, his fingers in her, rubbing her, invading her. He moved to her mouth, back to her nipple, to her mouth, her other nipple, and all the while his hand was working its magic, fingers in and out, palm or thumb massaging her most vulnerable spot. She stiffened, threw her head back, groaned deep in her throat and he said, "Let it go, baby. Come for me." She grabbed his shoulders and obliged.

The tenor singing in the background reached some kind of emotional crescendo and the sound throbbed through Clay's body as Lilly's sweet center clenched him; her fingers dug into his shoulders, her nipple puckered in his mouth and she came. And came. And came.

It lasted so long, he lost his breath. The second it seemed to begin to let go of her, he kissed his way down her body and put his mouth on her, licking, kissing, sucking. She still quivered there; she'd loosened his long hair and it fell in a canopy around her hips, her fingers threaded into it at his temples. She came again. Above the loud, thrumming music he heard her cry, "Oh, God, oh, Clay!" And he lost it. He went off like a rocket, pressing his throbbing erection against her leg, letting it come and licking her until they were both complete.

She had cried out his name. Maybe, if all his wishes came true, it was more than just sex for her. He'd hoped to perform better, but the second he had her on his tongue, there was no help for it.

He kissed his way up her body, ended on her lips, lay on his side and pulled her against him. He was breathless; she was flushed. He kissed her cheek, her lips, her ear. He whispered, "I didn't even know I liked opera." And she laughed, digging her fingers into his hair and pulling his mouth onto hers again.

at all what you think, Clay, or I wouldn't be with you like this now. About us…?"

He took her small hand and pulled it to him; he was already becoming aroused again. "Just the beginning of us."

She reached past his shoulder to the bedside stand and lifted the little foil package. "It would be a bad idea to forget really important things," she said, ripping it open and taking it upon herself to apply the condom.

At her very touch he let out a breath. He raised himself over her, covered her lips with his, even as he separated her legs with his knees and teased her very center with the tip of his sheathed penis. He held his weight off her as he probed her. "We'll get to all the other things later. There's nothing at all complicated about this. I need to be inside you."

And she needed him there. She already felt a lovely, satisfying intimacy with him, but there was a need deep inside her that she'd ignored for so long, that need to be *possessed*. She didn't answer him, but simply tilted her hips toward him and he lowered himself carefully. Slowly. Gently. She was so small and he was so big; it brought tears to her eyes as he moved within her with such caution and care.

"Are you okay, Lilly?" he whispered. "Tell me if it's too much."

As she shook her head, a tear loosened and rolled into the hair at her temple and a little squeak of emotion escaped her. "Please," she said softly. "Oh, please, Clay. I want you. All of you."

He growled with passion so hot, he trembled to control himself. With his hands on her hips, his lips on her lips, he moved inside her with precision, deep and strong. After the first few strokes a rhythm took over and her hips moved against his. He was astonished at her power for one so small, so sweet. He felt her hands on his hips, pulling him into her; he had to grit his teeth to hang on. Waiting for her was going to be difficult, even when it wasn't the first time tonight—there was such a force in her supple little body. "Lilly," he said in a drawn-out whisper. "Oh, my God, Lilly…"

"Yes," came out of her like a hiss. *"Yes!"* With her hands plunged into his long hair and gripping him, she led his head downward, his mouth to her nipple, and he went there willingly. He sucked hard, pulling that erect little knot into his mouth, and he pumped into her with gusto, rubbing his shaft against her clitoris as he penetrated her as deeply as her body would allow. "Oh, my God, yes…" she said. And he felt it begin in the deepest part of her core, gripping him with hot, wet, desperate tightness. She dug her heels into the bed and pushed against him, locked onto him. Her legs came around his hips to hold him there and she shattered. It was a small but powerful explosion of ecstasy that grew and grew; she held him inside her, held his head to her breast, and she clenched him in spasms of pleasure.

Clay held on for a moment, enjoying her orgasm, then he let go and throbbed with his own release. He heard her again, in the faintest, weak whisper. "Yes… Oh, yes…"

He couldn't even force himself to leave her body so he balanced himself above her. He gently stroked her face. Her eyes were closed and there was a small smile of satisfaction on her lips. "See?" he whispered. "We can do it justice even without opera."

Her eyes popped open and she let go a big laugh.

* * *

Clay insisted on taking Lilly out for dinner, though she'd have been just as happy to pull on those soft yoga togs, stay comfortable and half-naked and finish the meal she'd started in the kitchen. He had a double purpose, he said. He wanted some meat and more condoms. Neither were items Lilly had on hand.

He took her to a Mexican place, a little hole-in-the-wall where the carne asada was fantastic and she could have her fill of beans, rice, tortillas and cheese. He wanted to know all about the man he was competing with, the man he meant to take her away from, but he used great restraint and didn't raise the subject. Probably she had things to work out about that. There might be choices and decisions that weren't easy for her. He wanted to say, "Tell him it's over and we're together now," but he didn't. They'd talk about it before too long. Until they did, he didn't want to appear a brute.

He wanted her to come to him, not succumb to him.

Instead, he asked, "How long have you been in your little house?"

"Two years. I rent it. I had always lived with Yaz and I thought at twenty-five I was past due for a little space of my own. Yaz isn't crazy about the idea, but I like it."

"He wanted you in his house forever?" Clay asked.

"Of course he did," she said with a laugh. "He might still be plotting my return."

"I was thinking how perfect that little house seemed for you. And you need your privacy."

"What I needed was independence, and sometimes solitude."

He reached for her hand. "Do you need solitude tonight, Lilly?" he asked softly.

Her eyes twinkled and she smiled. "I think I'll have solitude tomorrow. That's soon enough."

So Clay stayed the night with her and made sure she was very well loved. It thrilled him that she reached for him in the night and when he opened his eyes he saw that hers were glistening and bright; she hadn't reached out of habit, but out of desire. He was quick to reward her longing, to satisfy her. She was so hungry, it couldn't escape his notice. Hungrier even than he, and that made an impression on him. Lilly had been left wanting, and a woman with her passion and responsiveness should never have found herself in such a state.

In the morning he kissed her sweetly before leaving. "I don't want to go, but horses aren't known for sleeping in," he whispered. "I'll see you later, when you're free."

The hours dragged for him until the afternoon. Annie gave some riding lessons in the morning, Nathaniel went out to a couple of ranches to see about sick animals, Gabe came to the stable in the early afternoon to do chores, and finally at midafternoon she appeared. While they readied a couple of horses for a ride, he stole a few deep, hot kisses and then took her out on the trail. On the trail there was some desperate groping and kissing when they were away from prying eyes.

"Let me come to your house tonight," he begged.

"But Gabe is here. Don't you go to your sister's most nights?"

"Most. Not tonight. Tonight I want to be with you."

"Will you eat a veggie meal with me?" she asked, teasing.

"I'll eat tree bark if it makes you happy."

"Hmm. I think you might work out...."

When they returned to the stable, took care of the horses and Lilly departed, Gabe didn't waste any time nudging his dad.

"Looks like something's happening there with you and Lilly."

Clay lifted a brow, peered at his son and asked, "How would you feel about that?"

Gabe shrugged and said, "To tell the truth, I really didn't think she was too old for me. But you beat me to it." When his dad went pale, Gabe laughed at him. "Lighten up, man. Lilly's cool. Go for it."

And Clay thought, *I did, I am, and I will....*

Lilly's weekends till now had been very predictable and dull. She spent Saturdays shopping and cleaning, both her house and her grandfather's. She made sure his laundry was caught up and his house clean. Yaz was far from helpless; he always made his bed, washed his dishes, swept his floors and put things away. But he was sixty-nine and no longer noticed the finer grit—the dust or smears or stains. He made apologetic comments when he realized she was cleaning something he had missed. "I didn't notice the spill, Lilly." "You could ignore the sheets for another week—they're clean enough." "I already mopped there—but I suppose I'm not as fussy as you."

Even though she had moved into her own little house, she was still the only woman in his. If she didn't chase away the dirt, no one would. But on this Saturday, after her chores, she had gone to the stable for a ride and later had that hard, strong Navajo in her bed all night.

On Sundays she shared a meal with her grandfather, a meal that she prepared at his house. He made his usual snide remarks about her vegetarian dishes; he said his doctor ordered him to have meat in his diet. She knew perfectly well he didn't have a doctor. No amount of badgering would get him to go for a physical.

"When are you going to let it out, Lilly?" he asked her. "The thing that's got you smiling to yourself and avoiding eye contact?"

She shrugged. "I don't want a lot of crap about it," she informed him.

"Take your chances. I'm a blunt old man."

"You use age as an excuse. What if I told you I think I like the new man who works for Nathaniel Jensen? You know who I mean—the Navajo vet tech."

He looked at her levelly for a long moment. "I could die a happy Hopi," he finally said.

"See? What a pain you are! I just said I like him, that's all!"

Yaz ignored her and became serious. "Lilly, when a man and woman are right together, the earth stands still for a moment," he said, almost solemnly. "That's how it was with your grandmother and me. Time stopped and a bright light protected us. We wore halos and could only see each other. There was impatience in every glance between us. Our fathers hurried our marriage to keep us from making a lot of big mistakes. She was not my first girl. I was not the first boy she had been attracted to, but when we met it was done. That was the last. The best and the last." He had a lot of wrinkles around his eyes. He stared at her hard. "I never saw this with you and any young man. Never. If I saw you with that new man, that vet tech, is that what I'd see?"

She glanced away. "I doubt it. I just think he's nice, that's all. We have horses in common." She shrugged and muttered, "It's probably a mistake, but there it is. I like him." She glanced over her shoulder at her grandpa. "Do you? Like him?"

"Ah, I think he's all right," Yaz finally said. "Nothing wrong with him that a little Hopi blood wouldn't fix, huh? Truth? I don't care who he is or what he is—I care about *you*. When we came here, you changed yourself as much as you could, making yourself as different as possible so you would never risk making a mistake. *Shiyazhi,* little one, don't you know you can't make a big enough mistake to turn me away from you?"

That's what she had done and she knew it. Starting at an early age she chose discipline; feeling she'd failed her only family, her grandpa, with her dangerous fling, she pursued perfection. She studied, built her body strong, took perfect care of the house and meals. She even denied herself—she ate sparsely, rationed possessions and friends, worked hard since before she was fourteen, before it was even legal to employ her. She gave up horses. Her grandpa offered to find her a stable where she could do a little riding for fun, but she declined. It was a long time before she relaxed and even began to enjoy life. To let herself enjoy life.

Even now, she was denying how deeply she felt for Clay, telling her grandfather she just sort of liked him. Why couldn't she just let herself go?

She couldn't help the gathering moisture in her eyes, nor her smile. "I know that, Grandpa," she whispered. "Thank you."

He stood from their table and with a deliberate lack of

sentiment, he carried his dishes to the sink. "Don't thank me. Do what you must. Before I die, if you please."

She laughed at him. That old Hopi would be dancing on her grave. He might look weathered from too many years of work and too much sun, but he was healthy as an ox.

She was pulling into the drive of her little house at six in the evening when her cell phone chimed in her purse. She didn't recognize the number, but answered. "Hello?"

"There is only your car in the drive," Clay said. "Is it safe to assume the boyfriend is still down with the flu?"

She couldn't help but laugh at him. "I imagine so," she said.

"Can I come to you?"

She turned her head right and left, back and forth. "Where *are* you?"

"Down the block, being circumspect. Giving you time and space. But I just couldn't stay away. Will you be on your own tonight or should I drive away?"

She got out of her car, looked over its roof and spied his big truck down the block. She waved and then she wiggled her finger at him, inviting him to come to her house, to park in the place he probably assumed her boyfriend usually parked.

All that mattered was that he parked and walked toward her. Time stood still while she took in the sight of him. It was dusk, but he seemed to walk in a beam of light.

Oh, God, she thought. *I'm already in love. In love and so done for.*

* * *

Every night for three long nights, Lilly slept in Clay's arms, whatever little sleep they actually got. Before sleep, he'd work her out in a way she had never experienced before, then hold her trembling, satisfied body close until she calmed, until she dozed. Invariably, she would reach for him, her hands begging him for more. With a groan of helplessness, he'd make love to her again and again. And again.

When his hands were on her, when he was inside her, she went to a place she could never remember being before. The man had a way with her body that defied reality. And from the sounds he made and the sheen of perspiration that covered him, she was not disappointing him.

She fought his hair during sex; he bound or braided it to keep it under control and she pulled it free, letting it flow. When he was above her, it fell like a curtain around her; when he was on his back, she found herself lying on it as if it were a soft mat, sometimes tugging it. It was a constant battle, but she wanted that thick black hair that marked his ancestry all around her, beneath her, over her, beside her. She caressed it as if it were a pet.

While he held her close on that third night he whispered, "I haven't wanted to ask…"

"You'd better. I can't read your mind."

He paused a moment to form his words. "Is your… Is what's-his-name still under the weather?"

Lilly chuckled. "I've spoken to him a couple of times. He's getting better. He'll be fine."

"I want to know about him," Clay said. "I want to know how you met him, what you like about him, if you're going to tell him that you've been having days of endless, mind-bending sex with me?"

"I wasn't planning to tell anyone," she said. "That would be indiscreet."

"I tried not to ask about him," Clay said. "I lasted as long as I could. Tell me some things. Like—is he Native? Did your grandfather pick him out for you?"

She burst out laughing. "No!" she said. "He might be German—I can't remember. Listen, I gave you the wrong idea. He's not a boyfriend, not technically. He's my *best* friend. His name is Dane, he owns a coffee shop near my yoga studio. I've known him for a few years, since he opened the place. We go to movies, sometimes we hike, we have long talks, political arguments, discuss books we like. When there's live music around here, we try to go. He has a sister, niece and nephew I love. I can talk to him about anything. We have the same kind of education and—"

"What kind of education?" Clay asked.

"We enjoy the arts. Music, literature, theater, art. My degree is in classical studies."

"But you're the accountant for your grandfather's store!"

"Well, not exactly," she said. "I'm the bookkeeper. My grandfather taught me and I've been doing it for a long time, since before college. I didn't exactly need to study it in college. I already knew what I needed to know."

"Do you love him?" Clay asked.

"My *grandfather?*" she asked, confused.

"The *boyfriend,*" Clay said impatiently.

"I do, as my closest friend," she said with a smile. She brushed his hair back from his brow. "I adore and admire him—he's such a good person. But please don't think of it as… I know I called him my boyfriend, but we're not a couple. We've never been and never will be lovers. He's gay."

"Gay?" Clay asked.

"Totally. I tried to get him to switch—we're so compatible and neither of us was attached. But switching—not an option."

"Good. I can deal with you loving the guy as a friend. You having another man in your bed is what I can't deal with."

"Believe me, that's something you don't have to worry about," she assured him.

"I should meet him," Clay said. He turned toward her, pushing her dark hair over her ear. "Even though you're not lovers, I invaded his territory. I should meet him and talk with him. I could let him hit me or something."

A burst of laughter shot out of her. She gave him a slug in the arm. "Could you be any more old-fashioned?" Then she planted a kiss on his beautiful mouth. "Besides, I would never put you in that position."

"Go ahead," he said. "Put me in that position. You've had me in every other position imaginable." He smiled lazily. "I'm not complaining, just making a statement."

A few days later, Lilly went to the Loving Cup for lunch after her yoga class. She jumped up on her favorite stool at the counter, leaned elbows on the bar and rested her chin on her clasped hands. Dane was standing in front of her in a matter of moments. He'd been away from work with his cold or flu, and although they'd talked, she hadn't seen him in almost a week.

"Greetings, little sister. The usual?" he asked.

She nodded and he went for the green tea.

"I'm sorry I stood you up Friday night," he said. "I didn't think the scourge would ever pass, but I guess it wasn't as bad as it could've been, given what I've heard about the swine flu. Darlene said whatever I had was definitely the whine flu. Frankly I—" He stopped suddenly, looked at Lilly closely. He took in her sparkling blue eyes, her flushed cheeks, her secret smile. Yoga wasn't singularly responsible for this new look of health and happiness. "Whoa," he said. "Someone is back in the saddle."

Ten

In the early fall, when the pumpkins were still green and the Halloween costumes hadn't yet been sewn, when the Valley High School football team was practicing for their homecoming performance, when the leaves on the trees that stood dwarfed under sequoias had barely started to color, the biggest item of interest in Virgin River was Hope McCrea's house.

The Presbyterian Women got the job of sorting, cleaning up and organizing, but half the town wanted in that house out of sheer curiosity. Of course, either Jack, Preacher, Paul or Mike Valenzuela stood like sentries at the door making sure whoever showed up *worked*. Those who wanted to satisfy their curiosity about what Hope left behind had to pitch in. Noah turned out to be a better tour guide than sentry, but he wasn't afraid of work himself.

Since the town meeting, the friendly neighbors of Virgin River were a lot less cordial toward Jack than they had been before he'd been named Hope's executor. They were a little surly, in fact, and there was the occasional snide comment. "That a new shirt, Jack?"

"I notice the truck has new tires…you didn't get a low-interest *loan* for those, did you?"

And Jack, being Jack, responded in his ever-patient way with comebacks like, "Wanna bite me, Lou?" and "Up yours, Hugh."

It was fair to say that certain relationships were strained these days. As for Jack, the usually helpful, loyal friend was just a mite put out with his neighbors.

This spirit of Open House lasted only a few days before it had to be shut down, and not because of Jack. Hope had been a collector of sorts and no one was sure of the value of some of the things she had rat-holed away. The women found odd and interesting items they just didn't know how to handle. There was a huge wardrobe stuffed with old china pieces, mismatched, some even cracked and chipped. She had a shoe box full of odd-looking, colorful stones, for example. There was an attic full of paintings, oils and watercolors, protected with cheap grocery store plastic wrap. This was art that Mel and Paige agreed they would have let go in a garage sale but then Preacher looked up the name of one artist on the Internet and informed them his paintings had actual value. It wasn't a Van Gogh, but it was probably worth a few grand—the artist was a Northern Californian watercolor impressionist from the Depression era. They found an old spiral notebook stuffed with crinkly paper that held odd, illegible signatures. She'd had first editions of popular novels, some of them signed. There were ancient photos, postcards and very retro jewelry. Hope had never worn jewelry that anyone could remember. There was an entire closet full of what appeared to be old teapots. Hope left behind tons of silver flatware and no one could remember a time she'd ever had a guest to dinner. And that didn't even include odd pieces of well-built furniture that the women suspected were valuable antiques.

Even though Mel had a nagging feeling that some of this old stuff was valuable, she had no experience with this sort of thing. Mel was good with five-star chefs, designer clothing and posh vacation spots—at least in her past life, before moving to Virgin River and marrying the owner of a bar.

But Muriel St. Claire, a local who had restored her hundred-year-old farmhouse, spent weekends antiquing and scouring the mountain and forest towns for "finds." In her house she had period paintings, tintype photos, refurbished fixtures, dated needlework and antique furniture. So Mel called her.

"I've spent every weekend off I've had for forty years going to estate sales," Muriel said. "Plus, I'm addicted to the *Antiques Roadshow*. I'll be right over."

Muriel must have flown around the mountain curves, she arrived so quickly. She wore her usual jeans, boots and hat, but as always she looked stunning. Muriel was a retired, or at least semiretired, Oscar-nominated actress who looked a good ten years younger than she was, and she could look elegant in a sack. On this afternoon, with a flush high on her cheeks, she burst into Hope's, found Mel and some other women in an upstairs bedroom stacked to the ceiling with miscellaneous stuff, and said, "Show me!"

It took Muriel two full days of plowing through pots, dishes, documents, little rocks, art, furniture and weird things—like ball caps from every professional ball team in the country—before she said, "I don't think this stuff is going to Christie's, but there's definitely money here. Not in everything, but generally speaking."

"How do you know?" Mel asked her.

"I can *smell* it."

"Like the colorful rocks?" Mel said expectantly. "Are they *gems?*"

"I wouldn't know," Muriel said. "But that wardrobe full of china? Antique Belleek. Very expensive Irish china. And the teapots? I recognize a couple of English sterling pieces, which tells me there's lots of hidden value there."

"Hundreds?" Mel asked hopefully.

"Thousands," Muriel said. "If I know my antiques at all."

One of the advantages of going to garage sales, estate sales and auctions as a hobby, Muriel was armed with business cards from consultants and appraisers from all over the place. The experts in this particular area seemed a reasonable place to start, but there was no evidence that Hope, who'd been computer savvy and obviously liked eBay, had been committed to Northern California.

And nothing could bring appraisers and consultants for estate sales and auctions running like the name Muriel St. Claire.

"We're going to start getting company right away," she informed Mel and some of the other ladies. "The thing to do is let them appraise the value of this stuff, run up the numbers, and then negotiate fees. It's possible much of this stuff—the art, for example, china and small antique pieces—will have to be moved to San Francisco for the best price. Or some of this could be purchased outright by an auction company that chooses to make it part of a moving sale or auction. Advertising will be necessary. Oh, this is very exciting! Benedict Compton of the San Francisco Pavilion Auction company—the president, thank you very much—is coming himself." Muriel rubbed her hands together and laughed.

Mel was stunned. "Did you just cackle?" she asked Muriel.

"I have to admit, this could be way more fun than actually attending an estate sale or auction."

"We could have a problem here," Mel said. "In this whole town I can't think of one person besides you who might know anything about this sort of thing. No matter how many appraisers come to look the stuff over, I wouldn't know how to negotiate a contract with them—I called you because I have a feeling there's valuable stuff here, but I don't know anything about it. Plus, I have patients. And these other ladies have work and families. And—"

"Well, I'm not an expert, but I do have a clue," Muriel said. "Want me to manage the appraisals?"

"Would you? Do you have the time?"

"As long as I get the horses fed, I can be here. For that matter, I'm sure Walt would take care of the horses for me. In fact, he might jump at an alternative to going antiquing with me," she added with a laugh.

While Muriel managed experts and appraisers, Preacher was studying Hope's computer records. It turned out that the local church wasn't the only thing she bought on eBay—the old woman had made a hobby and pastime of buying and selling, and her purchases and sales reached as far as China. And as for china, the Belleek was worth tens of thousands. A couple of the teapots were old English sterling worth a couple of

thousand each, and a couple were ancient Chinese teapots that were also very valuable. She didn't actually
have a Ming vase, but she'd bid on many.

"And gems?" Mel asked hopefully.

"Pretty rocks," Muriel said, shaking her head. "But
that notebook full of scrawls on crinkly paper? Famous
signatures. U. S. Grant among them. They should've
been framed and preserved but were instead stuffed
in a spiral notebook." She tsked. "I'm sorry to say that
Hope's treasures will be better cared for out of her
hands."

"I think she must have been just entertaining herself,"
Mel said. "She always acted like a woman with a million things to do, but she looked like a vagrant. Well,"
she said with a laugh, "there was never a question in
my mind that Hope was happy. Cynical and cranky and
self-indulgent and totally happy."

"By the way," Muriel asked. "Where *is* Hope?"

"She wasn't specific about her wishes, except that she
be cremated. So far no one has even picked up a hint
of what she'd like to have done with her ashes, so the
funeral home in Fortuna is keeping them for us. Jack
is trying to think of something that would do her justice, that would honor her, but he hasn't come up with
anything yet. And although the town is all pissy about
not being able get their hands on her money, no one has
asked if there will be a funeral."

Muriel looked very sad for a moment and just shook
her head. "Don't people disappoint you sometimes?"
she asked Mel.

"Sure," she said. "But fortunately not as often as they
surprise and impress me. This whole thing isn't over yet.
The town will come around—come through."

* * *

It took a very dedicated team of people to complete the process of dealing with Hope McCrea's possessions. Muriel St. Claire and her boyfriend, retired general Walt Booth, along with Mike's wife, attorney Brie Valenzuela, managed to select and negotiate a contract from a reputable auction company. The most expedient method was recommended by the appraiser and then approved by Jack—the company would pay a flat rate for the most valuable items, which they would remove from the big old Victorian in the country and take to auction in San Francisco. Preacher and Paige Middleton worked as a team to research some of those items that had been identified, looking up a large percentage of them online; they found the prices quoted by the auction company to be very reasonable. Away went the Belleek, paintings, teapots, collectible signatures and several pieces of furniture.

Pastor Noah Kincaid and his wife, Ellie, worked with their good friends, Jo and Nick Fitch, to create advertising fliers for a sale of what was left; the fliers would be scattered around the towns and cities nearby. They also bought ads in the five largest local newspapers, identifying a weekend estate sale. Items left to be sold were priced and tagged with the help of Muriel, the visiting appraiser and Preacher, checking and cross-checking on Hope's computer.

Then there was the enormous task of separating items that could be sold from items that had to be donated. It took all the Presbyterian Women, the Presbyterian Husbands and many a Presbyterian pickup truck.

And then all was ready. It was a garage sale of grand proportions, most of which took place in the house and on its front and back porches. Cars started to arrive early on Saturday morning and kept coming through the day. It was like a parade—weekend garage and estate sale shoppers from miles and towns away. The sale would be extended through Sunday if anything remained to be sold. A table was set up with several large coffee thermoses and pastries in the morning, and Preacher, Mike, Jack and a couple of friends set up barbecues in the yard and sold hot dogs, hamburgers and drinks in the afternoon. One of the Anderson sons, a family of local sheep ranchers, brought a couple of ponies for rides and Paul Haggerty had rented a little merry-go-round from an amusement company that leased equipment for parties.

Lawn chairs were pulled out of the backs of trucks, coolers full of soda, water and beer were added to the refreshments Jack and Preacher provided, baseballs and gloves appeared, a football was tossed around, a soccer ball was kicked between a couple of young boys.

It was a circus. A town fair. Most of the people, especially all those from Virgin River, were only there to watch, not to buy.

In and around Hope's house volunteers were posted to watch over the items for sale—furniture, dishes, flatware, quilts, old linens, that bag of dozens of ball caps, the old purple velour couch.

Mel Sheridan felt her eyes moisten with tears when she saw that old, jacked-up beige Suburban drive away with its new owner. It was still wearing mud on its frame from Hope's driving around the back mountain roads in the rain. It was hard to watch the memory of her vanish, piece by piece.

* * *

Lilly heard about the estate sale from Annie. She knew someone who would love poking around all that old, retro stuff, especially the tables, chairs and accessories. She planned to put off her cleaning and shopping chores to accompany Dane to the sale; not only did Dane love haunting oddball sales, he was always looking for furniture for the Loving Cup. If he could pick up a chair or two or old side table, he'd be like a kid in a candy store.

Dane worked out his schedule with Darlene to take a few hours off and Lilly picked him up. He was almost giddy with excitement and happy they were getting an early start. As they drove up Highway 36 toward Virgin River he yammered about the sorts of things he'd be happy to find—furniture, old pitchers, a pie safe or dry sink as a serving accessory, trays, linens, good flatware at a nice price.... The list went on the more excited he got.

"Hey, you've been doing more riding than yoga lately," he said suddenly. "How's the new guy working out?"

Lilly kept her eyes on the road, but she smiled and said, "I like him."

"*Like*...him?"

"I've seen a lot of him the last couple of weeks. We work together at the clinic, ride sometimes. I've been to his sister's house for dinner a couple of times. I'm thinking of letting my grandfather have a crack at him over Sunday dinner."

Dane whistled. "This is progress. When am I going to get the more *interesting* details?"

She just laughed at him and didn't answer.

"Seriously," Dane said. "I have stuck by you through everything for years now—why are you so cagey about this guy? Is it just because he's Native American?"

"Maybe," she said. Then she turned toward him and she knew her eyes glowed. "We have some traditional stuff in common, but I've been trying to avoid that stuff for so long. It's hard to let myself go. I'm just trying to keep my head. Stay sane."

"Not go over the deep end?" Dane asked. "Oh, cupcake, the deep end can be so much fun!"

"Yeah, I know. I have some experience with that. But there are big differences this time. Huge," she emphasized. "Clay is a beautiful person. He has a very old soul. He wants to meet you."

"Really?" Dane said, grinning stupidly. Clearly he was touched by this.

"Don't be so optimistic," Lilly said. "He offered to let you hit him to, you know, even the score or something."

"*Real*ly?" he said again, his grin growing. "Well, that's unconventional. Does this very old soul you're involved with know that I swing the other way?"

"He does," she said. "I even admitted to him that I've spent a lot of energy trying to turn you straight." She grinned at him. "I explained that you're hopelessly gay. He seemed to take that in stride."

"Ah, a secure straight guy," Dane said. "My absolute weakness…"

Lilly bit her lower lip, serious. "I intended to go very slowly," she finally said. "There's just something about him that makes going slow awful hard."

There was a colorful sign on the road that read Sale! Some balloons were attached, but they weren't helium so they drooped, hanging down by their ribbons. She maneuvered her little Jeep down the one-lane drive, passing some cars and trucks parked along the slanting road. All conversation between them stopped as the house came into view. Neither Lilly nor Dane had ever seen it before, but then, except for the locals who had lived in Virgin River a very long time, most of the people present— browsers, shoppers, collectors—would have had even less reason to have visited this property before today.

"Oh, my God," Dane said, his eyes running from the front porch to the top of the third story. The paint was peeling, the wood on the porch and rails was faded gray, the siding a faded dirty white, and some shingles on the roof were curling, but it was an amazing structure—three stories with turrets and decorative wood accents. It was only September and the grounds were still beautiful. Flower beds surrounded the front porch and flanked the stone walk, full green bushes grew alongside mature pines, oak and maple trees. With just a little exterior sprucing up, the old Victorian could be stunning. In its day it was probably quite a mansion. "Look at that *house!*"

Dane left Lilly in his dust. He was anxious to get inside the house and poke around, both at the items for sale and the architecture. He turned back when he was halfway to the front porch, a questioning look on his face. She laughed, shook her head and waved him on. He was far more excited about the event than she. She spotted Annie standing across the lawn talking to a man she didn't know, so she wandered over that way.

Once Lilly was standing beside Annie, she began to meet more people from Virgin River. Nathaniel joined them, then Jack Sheridan, who owned the bar and grill in town—the man who apparently had been made responsible for this deceased woman's estate. She was introduced to Preacher, Noah and Paul and their wives.

Someone handed her a soda and a couple more people joined them—Walt Booth and his lady friend, Muriel, who looked familiar and, Lilly learned, had had a hand in setting up the weekend sale. Lilly heard more about how Hope McCrea had been so well-known in the town and yet a mystery to so many.

"There was a lot more to Hope than met the eye," Muriel said. "We found some valuable art in her house that has been taken to auction, and some stories have come out of the paintings. One artist, whose estate has established an impressive online catalog, began her watercolor career just south of here. During the Depression she painted in exchange for food for her family—Hope actually had four of her paintings, which have become very valuable. Not only did Hope have a good eye for art, she was helping neighbors a long while before this was even a real town."

All around them was the atmosphere of a fair—the kids on ponies or the little merry-go-round, chasing each other through the big trees, people lounging in their lawn chairs with a beer or hot dog, watching as people came and went out of the house, happily carrying their finds. Lilly wasn't sure how long she'd been standing with new friends and old, maybe over an hour, when it happened.

She saw Clay coming up the drive; he must have parked down the road and walked the rest of the way. She filled her eyes with him; there was no more beautiful man on the face of the earth.

"There's Clay," Annie said to Nathaniel. "Did you know he was coming?"

Nathaniel laughed and glanced at Lilly. "I doubt he's here for the antiques."

Lilly barely heard; a slight smile touched her lips. She knew he hadn't come to shop, and it was such a nice surprise.

Clay saw them, waved, smiled and continued toward Lilly. He wore jeans and boots; it was unusual to see him in anything else. His shirt was denim, his hat bore the eagle feather and his hair was loose. Some of it fell over his shoulder while the rest flowed down his back.

"Good," Nate said. "He can meet Jack and some of the Virgin River guys."

"Oh, I know Clay," Jack said. "He's eaten at the bar a few times. Very nice guy." Jack waved a hand in front of Lilly's face to get her attention. "I don't know too much about Native American culture—I don't even know if this is a dumb question. Are you two from the same tribe or something?"

Lilly laughed lightly, sentimentally. "Our tribes are legendary enemies."

Jack watched her face. "You gonna be able to work that out?" he asked with a sly grin.

"I don't think we have a choice," she said, her eyes moving back to Clay.

Clay neared, aiming right for her, his smile broadening just as she felt a light seem to shine from within her. Clay went first to Lilly before acknowledging anyone else and the very moment his hands reached for hers, there was a crash.

Lilly spun around and saw Dane sprawled on the steps of the porch, looking shocked and a little wild-eyed, surrounded by the scattered sterling flatware that had spilled out of the leather case he held against his chest. His eyes were locked on Lilly and Clay and his long legs were splayed down the stairs.

"Dane!" she shouted, running to him.

Clay looked at Annie with a frown. "That's Dane?"

"You don't know Dane? He owns a coffee shop near my beauty parlor—he's a good friend of mine. And Lilly's."

Clay gave a nod that was more a lift of his chin. "I haven't met him yet." Then he began to slowly walk toward Lilly and Dane.

When Lilly got to Dane, she knelt on the step. "What in the world *happened?*"

Dane looked a little flushed. "Is that *him?*" he whispered, nodding over Lilly's shoulder. Lilly took a quick glance, then nodded back at Dane. "Good Lord! You didn't mention he was friggin' Adonis!"

She chuckled a little. "I told you he was handsome."

"Lilly, *I'm* handsome. *He's* a friggin' Adonis!"

"Yeah, and then some," she agreed.

"No shit. Whew." Dane wiped his forehead. "I went into a trance when I saw him walking up the road. Then when he reached for you and I realized—"

Clay towered over them. "You okay, man?"

"Um, yeah. Okay," Dane said, sitting up on a step. "Guess I slipped. I must have had… I don't know…"

"Maybe it was the vapors," Lilly suggested wryly. "Let's pick up your silverware. I can take you home."

With Clay lifting one elbow and Lilly lifting the other, Dane seemed to stand a bit shakily, but his head was twisted toward Clay, looking up at him in sheer wonder.

Lilly gave his arm a shake. "Did you hit your head?" she asked sharply.

He finally relaxed his intoxicated gaze and turned toward Lilly. He grinned stupidly. "No, not exactly. I don't have to go home. I just, I don't know, caught my heel on the last step." He shook himself. "I am going to put this silverware I just bought in the Jeep, however."

"You do that," she said, crouching to begin picking up pieces. Between the three of them, it didn't take long to gather up the spilled items. Then Dane was off down the drive to Lilly's vehicle with his treasure. He looked back over his shoulder a couple of times, as if to be sure he'd really seen Clay. On about the third glance, Clay gave an abbreviated wave.

"I'm starting to catch on," he said to Lilly.

"Are you, now?"

"Men don't usually gaze at me that way," Clay explained. "Shew."

"When he thinks about this later, he is going to be so embarrassed."

Eleven

Jillian maneuvered the van into the Riordan cabin compound, her sister Kelly riding shotgun, her friends Penny and Jackie in the backseat. They drove past the river, wide and flowing strong beside the cabins, surrounded by trees, shrubs, autumn flowers with mountains rising behind it. Six small, quaint cabins lined the drive; there was a two-story house with a wide porch at the end of the compound.

This was the last leg of their annual vacation, one they were committed to and had taken every year since college. She drove past the cabins right up to the front of the owner's house. When she parked, a young woman holding a baby stood from her porch chair.

Jillian and Kelly were the first out of the van. "Hi," Jill said. "I'm—"

"Jillian Matlock?" she asked. "Hi, I'm Shelby Riordan. Welcome." She turned away and shouted into the house. "Luke, they're here."

"How did you know it was me? There are four of us!"

Shelby laughed. "I didn't. You were the one who

called ahead, the only name I knew." She walked down the porch steps, baby held against her. "We have cabin number four ready for you and because today's a busy day for the town, Jack's Bar won't be open. It's the only place to eat in town, so I took the liberty of putting some food in your refrigerator—some bread, cold cuts, eggs, cheese and milk. Also some colas and coffee. You'll have to go as far as Fortuna for a restaurant meal—I'm sure you came through Fortuna on your way here. Just on the chance you don't feel like any more driving, I wanted you to have an option. There's no obligation— if that doesn't suit you, just leave it and Luke will take care of it."

Just as she said that, a man came out of the house carrying a diaper bag. "Can you think of anything else you need?" he asked.

"Um…a key?"

They both grinned. "The key's on a hook just inside the door—the cabin isn't locked."

"Oh," Jillian said. "Don't you ever lock up?"

"Sure we do," Shelby said. "We can't vouch for guests, so you should lock up your stuff after you unload and leave it. We're headed out."

"We'll be back by around five," Luke said. "There's Internet hookup, but your cell phones won't work here. I have a working phone in the house if you have calls to make later. We're headed to a garage sale—"

"*Estate* sale," Shelby corrected. "An elderly woman from town died recently and left a big old house filled to the rafters with interesting stuff. Not only will the whole town be there but probably most of the county. That's why Jack's is closed—he's flipping burgers at the estate sale."

Kelly stepped forward. "Is it open to the public?"

"Not only open, we've been advertising! It's free and with potential to find interesting stuff at rock-bottom prices. Most of the town just couldn't wait for a look inside that house—closest thing to a mansion we have around here. And no one from Virgin River was ever in it before she died."

"Interesting..." Kelly said.

"Have you heard of Muriel St. Claire? The actress?"

"Everyone's heard of her," Penny said.

"Well, she organized the sale. She's dedicated to yard sales, estate sales, antique sales... It's kind of her hobby."

"Did you hire her?" Penny asked, wide-eyed.

Shelby laughed. "She lives here. She dates my uncle Walt."

Jillian looked over her shoulder at her sister and friends. "Ladies?" she asked.

"Oh yeah, I'd like to see this," Penny said.

A few minutes later, after Luke fetched Art, a man with Down syndrome, to ride with him, the girls were back in the van and following the Riordans out into town.

Jillian and Kelly Matlock, sisters aged thirty-one and thirty-two, had a ritual annual vacation with girlfriends Penny Gerhard and Jackie Davis. All four of them had been friends since high school and were very successful in vastly different arenas—VP of Corporate Communications for a large software manufacturer, a well-known sous-chef in a busy San Francisco restaurant, a PR director for a large banking chain and a political analyst,

respectively. Four highly compensated, extremely pres-
sured single women.

Come hell or high water, they managed a full week
to ten days away together every year. Kicking back,
laughing late into the night, just like when they were in
high school, bleeding off some job stress, then going
back to their challenging work worlds feeling renewed
and ready to do battle for another fifty-one weeks. They
had all gone to the same university, except Kelly, who
attended various culinary institutes around the world.
They'd been taking these trips since the year they'd
graduated college. The destinations varied greatly, from
spas to sailing and diving trips to camping. One par-
ticularly memorable vacation was spent at a lodge in
the Boundary Waters of Northern Minnesota and it had
been one of their best—they had indulged in everything
from canoeing, hiking and tracking large animals to just
lying around in chaise lounges at the water's edge under
leafy boughs of trees, and delighting in the magnificent
talents of the lodge chef.

This year they'd rented a roomy van and taken a road
trip from the San Francisco area, where they were from,
to Vancouver. A restaurant owner in Portland who liked
to hunt and fish tipped them off about a beautiful little
mountain town off the beaten track in Northern California, and Jillian called to see if there was room at the
inn. A final two-day stay on their way back home in a
little cabin along Virgin River seemed like a great idea.
It'd bring back memories of the Boundary Waters, and
they could enjoy the early fall weather, warmer here
than in the Bay Area, and rest up from their vacation
before heading back to their demanding careers.

Jill was ready to end the reunion and get home

because she had a guy in her life and she missed him. The others were "between men" at the moment and not in any hurry to get back to their demanding jobs. Kelly worked in a five-star kitchen under a head chef as mean as Mussolini, Penny's banking chain was in a severe money crisis that made her PR job a living hell and Jackie, the political analyst, was gearing up for an election campaign as spiteful and bitter as any third world coup. Job pressure trumped boyfriends and the girls had headed to Virgin River for a couple of days before the annual vacation had to end.

None of the four would plan a vacation around an estate sale, but since the owners of the cute little river cabins mentioned this was a big event for their town, they decided to drop in. And it was *far* more interesting than any of them had expected.

There were people everywhere, and those who weren't just arriving or carrying purchases down the long drive to their vehicles were lounging around, watching the action or standing in clumps visiting and enjoying picnic food and drink or minding children's activities and games. Luke and Shelby Riordan were kind enough to introduce them around a bit as if they were old friends rather than strangers who happened to be renting one of their cabins for a couple of nights. They heard many different versions of the story surrounding the deceased elderly woman's estate and town trust. Each one of them gravitated to their own personal interests. Jackie spent a good deal of time chatting with Jack Sheridan, hearing about his adventures as the executor of the living trust. Penny met Muriel St. Claire, who considered herself an active part of the community.

Kelly was drawn into conversation with the cook

from Jack's bar. This was very typical of the sous-chef, to gravitate to the food, even if in this case it was hot dogs.

"We're a town that caters to hunters and fishermen," the man called Preacher told her. "Once word got out that we stocked quality liquor just for them and the food was delicious and hearty, they started making it a point to drop in for at least one meal with us when they were in our area for hunting or fishing. We have hundreds of regulars we see every year."

"And your menu?" Kelly asked.

"I don't have a menu," he told her. "I plan about a week ahead, make sure I have a different breakfast, lunch and dinner special every day. There's always some leftovers, and then I like to bulk it up."

"Bulk it up?"

"They're hunters and fishermen and women—they're not looking for light meals. They're tired and cold and hungry—looking for food that sticks to their ribs. I make a lot of fresh breads, pies, cakes.... Oh, and breakfast pastry—I'm really working on the pastry."

"And the town?"

"We serve the town," he said. "Jack's is pretty much the gathering spot for a lot of them and we try to keep the costs down so they can afford it. We have a dependable group of locals and visitors just about every day. Unless it's really wet. People don't come out in the rain that much. Jack says they're busy putting buckets under the roof leaks." He grinned at her. "We're not a fancy bunch. Pretty laid-back. But I take my food seriously."

Kelly was quiet for a moment. "I would *love* to work in such a place," she said, almost breathlessly. "I've been carrying around my great-grandmother's recipes for years. Some of them I've fooled around with a little, but they're hard to improve. I've brought a few to the restaurant where I'm currently sous-chef, but it's dicey—I won't give them up and the head chef doesn't want to serve anything his name isn't on."

And with that, they were bonded. "I'd give anything for a great-grandmother's recipes," Preacher said. "Or a grandmother, for that matter. I taught myself to cook. I wasn't a cook when I came up here. I was a marine. I just came up here to fish with Jack and ended up staying."

"I took a vacation to the Boundary Waters a few years ago. Up in Northern Minnesota. Rugged country and so beautiful. And they had a chef on-site whose food just knocked me out!"

Preacher grinned. "Bet they got nothing on us," he said.

"Maybe not," she agreed. "We stayed at a lodge on the water. That chef didn't have a menu, either, but he surprised me every meal. He served what he wanted and lots of it. Now, I've been to Paris, but the Boundary Waters was the most indulgent, fattening trip I've ever had. And I thought about what it must be like to be that chef.… I would love to be the only chef in a kitchen where there's no yelling.…"

Preacher stiffened his back and stood to his full six-foot-four-inch height. "Yelling?" he repeated.

Kelly laughed. "I guess there's no yelling in your kitchen."

He drew his heavy black brows together. "Who would yell at me?" he asked.

"Right," she said with a chuckle. "Where I work, the wait for a table is two hours if you have a reservation. If you want to sit down early, a couple hundred bucks in the maître d's palm might help, but no guarantees. The head chef is a sociopath and the manager is a Don Juan who can't keep his hands to himself." And then she laughed again. "It's a steep climb in the kitchen."

But Preacher was frowning. "Where are you climbing to, exactly?"

"Head chef. Head chef of a restaurant that's written up in every gourmet and travel magazine in the marketplace. Eventually, my own restaurant. I've been working toward that for twelve years with very little time off. I'm going to get there. And when I get there my manager will be civil and my kitchen will be sane." Then she smiled and said, "But I do envy you. You and the chef at the Boundary Waters lodge. That's got to be the best of both worlds."

"It's a good life. But I'm no chef. I cook the best I can. That's all."

"If they're coming back year after year, you're making it work. Isn't that what it's all about? People enjoying your food?"

Preacher gave a boyish shrug and shy smile. "We're not open tonight on account of all this, but I'm cleaning and loading the barbecues before dusk and I have some venison chili in the freezer if you and your girls want to come by and do a little sampling."

She reached out and impulsively touched his arm. "Seriously?" she said, her eyes wide. "Oh, that would be fantastic! "

"Might even be a couple of stuffed trout tucked away, too—stuffed with corn bread, rolled in bread crumbs, seared in a little extra virgin and simmered in beer. And there's always pie. Hardly anyone beats my pie. In fact, come to think of it, Buck Anderson gave me a big lamb shank and there's some of that left.… It wouldn't be as good reheated, but it's still pretty fine. I don't think I ever fed a chef before. I'd do it, though. Professional courtesy."

"That would be so wonderful. I hate for you to open up the kitchen just for us, but…"

"Open up the kitchen?" he asked. "My kitchen never closes. I feed my family from that kitchen—our house is attached to the bar and we don't have any other kitchen. It's open twenty-four hours. The front door of the bar has a lock."

"Front of the house," Kelly said.

"Huh?"

"That's what we call the restaurant, the seating, where the food is served—the front of the house. The kitchen is the back of the house."

"That a fact? Well, it's simpler here—it's a kitchen or a bar or a house. And we pretty much do as we please."

Kelly laughed. "I like that."

"Have you been in Hope's old house?" Preacher asked her.

"Not yet," she admitted. "I always seem to talk to whoever is cooking before doing anything else."

"Well, I don't know that Hope was much of a cook. Never heard her mention it and never knew anyone invited to dinner. But that house has a very neat kitchen. Looks like Hope pretty much lived in it the last ten years or so. I have to stay with the grills, so let me get my wife to show you around. Paige," he called. A woman with a toddler on her hip wandered over to Preacher from a short distance away. "Paige, this here is Kelly and she's a cook like me. Can you show her Hope's kitchen?"

"Sure, John," the woman said. She stuck out her hand. "Pleasure to meet you. Did you come to Virgin River for the estate sale?"

"Actually, I came with my sister and friends just to enjoy the mountains for a day or two before going back to the city. I'm from San Francisco. I work as a chef and your husband and I were just talking food. He even offered to open up his kitchen to give us a sample of his best chili and trout."

Paige laughed and her eyes twinkled. "John likes to show off his cooking. Wait till you see this kitchen. In fact, wait till you see the house...."

"So...the woman who died," Kelly said, "she was a hermit?"

"Not at all," Paige said, leading the way up the front porch. "She was around all the time, in everyone's business, looking out for the town. She was in the bar almost every evening—she liked a shot of Jack Daniel's to go with her cigarette. But she definitely had her secrets. Even though she was present for every town event or gathering, none of us has run into a single person from Virgin River who's ever been in her house. Though lots of people have been as far as the front or back porch or garden.... Hope used to garden like a madwoman and complain about the bunnies and the deer, but she'd give away most of her vegetables."

As Paige talked, Kelly followed her through the house toward the back and finally they stepped into a massive kitchen. The appliances were old but clearly of the type to service a manor house and not a house for a single inhabitant. There was a large worktable that had a Not For Sale! sign on it in the center of the huge kitchen. There were two sinks, a six-burner stove, two ovens, two refrigerators and a large, walk-in pantry. Kelly also saw a stairway that went to a cellar. "What's down there?" she asked.

"There were mice and canned goods that expired forty years ago," Paige said. "It's pretty much an unfinished cellar with a dirt floor. This house was built long before people thought of rumpus rooms."

One end of the kitchen was for cooking while the other was for eating and contained a very large stone fireplace. There was no furniture there.

"It appeared Hope stayed here. There was a big old easy chair and ottoman along with a couple of quilts. From this spot she could look out over her backyard, see the mountains rising back there behind her property. Anytime anyone came to see her, she met them on either the front porch or back porch. As close as we can figure out, she chopped her own wood, too. She had a desk, computer, files and television here; John took the computer home to see if he can help find if there's anything on it that Jack should know—like relatives, special charity interests, lost accounts or deeds, that sort of thing." Paige pushed open a door off the kitchen to reveal what would have been maids' quarters in its day. "Even though there are like seven bedrooms in this old house, Hope lived in the kitchen."

"That's what I would do," Kelly said somewhat absently. She turned to smile at Paige. "I fall asleep in my recliner almost every night. I mean morning. I work till three or four in the morning. I go home, turn on the TV, which by that time is usually showing infomercials, and zonk out. I wake up just before lunch and start over. My bed doesn't see me that much."

"But of course you have days off," Paige said.

"Yes, of course," she said because she knew she should. But not really. The restaurant was open seven days a week and while it was reasonable that she take Mondays and Tuesdays as her own, there was a thing about turf and she liked protecting hers. She was the senior sous-chef and it was a political position; some of the line chefs who worked under her would cut her throat for her spot in a second, and Durant, the head chef, would hand them the knife.

For the millionth time she said to herself, *I live this life because I love my work and if I hang in there I will be the Durant of the kitchen, and when it's my kitchen it will be a sane kitchen.*

It was at that very moment that she happened to glance out the kitchen window and see what she recognized as her sister's head. Jillian was sitting on the back porch.

"Have you met my sister, Jillian?" she asked Paige.

"I don't think I have," Paige said.

"Come with me," Kelly said, leading the way out the back door.

When she found Jill on the back porch, she was sitting in an old wooden chair beside a round, rusting metal table, just gazing across the backyard. It was about the size of a football field and led up to the tree line. Most of it was taken up with a garden.

"Hey," Kelly said. "Whatcha doing?"

Jill turned sentimental, round eyes up to her sister. "The woman who lived here," she said. "She died in this chair."

Paige stood just behind Kelly, bouncing her little girl, Dana, on her hip. "Um, yeah, that's probably right. She spent a lot of time on her front or back porch, weather permitting. The table and chair are in such sad shape—I don't imagine anybody would want them—so after the sale we'll take them to the dump."

"Her melons and pumpkins are in," Jill said, standing.

"We'll harvest them when they're ready. She liked to give them away. I'm Paige," she said, sticking out a hand.

"Jillian. Nice to meet you. So—was she very lonely? The woman who lived here?"

Paige shook her head. "She kept herself pretty busy. She spent hours on the computer and phone, running up deals. She bought and sold the church in town, brought our midwife and local constable to town, and even though no one seemed to know much about her, she knew about everyone. She supplied a lot of ranchers and farmers with land that had been left to her that she didn't use."

"That's one helluva garden out there," Jill pointed out, gesturing to the large plot behind the house.

Paige laughed. "Truly. She was a kick about the garden. The bunnies and deer drove her crazy and she used to show up at the bar and tell Jack she was going to start shooting them for the bar to cook and Jack would just tell her he couldn't accept illegally murdered wildlife. She loved her garden, and a few other things, like local art, which she collected. There was so much about her we didn't know until after she passed, but I think that's the way Hope wanted it." Paige smiled. "There is no question in my mind—she knew she was the most eccentric character in town and loved it."

"Do you think she liked being a mystery?" Jillian asked.

"Maybe," Paige said. "Mostly, she was a completely unsentimental, crotchety old woman who constantly tried to cover the fact that she had a huge, soft, sweet heart in her. We found some old pictures—she was widowed in her thirties and an attractive, rich woman. It's a wonder she never remarried."

"Mama," little Dana said, patting Paige's hair. "Mama! Potty!"

"Good girl!" Paige said. "Please excuse us—we're in training."

"By all means," Jillian said.

When Paige had taken her little girl to find a bathroom, Jill sank back into the chair. Kelly took a seat on the steps of the back porch and looked up at her sister. "Kinda moody there, Jill. Dreaming of getting back to Kurt The Wonderful?"

Jill sighed. "Actually, I was doing some reminiscing. What does this place remind you of?"

Kelly shook her head. "Couldn't say."

"Nana's house," Jill said.

"Oh, please—this place is huge! You could probably fit three of Nana's house in this one."

"But when we were five and six, didn't it seem like a castle? Like a mansion? I'm still sorry we let that place go. I'd give anything to have that old house to visit."

"Um, and when would either of us visit it? We both work all the time…."

"I know. You're right. I just miss it."

In fact, Jillian often missed the life she had growing up there.

When the sisters were five and six there had been an accident in which they lost their father, and which disabled their mother, confining her to a wheelchair for what remained of her life. They went to live with their father's grandmother. A seventy-year-old widow at the time, she suddenly inherited two small children and became a full-time caregiver. At what should have been one of the darkest times of their young lives, Nana gave the girls the boost they needed. She told them they were going to work very hard to take care of their mama, the house, the garden, be good neighbors and good students, but it was going to be okay because they were going to make work *fun*. Every chore became a game, every challenge was a contest. She took them in hand and taught them both the best of the kitchen and garden and then she, a French and Russian immigrant who had very little formal education but spoke five languages, taught them to read so they could take turns reading to their mother.

"Doesn't it remind you of Nana's house and yard?" Jillian asked again.

"Nana's house on steroids," Kelly said. "Besides Mom and Nana, what do you miss, exactly?" Kelly asked.

Jillian shrugged. "It must have been really hard, all we were going through back then, but it sure seemed easier. Simpler."

"Poorer. Much poorer…"

Jill laughed. "But we did learn how to make money, didn't we? Something Nana never had."

"That's the one thing I would have changed about her life if I could."

But their nana had to be moved out of that big old house when she was ninety and their mother passed years earlier. The stairs became too much for Nana, but she couldn't be trusted to stay off them. They put her in a cushy, ground-floor assisted-living apartment, paid for it themselves even though they were only twenty-five and twenty-six at the time. And she had *hated* it. "I'd rather stick to one level than live in this little toilet with shelves!" Nana had said. "They've poured cement over their garden!"

She had died in her sleep at ninety-four just a couple of years ago. They hadn't let go of the house until she was gone.

"Better get me back to civilization," Jillian said. "I'm starting to remember what was surely the most difficult time of my life as sweet and uncomplicated."

Kelly laughed a bit cynically. "With the way we work, I don't think I'd argue about the sweetness when we were kids, and we were too young to fully understand the complications. But there's no going back, Jill, so let's just remember it fondly and get back to the concrete jungle." She took a deep breath. "I've been out of the kitchen for almost ten days. By now Durant has probably replaced me."

"And my department has probably voted in a union or something," Jill said.

Luke, Shelby, the baby and their helper, Art, returned to their home along the river before sunset, in enough time for Art to get a little fishing in before dinner. When Art was headed for his cabin next door to grab his rod and reel, Luke said to Shelby, "Did you notice that Jack was getting the freeze treatment from some of his friends?"

"We should have gone to that town meeting," Shelby said. "As Mel tells it, some of the Virgin River folks have it in their heads that he should just divvy up the money Hope left the town and write everyone checks.

And Jack, being Jack, got pissed and stormed out of the meeting."

Luke lifted the baby out of the car seat. "That's what I would've done," Luke said. He held the baby against his shoulder for a moment. "They should be thanking Jack for taking care of this whole thing. I mean, it's not like Hope *asked* him."

Shelby laughed. "She obviously knew better. Mel said it's just a little lover's spat between Jack and some of the town. It'll pass." She reached for the baby.

"I'd say screw 'em," Luke said. He handed over the baby. "Let 'em be mad."

"You have a very cranky side that's not all the way softened up yet," Shelby pointed out to him. "I have an idea. Before we think about dinner, let's sit on the porch with a glass of wine. The baby is zonked from all his fresh air today and I bet we get a good half hour of this awesome weather."

"Consider it done," Luke said, pulling the baby carrier off its base to carry, along with the heavy diaper bag, up to the porch. "I'll pour you a nice glass of wine." Then he grinned. "Kinda nice that you unloaded and now can have fun things like wine and lotsa sex, huh?"

She made a face at him. "Actually, I think this is kinda nice for *you*. And I'm not referring to the wine."

"Well, if you don't want a lot of sex, stop being so freaking sexy!" he said, walking into the house.

Shelby sat in one of the porch chairs, snuggling the baby close. She'd put him in his infant carrier in a second, but she never really tired of holding him close. Since she'd started back to nursing college and Luke was in charge of Brett, Shelby missed him during the days she was at school.

She heard Luke open the refrigerator and get out a chilled bottle. Then she heard her brother-in-law Aiden's voice on their answering machine.

Luke, I need you to call me when you get this message—there's been an accident. Colin. I'm on my cell and I'll give you what details I have when you call.

As Aiden's voice poured out of the answering machine, Shelby stood from the porch chair and wandered to the doorway. She found Luke standing at the work island in their kitchen, a bottle of wine in one hand and the opener in the other, frozen, a stricken look on his face. His eyes were wide and definitely afraid, a look he tried to erase the second his wife's eyes were on him. "I know what it is," he said. "Colin drives like a lunatic, always has. I've been telling him for years, he's gonna ride that bull just a little too long and zap, he'll get hurt."

"Luke," Shelby said, "just call."

"'Course I'll call," he said. "But I bet it's a fender bender and he broke a couple of bones. Aiden didn't say he was—" And there he stopped, because he couldn't say it or think it. "Want me to pour your wine first?"

Shelby shook her head. Her expression was serious. She knew her husband's predilection for trying to make things turn out a certain way by just lending his voice to them.

He picked up the cordless and dialed. All he said was, "Aiden."

"Aw, Luke, he augured in. They were in exercises at Fort Hood when some crazy civilian airplane crossed protected airspace, flew right into a crop of Black Hawks and Cobras. Ran right into the tail-boom of Colin's helicopter..."

"How the hell did a civilian aircraft—"

"I don't have any details, but the sergeant who called me said the plane was erratic and flying out of control. Maybe the pilot had a stroke or coronary."

"And Colin?"

"Critical. Broken bones, possible internal injuries, burns. All messed up. Unconscious."

"Aw, Jesus!"

"Sean is closest to him in Alabama and he's on active duty. He's already on his way to Fort Hood. The rest of us are going to sit tight till they stabilize him. He could stay at Fort Hood, end up back at Fort Benning or even be airlifted to Fort Sam in San Antonio, depending on the extent and type of his injuries. If they airlift him out of Fort Hood, chances are Sean can catch a ride on a military aircraft. So… Go ahead and throw a few things in a bag and when I know more, I'll call you."

"Aiden," Luke said. "When you say *critical*… Is he gonna make it?"

"No one knows yet, Luke. He's in real bad shape, headed for surgery."

"Did you get a hold of Mom and George?" Luke's mother and her boyfriend were traveling the country in their RV.

"I did. They're in Florida visiting one of George's stepgrandsons, so I was able to convince her to stay where they are for now. I had to promise to call her first when I have more news, but…"

"But call Sean, since I assume he has his cell and is headed that way. Then me so I can get going. Then call her and tell her she was first. Listen, maybe I should just head for Florida right now, drive Mom and George in that bus of theirs. I don't like two old people driving somewhere all upset."

"I doubt you could get there fast enough to chauffeur them. Sean should be at Fort Hood by early morning," Aiden said. "Let's get more information before we react."

"I just don't want Colin alone if—I want one of us to be there if—"

"Luke, he's in surgery and *no one's* going to be with him but the doctors. Don't worry about things it's too early to worry about."

"Was he unconscious or in a coma?" Luke asked. "Did he have head injuries?"

"He was conscious when they pulled him out of the wreckage, but they put him under because of the pain. He went into surgery right away for serious fractures— and no, I don't know which bones—and to assess him for internal bleeding. We're going to have to wait, Luke. The crash was only a few hours ago. Just hang on. I'll get back to you."

"Yeah," Luke said, running a hand over his head. "Yeah. Thanks. I'll get ready to travel."

When he hung up the phone and turned toward his wife, all he could do was shrug helplessly.

"It wasn't a car accident," Shelby said.

"Helicopter crash. He's in rotten shape, baby. I won't even know where to go to him until he's assessed and stabilized. Broken, bleeding and burned. Critical, Aiden said. In surgery. And not very many details."

"Do you have to go now?" she asked.

"I'm going to pack now, but there's no going anywhere till I know more. They could airlift him to a different post, depending on his injuries and what he needs.

Baby, I do some things real well, but I don't wait real well."

She smiled with affection. "I know, Luke."

"Maybe I should just drive to Aiden in Chico, then we can go wherever we're going together. I'm probably going to have to head for Sacramento for a flight anyway and Chico is on the way. It's turning night. Sacramento doesn't have so many flights at night."

"There's always San Francisco," she said. "If you want to just get started, I understand. If Aiden calls while you're driving, you have that cell phone that works everywhere but here. Charge it in the car."

He stepped toward her. "Shelby, I want to," he said. "I want to get to him. The thing I'm most afraid of—" Again he couldn't finish.

"He's not going to die, Luke," she said. "I really think it helps if you believe that. If you envision that."

"I can't lose him," Luke said emotionally. "Colin has always been the one brother hardest to pull into the fold, the hardest to get close to. He was always the wildest one."

"Wilder than you?"

"Oh, God, yes!" He pulled her into his arms, baby and all. "If I throw some stuff in a bag and start driving south to Aiden, will you be okay?"

She nodded. "I'll call Uncle Walt to help Art around the cabins. Uncle Walt will babysit if I ask him to, but I can take the baby with me to class. And if I have to skip a class or two, not that big a deal. Brand-new mommies get slack." She touched his face. "Luke, please try to believe he'll be all right."

"I'm trying, Shell. I'm trying."

Twelve

Preacher had explained to Kelly that the Closed sign would be lit at the bar, but the door would be unlocked until they arrived. When they pulled up, Kelly driving this time, she took a moment to look at the building. It appeared to be a refurbished log cabin with a wide porch with several chairs. She could see the two-story house built onto the back. It was rustic, yet in perfect condition.

Caught studying the bar from the outside, she was the last one out of the van, but the other women stood aside on the porch and let Kelly pass. She pushed open the door and yelled, "Hello?"

A swinging door in the back of the bar glided open and Paige smiled at them. She held her little girl, wrapped in a big, fluffy towel. "Hi. Come on back. John's been waiting for you." She gave her little girl a squeeze. "We're getting baths. When the kids are settled, I'll join you in the kitchen."

The room was dimly lit by a light that ran along the top of a very long bar of beautiful, ornately carved dark wood. Kelly counted at least a dozen tables at the front of the store.

Penny gasped, and that's when Kelly noticed the animal trophies—a buck's head over the door, a bear skin, a large stuffed fish in back of the bar.

"Hunting country," she said. "Kind of like the Boundary Waters."

The women filed into the kitchen to find Preacher standing behind his worktable wearing a white apron. He said, "Welcome," with a smile. "Have a seat. We'll start you off with some wine. Jack always keeps some good stuff tucked away." His worktable was set with four plain white soup bowls sitting atop four plain white plates. The utensils were wrapped in white linen napkins. "This Raymond 2005 Small Lot Meritage will work with your venison." He poured a small amount for Kelly to taste.

She rolled it around in her mouth. "Very nice," she agreed.

"Good," he said. "I'm not that good with wine. I'm not called on to serve the drinks with the meals—Jack does that. And until the hunters and fishermen fill up the bar, it's not an issue. A lot of our sportsmen know their wine and liquor and have requests. Jack can handle that."

He pulled a basket of bread from the warmer and put it on the table, adding a flat dish of butter.

"Should we wait for Paige?" Kelly asked.

"Nah, she'll be around for dessert. Cobbler—the apple crop is in. Do you get your food fresh at the restaurant?" he asked Kelly.

"We do. When possible I order most of it myself. Sometimes the head chef takes on that chore, but I like doing it. I go to the wharves myself to look at the catch."

He grinned. "And here, we just go ahead and catch it. Or shoot it. Or get it straight from the ranchers." He donned a mitt and lifted the pan from the stove. With a ladle, he spooned some venison chili into their bowls. Then he stood back, arms crossed over his huge chest.

Kelly stirred her chili while the others just dug in. She noticed that in addition to the kidney beans there were black beans and a smattering of corn, some scallions. The tomatoes were diced; onion minced so finely it was barely visible. She pushed a piece of venison against the side of the bowl with her spoon and it fell apart. She heard the others humming their approval, then she took her taste. Her eyes dropped closed. When she opened them, she said, "It's not gamey."

"It can be and most of my folks like it a little gamey, but I soak it in buttermilk—calms it down a little."

"I've never heard that one before," she said.

"Chances are you don't deal with a lot of venison. When you live in the mountains, on the river, you eat off the land as much as possible. That's what makes this place work. Is it any good?" he asked.

"It's the best I've ever tasted," she said with a grin.

"Tomatillo—better than tomatoes."

"Ahhh," she acknowledged. She never would have thought of that. "How are you fixed for fresh fruits and vegetables?"

"Most of what we grow around here is silage for the ranches. And we've got lots of orchards—apples and nuts. Berries of all kinds everywhere, but only in season. But everyone has a big vegetable garden. When the locals who don't have health insurance pay the clinic for services in fresh produce, a lot of that comes over to the bar, where we feed whoever serves the town for free—the doctor, the nurse midwife—that'd be Jack's wife—the local police. If Jack or I help out some neighbor, we get whatever's in season or a cut of meat—beef, lamb, chicken, eggs. In the fall we fill the freezer with so much salmon from the river it keeps us at least half a year, but it's best fresh. It all comes full circle."

"But you get it in season?" she asked.

"Always," he said. "Next I have some stuffed trout for you, but we have to wait a few minutes. Try the corn bread with your chili. It's nothing special—I use package mixes when it's the most practical."

But the corn bread was delicious.

Next came the stuffed trout. He managed to beat the chef at the Boundary Waters lodge. He explained that the asparagus was "up" so he served that with the trout; he apologized that the fish had been frozen and wasn't as good as fresh, but it was still so good. He took away their bowls and wineglasses, serving them a chilled Chardonnay that was outstanding.

Next came the lamb, so tender you could eat it with a spoon, and while he didn't ordinarily serve garlic mashed with his lamb, that was one of his most popular dishes so he pulled some out of the refrigerator. Indeed, best garlic mashed Kelly had ever tasted; she detected flavors of butter, cream instead of whole milk, cream cheese, fresh garlic and parsley.

The girls were moaning, holding their stomachs, raving. Paige joined them just in time for the cobbler and some coffee. "We're known for our coffee," Preacher said. "Best in three counties."

It was.

While Jillian, Penny and Jackie were visiting with Paige, Kelly was focused on Preacher. "I don't know how I can ever thank you for this amazing demo. Can I pay for dinner? Pay for the wine at least?"

He shook his head. "It's fun to have an expert like my stuff."

"I'm going to do something special for you," she said. "I don't know quite when or how, but I'm going to come back up here. And if you'll let me use your kitchen, I'll share my nana's vegetable soup and rhubarb pie."

He leaned his big hands on the worktable and said, "Really? How much meat in your vegetable soup?"

"All straight out of the garden, but it's thick and delicious."

"That would be great. I can't get it right without a side of beef. And I've been trying to figure out rhubarb pie for a long time."

"There are old Russian tricks. I'll show you if you promise not to publish a cookbook."

"You have *nothing* to worry about," he said.

When the four women were driving back to the Riordan cabins that night, Kelly said, "This place. It's a diamond in the rough."

Aiden, Sean and Luke Riordan stood outside their brother's hospital room in the Fort Hood hospital, talking with his surgeon. Patrick, their fifth brother, would have been there, as well, but he was a Navy pilot stationed on an aircraft carrier.

Colin was almost twenty-four hours postsurgical, in a deep, drug-induced sleep to control the pain. His humerus was broken in two places, his elbow all messed up, his pelvis cracked, femur fractured and he had three broken ribs. He now had a titanium rod in his femur and screws in his elbow. Ironically, the elbow was probably the worst for pain, and would be the hardest to heal healthily.

"He's suffered some burns—second-degree burns on his cheek, neck, shoulder and back, but the fractures concern me more right now. He was thrown hard onto his left side. All the bone injuries are on that side, burns on the right."

Luke just stared at his feet and shook his head. Sean asked, "Any good news in here anywhere?"

The orthopedic surgeon, who had a lazy Texas drawl, said, "He's right-handed." It sounded like *He's raght handed*. And then he grinned slightly. "Nah, I'm sort of kidding. Good news—no internal injuries that we're aware of. He had a clean CT scan. No skull cracks, no paralysis. Barring complications, he'll recover. Could be a slow, painful, difficult recovery, but he has an excellent chance of making a full recovery with all his limbs intact. Now I might be just a cockeyed optimist, but I think your boy could get out of this without any disabilities. If I were a bettin' man, I'd say not so much as a limp." Again with the grin. "I'm damn good with a titanium rod, if I do say so myself."

"He was burned," Sean said solemnly.

"He was pulled out of a burning Black Hawk. The extent of his scarring will take a little time to figure out, but the area affected is under twenty percent of his skin and should heal up real nice. Your boy had a head-on with a Cessna—it's a fucking miracle we're standing here talking about him. Don't tell him that," the doctor drawled. "At least not anytime soon—he's gotta be in one piss-poor mood. He's gonna feel like he's been dragged behind a truck over a rock bed."

Aiden was the first one to stick out his hand. "Thank you, Doctor."

The doctor smiled and took his hand. "My pleasure, Doctor. You have my cell number. I'm not on call, but you call me if you need anything. I'm on call for this guy."

When the surgeon walked away, the three brothers just stood in their small circle for a few moments of silence. "You two, go get something to eat," Luke said. "I'll sit with him in case he wakes up. Take your time— he's drugged out of his mind. Then one of you can take a turn while I eat."

While Sean and Aiden turned away, Luke headed back into the critical care unit. There was a chair beside the bed.

Colin's leg was immobilized, but not in a cast; his arm was not only in a cast, but also a brace that held his elbow away from his body. There were gauze bandages stained with yellow salve and some blood covering the right side of his head down to his shoulder.

And he was out cold.

Luke reached out and touched the hand that was uninjured. Colin had been awake a couple of times since surgery, and one of those times he'd become agitated, angry, maybe hallucinating. He'd started yanking at the IV and catheter, trying to pull them out; it took two nurses, Luke and Aiden to control him long enough for the dope to work its way through the IV. Luke hated that he had to be heavily drugged like this, but he hated more the thought of the damage he could do if he yanked out that catheter, or if, God forbid, he managed to get out of the bed and did worse damage to his arm, leg and ribs.

When Luke touched Colin's right hand, his one exposed eye slowly opened.

"Hey," Luke said.

Although half of Colin's face was bandaged, his scowl was unmistakable. When it came out, his voice was raspy, probably from the intubation during surgery. "I'm not done flying," he said in a threatening tone.

"Fine," Luke said. "You're done for today. Let's take this one day at a time."

"I'm flying again," Colin said, sounding as if his tongue was very thick.

"For right now the only flying you're doing is on OxyContin. For the rest, you have to heal first."

Colin's eye drifted shut slowly, then opened again. "I'm not being put out to pasture like you," Colin said, his words slow and thick. "First off, I'm not done. And second, I got no pretty little mama who thinks I'm a god waiting out in that pasture for me."

Luke chuckled. "Well, you manage to outdo me on everything else, so I imagine you'll find yourself some pretty little mama. Hard to come up with one better than Shelby, so your days of trying to beat me might just be over."

"I'm flying," he said.

"Whatever," Luke answered.

"Doctor say I'm gonna live?"

"And live pretty well—once you get better," Luke affirmed with a nod.

"Then you can leave. Nothin' for you to do here but watch me breathe."

"Y'know what? After what you just went through,

watching you breathe is a mighty fine pastime. But listening to you talk is wearing me out. Why don't you go back to sleep?"

Colin swallowed and then smacked his lips. "Water," he ordered.

"Ice chips," Luke replied, leaning over the bed to spoon a couple of small chips in his brother's mouth. "See? There's things I can do. I'll be your battle buddy."

Colin sucked the ice hard, then swallowed. "There's nurses for that," he said.

"You've been kind of a load for these nice nurses. They're gonna fly one in special—from Samoa. Big guy, long ponytail down his back, built like a refrigerator. You'll like him—he's sweet."

"Go. Away."

"Shut your eyes and pretend," Luke said.

"Isn't this bad enough? You think I need a Riordan family reunion, too?" Colin grumbled.

Luke leaned forward in the chair. "Where would you be if I was lying in some hospital bed under a pile of bandages?"

"Hopefully on a sandy beach with a big-breasted nymphomaniac."

Luke shook his head. "You're adorable, you know that?" He stood up and turned away.

"You leaving?" Colin called.

"I'm asking for more drugs for you. Or duct tape. Don't go anywhere."

Luke made his way slowly to the nursing station, but the real reason he had to turn away from Colin was because tears of relief had gathered in his eyes. It was so good to have him back; such a miracle to get a second chance with him.

All five Riordan brothers were close, some closer than others. Their connections weren't based on their ages or their common interests so much as quirks of personality. Luke was the oldest, Colin second in age. Maybe that explained why the two of them had always butted heads. They'd always been competitive. Or maybe it was just Colin—he was the most likely to remain aloof and out of touch with all of them. But like any Riordan, if there was a celebration like a wedding or an emergency call like an accident or illness, Colin would come through. He might be last to arrive, first to leave, likeliest to pick a fight—usually with Luke—but he'd come through.

If Luke strained his memory, it seemed they started to rub each other the wrong way about the time Sean, fourth born in eight years, came along. That was about the time Colin did the most despicable thing—he shot up about three inches taller than Luke and managed to keep that advantage all through life. Luke was a respectable six feet and nicely muscled, but Colin was a six-foot-three-inch giant with big arms and long legs. Then, if that wasn't enough of an insult, Colin made it his life's work to do just slightly better than Luke in school and at getting girls. And the icing on the cake—Colin followed Luke into the Army, got into the Warrant Officer program and flight school and, as one could predict, outscored his older brother. Not by a lot, but still.

Luke had always had an attitude because no matter how well he could do at anything, Colin could always do just a little better. And if he wasn't *doing* better, he was taller and more handsome.

Well, now Colin was broken and scarred. Luke was ashamed that it had taken this to feed his determination for a fresh start with Colin. They should be best friends—they had so much in common! Twenty years in the Army, both of them helicopter pilots, both very successful with the ladies.

Well, that was in the past for Luke, but happily so—no man could ask for more than the life he had with his young wife.

But it wasn't in the past for Colin yet. It wasn't necessarily over for him. The recovery ahead might be difficult, but he could get back in the Black Hawk. If his arms and legs worked, why not?

Luke faced a very nice, very patient nurse. "Any chance my brother can start having some water? Or something?"

"Not too much longer, Mr. Riordan. That's something we really don't want to rush—not with the anesthesia and pain meds. He's actually going to have his first meal pretty soon. Jell-O and broth."

Luke grinned because the devil inside him was feeling slightly vindicated by Colin's comeuppance. Not the injuries—he'd never smile about that. But Jell-O and broth? Sweet. Really, Colin had come in first for a *long* time. "He's gonna love that."

The nurse just shook her head and smiled. "Oh, you kids," she said.

He went back to his brother. "Guess what, pal. You're going to get dinner."

"I hope it's a steak and beer with a shot."

"It's Jell-O and broth," Luke said. "Want me to request beef broth or are you okay with the chicken?"

"Can you please go away?" Colin said, turning his

head. He turned back. "Aren't you just about cleared for sex with that hot little mama you married? I mean, the kid is what? At least six weeks, right?"

"Over eight," Luke said with a smile that was both victorious and taunting. There was another thing he'd finally gotten over on Colin—the perfect wife and a son.

"Oh, for Jesus's sake, go home!"

"Not just yet," Luke said. "Not until Mom gets here to take over."

Colin's unbandaged eye grew round for a second, then slammed shut. He groaned loudly enough to bring one of the nurses out of the nurse's station. With a scowl, he said to Luke, "Why couldn't I just die?"

Blue Rhapsody was shaping up to be one of the most dependable and responsive horses in Nathaniel's stable. She was excellent with a young rider, as if she knew by the sheer weight that this was precious cargo. Yet when Lilly rode Blue, she was a little more energetic and sportive.

Blue was not officially Lilly's yet, but nearly so. Lilly paid her board with cash and work. She had an arrangement with Annie to help with some young riders' classes and activities in exchange for boarding costs. Lilly and Annie were planning an overnight trail ride for six eleven-year-old girls and that brought back such wonderful memories for Lilly. She always knew she loved horses and that riding brought her untold happiness, but it was with the planning of a trail ride that she recalled how much her horsemanship fed her confidence and gave her a sense of mastery.

Lilly had always been smaller than other girls her

age, and her grandfather must have seen the struggle that brought her. He was the one that arranged for her to start riding and helping with the horses on the ranch next door. He had never admitted to paying for this luxury, but she seemed to remember him running errands for their neighbor, delivering anything from hardware to feed, and once Lilly was grown she realized there could only be one reason for that—a barter for her riding. And giving his little granddaughter the opportunity to learn to control and manage the thousand-pound animals gave her just the boost she needed to feel taller, stronger.

As September came to an end and the weather cooled down, the sun was setting earlier in the evening. It was hard for Lilly to finish her bookkeeping at the feed store early enough to take Blue for a ride, but she never missed a day of seeing her.

One evening as she tidied up her desk across from her grandfather's desk, he asked, "On your way to the stable, Lilly?"

She glanced at her watch, then shut down her computer. "If I hurry, I'll be the one to feed Blue and maybe have time to exercise her just a little bit."

"You might want to bring that Navajo around for a meal one of these days."

"You've met him and you know his name," she teased. "He doesn't call you *that Hopi*."

"Of course he doesn't. He wants my granddaughter. He'll be cautious. I could forbid it."

She flashed him a grin and then chuckled. "And I could go to work for another feed store," she taunted.

Yaz seemed to drop the teasing, at least a bit. "Has he asked to see me? To spend some time in discussions with me?"

Lilly just tilted her head to one side and smiled tenderly at Yaz. This was his old traditional way of asking if Clay would be speaking for her soon. And all that old tradition, as she'd said a hundred times, wasn't important to her. She found it completely respectable—and it made the most sense—for a man to actually ask the woman he was interested in, considering that her acceptance really was the most important issue. But it was pointless to argue with Yaz. "I haven't known him all that long, Grandpa."

"It doesn't take all that long, Lilly." Their eyes were locked together for a long moment. "You'd better get to that stable before you miss seeing the horse that occupies so much of your brain these days."

"I suppose I'll see you in the morning," Lilly said.

"Where would I go? I'll be here," he returned. "I don't have a horse to visit." And then he winked at her.

It was dusk by the time she got there; with the mountains to the east and west and the sun beaming across the stable and pastures, it looked like a movie set, an idyllic setting for anyone who loved animals and the outdoors. She saw Blue out in the far pasture with Annie's mares. She assumed they'd all been fed and turned out; Nathaniel and Clay operated on a very strict feeding schedule to avoid digestive problems.

She was going to take a shortcut through the stable to the pasture, but before she got very far she heard music and stopped. It was the high, haunting, magical Native American flute, the kind she'd heard many times at celebrations and ceremonies and programs for tourists. Soft and pleasant, sometimes eerie, the rhythm slow. Lilting.

She walked through the stable and saw that Clay was

perched on the top rail of the fence surrounding the pasture, facing away from the stable, playing the flute in the dusk. His silhouette cast a long shadow and the music he made caused her to quiver low in her belly. He'd been working all day so his hair was braided and hung down his back. He wore the hat with the feather. His fingers worked the flute while his pursed lips rested on the mouthpiece. Rawhide ties and beads hung down from the end of the instrument.

She leaned against the opened doors, her hands behind her back. He didn't notice her; he was completely at peace. The melody was no doubt something from his childhood, perhaps his grandfather's childhood. And it was flawlessly done, as though he'd been playing that particular piece for many years. Perhaps many lifetimes.

Lilly had spent so much energy fighting the old ways, but by degrees she was being reunited with her roots and she couldn't deny a feeling of coming home. Clay was bringing her comfort by way of reunion and familiarity every day, in so many small but significant ways.

She tilted her head back and closed her eyes, allowing herself to be seduced by the melody, so ghostly and captivating. She could almost see the men of her community in their Native garb, moving to the flute's music, the women swaying. She was lost in her own fantasy for a long time, and then the music stopped. She opened her eyes to find Clay walking toward her.

When he reached her, he put a finger under her chin and lifted it so he could place a light kiss on her lips.

"That was very beautiful, Clay," she said.

"My father's instrument. He taught me and I find it soothing."

"Music is such a big part of our relationship—the opera and now this. But I can't think of a way you can seduce me with the flute and make love to me at the same time."

His smile was teasing. "I like the music we make together whether there's music or not."

"Have the horses been taken care of?"

He nodded. "Annie and Nathaniel are out for a few hours, so we have to stay here. There's a pizza in their oven for us. Then we can grab a shower and I have plans for you. If you can stay, that is?"

"And go home later?" she asked.

"Stay the night," he said. "We'll get up early, feed the horses, go for a ride."

"I didn't bring a change of clothes, Clay."

"You don't need a change. I'll give you a T-shirt to sleep in. Or maybe I can keep you warm, myself. You can wear the same jeans in the morning, can't you?"

"What if Annie or Nate comes to your room?"

"Lilly, with your Jeep parked by my truck, they'd know to knock! If there's an emergency, we can get up and help."

She thought about this and then smiled dreamily. "What kind of pizza?"

"Half pepperoni and sausage, half pineapple and double cheese."

"You cater to me," she said with a smile. "That's good. You're very well trained."

"Do you have any idea how spectacular my life is when you're happy?" he asked.

"I must be quite the Hopi princess—it pleases me that you want to please me."

"I'm very hungry."

"Then let's eat," she said.

"And after that we can get to what I'm really hungry for."

There were only two people in Jack's Bar even though it was that time of day when the regulars usually gathered. Mel had stopped in before going home to the children and Mike Valenzuela, Jack's brother-in-law, had just come by for a beer.

It was easy for family and friends to see Jack Sheridan being jovial and teasing—it was his natural state. What was difficult for his friends and family to see was him being *morose*. Sad. Disappointed. Jack wasn't a guy who felt sorry for himself, so that kind of unhappiness was difficult to take. And he was under the weather emotionally because a pretty significant portion of his town, his friends, neighbors and regulars at the bar, were distancing themselves—all because Jack wouldn't provide information about the substance of the Virgin River Trust, and he wasn't willing to turn it over to townsfolk for their personal use.

"Maybe I was wrong," he said to Mike and Mel. "Mel and Preacher were right—I shouldn't have held a meeting, shouldn't have opened up the whole thing for discussion. I didn't know Hope that well, but I know she wouldn't start writing checks to clear equity loans and second mortgages."

"It's water over the dam," Mike said. "They'll get over it."

"Or not," Jack said.

"They'll get over it or have to drive a long way for a beer and good food. This is the only game in town, this bar."

"Ron and Connie used to eat here once, twice a week. Harv doesn't have breakfast here anymore. Haven't had any traffic from the Andersons, Bristols or Fishburns. And out at the estate sale, most people who came just to watch brought their own food and drink even though we'd set up the grills. I think that bothered me more than them not talking to me—that they don't want what we're offering as friends."

Preacher came out of the kitchen just at the end of that comment. He walked up behind the bar next to Jack. "Screw 'em. We need a sign for this town all right, and it needs to say You'll Catch More Flies With Honey."

Right then the door opened and Walt Booth came in. After a round of greetings, the general was up at the bar and without being asked, Jack served him up a beer. Right behind him the door opened again and Nathaniel and Annie came in.

"What are you two doing here?" Jack asked.

"We heard there was plenty of open seating," Nate said with a smile as they took their places at the bar.

"Oh, so that's it," Jack said. "Everyone is feeling sorry for Jack? I hate that worse than not being talked to!"

"They'll all be back, Jack," Walt said. "They're acting like a bunch of kids."

"Let's see how far old Ron gets when he gets sick of fish and wants some leftover brisket," Preacher said. "Or how about when Hugh pulls up in that big old dually he'd like Jack to pay off for him, hops up to the bar and wants to run a tab for his boilermaker and dinner?"

That brought a slight grin to Jack's face. He tilted his head toward Preacher. "Always makes me feel better when Preacher's ticked off," he said. He put a hand on the big man's shoulder. "Did you hear about Preacher's dinner party?"

"Huh?" Mike said. "What's that?"

"Aw, it was just one of those things," Preacher said, looking down shyly.

"Preacher met himself a five-star chef from San Francisco at the sale. She was staying out at Luke's cabins with some of her girlfriends on their way home from Vancouver, and Preacher opened up the bar so they could taste some of his favorite dishes."

"How'd you rate?" Mike asked.

He stood a bit taller. "I'd say she was impressed. She gave me a few tips, too. Little ginger in the beans, a sprinkle of thyme on the roasted vegetables. And she offered to come back and cook up her special soup and show me her rhubarb pie, which she says is good. Mine's always sour, no matter what I do. She said just try 'em and if they're not way better than the recipes I'm using, no hard feelings." He grinned. "I don't think another cook has ever eaten here."

"How'd the girlfriends like your food?" Mike asked.

"They were all groaning and holding their stuffed bellies when they left. I set 'em up right at the counter in the kitchen and kept it coming till they begged me to stop." He sniffed the air, lifted his chin and said, "I think it's fair to say I knocked their socks off."

The men laughed at him, but Preacher took it in stride. Truthfully, nothing could have made him more proud than to have a *real* cook admire his work.

"How are things at the cabins, General?" Jack asked. "And how's Colin getting along?"

"Luke's been there with him almost a week and he's

coming back in a couple of days. Colin is doing better. Boy took a heavy crash and a lot of broken bones are hard to heal. Their mother, Maureen, is there now. George is with her. Luke says Colin can be discharged within the week, but he'll be transported to a wounded warriors support center at Fort Benning, where he's currently serving. Luke's a little nervous about leaving Colin in Maureen's hands—she and George aren't strong enough or experienced enough to take care of a big man like that who's in an arm cast and a whole bunch of bandages. Luke wants to make sure the arrangements for his transport are complete—guys from his unit will make sure he's taken care of." He chuckled. "And Colin is begging Luke to throw him out a ten-story window rather than leave him at his mother's mercy."

"But he's going to recover?"

"So they say." Walt shrugged. "You know how that goes—a lot of it's up to him. He needs physical therapy. He has to build strength. You know what Luke says he complains about the most? The elbow! He's got screws in his elbow and it's driving him crazy."

"And Shelby and the baby?"

"Oh, they're getting along fine. I go out there every morning and stay till dinner. Sometimes Muriel comes out and eats with us. Cabins are going to fill up next week—hunting season."

"The bar might see some action, too, when the hunters come."

"So you're not going to go broke while the town is in a snit?" Nate asked.

"Nah, we got hunters and fishermen," Jack said. "But I'll tell you what—if these folks don't get over themselves real quick, they might find they're just not so welcome here. Doesn't make you want to be the good neighbor, if you know what I mean."

"It's going to pass real soon," Mel said, lifting her beer.

Nate leaned an elbow on the bar and peered at Mel. "Is your business suffering, since you're consorting with the executor?"

She shook her head. "Couple of the old boys are a little put out that Jack didn't open up Hope's trust for them, but for the most part the women are fine with things the way they are. It's not that many of the guys, really—just seems like a lot to Jack—he's not used to being viewed as the bad guy. By anyone."

"Because I'm *not,*" he said emphatically.

"Of course you're not, darling," she said. "But you just can't please all the people all the time. It's such a thankless job to be in charge of anything, isn't it?"

"I liked it best when I was in charge of this little space back here," Jack said, throwing his arms wide, indicating the area behind the bar. "I don't even have many opinions about what goes on in the kitchen."

"Very wise," Preacher said.

Suddenly there was a slight vibration, a distant and faint rumble, and the bottles on the shelf behind the bar clinked up against each other. It lasted only a few seconds, during which time everyone was stone still and silent, experiencing it.

"That was either the biggest rock slide we've ever had around here, or an earthquake," Jack said when it had passed.

And Mel, who had lived many years in Los Angeles before coming to Virgin River, said, "It was an earthquake, I believe. But thankfully not much of one."

Thirteen

When Lilly was lying in Clay's arms, flesh to flesh, with nothing heavier than a sigh between them, it was a time made precious by more than just physical intimacy.

It was still early evening. They'd had their dinner, showered and climbed into bed together.

"Tell me something from your childhood on the reservation. Something I couldn't guess—like the happiest day of your life."

"I could say it was the day I had Gabe, but the truth is I didn't know that was a happy day until he was a little older and I could get some sleep. It was probably the day my father told me the new stud colt was mine to break, to raise and ride. He's still on the Tahoma ranch, almost to the end of his breeding days, but not quite. A handsome blue roan. He taught me everything I know about a stallion's temperament and drive. There were lots of horses on the ranch, but he was mine."

"Are a lot of your happiest days from your life back on the family ranch?"

"Mmm-hmm," he hummed, nodding. "We worked hard, played hard."

"Tell me the most terrified you've ever been in your life," she said.

He thought for a moment. "When I was real little, about ten, I went into a pasture I'd been told to stay out of. I was with a couple of my cousins, but they were older, faster. We were supposed to stay away from this old bull, but we figured he was too old to give us much game. Turned out he was pretty fast. One second he was lying there, looking like he was asleep, and the next second he was charging me."

"What about your cousins?" she asked.

"You know that old joke about the two campers who come upon a bear—*I don't have to outrun the bear, I just have to outrun you?* They took off, left me for the bull. I scrambled up a tree. He butted the trunk a few times and almost shook me out, but he got bored and went back to lie down. I sat up in that tree for hours. It was almost dark when my dad came for me. He walked into that pasture like he had all day. He was carrying a pitchfork, but he didn't seem worried about anything. He looked up into the tree and said, 'Get down here.' I tried to warn him about the bull, but he insisted. Well, I was coming down, very slowly and carefully, and right then the old bull got up and kind of wandered over toward us. When he was standing about six feet away, my dad turned toward him, made eye contact with him and just stared him down, and the damn bull lay down. And my dad took me by the hand and walked me out of the pasture."

"Just like that?" Lilly asked.

He nodded. "He said, 'Weren't you told to stay out

of that pasture?' and I asked, 'What did you *do?*' He just looked straight ahead and said, 'That's an old bull. Mean, but old. He wouldn't have known what to do with you if he caught you. I just wanted to make sure. We sort of came to an agreement—when he didn't charge me, we made our peace.' And so I asked him why he brought the pitchfork and he said, 'Just in case he didn't listen to reason.'" And then Clay laughed.

Lilly didn't laugh. "Did your father talk to animals, too? Did you get it from him?"

"I don't know what I have, Lilly, or where I got it. I get feelings from animals, like if they're in pain or afraid. All I got from that bull was that he was *mad*. Territorial and pissed off. But the things my dad seemed to always have were confidence and understanding. I don't think I've ever had his kind of confidence. He took a pitchfork into that field—my hundred-and-eighty-pound father—and he faced off with a twenty-five-hundred-pound bull. He walked slow and easy, kept himself between me and the bull, and somehow with just his self-possession he let the bull think he could kill him with the pitchfork if they didn't come to terms." He shook his head in wonder.

"What?"

"When we got home, all he said was, "Next time you can stay in the tree until you're old and gray."

"No punishment?"

"There was rarely a real punishment at our house. Disappointment was punishment enough. Discontinued praise was punishment. I lived to please my parents. And sometimes I resented that and rebelled, but not for long. The Tahomas are strong and very proud. They're influential. If I rebelled I got over it fast. They were always there for me."

"When were they there for you?"

"Well, you know all about Gabe's sudden appearance. They rallied for that boy, for me. My father gathered his brothers and his lawyer and they went to town to meet the maternal grandparents of my unborn child. He didn't carry a pitchfork, he carried a leather binder containing a photocopy of some adoption law the lawyer had given him. The whole ordeal didn't take long, but once I had Gabe home there was a definite chill in the air around me and a distinct reluctance to help me with my son—I had to take my medicine. I think Gabe was six months old before my parents finally lightened up. I knew they were disappointed in me, but at the same time they didn't want Gabe to suffer any lack of affection because of me, so we had to make peace. Then there was..."

His voice fell off and she jiggled him.

"What? Then there was what?"

He took a deep breath. "There was a time when I was following rodeos as a farrier. I was about twenty-three, on a job in Houston, and I got jumped by a bunch of cowboys. I don't know who they were—I don't think they were competing. They were drunk and mean and looking for trouble—they sneaked up on me, cut off my braid. They had a good advantage and I fought back, but I didn't do much damage. I was pretty whipped by the time someone broke it up. They said I was a crazy, drunk Indian who attacked them and the police threw me in jail. I gave my father's number just before I passed out cold in a jail cell." He shook his head. "As far as I know, the police never even detained the cowboys."

"Oh, Clay..."

"It took my father and uncles about twelve hours to

get there. My father asked one question of the police. Did you test his blood? The deputy said, 'Sir, we have a rodeo in town. By the time we could get to that, too many hours had passed for an accurate blood-alcohol level. But the boy passed out.' And my father, who carried his leather folder, calmly asked the deputy if he thought I'd cut off my own hair. Then he explained that it had been twelve hours—they could do the blood test immediately and if there had been enough alcohol in me to have caused me to pass out, at least trace amounts would show up. But if nothing showed up, they'd know I was unconscious from the beating and they were at fault for taking me to jail instead of to the emergency room—that would open up an interesting dialogue with the courts. He said, 'Either do a blood test or release him to us now.' And they let me go. I had a concussion. And this," he said, running a finger along a faint scar under his eye on his cheekbone.

"Did your father ever ask you if you were drunk?"

Clay shook his head. "He knew that if alcohol was a problem for me, it wouldn't be long before he'd see it again. And again. And again." He smiled. "He didn't."

"Did you have problems like that a lot? Because of being Navajo?"

"No," he said. "Fascination. Curiosity. People ask questions cautiously, as if they're afraid to offend me. I always answer and invite them to visit the reservation." He smoothed her hair over an ear. "Have you ever had any problems?"

"No," she said, shaking her head. "I would give anything to see all those big, stern Navajos bearing down on the police. Or the parents of your girlfriend. I bet when people remember those events, they imagine the Navajos wearing buckskin and feathers."

"They fully intend to appear as a tribe. There is pride in the tribe. I grew up hearing that. It's in their eyes...."

"It's in your eyes," she said softly.

He looked surprised for a second. Then he relaxed into a smile. "I don't mean any offense, but it's not in your eyes, my blue-eyed girl. Tell me your secrets. Tell me when you were most afraid."

She inhaled deeply and rolled on top of him. "I will, but not right now. Right now I want to thank you. I had a very bad romance when I was young and it left me scarred and broken. I'll tell you all about it some other time, but tonight I want to make love and then sleep on your hair, pulling it when I move in my sleep and making you whimper and grunt." She laughed and ran her fingers into the hair at his temples.

"Why must you do that?" he asked. "I could braid it and we could both sleep."

"I love your hair. I love it free. That's how I see you when I dream about you."

"And...why exactly are you thanking me?"

She gave him a little kiss. "I wasn't sure I would ever trust a man again. I stayed far away from men. I buried myself in work and school. I wasn't going to take any chances. But then you came along and..." She shrugged and smoothed a hand over his bronze, hairless chest. "Maybe I'm just a naive fool, but I believe everything you tell me. I trust everything you say."

"Then trust this, sweetheart. *Ayor'anosh'ni*. I think I'm in love with you."

"I think you've been in love a hundred times before..."

"No. No, that's not true. I thought I was in love a
couple of times, but it was such a struggle—there were
so many barriers. This time, this is as it should be—
easy. Free. Pleasant and comfortable." Then one side of
his mouth lifted in a sexy grin. "Hot, wild, crazy and
amazing, too." His voice lowered to a whisper. "This
time is different for me, Lilly. Is it different for you?"

"It is," she whispered back. "It is."

And then they felt a slight, brief vibration beneath
them, from under the bed; there was a definite disturbance in the stable. "Earthquake," Clay whispered. "A
small earthquake."

"We haven't had an earthquake since I've lived here,"
she said.

He rolled her off him and sat up. "Oh, that's what it
was. I experienced quite a few in Los Angeles. Don't
move. Don't dress. I'm going to check on the animals,
then I'm going to come back here and rock your world
for real."

Colin Riordan had many visitors while he was hos-
pitalized—three of his brothers plus several phone calls
from his fourth brother, Patrick, who was sitting alert
on an aircraft carrier. His three-month deployment was
winding to a close and he promised to visit Colin at
Fort Benning as soon as he was stateside. Maureen and
George had parked their fancy motorcoach at an RV
park near Fort Hood and were at the hospital every day.
Other visitors included men from his unit who had been
with him on exercises. At first they came because they

were still at Fort Hood, and then a couple of them caught
military hops from Fort Benning.

Sean was the first to leave Fort Hood and head back
to Maxwell AFB after a few days; Aiden was second
to leave, returning to Chico to meet with a group of
physicians whose ob-gyn practice he was considering
joining. Luke stayed on until the arrangements to send
Colin back to Fort Benning were nearly complete. One
of Colin's buddies was going to accompany him on a
commercial flight out of Houston, see that he was settled
in the Wounded Warriors Resource Center where his
full-time job for the Army, for now, was getting well.
Maureen and George had plans to follow in the RV and
park there for a couple of weeks, until Maureen had
peace of mind that Colin was on the mend and didn't
need his mother for anything.

But Colin, in pain and bored out of his skull, wasn't
exactly the best company. He was also struggling with
some stress about his future, because although he should
be able to heal and get back in the cockpit, the idea of
everything being different from now on was doing a
number on his head.

"Can't you talk Mom out of going to Fort Benning?"
Colin asked Luke.

"I doubt it, buddy. Why don't you relax and take advantage of it? You know she'll do anything she can for
you—ask her to bring you stuff from home, run errands,
do laundry, anything you need."

"I need to be left alone," he said.

"Well, I'm sure after two weeks of your charming
personality, you'll get that."

But when Luke called home that night, he discovered
he'd have to cut his own stay in Fort Hood short.

"We had a little excitement today," Shelby said over the phone. "An earthquake!"

"Are you *kidding* me?" Luke nearly roared.

"Just a very little one, off the coast in the Pacific, but we all felt it. It was kind of cool."

"Cool?"

"There wasn't any damage reported anywhere," she assured him.

"Were you alone? You and Art and the baby?"

"Uncle Walt had just left for the day and Art was still at the river even though it was almost dark."

"Was Art upset? Scared?"

"Just the opposite," Shelby said. "He said some fish jumped out of the river—more than he's ever seen jump at once. I've always heard that animals get all revved up when there's an earthquake or even when one's coming."

"All right," Luke said. "Things are handled here. My mother is here and arrangements have been made to get Colin home. I'll be on the next plane."

"Luke, I miss you, but everything is fine! It wasn't a scary earthquake or anything. I've had plenty of company, plenty of help, and I don't want you to leave Colin until you're sure it's time."

"It's time—I don't want you and my son left as the responsibility of someone else. Colin's got a lot of work to do to rehab his body and he's a giant pain in the ass. It's time for him to be someone else's pain in the ass. I'll be home as fast as I can get there."

"Well, whatever makes you happy—but be sure to tell Colin that I haven't called you home! Because I'm no wimp and I'm doing just fine."

Luke did tell Colin that, and Colin said, "Good—go home. And did I thank you for coming?"

"No," Luke said.

"Well, thank you for coming," Colin said. "And please don't come again until you're invited."

"I guess you didn't get that gracious Irish gene," Luke said. "I'll call."

"Be sure to leave a message if I don't pick up. I hear they have a great soccer team at the Wounded Warriors hotel...."

Lilly wanted to tell Clay a few things—like the fact that she had done very, very little dating, that there hadn't been a serious relationship with a man in her life in fourteen years, that there were things that haunted her and had kept her from forming a strong, healthy relationship with a good man. And she planned to. She knew there would be a perfect moment and when she found it, she wouldn't hold anything back. It was easy to put off; she was enjoying the finest time of her life and just couldn't let a negative thought or memory interfere.

It was fall; the weather was cooling and the colors emerging. Lilly and Annie took six eleven-year-old girls on an overnight trail ride before the first real freeze. Nathaniel wanted to go with them or at least send Clay along, but Annie and Lilly had agreed, that was not the message they wanted to send their troop. Annie was very good with a rifle if there was any wildlife threat, and they had planned a ride only into the foothills, so they would never even be at a high enough elevation to contend with any freezing weather.

Both women appreciated the concern their men showed, but Nate and Clay didn't push too hard. They trusted their competence, while still waiting anxiously to welcome the riders home.

The trail ride was one hundred percent successful; the little girls returned to their parents wild with excitement, all gamy and rosy cheeked, happy and feeling self-reliant.

A few days later Lilly took Yaz to the Toopeek house for one of those big family meals. It was no surprise that Yaz and Lincoln gravitated toward each other. Tom Toopeek, ever the politician, seated one elder at each end of the long oak table. They both started out stern and cautiously observant, but before long they were laughing with the family, making jokes at the expense of Lilly and Clay. And when dinner was done, the old men went outside, where Lincoln liked to enjoy a small fire. It was one of his old traditions and even though there were very strict burning laws in the mountains, Lincoln's fire was safe from prosecution because the police chief's father had a Get Out Of Jail Free card.

Inside the house, the women cleaned up—a tradition Lilly hoped to change if she ever had a family. The men and kids played Scrabble noisily. It seemed as though Gabe and eighteen-year-old Johnny Toopeek were beating their fathers.

Lilly hadn't ever allowed herself to fantasize about what it would be like to have a lover, a partner, a family. She had always considered it practical to stay away from romance; after all, she had Dane and she'd been happy. Now there was love and family all around her—at the Jensen clinic, at the Toopeek household, in Clay's sturdy arms. She enjoyed a kind of contentment that was fresh and new. On the days she delivered feed to the clinic she made sure it was her last delivery of the afternoon and she would stay long enough for a ride, often with Clay if he didn't have other work-related duties. Even if she went riding alone, the joy of it was sheer bliss.

On days she didn't deliver, she was often at the stable for at least a couple of hours. She frequently had dinner with Clay—either at her house or out. There was the occasional dinner with Annie and Nathaniel, sometimes at the Toopeek house, and she'd finally brought Clay to her grandfather's house for their Sunday meal together.

Clay took her to Jack's Bar, where just about the only vegetarian dishes were pie and coffee. Although the big, scary-looking cook scowled, he could be talked into serving her something that hadn't been simmered in the juices of animals. And then with his heavy dark eyebrows furrowed, he said, "I'm going to make up some mac and cheese—three cheeses—and before I add the ham and bacon, I'll put some aside in the freezer, in case you ever come back."

The best part of her life was that time she spent in her lover's arms. He was so right—their bodies together made music. And then in the still of the night or early morning, they would hold on to each other and whisper. Clay said to her, "You'd better never leave me, because I'm sure I'll never be able to stop loving you. I'll love you forever, Lilly."

It had only been a couple of months since they'd met and a couple of weeks since he'd told her he was in love with her. A matter of days since he'd said he'd love her forever… And it was a bright, crisp, clear and sunny afternoon in mid-October when it all fell apart.

Clay was in the veterinary office, doing some online charting Nate had left for him when he heard the growl of a diesel engine. They weren't expecting a patient, and Nate had gone to Mendocino County to check on a pregnant mare who'd previously had a couple of stillbirths. Clay pushed back from the desk and looked out the window. There, in the large parking expanse between the house and clinic was a late-model pickup with dual rear wheels pulling a custom horse trailer. And he knew whose it was.

He stepped out of the office just as Isabel shut off the engine and jumped down from the cab of the truck.

She looked lovely, as always. She beamed when she saw him—all smiles and pleasure. She had what appeared to be a healthy tan, but Clay knew it was from her expensive, custom-formulated tanning cream—Isabel was afraid of aging, and would never surrender her skin to the sun's rays. Her ideal shade of blond also cost a fortune. In fact, everything from her perfect body to the clothes on it was very expensive, very chic. But the effect was breathtaking to just about anyone, and very few people knew how much time and money she threw at it. Her ex-husband, of course, was privy to this information.

She came toward him, reaching for him. "Clay," she said, smiling warmly. "Oh, *Clay!*"

He returned the gesture, giving her a hug and exchanging cheek kisses. "What are you doing here?" he asked.

"I have a problem—with one of your favorite horses," she said, but she didn't let go of him. "It's Isa Diamond Two. She's got a slight limp. The vet's seen her, we've done X-rays and ultrasounds and can't find a problem, but her gait is off—unpredictable and uneven."

"You could have called me," he said.

"But I knew you couldn't come to me, not with your new responsibilities. And I needed a getaway. Besides," she said with a laugh, giving her silky, shoulder-length blond hair a toss, "I wanted to see where you are now." She craned her neck to look around. "I have to admit, beautiful country."

"But you should have at least told me you were coming."

"Hey, listen, if you and your vet are too busy, I'll wait. I have excellent accommodations," she added, throwing an arm wide to indicate the horse trailer. He'd been in this one plenty of times—the rear was outfitted with two enclosed, padded stalls while the front section had upscale living quarters with full kitchen, bath, king-size bed, leather couch, small table and plenty of electronic equipment. Nothing but the best for the Sorensons. Actually, they only used their custom trailers for relatively short hauls—Frederik Sorenson had private jets to transport his horses to races. The money in the Sorenson family was nothing short of astonishing.

The horse in her trailer was a famous, prizewinning quarter horse, a blond bay with one white stocking, a white mane and a blaze. She was not only a beauty, but skilled and accomplished. And she had lent her eggs to more prizewinners, mated in a petri dish and carried by a surrogate to save her body from the strain. Diamond was only eight years old and could yet win quarter-mile races. If she wasn't lame.

"Let's bring her in," Clay said, pulling out of Isabel's grasp and going to the back of the trailer. "Nathaniel is on a call, but he should be back before long."

"Thank you," she said with her customary grace. "I knew you'd help."

"And I know there's more going on than the horse," he answered without looking at her. "You came unexpectedly for a reason...."

"You've never required notice before," she said. "All I ever had to do was ask."

"True. That was before," he said.

He opened up the back of the trailer, put the harness and lead on the horse and expertly backed her out. He talked softly to her and she responded with familiar friendly nickering. Isabel was right about this much— he loved the horse. And the horse loved him. As he led Diamond into the stable, Isabel followed at a distance, giving him charge. Part of her charm was knowing when to step back and let a man take over. No doubt she learned that technique from a father who demanded it and praised it, and it worked.

It had stopped working when her vulnerability and weakness took over. A man would naturally want to protect her and take care of her, until that job became so overwhelming it was suffocating.

Isabel was ten years older than Clay, but she looked ageless. She had been thirty-eight when they'd met, forty when they'd married, and although she'd never been married before, she had a long history of very bad relationships with men. Cheating men, abusive men, greedy men. And who could blame her for falling for them? That was the man her father was and women so often marry the male role model they worship, and she did worship Frederik. On another level, she hated him, but that had taken a long time for Clay to understand.

The first few times Clay had encountered Isabel, she'd just triumphed in horse shows and she was radiant. Then one time she'd lost, and he'd found her broken and despondent, not from the loss so much as her father's abusive disappointment. Frederik was a demanding, egotistical ass. His wife had left him when Isabel was small and he'd never treated his daughter with an ounce of gentleness. He'd tried to train her into a tough horse-woman. When she won, he lifted his chin and walked away as if she'd simply done as he expected; when she lost, he berated her as though she was a complete fail-ure. She craved her father's attention and approval, but it was hard for her to get both simultaneously with one accomplishment. Any attention he showed her was nega-tive; his approval was too rare.

Because of the way Clay was raised, because of the way Tahoma men regarded the women in their lives, this injustice purely broke Clay's heart.

Generally, when Clay worked for anyone, he tried to stay in the background unless his specific skills were called upon; he never pushed his way into the personal lives of his employers or their families. But after he congratulated her for her wins and consoled her for her losses, Isabel began to seek him out. He gave her the emotional support she so desperately craved. And after about a year of brief meetings, she seduced him.

"Your father will fire me for this. Or kill me," he had said before succumbing to the seduction.

"No, he won't. He only cares about the horses, not who I dally with."

It had taken Clay a very long time to learn and accept that truth, and to understand that even though they'd married, Frederik still considered him a mere dalliance. While Isabel was so like a hurt little girl, he gravitated toward her, prepared to offer comfort. Eventually, he could see that she needed so much more—a partner who could give her the kind of insight he had, a person who could tell her whether the training was working or if the horse would be a good candidate for a certain race or type of competition. He could help her win more often. But by the time he actually understood the complexity of her relationship with Frederik, he had married her, pledged his life to her. The marriage was at her insistence and with her hardheaded father's partial blessing.

Partial because Frederik had said, "There'd better be a prenup! I'm not going to have some blacksmith part me from my money!"

Clay had shrugged and answered, "Aside from my wage, I don't want anything from you."

But Isabel fought her father and said, "No! Clay said he doesn't want the family money and that's good enough for me!"

It was years before Clay understood—every decision Isabel ever made was in reaction to her sick and alienating relationship with Frederik. Isabel might indeed have loved Clay, but she had married him to rankle Frederik, to get his attention. And while Clay thought he should have been angry with her for putting him in the middle of that twisted relationship with her father, instead he felt profound pity. He knew how needy she was, how much she hurt, and he did all he could to reassure her.

But that relationship was unhealthy for both of them and had to stop sometime.

"Leave Diamond with me, Isabel. I'll give her a workup and have Nathaniel look at her. He might recommend an MRI...."

"I brought the films," she quickly supplied.

"Excellent. Leave them with me and come back

tomorrow. We'll have a full report and recommendation."

"Leave?" she asked. "Can't I stay here?"

"You mean, park your trailer here?" he asked with a lifted brow.

"No, I mean…can't I stay with you?"

"We're divorced, Isabel."

"That didn't seem to matter to you before," she said, smiling very shyly for a forty-four-year-old woman wearing a hundred thousand dollars' worth of upkeep.

"It matters now, Isabel. I've met a woman I care about. I don't think she'd appreciate a little ex-wife maintenance."

She stiffened and glowered, insulted. Apparently, the truth angered her, even though that was clearly the reason she was here. Isabel wanted to get laid, preferably by someone she trusted. If this visit had really been about the horse, she would have sent a trainer or at least had a hand drive her. Isabel didn't usually take off on long trips *alone,* pulling a trailer. In fact, Clay realized, he might not find a problem with the horse at all.

"I won't cross that line," he said to Isabel. "I wouldn't have done it to you and I won't do it to her."

"I see," she said curtly. "Well, now. So, will it insult your new woman if I park my trailer on the property?"

He tilted his head and peered at her. He couldn't believe there was still more to learn about her after all this time, but sure enough—she was behaving exactly as her father would. Frederik would cajole what he wanted and if he didn't get it, he'd throw a little temper tantrum, and people would scramble to please him.

"Fine," Clay said. "Pull down the road to the east

pasture. I'll tell Nathaniel who's parked there. As for me, I won't be here tonight. I'll put Diamond in a stall and I'll be back early to tend to her."

"Clay…"

"No, Isabel," he said, shaking his head. "You must know that we can't continue. Not if either one of us is to have an authentic life."

"I thought it was pretty authentic!"

He shook his head. "I was a placeholder, that's all. But we both deserve something better than that."

Fourteen

Clay knew it was important to explain to Lilly about Isabel, but he couldn't bring himself to do it until their business with Diamond was finished. He also knew if he stayed in his quarters he would be faced with Isabel again, and there would be a very uncomfortable confrontation.

He explained to Nathaniel who was staying in the fancy horse trailer. "She could stay in the house with me and Annie," Nathaniel said. "I'd be happy to extend our—"

"It's complicated, Nathaniel. I think there's more to this visit than the horse. If it's okay, I'm not going to spend the night here tonight."

"Of course, that's fine," Nate said. "I've got your cell number."

He went to Lilly's little house; he was so comfortable there. He was content with the veggie-bean chili, rice and tortillas she made for them. They went to bed together and made love, but languidly, slowly, sweetly. He told her he was tired. He teased that she was wearing him out. And while he held her close as she slept, he prayed that he could be finished with the difficult part of his past and move ahead with Lilly, because she was all he had ever wanted.

In the morning he got up and dressed early.

"I can get up, too," she said sleepily. "I'll drive out to the stable and have a short ride before work."

"Sleep, sweetheart. We'll ride later. I have so much on my schedule today and I want to be free of it so I can concentrate on you."

She smiled and snuggled in the sheets. "I like the sound of that," she murmured.

That morning Clay was surprised by two things. There *was* a problem with the horse—one that explained the occasional limp or hitch in her gait. The mare's MRI showed a very slight bowed tendon, often seen in race-horses and sometimes caused by overtraining.

Clay wondered if his replacement at the stables was trying to prove himself, and in so doing was pushing the horses too hard.

The other thing that surprised him was that Isabel didn't show herself all morning. She was obviously there—the truck and trailer were still attached and parked on the road to the east pasture. But she didn't come to the clinic to confer with the doctor.

"Tell her the injury is minor," Nathaniel said, "but this horse can't train for at least three months. To be safe, longer. She needs more turnout time, less time in the stall. And that's all I've got for her." He handed Clay the large folder of MRI films.

"What's the charge?" Clay asked.

"Come on. It's your ex, man—it's on the house."

Clay sincerely wanted to argue that Isabel had more money than God and could certainly pay, if only for the inconvenience. But he kept quiet because the most important thing was to pack her and Diamond up and get them on the road home.

Throughout the morning he wanted to go bang on that trailer door and tell Isabel it was time to get the show on the road, but he resisted, sensing that's what she was hoping for.

It was just after noon when Nathaniel got a call about a nearby rancher's horse. "Sounds like colic," he explained to Clay. "Can you give me a hand?"

Clay looked at his watch.

"Got an appointment?" Nate asked.

"Sorry. I should have dealt with Isabel, but I've been putting her off. I'd like that to be behind me before Lilly comes by with her delivery later."

"I just might want a hand with the injection and mineral oil. We'll go in two trucks and after we get the gelding dosed, I'll have the owner walking and watching him. Shouldn't take too long, then you can come back here and take care of business."

"Thanks," he said. "I'm sorry for the inconvenience, Nathaniel. It's just that…"

"I've never had an ex-wife. I'm sure it's complicated."

"You have no idea," Clay said. "Let's go."

Because the weather was exceptional, Lilly rushed through her deliveries. She hoped to get to the last one at the clinic a little on the early side today; a ride sounded like a perfect plan, whether Clay was available to join her or not.

When she pulled into the clinic parking area and found an amazingly beautiful late-model truck and horse trailer, it made her briefly happy—it would be good for Nate's practice if his clientele included wealthy horse people. It wasn't until she noticed the woman pacing along the length of it that she realized both Clay's and Nate's trucks were missing from the front of the barn. Lilly was instantly taken with the woman's beauty, but not surprised. Wealthy women who owned expensive horses tended to be richly dressed and gorgeous.

She backed in and went about her duties, dropping the tailgate, opening the barn doors, hefting the bales and feed, putting them away in the feed room. Since there was no one there to sign off on the delivery, she folded the paper in half and slid it under the office door—she could pick up the signed copy when she was there next. To do that, she walked past the woman. On her way back to her delivery truck, she paused. "I guess the vet isn't here, but did you try the house? His fiancée might be home, might be able to tell you when to expect him back."

"Fiancée?" she asked, smiling. "Nathaniel is engaged?"

Lilly nodded. "For a while now. He met Annie almost a year ago and they're planning a spring wedding."

"That's wonderful," she said, smiling. "Good for him! But I won't bother her. I was actually waiting around for my husband."

"Husband?" Lilly asked, stunned.

"Well, technically ex-husband," she said with a laugh. "He's a tall Native American by the name of Clay Tahoma. We divorced before he took this position. But aside from his move up here, nothing has really changed between us. We at least talk every day."

Lilly's smile was weak. "How nice for you both," she

said. And her brain turned over the *at least*. Since she'd become intimate with Clay he hadn't left town. And Annie was a friend—if Clay had had female company here, Annie would have told Lilly.

Yet here was a woman who believed her ex-husband was still her husband in almost every sense of the word.

"Of course I had another reason for coming so far to see Clay," she went on. "Clay's the best—we hated to lose him at our stables. But if he's the best then the vet he chose to work with must also be the best. And I have a lame quarter horse that the vet my stable has on retainer can't fix. Clay loves that horse. She's worth half a million dollars. She has many more wins in her if she gets treated. So," she said, grinning, "I get the horse treated properly and I get to spend a couple of nights with my husband."

First Lilly's stomach did a flip—a couple of nights with Clay? Then she got stuck on that figure: half a million. She tried some quick math—had she earned that much in ten years? More to the point, would she earn enough to equal the cost of this truck and trailer in a dozen years?

"Clay should be back before long," Lilly said. "It's unusual to have everyone away from the clinic for long."

"Thanks, dear," the beautiful blonde said.

"Sure," Lilly said, heading for her truck. As she did so, something nagged at her. She turned back to the woman. "Where's the horse?" she asked.

"Oh, she's in the stall. I got here yesterday—Clay already looked at her, we spent some time together and Nate was going to read the MRI study that was done. And I might stay a few days, depending on Clay's schedule."

"Ah," Lilly said, putting her hands in the back pockets of her jeans as she backed away.

He was different last night, she thought. Tired. Slow. Maybe not interested? Maybe well satisfied by the blonde with the expensive gear and winning horse?

No. No, surely not.

But after she drove away, she took an unnecessary turn down a country road, pulled off to the side and tried to think it through. To get her bearings.

He said he'd been divorced a couple of years; she assumed that was the end of the relationship he'd had with his wife. He'd been different last night, but still loving and sweet. But the woman…the ex…she was irresistible. Did the woman, whose name she didn't even know, still have a hold on him?

Lilly didn't know how to answer these questions or how to find the answers. After about an hour of thinking it through she decided to go back to the clinic, even if it meant confronting Clay while the woman was still there. Whatever the challenge, she needed to know what was going on.

When Clay pulled into the clinic, he saw Isabel's truck and trailer, but she was nowhere in sight. He parked and found her leaning into one of the small paddocks, looking at Streak. She turned toward him.

"What an incredible horse," she said. "What's his story?"

"He came to us a difficult, unfinished stud colt," Clay said. "Let me bring him in and I'll talk to you about Diamond." He got the bridle and lead, put Streak in the stall, and stood in the aisle between the stalls. Isabel followed. She stayed quiet and back while he took care of the horse and put up the tack. Then he brought Diamond out of her stall. He explained about the minor training injury that Nathaniel had seen on the MRI and confirmed with examination. "Is it possible her trainer overworked her? That's the most common cause, and it's usually in a younger horse."

"Possible," she said with a shrug. "I usually pay close attention to detail, but lately... I admit, I've been a little lost without you at the stable...."

He tried to ignore that and said, "Well, the cure will cost you—she can't train for at least three months," he said. "Which means she won't race."

"How'd he see it?" she asked. "My vet didn't—"

"You could use a sharper, more conservative veterinarian. And why a stable as rich as yours doesn't have an orthopedic specialist on retainer is a mystery to me. Nathaniel spent some time at an equine orthopedics clinic, studying for a specialty. If a horse like this doesn't work for a living—"

"Can we please talk about...us?"

He was caught off guard. He gave Diamond a stroke. "Isabel, there really is no us."

She moved closer to him. They both stood beside the magnificent mare. Clay was tall at six-two, but Isabel was a good five-eight in her bare feet, and in boots she stood up to him admirably and could look in his eyes.

"I didn't realize how much it would hurt when you left," she said.

"And it also hurt while I was there. You needed that divorce to appease your father."

"Not just my father, Clay. You were so unhappy."

He let a huff of laughter escape. "Was I the only one who was unhappy? Come on, Isabel—we came from different worlds and couldn't live together in either of them. I couldn't make it in that mansion, inside your social life. I did put a tux on for you on several occasions. But for your part, you've never seen the inside of a reservation."

She laughed and her eyes actually sparkled. "Yes, a tux, with all that hair flowing down your back. You stood out, that's for sure. If it was your intention to be different…"

"Here's where we parted company from the start. I'm not different. I'm *Native*. There isn't anything about me that's contrived to fit in."

"And yet, we fit together so well…" she said in a sultry voice.

"For a while it seemed as if that was the case. Isabel, I think you chose me to challenge your father. You have a long history of love affairs that haven't worked for one reason or another and Frederik hated all of them. I don't know if you've spent a lifetime trying to meet his expectations or trying to provoke him. Whatever the case, I don't want to be a part of it anymore."

"But I love you," she said softly. "And you said you'd *always* love me." A tear spilled out of her eye and rolled down her beautiful, smooth cheek.

He put his big hand on her cheek and leaned down to kiss her forehead. "Of course I'll always love you, but…"

He heard a gasp from the stable doors. Clay turned to see Lilly standing there, her hand over her mouth, her blue eyes wide. "Lilly," he said.

She backed away. Then she turned and ran. Before

he could get to the doors, she jumped into her grandfather's delivery truck, started the engine and roared out of the clinic compound. Of course she didn't wait long enough for him to follow her, to speak to her. He hung his head and said, "God!"

"Oh God, is right!" Isabel said from right behind him. To his utter astonishment, he heard her laughter. He turned to see her face alight with amusement. "Clay! Did you hook yourself up to a little Indian girl? I knew it!" And then she laughed as if highly amused.

His eyes and nostrils flared and he took a giant step toward her. "She is not a girl! She's a *Hopi woman!*" he said in a low, menacing tone. "She is Native American! Of indigenous people! I want you to take your horse, your diagnosis and recommendation and go home now. And if you want help for your horses again, make an appointment and send one of your hands!" He strode away from her and the stable, digging in the pocket of his jeans for the keys to his truck as he went.

As Clay was pulling away from the clinic, Gabe was arriving in his little green truck, having just passed Lilly, who was flying down the road at high speed. Clay never looked at Gabe; never waved, never slowed. And even before the attractive blonde stepped out of the barn, he knew who the fancy truck and trailer on the property must belong to. And he knew something bad must have happened.

He parked his truck and got out, approaching the woman.

Her smile was bright and welcoming; she held her arms wide for an embrace. Both things were a first. "Well, hello, young man! It's been a while since I've seen you."

He really didn't want to touch her. Isabel had always repelled him. But not knowing what had gone on between his father and former stepmother, he allowed her to embrace him, kiss his cheek, give his dark hair a pet. When she touched him he realized that's what bothered him most—she made him feel like a *pet*.

"You're looking well," she said sweetly.

"What happened with my father?" he asked. "He looked upset or angry. And Lilly…"

"I'm not really sure," she replied, arching her eyebrows as if confused. "We were just talking when the girl—Lilly you say?—when she saw us and ran off. And I think I said the wrong thing—I asked your father if she was an Indian girl and he barked at me that she was Hopi." She shrugged helplessly. "I seem to have offended him, Gabe. I'll have to make amends."

Gabe put his hands in his pockets and hung his head. His father was not overly sensitive about such vernacular unless it was meant disrespectfully. He lifted his eyes and looked at her. "And that's all it was? You asked if she was Indian?"

Again the shrug, but Gabe didn't miss the shifting of her eyes. "As far as I know. I'll give him a day or two to simmer down, then call him and try to sort it out. You know, one of the things I'm most proud of is that we managed to separate, end our marriage, so amicably. We've always maintained a good relationship, a very strong friendship. I wouldn't want it to all crumble away because I stupidly chose the wrong word. Surely he'll accept my apology?"

"I didn't know you were here," was all Gabe could think of to say.

She laughed. "Well, we're even. I speak to your father

regularly, but I didn't know you were here, either. Are you visiting?"

"No. I'm staying with my aunt and uncle in Grace Valley. My father arranged it so we could see each other every day. I didn't know you and my dad were in touch."

"I guess he wouldn't think to mention," she said with a shrug. "Now, what are you going to do while you're here?"

He knew she was lying. They weren't in touch much, if at all. "I work at the clinic and stable and will be be finishing high school here."

The shock was evident on her face. "Oh? Why, that's wonderful! You must be so happy!"

"My father has worked many hard years so we could be together," Gabe said.

"Yes," she said solemnly. And wisely she didn't say any more. Clay had brought Gabe to the Sorensons' after his marriage, brought him to that big, cold, unfriendly house, and after just a few weeks sent him back to his grandparents. Gabe had occasionally visited the Sorensons' ranch in L.A. but he never again attempted to live there. His dad had said, "Surely you can see this isn't the right place for you."

And Gabe had said, "Is it the right place for you, Dad?"

"You know, Gabe," Isabel went on, "there are opportunities for you at our ranch when you've finished school. I would sponsor you myself. Hire you, that is. We're connected to many important breeders, training programs, et cetera. It might give you the right connections to establish your own equine business. You have only to call me if you're interested."

"Thank you," he said politely, knowing he'd never take her up on the offer.

"Well, I'd better be on my way then," she said, turning away. "Very nice seeing you, Gabe." And she strode back into the barn.

He called after her. "Are you loading that horse?"

"Yes," she said over her shoulder. "I brought her up here for your father and Dr. Jensen to have a look at her leg. I wasn't satisfied with our vet's diagnosis and for good reason—Clay and Dr. Jensen had a better idea of what was wrong with her. I'm glad I made the trip."

She is so full of shit, Gabe thought. Isabel Sorenson didn't have to cart her own champion horses around the state in a trailer to get second opinions. She could bring half the high-priced vets in the nation to her door; they'd be panting for a chance to give their opinions, to find a niche in that wealthy breeding and racing family. Isabel had come for his father. And at the moment Gabe was very happy he'd seen his father leaving angrily.

But he said, "Can I help you load her?"

Isabel stood aside, her hands behind her back. "Thank you. That would be so nice of you."

Gabe took the lead and put the horse in the fancy trailer. He closed it up and turned to Isabel. "Is there anything else I can get for you before you're on your way?"

"Not a thing. But do remember what I said, Gabe. If you want a chance with a big breeder, you have only to give me a call. I'll set everything up for you. You'll never have to worry about a thing. Being your father's son, I know you're a talented young man."

"Thank you," he said with a slight nod.

He watched her climb in the big truck, turn it around

to face the road and roll down the window to give him a winning smile. "Call anytime, Gabe!"

"Thank you," he said. And as the truck and trailer exited the lot, heading down the road, he said, "When hell freezes over."

Lilly drove away from the Jensen Clinic as though her tailgate was on fire. She had trouble breathing. Hadn't Clay just told her he'd love her forever? Exactly how many women had he pledged to love forever? Did he envision a harem?

She had a flashback to her old boyfriend. To the time she'd seen him flirting with another girl and had thought to herself, *He's just a boy. When I tell him we made a baby, that will be over.* But a different outcome was in store for her. She told him and he laughed and said it couldn't be his—that he'd been careful. Lilly never understood what he meant by that—he certainly hadn't used a condom!

She tried again and again to direct his attention to that baby, but when all else failed, she'd gone to her grandfather. Yaz was incensed. He loaded his rifle and headed for the boy's home to confront the whole family at gunpoint. There was no tribe like Clay's father and uncles with a lawyer and leather binder, just her infuriated grandfather.

But the boy had run. And Yaz had pulled her away from the only home she'd ever known before she had a chance to even hear whether he came back around.

She lost the baby and for a few months she grieved. For a few more she fantasized that he'd returned to the reservation to reclaim her. For still longer she dreamed that he was searching for her. It took such a long time for her to face the truth; he didn't love her, but had used her and had no concern about her once he was done with her.

This thing with Clay, she thought it was so different. But it felt so *familiar!*

When she reached her grandfather's feed store, she jumped out of the truck. Her grandfather wasn't expecting her back today, except to pick up her car before heading home. She grabbed her purse from the truck and headed for her Jeep. She saw one of her grandfather's employees and yelled, "Hey, Manny! When you go back inside, tell my grandpa I'm done for the day, will you?"

"Not riding today, Lilly?" he shouted back.

"I was going to, but something…" *Something ripped my heart out!* "Something came up!" She had barely made it to the driver's door of her Jeep when a big truck pulled into the feed store lot and blocked her departure.

She had been hurt before, but as she watched Clay jump out of his truck and stride toward her, her anger flared. She tried to make herself taller by straightening her spine and lifting her chin.

"Lilly, you have to let me explain," Clay said.

"I can't wait," she said, shaking her head. "I can't imagine there's anything about what I heard that could be explainable."

"She's my ex-wife, Lilly, and her horse was hurt. She didn't realize that so much had changed since I left L.A."

"That's basically what she said when I met her," Lilly said, crossing her arms over her chest. "That the divorce was a *technicality,* that she came up here to spend a few days with you…*if I knew what she meant.*"

"You met her?" he asked, clearly stunned. "When—"

"When I delivered feed. I was going to take Blue out, and there she was, waiting for you. Oh, let me be clear—she said she was waiting for her *husband!* She told me she arrived yesterday, that the two of you spent some time together!"

"A half hour, tops," he said, stepping toward her. "She might have had the idea she was going to be with me, but I told her to park her trailer on the back pasture road and I left the clinic to be with you. Isabel is used to getting what she wants. Now she'll have to get used to something else. I don't have a relationship with her anymore, Lilly."

"No?" Lilly asked. "If it's nothing then why didn't you say anything about her arrival last night?" She shook her head as tears sprang to her eyes. "You told her you'll love her forever, Clay. What do you take me for?"

She turned toward her Jeep, but he grabbed her arm and turned her back. "We have had a complicated relationship and what you heard isn't what you think."

She shook his hand off her arm and put both hands on her hips. "I think I heard you tell her you'd always love her. And that doesn't sound complicated. That sounds very direct and to the point. It also sounds like exactly what you told me a few days ago."

Manny had been standing on the loading dock and two more men who worked in the feed store joined him there, all three watching Lilly and Clay.

"Not as a husband or lover, but as a friend who will

care about her and be there for her when I can. Lilly, let me follow you home. Let me tell you about my relationship with Isabel and why I'd say something like that. Let me explain how that doesn't threaten what we have....''

She put up her hand. She gave her head a shake. "She didn't look like the kind of woman who needed a friend. She's beautiful and rich. I'm sure she has plenty of friends. There might be a real shortage of hot Native men with thick black hair down to their butts, however." *And a working man's callused hands that are still soft and sweet on a woman's skin.* "She seemed very sure that she'd find what she wanted here. Why don't you hurry on back to the clinic so you can continue the conversation?"

"I sent her home, Lilly. What you heard—it was a complete misunderstanding. We have to talk!"

"I don't have to do anything," she said in a fierce whisper. She glanced at the loading dock and saw that now Yaz had joined the men watching them. "And *nothing* is exactly what I intend to do. And I'm doing it alone. If you're half as smart as you seem, you'll give me space."

"You don't want an explanation," he accused. "You want to be angry."

"Oh, you're *wrong!* I don't want to be angry or hurt or disillusioned, so I'll do this for you—while you leave me alone, I'll think very, very hard about whether I want to take a chance on a man whose ex-wife thinks their divorce is merely technical! I'll let you know what I decide."

"She deliberately misled you, Lilly. She's a spoiled, self-centered woman."

Lilly turned and took a step toward him. "Look into my eyes, Clay," she said softly. "Did she deliberately mislead me into believing that there was still a relationship after your divorce? Or is that true?"

"Isabel assumed too much. Part of the reason I moved here was to be sure that was ended for good. And when I met you—"

It was like a sucker punch to the gut, and Lilly winced. It was true. It hadn't been a couple of years; he'd *barely* left his wife. Yet he hadn't told her that. She turned away from him again.

"Don't do this, Lilly. Don't walk away like this."

She opened the door to her Jeep. "Move your truck or I swear to God, I'll *ram* it!"

There was a part of her that wished he'd hold fast and refuse to move his truck, even though ramming it would have been beyond ridiculous. First of all, his truck was far bigger than her little vehicle and the bumper was huge; only Lilly would sustain damage and probably injury. And second, it would prevent her escape, and she needed to get away from him. She drove away from the feed store as though hornets were after her.

She could see him following her in the rearview mirror. If he dared follow her home, he'd live to regret it! She watched him closely as they came to the intersection where she would normally go right and he would go left. She held her breath as she made her turn. And as she watched him go the other way, she sucked in her breath in a jagged gasp. Oh God. Oh God, oh God, oh God!

This can't have happened to me again, was all she could think. *I've been in love exactly twice in my entire*

*life and both times I'm betrayed? Left in pain? This
can't have happened to me* twice!

There was no possible way she could eat; her head
began to pound and she knew it was from the effort she
put into not shedding a tear over him. But she bolted
both the front and back door so he couldn't enter, put
on her opera CDs, shut her eyes and tried to drive the
image of him making love to her from her mind. She
barely slept.

The next day she called her grandfather and excused
herself from work on account of the flu.

"Lilly, I saw—"

"You don't know what you saw, Grandpa, and I don't
feel like trying to explain it until I've had a chance
to think it through. Please. Give me a little time and
space."

"If he's wronged you, I will—"

"I know how far you'd be willing to go to avenge me,
Grandpa. But this time I'm going to take care of myself.
I'll check in later."

Then she called Annie. "I'm afraid I can't help you
with lessons the rest of the week, Annie—I'm under the
weather."

"Lilly, we all know something's wrong," Annie said.
"You're not here, Clay is miserable, Gabe is upset, and
everything is upside down. Won't you tell me?"

"Will Clay tell you?"

"He won't say anything and I'm worried."

"No need to worry, Annie. Just please excuse me
from my commitment the next few days. I'm sure I'll
be fine soon. I'll give you a call."

She stayed home from the feed store for a couple of
days. Clay waited almost twenty-four hours before he

started calling her cell. Despite her desire to ignore him, she listened to his voice mails—he left several. *Lilly, I have things to explain to you, but you have to give me a chance. Lilly, maybe I was wrong not to tell you more about Isabel, but honestly I didn't want her in our lives. Please forgive me. Give me a chance.* And her favorite, *Lilly, you're giving up on us too soon—we only need to talk to make this right.*

She just wasn't going to do it, wasn't going to trust him again only to find out he was lying. She didn't take his calls or return them.

On the second evening after their confrontation, Clay came knocking at her door. She crept to the door and told him to go away, but he persisted.

"Please, just talk to me. Fifteen minutes, that's all I ask, just fifteen minutes. You have to understand about Isabel—she looks like she has everything, but she doesn't have any of the important things, Lilly. She's insecure and in so many ways she's childlike."

Hmm, Lilly thought. I wonder how childlike her bank account is. Or how childlike she is in bed. "Go away. I'm not letting you in. I don't want to talk to you!"

"Lilly, you mean so much to me and I know you care about me, too. Let's work this out. Let's hear each other out, clear the air. I'll try to explain. I just need you to try to understand…. We'll start over. We can't let this thing we have end so soon. Not now, not when we're just getting started."

She had to admit this was a vast improvement over the boy who said, "Baby? Well it can't be *mine!*"

But having him bang at her door threw her and she lost her mind. She wanted him to know she meant business, that she wouldn't be a naive little girl both he and

Isabel could manipulate! So after she called the Fortuna police, she went into her bedroom and closed the door. She heard him pounding on the door, but his voice, which tempted her and angered her at the same time, was blissfully muffled.

And she thought, *What have I done? What if they take him to jail?* If anything could bring a final end to their relationship, calling the police on him would surely be it!

Clay had been knocking and talking for about twenty minutes when the squad car pulled up in front of Lilly's house. A cop equal to Clay in size got out, sauntered up to him and asked, "Sir? Did the lady ask you to leave?"

"I haven't done anything wrong," Clay said.

"You're creating a disturbance and it looks like you might be harassing her. How about you either leave or we go to the station and talk about this?"

"Damn," he said.

"Buddy, you gotta leave the girl alone. She's not into you, all right?"

"Yeah," he said, hanging his head. "Am I free to just go?"

"I'd like you to go. By the way, in case there's any confusion, Mr. Tahoma, I ran your plate and the young lady told the dispatcher where you work, so let's not give the woman any more trouble. We on the same page here?"

"Same page," he said over his shoulder as he headed for his truck.

And inside, Lilly lay on her bed and, for the first time since their dreadful confrontation, she cried.

Fifteen

When the phone rang in the office of the Jensen Clinic, Nathaniel picked it up, even though his assistant was in the same room working on the computer.

"Dr. Jensen," he answered. "I'll see if he's available, Isabel. Hold the line, please." He punched the hold button, turned to Clay and said, "It's Isabel. For you."

Clay nodded and reached for the phone.

"Clay," Nate said. "I can step out."

Clay thought about this for just a second, then nodded and said, "Thank you." He waited for Nate to leave the small office before he connected with the call. "Hello, Isabel."

"Well, hello," she said. "I hope you've simmered down a little."

"What's on your mind?"

She laughed lightly. "I'd have to be blind, deaf and stupid not to see that I really pissed you off. I've never seen you so angry, certainly not with me, certainly not from some offhand remark about an Indian girl! We had talked about this stuff before and you said the term was not offensive to you. I called to make amends."

"Forgiven," he said.

"But Clay, I'm still not sure what I did, what I said," she argued.

"I said, forgiven. Let's move on, please."

"Not until I understand," she begged.

"I told you there was a woman and you treated her with disrespect. It wasn't what you said so much as the way you said it, laughing at her, as though she's *nothing*. Some little *Indian* girl. Shame on you, Isabel. I expect that cruel side from Frederik, but not from you."

"Ah. So an apology won't quite get it with you. Clay, you know I'm not savvy with these Native American issues, the vernacular. Come on, give me a break here. We were together a long time and we talked about this stuff a lot, but I didn't grow up in the Native community and—"

"It isn't about the Native community, Isabel. It's about mocking another human being."

"And she heard you say you'd always love me, she's angry, and you're upset. How can I help that?"

"Somehow you knew who she was before I even arrived at the clinic," Clay said. "You made sure she was aware that our relationship didn't exactly end with our divorce. Was that to taunt her? To anger her enough so that you'd get what you want out of me? Ah, never mind—what goes on between Lilly and me isn't your concern, so just drop it. Is there anything else you need from me?"

She sighed audibly. "The stable vet and trainer disagree with your recommendation for Diamond."

"Not the first time there's been a difference of opinion," he said impatiently.

"Will you please come? Just for a weekend? Talk to them?"

"I'm afraid that's not possible, but if you'd like me to ask Dr. Jensen if he's available for a quick trip to L.A., I could do that."

"You know it's not *Dr. Jensen* I need right now. I'll pay. Top dollar."

Clay leaned his elbow on the desk and applied his thumb and forefingers to his temples. "You never understood about that, did you, Isabel? I'm not for sale."

"You have your son there now," she said. "Your son and your girlfriend."

"Gabe is working in the clinic and living with my sister in Grace Valley. He told me he talked to you briefly before you left, so I'm sure you already know those details."

"And the girlfriend?"

He was silent for a long moment. "Do you want to talk to Dr. Jensen about a consult?"

"I want you to stop treating me as though I'm some horse breeder you don't know! I have a problem with a very valuable quarter horse."

Clay stayed stoically quiet for a moment. "Yes, I know. I think we addressed that problem. Didn't we?" There was no answer on the line. "Do you need the doctor?" he asked.

"I thought I was clear. I need *you*."

"I'm no longer available to you."

"What about my *horse?*" she asked indignantly.

"The doctor has given you a course of treatment. If you'd like to discuss it further, I'll call him to the phone. Otherwise, good luck."

The sound of the phone slamming several times

against a hard surface answered him. Then there was a dial tone. He stared at the phone for a moment, then the door to the office opened and Nathaniel stood looking at him.

"You didn't step all that far out," Clay commented.

"Landlord rights," he said. "And maybe the only way I'm going to find out what's going on around here." He nodded toward the phone. "What's that all about, Clay?"

Clay put the cordless on its base. "That is proof positive that material wealth does not guarantee happiness. Isabel has many needs, and right now what she needs is to have me at her beck and call." He shook his head and didn't smile. "Poor Isabel."

"She's having trouble with the horse?"

"Possibly, but more likely she's having trouble accepting the fact that I moved on. This is my fault, Nathaniel. I thought patience was the way with Isabel. Patience and understanding. But I only enabled her."

"Enabled her to do what?" Nate asked.

"I've always seen her as a woman who needs love and acceptance, who needs reassurance that love wouldn't be withdrawn, that it would be permanent. But there's more to her. Isabel was raised by an abusive man and I can't even imagine the extent of that abuse. There are things she's never been able to talk about. I do know that as a child she was treated too harshly—affection was continually withheld. Earning a kind word from Frederik was impossible, even when she became an accomplished adult. And I see now there's a side to her that's...that's very like the man who raised her. It's not something I witnessed often, but her many needs can push her to behave as a selfish, self-pitying bigot. And

I should have been clearer when I left L.A. that I was permanently leaving her and our relationship. Like I said—my fault."

"Bigot? A bigot who married a Native American?"

"Exactly. If Isabel is a bigot her father is a full-blown racist. It suited them to have a Native farrier and stable manager—it was interesting for them. I was a conversation piece, more so when I married Isabel. It escalated again when we divorced but I stayed on at the stable. This move was long overdue."

"This used to be a happier place," Nate said. "No one's happy these days. What are we going to do about Lilly?"

"We?"

"It's not just you and Lilly who are unhappy. My Annie is down—Lilly isn't ready to talk about this whole mess. Annie had just found herself the perfect training partner and had big dreams for what they could do for young girls when you and Lilly fell out. I used to have a much more content assistant. And poor Gabe— he walks around like he's afraid to sneeze. So, what are we going to do?"

"Nathaniel, I apologize. If I'd dealt with Isabel a long time ago none of this would be happening. I carried on with Isabel for a long time after our divorce. I was married to her, after all. There was no one else in my life and I didn't see the harm.... Isabel was here when Lilly came to deliver feed the other day and somehow she knew. She knew Lilly was my—" He took a breath. "Isabel made sure Lilly knew that even though I'd been divorced a couple of years, we'd continued on until recently."

Nate had a shocked look for a moment. "That's what you meant," he said. "When you said you were divorced but not that much had changed." He ran a hand around the back of his neck. "Jesus."

"This is all my fault, all of it. I apologize. I brought unhappiness to all my favorite people. Maybe if I'd truly ended it with Isabel, or at least been more honest with Lilly before Isabel showed up…" He shook his head. "I'll do whatever I can, Nathaniel, but in the meantime, I'm sorry. I take full responsibility."

Nate looked at him for a long moment. "Oh, boy, do you have your work cut out for you."

"Tell me about it."

Jack was getting pretty used to the bar being quieter than usual at around the dinner hour. In fact, if some of his close friends didn't drop in, if hunters didn't come by, there wasn't very much to do. Mel kept trying to re-assure him that he'd done the right thing by refusing to buckle under to the obviously selfish wants of individu-als. "And I know these people almost as well as you do, Jack—they're going to come around. You were true to what we all believe Hope would want. She has always wanted to improve the town, not improve a few personal fortunes."

He believed in the town, too. But he had believed they'd come around a little faster.

When a young man walked into the bar, Jack thought he probably grinned foolishly. He was a little too glad for the company. "Hey there, how you doing?"

The guy dragged his hat off his head and actually looked around, as if to be sure Jack was talking to him. He was tall, had short brown hair, dark eyes and a shadow of a beard. He wore a khaki jacket, jeans and lace-up boots. He smiled at Jack and cocked his head. "Good," he said. "How about yourself?"

"Excellent," Jack said, giving the counter a swipe. "What can I get you?"

"How about a beer? Whatever's on tap."

The beer on tap was stale from under use. Jack reached into the cooler and pulled out a Heineken in a bottle. "I'm ready to change out the keg—try this at on-tap price."

The guy chuckled. Kid, he was just a kid. Jack would put him at about twenty-three, twenty-four. "Can't argue with a deal like that."

"If you like Heineken, that is," Jack said. "If that's not your brew, just say so, I'll get you something else."

"You're the most accommodating bartender I've run into in a long time."

Jack just gave his head a shake and realized he was so damn happy for a nonjudgmental customer, this was a little embarrassing. "Yeah, we aim to please. So what brings you to town?"

The kid took a long pull from his beer and put it down on the counter. "That's nice," he said, admiring the beer. "I heard about this place from a buddy who likes to hunt up here. I was gonna come hunting with him, but he couldn't get a kitchen pass from his wife, so I came up just to look around. That's all," he said with a shrug.

"It's deer season," Jack said. "You decide not to hunt?"

"Not this time, but I wanted to look the place over."

"We get quite a few hunters in here, but not usually till after nightfall. Dusk is a good time of day for hunting and they wait it out. In fact, most of them stop here on the way out of town, when they've done their hunting and want to enjoy a good meal." He frowned slightly. "You look kind of familiar. Have you been around here before?"

"No," he said with a laugh. "I've been a long way from here. Afghanistan. I just got discharged."

"What branch?" Jack asked.

"Marines."

"Ooo-rah," Jack said, putting out a meaty fist. "Lotta us around. Welcome aboard. So, when you're not in Afghanistan?"

"I grew up around San Diego. I was born there. Not far from Camp Pendleton, as a matter of fact. So what else was I gonna do? I didn't want to join the Marines, but it was the law." Then he grinned handsomely.

Jack laughed at the boy. "I guess you look like every kid I ever took into a training program, exercise or war. I must be getting old. Thanks for serving and welcome home." He put out his hand. "Jack Sheridan."

The young man stuck out his own. "Denny. Denny Cutler."

"I think I might've had a Cutler serve under me. Did you have brothers in the Corps?"

"Nope," he said with a laugh. "Just me."

"I guess they're all starting to run together—the names, the faces. Sorry about that," he said. "But I'm glad to make your acquaintance, son. Wish you were gonna be around here a little longer."

"I think that may happen, as a matter of fact. Just how nasty does this place get in winter?"

Jack shrugged. "Not terrible. We're low enough elevation that we almost never get snowed in, but the roads, well… Just let me say, four-wheel drive comes in handy."

"I was afraid of that," Denny said. "I grew up on the beach."

Jack leaned his elbows on the table. "Then why on God's green earth would you hang around a place like this?"

Denny seemed to think about his answer. "How good are you at confidences?"

Jack straightened, got a serious look in his eye and held up his right hand. "On my mother's grave, I haven't let slip more than twenty-percent of the time. And never under enemy interrogation!"

"At least you're honest," Denny said.

"I like to talk—I can admit that. But the fact is, if I know it's a secret, I'm good."

Denny just stared at him for a long moment and then he burst out laughing. "I'm crazy, right? I'm going to tell you a secret when I don't even know you? And you're a bartender? You could tell everyone in the closest three towns!"

Jack straightened. "Well, that's not likely," he said. They don't hang out here so much anymore, he could have added.

Denny just chuckled. "Okay, here's the basic fact. My mother never got married. I grew up thinking the guy who lived with us since I was born was my biological father. He split when I was little. We weren't that sorry to see him go. My mom died about six months before I went to Afghanistan, and before she died she told me the guy was not my father." He gave a shrug. "This wasn't bad news."

"Oh, man, I'm sorry, Denny," Jack said from the heart. "Was it sudden?"

"No, it wasn't sudden. She was sick for years—she had cancer and would go into remission, have a flare-up, go into remission and… Well, when it was getting to be the end she knew it. She had lots of time to think about it. She wanted me to know who my real father was. He's around Northern California. He was a marine."

"Seriously? Have you found him yet?"

"Not yet," he said.

"Well, maybe I can help. I know most everyone. Around here, anyway. And most of the military folks around here at least stop in to say hello."

"I appreciate that, man, I really do. But here's the thing—I thought I'd figure out on my own where he is, what he's like. Two things here, Jack? Is it Jack? That's your name?"

"Jack, that's right."

"Thing is, Jack—maybe I find him, meet him, and I don't like him. Maybe he's not a real big improvement on the guy I thought was my father and was relieved to learn wasn't. What if he's a jerk? What if he beats his wife or something? I can walk away and he'll never know. And the other thing—what if he really doesn't want to know he has a son from a little fling twenty-five years ago? What if he's a mayor or something? A priest or police chief? What if it would really upset his life to have some long-lost son pop out of the woodwork, huh? Because I could understand that, too."

"I get what you're saying, kid—especially if he's a loser. But what man wouldn't want to know about his own son?"

Denny shook his head. "A man who never had the

first idea might be a little upset about it, don't you think?"

"Maybe for five minutes," Jack said. "But once he thought about it, he'd be glad for a second chance."

"You think?"

"That's what I think," Jack said.

The door to the bar opened and Mel came in. She held a little hand in each one of hers—David, almost four, and Emma, almost three.

"Hey there," Jack said, coming around the bar. He crouched to pick up Emma and with one strong hand, lifted David onto a stool. "Were you two good today?"

"They were excellent," Mel said. "We have a new addition at the clinic—Cameron put up a swing set in the backyard for our kids and his twins. I don't know why we didn't think of it sooner. So," she said, jumping up on a stool next to her son, "may we please have some juice? Please?" she said, nudging David.

"Please, Dad," he said in a very adult way.

"Pease!" Emma said, clapping.

"And maybe a short beer," Mel added. "Just a little less than half. Then I'll go home and feed the kids."

"We have some mac and cheese ready to roll," Jack offered. Then he looked at Denny and said, "Denny, this is my wife, Mel—she doesn't cook. And Mel, this young man is just back from Afghanistan. Denny Cutler."

"How do you do?" she said. "Welcome home. Marine?"

"Yes, ma'am. How'd you know?"

"I don't know," she said. "Jack's like a marine magnet. They all end up here eventually."

"I can see why," Denny said, lifting his beer. He

looked at Jack and said, "Somehow I didn't really see you with a young family."

"No one did, pal, including me. I was forty when I met Mel, and I was nowhere near interested in marriage and children, but she trapped me."

She laughed at him. "This is utterly untrue," she said. "I was running for my life."

"All right, then, I trapped her. Whatever, it ended up working out just fine."

"So, Denny," Mel said, "did you just move here?"

"Sort of," he said. "I came to look the place over on the recommendation of a friend and I like it. But there's one problem—I was recently discharged. I need a job. Any line on a job around here?"

"That's a tough one," Jack said. "With the economy the way it is, jobs are tight. Lots of unemployment."

"It doesn't have to be that much of a job. I'm not married—no girl waiting for a ring or anything. I'm still thinking about school. But I could rent a room and hang out for a few months. I saved a little per diem to see me through."

"A few months?" Jack asked.

"If I decide to get more permanent than that, I'll look around for an apartment or duplex or something. For right now if some little old lady would give me a spare bedroom…"

"We could give you a bed," Jack said. "We have a guesthouse or casita or whatever you call it—it's for my dad when he visits, but there's also an extra room for him in the house if he shows up unexpectedly. I mean, if it's not long-term." Jack shrugged. "And you're a marine."

"Wow. That's almost too good to be true."

"I'll give you some directions," he said, pulling out a napkin and writing on it for him.

Late that night, when Mel and Jack were in bed and the children asleep, she said, "Don't we usually talk about things like this?"

"Mel, his mother died, he found out his father wasn't his father, he went to war... He's a marine. We can do this for him—it doesn't cost us anything."

"What if that's not all totally true? What if he's never been a marine? What if his mother is alive and well? What if... Jack, remember Annalee?" she asked, recalling a beautiful con artist who had gotten the best of Jack not long ago. No harm was done—she wasn't after Jack, but someone else. Just the same, Jack was reeled into her con too easily. Jack loved everyone. "What if he's a serial killer or something?"

Jack just shrugged. "We lock the doors to the house, watch him for a while, and if he's a serial killer..." He chuckled low in his throat. His shoulder and arm muscles automatically flexed. "He picked the *wrong* guesthouse!"

She sighed and settled against him. It had been a long time since Jack had been in a war zone, a long time since he sat alert or on surveillance, but some things never went away. Jack would wake at the flutter of a feather, his reflexes were as sharp as ever and he was strong.

"Right," she said, snuggling up. "But next time can we talk about it first?"

"Sure, babe," he said, his arms going around her. "Try to relax. I like him, he's a nice kid."

After two days at home, Lilly returned to work at the feed store. For the first time in her life she took a very firm hand with her grandfather. "I'm not ready to talk about Clay, so leave me alone about that. And I think it would be best if you asked Manny to deliver feed to the Jensen clinic next week. I'm pretty sure I'm not going to be ready to do that."

Instead of riding after work, she returned to yoga in search of peace, calm and serenity. After yoga, she went to the Loving Cup, where Dane offered as much loving as he could. She'd told him all the grim details over the phone and, to her embarrassment, she'd cried on his shoulder a bit more than her pride easily bore.

There were just a few people in the coffeehouse, clear on the other side of the room, when she took her usual seat at the counter.

"Well," Dane said, smiling. "You're looking pretty good. Better than I expected."

"Don't lie," she scolded. "I've learned that falling asleep with a bag of frozen peas on your eyes can be a partial remedy, but you have to be absolutely sure you're done with the crying or your eyelids will stick to the plastic."

"Eww."

"How long do you think this will go on? This obscene, ridiculous, humiliating crying?"

Dane just looked down. When he raised his eyes, they were troubled. "Lilly, have you thought about sitting down with the man, hearing him out to either work it out or officially break it off? Before you invest any more money in frozen peas? I mean, he's begging!"

"He lied to me, Dane...."

Dane shrugged. "Sounds like he didn't tell you a few things, but that doesn't mean he intended to keep it from you forever. You two are pretty new, after all."

She shook her head. "He should have come clean before his *wife* informed me. Before I caught him pledging his forever love to her!"

"From what you told me, apparently he didn't quite end it with the ex after the divorce was final. Is that a crime? He hadn't even met you yet. And from what we think we know, he hasn't been with her since moving here." Dane leaned on the counter. "I think that happens more often than we realize. My sister? She had a rotten marriage, the worst husband you can imagine, but after they split up she hooked up with him a couple of times before we finally came up here and opened the shop. Just sometimes old habits die hard...."

"Really?" Lilly said. "And how do we know when they're finally dead?"

"I think that's the point in talking it out, or fighting it out, or whatever it turns out to be."

"I can't do that," she said in a strained whisper. "Don't you get it? I can't go through that again!"

"He didn't cheat on you!" Dane said hotly. "Before he knew you, before he was involved with you, he was with another woman! That's not a crime!"

"But he lied to me! Just like the guy before him lied to me!"

"This has to stop!" Dane said. Lilly looked at him, stunned. "How long do you plan to keep that tired old heartache alive? You were a little girl! You're a woman now. Grow up!"

She stared at him in wonder, shaking her head. "You can't really be saying this to me...."

"I love you, Lilly. Listen to me for once—you're not the first person to have a broken heart. You're allowed to feel sorry for yourself for a little while, but you've licked that old wound so long it's festered! For God's sake, no wonder you can't deal with Clay, can't let yourself face the truth. That would take strength and courage—and you're more comfortable acting like a whipped little victim!"

She withdrew from him, leaning back. She shook her head because she was speechless.

"A victim with enough self-pity to sink a ship," he went on. "You have to get over yourself, little sister. If you need help to do that, get it. If you keep this up, not only will you lose Clay before you even know if he deserves to be kicked to the curb, you will never allow yourself to find a good man! If you die old and all alone, it will be no one's fault but your own."

She was silent for a moment. Her eyes grew liquid and a tear slipped down her cheek. "How dare you!"

He leaned toward her. "I dare because I'm your best friend and I love you. It's time, Lilly. If you're ever going to be in a grown-up relationship, you're going to have to ditch the little girl self-pity, straighten up and face your situation like an adult. I'd like to tell you that once you find The One you'll never have problems, never face complications, never have to deal with a guy's fuck-ups. Oh, hell, no one can get through a serious relationship without contributing their own mistakes to the mess. It's never going to be easy, Lilly! People are flawed! Imperfect! They make mistakes! You have to be strong enough to face them, know when things can be worked out and when they can't."

Another tear ran down the other cheek; she felt the hair on the back of her neck prickle as if there was danger. Not knowing what to say, what to do, she grabbed her purse and whirled off the stool, heading for the door.

"Go ahead," Dane yelled after her. "Run away! It's the only thing you're brave enough to do!"

Out the door she went.

Dane leaned on the counter, looking down, almost trembling. He'd taken a huge chance…and might have lost his best friend forever. It took him a minute to regain his composure and straighten. When he did, he found the eyes of four patrons staring at him from across the room. He ran a hand nervously through his blond hair. "Sorry," he said. "Lover's quarrel."

Luke Riordan grabbed the phone on the second ring; baby Brett was sleeping and Luke wasn't in the mood to go another round of trying to get him down.

"Hey," Patrick said.

"Hey," Luke returned. "What's up?"

"Well, I got a couple of days in with Colin, but that's all. He invited me to leave. So…I'm in the inn suites up the road from Fort Benning."

"He's not in the best mood," Luke said. "I get that. His body hurts, rehab is killing him. He had a lot of company—Mom was there for two weeks.…"

"I think we might have other issues, Luke. He's popping pain pills like they're M&M's."

"Well, they're prescription, right?" Luke asked.

"I took him to physical therapy a couple of days ago, then to the clinic. The doctor told him it was time to wean off the good stuff and go with some anti-inflammatory and ice, but I don't see that happening. He's still on the strong stuff."

"Is he still in a lot of pain?" Luke asked.

"His leg aches because he's putting some weight on it now, but he's making good progress, according to the PTs. It's been a month. His elbow is killing him and the PT says that's a tough one to rehab, real painful. Luke, he's not using anti-inflammatory and ice. When I got on him about the drugs, he threw me out."

"Let me think," Luke said. Colin had been in the hospital at Fort Hood, where the accident had taken place, for ten days. He went back to Fort Benning to the Wounded Warriors Support Center, a convalescence center, for about a week and then he was cleared to go home—a small, comfortable house near Fort Benning. Their mother was there to help him get to physical therapy and clinic appointments; there were guys from his unit to chauffeur him, but he could also drive the short distance on his own, though it was recommended he get a ride as long as he was on heavy pain medication. He'd been home about a week when Patrick got back from his Gulf mission and had gone straight to Colin. "It's been a month since the accident," Luke said. "That doesn't seem like much for what happened to him."

"Maybe not," Patrick said. "But I'm a little freaked out by this—I heard the doc tell him it was time to get off the narcs and I heard Colin agree. But that's not what's happening. He glazes right over about five minutes after popping a pill, and, man, all is right with his world. But just suggest he might be taking too many pain pills and look out! He can't hardly move in PT, but if you piss him off, he can throw all your shit on the lawn without any trouble."

"He didn't do that," Luke said.

"He did."

"Aw, fuck. How long does it take to get totally hooked on pain pills?"

"Apparently about a month," Patrick said.

"Okay, let me think," Luke said again. But thinking wasn't as easy this time. What were the options? They could go to his commander and report the situation and the Army would say, *Oh, really? Buh-bye!* The deal is— turn yourself in for an addiction problem and get help, get caught on drugs you're not prescribed to take, and there is no help for your sorry soul. Was there wiggle room if you got banged up and hooked on drugs compliments of the Army?

"I could come out," he said to Patrick. "But he hates me."

"He doesn't exactly hate you," Paddy said. "But he doesn't want advice from you."

"It has to be Aiden," Luke said.

"Or Sean," Paddy said. "But I swear to God, he's taking too many pain pills. This isn't like Colin. Colin *likes* pain…sort of. He's always pushed himself real hard. He's been hurt before and he never tossed back a bunch of pills. This isn't good."

"But these *injuries* were bad, Paddy. You should've seen him. He was a mess—unconscious and hallucinating and… Maybe he's not acting that abnormally. Let's call Aiden. And while we're at it, Sean. You know how to do a conference call?"

"Yeah," Patrick said. "Yeah, I can do that."

A half hour later Aiden had agreed to go to Colin's house near Fort Benning. "I don't know that I'll be able to do much good," he said. "The last thing he seems to want right now is his brothers. I'll check him out and try to be circumspect. I'll try not to piss him off. But I guaran-damn-tee you he isn't throwing *my* luggage out the door."

"Good for you, Aiden," Luke said in great relief.

"Yeah," said Sean.

"Thank you," said Patrick.

Sixteen

A few days of not talking to Lilly or being alone with her was a few days too long. While Clay couldn't say he knew everything about Lilly after just a couple of months, this was not the Lilly he thought he knew—too stubborn to even hear him out. Out of complete frustration he found his way to that funky turquoise coffee shop in Fortuna, the Loving Cup, and hoped to get some enlightenment there.

Clay had no idea what days or times Lilly frequented the coffee shop or that she had a favorite place to roost when she did, but without knowing it he took the seat she usually claimed. When Dane saw Clay walk in, a flash of surprise registered on his face, but it melted quickly into understanding. He walked over to Clay. "Howdy," he said. "What can I get you?"

"I'm hoping for solutions. Peace of mind. An end to this misery," Clay candidly shared.

"Well, let's see. Does that come in a latte or a cappuccino? Maybe a double shot?"

"Just a cup of coffee. Black. And how about some answers?"

Dane poured the coffee in a big, masculine-looking mug. "I don't have any answers without questions," he finally said.

"I can't break through the barrier, Dane. I hope she talked to you because she hasn't talked to anyone else. I went to Annie and she knows nothing at all, except that Lilly took a little time off from helping out at the clinic. Annie was counting on her and the Lilly I thought I knew wouldn't let her friend down like that unless… unless she was in a very bad place and couldn't help it. Lilly won't take my calls or return my messages. She hasn't seen Blue in days—that's got to be killing her. When I went to her house, she called the police."

"I heard about that," Dane said rather quietly, as if disappointed. "That was a little over-the-top," he said. "If it makes any difference, I urged her to have it out with you—have a sit-down about whatever the problem is. I think it's foolish to refuse to communicate. I don't know how she's going to know, ten years from now, whether she made the right decision."

"Has she made some kind of decision? Because she hasn't said anything to me. Well, except that she doesn't want to talk to me. She doesn't want to listen."

Dane pursed his lips and stood very still on his side of the counter.

"Can you help me?" Clay asked. "Can you help me understand? Can you tell me what to do?"

Dane shook his head. "I'm sorry. I think I might've made it worse. We had a fight about it. All of it. I made her cry and she's not speaking to me, either."

"Swell," Clay said. "I wonder if I should go to her grandfather, but common sense tells me—"

"Oh, please," Dane said indignantly. "Even if Lilly

did confide in her grandfather, he'd never break her trust. Especially to you! You're the enemy right now."

"But why am I the enemy?"

"Seriously?" Dane asked with a laugh. "She saw you kiss your ex and tell her you loved her. That sort of thing just doesn't go down well, I guess. Silly Lilly!" he added facetiously.

Clay shook his head, a very slight movement. "No, that's not exactly what happened."

"She believes she caught you in a tryst," Dane said.

"No," Clay said. "No, she caught me sending away a fragile person I once cared about, as kindly as I could. And I regret that now, but not because Lilly misinterpreted it—because I've finally realized that to be too kind to Isabel sometimes carries a heavy price."

"But you *kissed* her," Dane said, leaning toward him in a threatening manner—threatening for a man a few inches shorter and a good forty pounds lighter in weight. "Girls don't like watching their boyfriends kiss other women, especially women they profess to *love*." He lifted one tawny brow, crossed his arms over his chest and peered at Clay. "Know what I mean?"

"I was trying to cushion the rejection. I kissed her forehead and said that I would always love her. I didn't get any further than that before Hurricane Lilly blew in and out of the barn."

Dane tilted his head. "Forehead?" he asked.

Clay gave a short nod. "I wanted to get her back on the road with a minimum of drama. I had already told her there was a woman in my life. I was trying to say that while I'd always love her, have affection for her, I was moving on to a new relationship and she would have to move on, too. But I didn't avoid the drama, after all—by the time I did send her on her way, it was *not* with affection. Or kindness." He shook his head.

"Forehead?" Dane asked again.

"Yes," Clay confirmed. "It was the kiss you'd give a sister. It was the love you'd give a sister. But I take that back—if Isabel was my sister, I would be insane by now."

A half smile flirted with Dane's lips. "Well, I got the impression it was a passionate, sweaty, sloppy, lip-lock."

Clay frowned. He shook his head.

"But there's that other thing—the ex told Lilly you'd been involved for a long time after the divorce…"

"Correct," he said with directness. "We didn't live together, but it was not a clean break. Bad judgment on my part—I admit that. But that was one of the reasons I took the job with Nathaniel. That postdivorce relation-ship wasn't a very satisfying place for me to be. I needed distance from Isabel. Of course I meant to level with Lilly, but honestly, I didn't see what that had to do with us. Isabel and I were over. That was before Lilly came into my life and it was over."

"I think my friend Lilly is going a little nuts." He tilted his head and peered at Clay. "You know, if you're lying about this and just trying to find a way to juggle two women at the same time, I could think of terrible things to do to you.…"

"Don't be ridiculous," Clay said. "Why the hell would I want *two?* One at a time is proving far more than I can handle!"

"Lilly said this Isabel is rich and beautiful. I think poor Lilly was intimidated by her…and her horse trailer.…"

"*Lilly* is rich and beautiful. Isabel's life is cluttered and heavy. She can barely breathe. And her beauty is a full-time job. Lilly's beauty is from here," he said, splaying his fingers across his chest.

"Ohhhh," Dane said, sighing and nearly swooning before he could stop himself. He cleared his throat. "I guess when a girl like Lilly sees the man she loves kiss another woman, no matter how innocently, she sees passion and true love even if that's not what it is."

Clay was quiet for several beats before he said, "A girl like Lilly?"

"Oh, you know," Dane said. "She's young, she's pretty innocent, she has her baggage.… She took a big chance on you and then—"

"What baggage?" Clay asked.

Dane shrugged and glanced away. Without looking at Clay, in a quiet voice he said, "She had a romance go rotten when she was younger.…"

"She mentioned that. But then, hasn't everyone?"

"Have you?"

Clay smirked. "Everyone," he repeated.

"What kind of terrible romance did you have?" Dane asked, leaning an elbow on the counter and his chin in his palm.

"Is that relevant?"

"It could be," Dane said. "Try me."

"I had a girlfriend when I was a teenager. We had a child. She wanted to give him up, but I raised him with the help of my parents."

That shot Dane up straight. "No kidding?"

"Gabe is seventeen now," he said. "It was a misstep with a very positive outcome. He's living in Grace Valley with my sister, working at the clinic part-time, and I see him every day. Finally, after all these years of working away from the reservation and only visiting and talking to him on the phone. Now, about Lilly…"

Dane took Clay's coffee cup and refilled it for him. He took a breath. "Much as I want to tell you what I know, I'd better watch it. Lilly's on shaky ground right now, trying to figure everything out. I'll tell you this— she was *very* young. The boy was older and he was a handsome Navajo—damn your luck. He hurt her very badly, Clay. Her grandpa saw that as a good time to move her away, but… But how many times can a girl be rejected, abandoned, before it really takes its toll?"

"Was there more than one guy?" Clay asked.

"No. But she never knew her father, her mother left her with her grandparents, her grandmother died when she was just a little girl, the boy dumped her…very cruelly, she was moved out of her home, and…" He coughed into his fist, stopping himself. He was going to be in enough trouble; he wasn't saying any more. "There are circumstances around the whole thing that I think Lilly should be the one to tell you about. I think Lilly has had too many losses and was playing it safe. Taking a chance on you was a big gamble."

Clay stared into his cup for a moment. Then he stood up, pulled his wallet out of his back pocket and put a few bills on the counter.

"Come on," Dane said. "It's on the house."

"Everyone has to make a living," Clay said.

"What are you going to do?" Dane asked.

"I don't know. But I'm not letting her go."

"Good. I was hoping you'd feel that way. And if you do get it fixed, maybe you could put in a good word for me. I chewed her little ass good—for being a baby about this and refusing to speak to you."

"If I ever get the chance, I'll do what I can." Clay put out a big hand. "Thank you."

"I might've just made it worse.…"

"Your loyalty to Lilly is a good thing. You are a very good friend to her. It isn't always easy to be honest—there's risk. If I can get her back, I might have you to thank."

"My pleasure," Dane said.

Clay walked out of the coffee shop to his truck. Dane watched his departure with a myriad of emotions—pleasure, wonder, admiration, perhaps desire—that tall, straight height; long black braid; wide shoulders. After Clay had backed out of his parking space and driven away, Dane collapsed onto the countertop. "Oh. My. God," he said very softly. "Whew."

Lilly couldn't decide whether Dane had hurt her feelings, infuriated her or disappointed her.…

Until she realized with sudden clarity that he was *right!*

For a young woman who despised weakness, she had been a wimp. A spineless victim. She should have realized long ago that the only thing to do about that old broken heart was to let it teach her what she wouldn't stand for in a relationship, rather than let it keep her from ever taking a chance on one. And while she might've wished Clay had opened up about everything that had ever happened in his life before she found out in other ways, there hadn't really been enough time for that—they *were* too new. And not only that, she hadn't yet opened up to him! He needed to know the kind of

childhood hurts that got in the way of her committing
to a man as powerful, as beautiful as he was. She was
terrified that she didn't deserve him, wouldn't be able
to hold on to him.

She had been at least as wrong as Clay. And it needed
to be faced directly, with courage and not self-pity.

She could call Clay at once and tell him that she'd had
a revelation, that she was ready to talk. But she wanted
to think it through a bit first, figure out what she'd say
to him, what she'd ask him.

She went to work at the feed store and got a lot of
thinking done while she worked at her computer, keeping the accounts. She also wanted to talk to Dane, tell
him she wasn't angry over their fight.

But she'd rather look him in the eye and tell him she'd
heard him loud and clear and had faced Clay. It would
be better still if she could go to the coffee shop and tell
Dane that they'd been able to work things out.

She left the feed store a bit early and drove to the
clinic. While she was on her way there she realized that
there were other people to make amends with—she'd
refused to confide in Annie, who she loved and trusted.
And she'd neglected Blue, who had brought her so much
happiness.

When she got to the clinic and saw that Clay's truck
was gone, she almost sighed in relief. At least that would
give her some time to talk to Annie and take Blue out
on the trail and bond with her anew.

She found Annie and Nathaniel in the clinic office.

"Lilly!" Annie said, jumping to her feet excitedly.
"Oh, thank God you're here! I've been worried sick
about you!"

Lilly hugged Annie while Nate looked on. "I'm so

sorry, Annie. I didn't mean for you and all our plans to be collateral damage from my falling-out with Clay." She held Annie away from her. "My fault, Annie. I think I went off the deep end. That woman—Isabel— her showing up like that had me so jealous and crazy, I practically hid under the bed. I've refused to talk to Clay, even though he's called a couple of dozen times. I apologize for how it must've hurt you."

"Are you going to talk to him now?" Annie asked. "Because he's completely miserable."

Lilly nodded. "Will he be back soon?"

"I don't know where he went, but he should have his cell phone. Want me to call? Tell him you're here?"

Lilly shook her head. "Maybe if he's not back in an hour or so. For right now I just need to see Blue. I'll take her out for a ride and when I get back, Clay will probably be here." She laughed a bit ruefully. "Here's how crazy that man made me—I was going to give up everything I love because I was too mad at him to listen to his explanations. I never thought I was that unreasonable."

"You must have had a reason...."

"Sure I did—I was scared to death! I didn't think I could bear it if the whole thing went south. There was a part of me that thought it would be easier to run for my life!" She shook her head and shrugged. "I think when you love someone, it can make you lose your mind."

Annie smiled at her. "Well, it seems like you found it." She hugged her. "Welcome home."

Jack Sheridan was behind the bar when Denny came in. He gave him a friendly smile. Jack had to give him credit—the kid was pretty smart. He didn't make himself too obvious around the home property—he got out in the morning, went job hunting, dropped by the bar for dinner and insisted on paying for his meals. Jack was sure Denny made it a point not to impose. Frankly, he liked him…liked having him around.

"How'd the job search go today?" Jack asked.

"Not bad. Filled out a lot of applications, met a lot of nice people. To tell the truth, I could take a simple job to tide me over while I look for something better, but I'm afraid it might cut into my searching time. How about a beer, sir?"

"*Sir?*" Jack laughed. He poured a fresh draft for his new friend. "What kind of jobs, just out of curiosity?"

Denny accepted his beer. "Well, there's a private school over in Redway that needs to replace its custodian and fortunately the old guy is still there, so he could give me some tips and training. Not that the Marine Corps didn't give me some *fine* tips on getting things straight—I just don't feel like using a toothbrush on floor tiles, if you get my drift. Thing is, it's minimum wage and full-time—when would I look for something better? And I wouldn't want to take the job and have them count on me, only to leave them in the lurch the second something better comes along. There are lots of jobs like that—good, hard, solid work that can't pay the rent." Then he grinned. "I realize I have a break right now and it totally embarrasses me that you won't take rent money, but I do have to think ahead. If the police or fire departments were hiring, I'd qualify and I guarantee you I'd pass their exams and do great in their academies, but…" He shrugged.

"You might have to take a minimum wage job till this economy picks up a little. Hardly anyone's hiring," Jack said. He lifted his coffee cup. He was starting to really like this kid. He liked the way the kid handled life. Liked his attitude.

"Yeah, I know," Denny said. "But I'm holding out for the best low-paying job I can find before I settle in. But I have to say, my friend was right about this part of the world—very pretty. And the people are nice. Friendly." He lifted his beer toward Jack. "Very accommodating. Especially you!"

"I got in a little trouble for that—offering up the guesthouse without even seeing your ID."

"Oh, really?" Denny asked with round eyes. He went for his back pocket.

"Nah, we're fine now. I guess Mel is right, I should at least check a person out before letting them on the property."

Denny pulled out his wallet and flipped it open. "Seriously, she's right! You should be sure about who you're letting hang around your house and your family! Even if I am in a separate building. I mean, I don't want any trouble with Mel. She's so nice and all—"

Jack put a hand over the boy's wrist. "It's okay, Denny. We're square. She's fine about it now."

"But look at it, Jack. Huh?" he asked, pushing the ID toward him. "That's me, my face, my San Diego address, which I moved out of so I guess it's not really my address anymore, but…"

"What about your mail?" Jack asked.

"General Delivery," he said with a shrug. He grinned boyishly. "If the Marine Corps has trouble finding me, I'm okay with that!"

"Done with that, are you?" Jack asked.

"Oh, man—I am so done."

Jack stepped back from the bar, chuckling. He lifted his coffee cup to his lips.

At that moment, the sound of tinkling glass emerged from the bar and the floor began to vibrate. Jack felt as if he was off balance, as if the earth moved beneath his feet. Liquor bottles on the shelf danced around; one fell. Glasses began to tumble off the shelf.

"Jack!" Denny yelled. Then the kid put a foot on his barstool, leaped over the bar and pushed Jack down, hovering over him, protecting him. He started to move him out of the bar area. "Get away from this glass! Hurry! Crawl! Front of the bar—come on!"

Despite the uneven feeling of the floor beneath him, Jack moved to the end of the bar, and not a moment too soon. Bottle after bottle smashed to the floor, glass flying, liquor splashing. In just seconds they were at the front of the bar, sitting under the overhang. The shaking went on and on; it seemed to last forever and the breakage continued. Then the vibration slowed to a stop.

From where Jack crouched he could see that the two men who'd been sitting at a table by the door had abandoned their beers and fled the bar.

"Whoa," Jack said, trying to stand, but his balance was still impaired.

"Yeah, don't stand up too fast. I grew up in earthquake country. It screws up your equilibrium for a while."

"How'd you get over the bar like that? With everything shaking?" Jack asked.

"I dunno," Denny said. "I saw a couple of bottles go and knew about fifty more would follow and I knew you had to get out of there. No offense, but you had a kind

309

of dumb look on your face, like you weren't sure what was going on."

Jack pointed a finger at Denny. "Do not tell anyone that!"

Denny put his hands up, palms toward Jack. "Absolutely not! But really, I didn't want you to fall and end up crawling out of there on top of shattered glass."

"Thanks." Jack sniffed. He looked at his young friend. "Really smells like a bar now, doesn't it?"

There was a loud bang and a shout as Preacher hit the swinging door and blasted through it from the kitchen. "Jack!"

"Yeah, we're fine," he said, slowly leaning over the bar to get a glimpse of the mess. "Paige and the kids?"

"I checked them first. They're okay. Mel?"

"She's at the clinic with the kids. I gotta get over there." He turned to Denny. "Stay here, will you, buddy? Help Preach with anything he needs? I'll be right back."

"Sure," the kid said, standing up slowly. He peered over the bar. "I'll get a broom and trash can. Lotta glass back there."

"I'll be back to help in a bit." Jack looked over the bar. "Um, you're gonna need a shovel."

Mel and the kids were outside by the swing set when the earthquake hit. She had huddled with them on the ground, so they were fine. Cameron had been in the clinic and reported a couple of broken glasses that had fallen from the kitchen counter to the floor, but that was all.

"The bar's a disaster," Jack told Mel. "I don't want

you or the kids over there—it's covered in glass. Denny happened to be there, having a beer—he's going to help us with the cleanup."

"We'll button things down here, but I think Cameron and I will have to wait here for a while, see if anyone calls with an injury. What will I do with the kids if that happens?"

"Preacher's place is stable, just not the bar. I'll check with Paige and let you know. In the meantime, if you need me, I'll come over here." He leaned forward and gave her a kiss. "That kid, Denny—he jumped over the bar and pushed me out of the line of falling bottles."

She tilted her head and lifted an eyebrow. "Good boy," she said. "I guess behind the bar isn't a good place to be during an earthquake."

"I'm going to have to think about that when we get around to repairs. Some kind of guardrail for the bottles and glasses."

There was very little damage in the kitchen; Preacher was fastidious about having dishes put away unless he happened to be creating. There were only a couple of bowls and platters on the work island. He had a big pot of soup on the stove top and as soon as the shaking started, he slid it into the sink where it was safe from falling and burning him. All they lost was one large mixing bowl.

By the time Jack got back from the clinic, Denny already had a large trash can at the end of the bar and was scooping up broken bottles with a flat-edged snow shovel. Preacher had donned his thigh-high fishing waders and was standing in a cleared space behind the bar, moving bottles and glasses off the shelves, putting what he could in closed cupboards, ready for aftershocks that could be as bad as the first earthquake.

"Good idea, Preach," Jack said. "We'd better tape those cupboard doors shut for the time being."

Jack went to the back of the kitchen for an industrial-size broom and began to sweep glass and liquid toward Denny, where the younger man scooped it up with the shovel. A half hour of this work saw them with a lot of cleanup left, but things were at least under control. When the door to the bar opened, Jack reflexively yelled, "Sorry—bar's closed."

"Jack," Buck Anderson yelled. "Lou's stupid old dually went off the road during the earthquake, right at that soft shoulder—same place the school bus went down a couple of years ago."

"He okay?"

"Split his lip on the steering wheel, but he got out and climbed back up to the road. Thing is, that dually is about all the guy has. That oughta teach him to put all his money in a fancy truck."

"How badly wrecked is it?"

"Looks to be in one piece," Buck said. "If it doesn't slide any farther down the slope. How long you reckon it'll take to get a tow out here?"

"Why wait for a tow? Let me see what Paul has available. We'll go out there—maybe we can pull him up."

"Wouldn't blame you if you let it just slide down the hill," Buck said. "Lou hasn't exactly been a pal to you lately."

Jack rinsed the grit and liquor off his hands, dried them on a handy towel and just shrugged. "I think we better try to get out there before someone drives past that soft shoulder, slips down and lands on top of that truck. Denny? Want to lend a hand?"

"You bet!"

They locked the bar door on their way out so no one would get inside and hurt themselves on the broken glass. It only took a half hour to find a bunch of guys to help and one of Paul Haggerty's biggest trucks. Paul used heavy cable to attach the frame of the pickup to the back of his flatbed. It took a lot of doing; a lot of cable, big hooks, and Jack and Paul both had to rappel down the hill wearing safety harnesses to get it all attached. Once that was done, Paul drove the truck slowly as far across the road as possible, inching that big pickup up the hill. When it was about twenty feet from the road, Jack worked his way down the slope to it, got in and revved up the engine. The dual rear tires were powerful, caught traction and began to slowly climb up the hill. When it cleared the surface of the road, all the men standing around cheered.

Jack got out of the truck. "There's a time those dual tires make a difference," he said. Then he touched his lower lip as he looked at Lou. "If you're fine to drive, I suggest you show that split lip to Cameron, see if it could use a couple of stitches."

"Aw, I don't need no stitches," Lou said.

Jack grinned at him. "Yeah, I guess you can't get much uglier."

"You coulda just left me down there, Jack. I mean, the truck. Left me to wait for a tow."

Jack shrugged. "You wouldn't have left me down there. Even if you don't much like the way I manage the town money. Now, before we leave, we gotta put up some blinkers or something around this soft shoulder. Paul, you bring anything?"

"Do I look like just another pretty face?" he asked with a grin. Then he proceeded to set up road construction blinkers around the soft shoulder, closing off one lane.

Jack was shaking his head thoughtfully. "We gotta get this taken care of."

Seventeen

Lilly took Blue Rhapsody up a narrow trail into the foothills. They reached a plateau from which she could see the entire valley below. She was so happy to be on this horse again, so relieved to feel that even if she didn't have a future with Clay, she'd manage to have a future with Blue. It was one of the best days of her life when she stumbled on that horse. And if she wasn't mistaken, Blue was thrilled to be with her again, too.

They'd been out for over an hour and the sun was lowering over the western mountains. It was breathtaking. The air was cool, the leaves in glorious fall splendor and the sky clear except for those few puffy white clouds along the coast, turning the setting sun pink.

Once she'd wrapped her head around the idea of talking to Clay and listening to him, things had begun to look better. From a new perspective it seemed pretty simple—they would either come to an understanding and move forward or they would learn they weren't meant to be. If it was the latter, would she cry? Feel hurt? Absolutely! Would it kill her? Keep her from her horse? Not a chance! Lilly was nervous about the confrontation, but she was determined. She was no longer a pitiful little girl.

She turned Blue back toward the clinic; surely Clay would have returned by now. She wanted to get off the plateau and down the narrow trail before it was almost dark.

The horse began to dance a little beneath her. "Easy, my love," she said gently, taking a firmer hold on the reins, tightening her knees. The horse relaxed, but in a moment she danced again. Just ahead a small flock of birds shot out of a bush and Blue shied again. "Birds, baby. Nothing but birds."

The horse was spooked; she threw her head, fighting the bit, and bounced on her front legs. Blue never acted like this! She was the calmest horse in the stable. "Whoa, whoa, whoa," Lilly said. She looked around for something that frightened the horse, something she hadn't seen yet, a snake or small animal, but she saw nothing. These nervous reactions went on every few moments. "Okay, it's okay, we're heading home," Lilly said. "No more acting up… Shhh. Shhh."

Lilly calmed the mare and continued down the trail. It wasn't too narrow and was made up of a series of switchbacks on the way down so if Blue was skittish, they'd still manage. They'd barely begun their descent when she noticed a white plastic grocery sack stuck to a bush and fluttering in the breeze just ahead of them. "Easy, easy," she said softly, using her legs and a calm but firm grasp of the reins.

It all happened at once. Lilly felt a shaking travel up the legs of her mount; what sounded like a distant rumble accompanied the vibration and the horizon seemed to blur. Blue began to dance backward, away, rearing slightly. At that moment a brisk gust of cool wind snapped that plastic bag off the bush and sent it flying right past Blue. The horse took a fright, whinnied and reared suddenly, unsteadily, throwing Lilly off her back.

Lilly hit the shaking ground with an *ooomph!* She bounced! She rolled away from the horse as quickly as she could to avoid getting trampled and in doing so rolled to the edge of the trail. Blue had trouble getting her footing and Lilly went off the edge and down the hill. She grabbed at a thorny shrub as she rolled by it, cutting her hands, but she couldn't hold on.

While the ground shook violently, she heard her horse scream in fear and take off like a shot, running from whatever danger there was.

And Lilly rolled out of control down the hill, her head bouncing off rocks, until she came to a stop against a big, thick, unforgiving tree trunk. She lay there, still, while the ground shook and gradually calmed beneath her.

Although she was banged up, her hands bleeding, and she had a big knot on her head, her first concern was Blue. If the horse lost her footing on that trail and fell down the hill she could break bones. And for a horse that could be catastrophic.

She started to make her way up the hill on her hands and knees, pulling with her injured hands on a tree or shrub here, bracing a foot against a rock or tree there. Even though it wasn't a real steep hill, her progress was very slow. It had been a long time since she'd been thrown. Her whole body hurt, though nothing seemed broken. By the time she got to the trail at the top, not even a puff of dust from her horse remained. Blue could be in Arizona by the time she stopped being terrified of the moving earth and the ghostly white bag.

The sun was lowering behind the western mountains. The temperature was already dropping. And it was a long damn walk back to the stable.

"Crap," she said. "If I didn't have bad luck, I'd have no luck at all!"

Clay had returned from the coffee shop to the clinic by 4:00 p.m., before the earthquake hit. They kept a very strict feeding schedule, but one of the first things he noticed was that Lilly's Jeep was there. His chest immediately swelled with hope that must have shown all over his face. When he found Annie in the barn the first thing she said was, "She took Blue out for a ride and will be back before long. She wants to talk to you. I hope you can make things right with her."

"I hope so, too, Annie, and I'll try. Because I love her, too."

"The last few days have been torture," Annie said, "I don't know all the details about what happened with you two, but she said you made her crazy."

He smiled. "Is that so? Well, she did her part to make me crazy, too. I went to see Dane. He helped me as much as he could without completely betraying her trust."

"Good for you," Annie said with a slight smile. "You're going to fight for her!"

"Of course I am, though she hasn't made it real easy. When do you think she'll be back in?"

"I thought by now—she knows we feed on a schedule. Soon, I would expect."

"Do you know where she went?"

"She just said she was going out on the trail. I assume

one of the ones that lead around the back pasture and into the foothills, but she didn't say. You're going to hang around and wait, aren't you?"

"Absolutely," he said. "I'll finish up with these horses and turn them out. I know you want to get to the house and draw Nathaniel's bath and chill his beer mug while he lounges around tonight." Then he grinned. "Go ahead. Leave Lilly to me."

"Cute," she said, turning to go. Then she turned back and said, "Try to do something productive tonight, like get our girlfriend back!"

She was already gone when he said, "I'll do all I can."

Gabe had football practice and wasn't coming to the stable today, so Clay busied himself cleaning stalls, sweeping out an already swept barn, even organizing the tack room, waiting. He frequently looked out the back doors and down the road that led around the east pasture. The sun was setting earlier and earlier now that fall was full on the land and by five-thirty it was turning to dusk.

Then he noticed the horses in the stalls getting restless; in the paddock where they kept him, Streak started dancing around. Out in the back pasture a flock of birds bolted out of the tall grass and flew off. There was an uneasy feeling in Clay's gut that he was getting from the animals. Something wasn't right.

Then he felt a vibration that turned into a rumble that became a wave beneath his feet, almost toppling him to the ground. He steadied himself in the frame of the tack room door while he watched equipment fall off the wall hooks and tools and small appliances dance across the countertop and crash to the floor. The hanging light from the ceiling swayed. He could hear the horses that were inside crying out and kicking at their stalls; he could feel Streak's terror as he tried to run, his gait awkward and legs spreading in a crazy effort to stay balanced.

Whoa, Clay thought. This is a big one. He looked at his watch and saw the second hand move around the face—a big one that lasted a long time.

He was no expert, but either this was bigger than the last one at 5.5 or the epicenter was right beneath them. It seemed as if a long time passed before things stopped moving and falling to the floor and the ground stopped rolling, but as was typical with earthquakes, it upset the balance enough so that walking seemed uneven and wobbly even after it had passed. Clay's first thought was that if a human who had the capacity to understand what was going on felt that way, how must the animals feel?

And where was Lilly during this?

Within a few moments, Annie was in the barn. "Clay! Everything all right out here?"

"Minor damage, stuff to clean up. As far as I can tell, no structural problems." He looked around the ceiling of the barn. "That wasn't little. How about in the house?"

"A little glass breakage, but almost everything was put away in cupboards so it's minor. How are the animals?"

"Upset. The best thing to do is leave them in the pastures. They get a little freaked out in a stall, ground moving and all."

"Clay..." Annie attempted.

"She'll come right back now," he said, as if saying it could make it happen.

An hour later, after two very minor aftershocks, Clay was saddling Streak and speaking to him softly. "I know you're a little upset, but I think we'd better go find your girl. I'm going to need you—you seem to gravitate to her and if anyone can—"

"Clay, let's leave Streak in the pasture and take the quads out," Nathaniel said from behind him.

"Quads won't work on the narrow trails where she might be, or on the downhill paths or overgrowth. You and Annie take out quads if you want to. It's almost dark and I'm not leaving her out there in the dark."

"Isn't Streak a little jumpy for this job?"

"He is, but I can handle him now," Clay said. "And he loves her. Have you seen him with Lilly? He loves her." *I love her,* Clay thought. *If there's a God, I'm going to find her and we're going to talk about the mess we're in and make sure it never happens again!*

"I'm not sure this is safe," Nathaniel said to his back as Clay tightened the cinch.

"Then shoot me in the back—that's the only way you'll stop me."

Clay went into the tack room and came out with an extra blanket, an industrial-size flashlight, rope, a couple of bottled waters and some protein bars to fill the saddlebag. He pulled on his heavily lined denim jacket and was leading Streak out of the barn doors when the sound of hooves stopped him. Nate came up to his side and they both saw Blue Rhapsody running down the road beside the east pasture, headed for the clinic barn. She was saddled. And riderless.

"Shit," Nathaniel said.

Clay put a foot in the stirrup and mounted Streak. "Call rescue. They're probably getting a million calls and are too busy for us, but call anyway. Then go out on the quads. Take blankets and water—it's cold tonight." And then he urged Streak forward. He went out of the front of the barn and down the road that Blue had just returned on.

Nathaniel let the mare into the round pen as Clay and Streak galloped down the road and away.

Clay looked at his illuminated watch; at almost eight it was dark and cold out. He wouldn't just get lucky and find her on one of the trails in the valley that Annie used for her new, young riders. He shouldn't have wasted his time—Lilly would have taken the horse onto more challenging trails. So he decided to head northeast, shining the flashlight on the trail ahead of him, scanning the sides of the trail for an unseated rider as he went. He called her name in case she was huddled in some rocky crevice or within some bushy growth to keep warm.

He'd been searching for a couple of hours when he saw her coming down the road. He shone the flashlight on her, then kicked Streak into a gallop. He stopped the colt on a dime in front of her and dismounted. She had a big goose egg on her head, grass and leaves in her hair, a large, unfashionable tear in one thigh of her jeans… and a scowl on her face.

"It just had to be you," she said, looking up at him. "Sometimes I think you're always one step ahead of me. I was planning to see you back at the barn."

He pulled off his hat. "I guess Blue dumped you in the earthquake," he said.

"I don't know where she is. We're going to have to find her."

"She went home, Lilly." He went to her. "You're hurt," he said.

She touched her head. "I fell off the horse and down the hill. I'll be fine."

"Once we get you home." He took off his jacket and draped it around her.

"I don't need your jacket," she said with an unmistakable shiver. She tried to wiggle out of it.

"Níwe!" he said in Navajo. Stop! He pulled the jacket tighter around her. He reached for one of her hands, then the other, examining the palms. "Trying to break your fall?"

"It didn't work exactly the way I wanted it to."

He lifted his dark brows and couldn't help but smile at her. "I think you're in a very bitchy mood for someone who's just been rescued."

"I guess getting tossed down a hill made me cranky. Sue me."

He pulled a bottle of water out of his saddlebag, a handkerchief out of his back pocket, and cleaned her palms. He closed up the water and stuffed the bottle in his front shirt pocket. "Isn't it amazing how there's always a bright side? Now we're going to get some things out in the open."

"Well, if you were looking for a captive audience, you managed that. But this isn't how I planned it," she said.

He wrapped the damp handkerchief around the hand that had suffered the most. "I'm sure you didn't. I bet it's been years since you've been tossed. I'm going to get on the horse and pull you up. I'll try not to hurt your hand. When I'm astride, put your boot on my foot for leverage. I have to get you back—Annie and Nathaniel are out on the quads, in the dark, looking for you. The sooner we can call them in, the better. Try to be as little trouble as possible."

She made an insulted sound and looked away. "And you try to be nicer. This may not be ideal circumstances, but I did come out to the clinic to talk to you. And to listen to you." She couldn't deny she felt good in the folds of his coat. Good and warm, and the scent of him rising to her nose was beginning to intoxicate her, just as it always had. "Does my grandfather know people were looking for me?"

"I didn't call him," Clay said. "I was anxious to find you. Now I'm anxious to get you back and call him to be sure there were no injuries at the feed store. That was a big earthquake." He put a foot in the stirrup, pulled himself up into the saddle and reached out a hand to her.

She didn't move.

"Come on," he said. "We need to get back and be sure Yaz is all right."

She sighed and put her hand into his. "Careful, please," she said.

He wrapped his hand around her wrist to avoid the cuts and scrapes on her palm. "Foot on my foot," he said.

She did so and he effortlessly lifted her onto the horse in front of him. He settled her around the horn, sitting sideways.

"There have been aftershocks," she pointed out. "How's Streak handling this?"

"He's a little jittery, but solid. Good, for Streak. I

think we're safe along the road." He turned the horse and went back toward the clinic. "Now, here's what I want to explain…

"Isabel and her family were so alien to me when I met them, I had no idea how complex they were. I mean, we have plenty of ordinary old dysfunction in the Tahoma family, but nothing that could prepare me for the Sorensons. I took the job for the exposure to other breeders and for the money, which was excellent. And she seemed a sweet woman with a cruel and domineering father, an absent mother who didn't care about her.… I had been a very long time without a woman in my life and it was natural for me to be attracted to her, to be willing to protect her. She's ten years older than I am, Lilly, and about a hundred times more screwed up. And that's comical—with my history, I should be the one messed up."

"You really don't have to make excuses for falling for her," Lilly said. "I saw her. I saw that horse trailer."

Clay smiled. Dane had suggested that the horse trailer had filled Lilly with envy. Well, small wonder—he had loved that horse trailer himself. He could live in that trailer for the rest of his life and be happy, as long as there wasn't horseshit in it. He laughed at his thought.

"Funny?" Lilly asked.

"Not at all. Damn fine trailer, isn't it? The Sorenson family wipe their asses with hundred dollar bills."

"How delightful," she said.

"Her looks and possessions haven't brought her much comfort. She…Isabel…was always at odds with her parents, especially her father. She was either in ecstasy because he praised her or in a deep depression because he was disappointed in her. This had nothing to do with me for a long time. She liked me, she seduced me, I was pretty easy prey—I was lonely and I worked hard. She asked me to live with her and I wouldn't without her father's permission, which came grudgingly. She was the one who wanted to be married, though she wouldn't visit my family on the reservation or have them at our private wedding. She wouldn't take my name. There was a long history of terrible relationships in her past and I stupidly thought that was the reason she didn't want to make a big deal out of our marriage, but it went deeper. I slowly realized that marrying a Navajo challenged her father. That was the only way she could stand up to him or get his attention. When she wanted a divorce two years later I wasn't surprised at all. But she couldn't let go."

"Ah! And was she the only one who couldn't let go?" Lilly asked.

"Yes," he answered. "Yes, she sought me out some-times, but I never went to her. That's one of the reasons this job and this move appealed to me so much—I really couldn't deal with Isabel's controlling nature, her sick relationship with her father, her manipulation of me. Lilly, I don't know what has made her the way she is—abuse, certainly. I can't explain why I was so involved with her—sucked right into the craziness, maybe. But I don't love Isabel. Now I'm not sure I ever did."

"But I heard you tell her you'd always love her!"

"Yes, I said that. If you'd just listened a second longer you would have heard the rest. I was telling her I'd always love her, care about her, but we had to move on, move away from the relationship we had, that I couldn't be there for her anymore. I had already told her there was a woman in my life. But she's always had a terrible fear of having love withdrawn from her. I was going to tell her I loved her enough to wish her well." He ground his teeth. "All that has changed now."

"Changed how?"

"I don't feel sorry for her anymore. I didn't realize how petty and selfish she could be. And why didn't I? The apple doesn't fall far from the tree. Her father is a horrible parent. Whether we like it or not, the people who raise us leave an indelible mark." He pulled Streak to a stop. He lifted Lilly's chin and turned her to face him. "Isabel is a sad and damaged woman, and I did my best to honor my commitment, Lilly. But that is far in my past. I love *you*."

"Are you sure?" she asked.

"Yes, absolutely. I'm sorry for the way she treated you. I can't say how she knew you were the woman in my life—"

Lilly laughed. "Somehow, women can just sense who their competition is."

"I can hear the horses think, but I never figured out women," he said. "I had no idea she was coming and I was telling her to go away in the nicest possible way. Once you ran from me I lost all my patience and told her to just get out of here."

"Why should I believe this, Clay?"

"There's a more urgent question," he said. "What happened to you to make you unwilling to believe me? To be tempted to throw away things that made you so happy, like our love, like Blue, like working with Annie? What the hell happened to you?"

"I just have so much pride—"

"Bullshit," he said. "Take a risk. See what happens

when you let me in, tell me the truth. So, you had a rotten romance. You mentioned it once. Is that it?"

"Bad relationship," she said with a shrug. "Painful breakup…"

"So who hasn't? I told you about mine—one when I was a kid, one more recent than that," he said. "Maybe we're both due a break."

"You might find I'm at least as screwed up as Isabel, and where would that leave you?"

"Try me," he begged.

"It was very bad," she said by way of explanation. "I was young."

He laughed lightly. "Younger than sixteen?" he asked.

She turned and looked up at him. "Thirteen," she said.

After a moment of shock, he tightened his arm around her. "Honey. I'm sorry. That's just too young for a girl to go through something like that. At least you weren't made a mother."

"But…but yes, I was. At only thirteen, a virgin who had given it up to a bad boy of eighteen, pregnant, and he ran like a fox."

He was so still that Streak stopped walking. Clay leaned down and nuzzled his cheek against hers. "Your child?" he asked in a whisper.

She looked into her lap. "I lost the baby. Probably a blessing—I wasn't ready to be a mother, obviously."

"I'm sorry, sweetheart."

"And when you came along, I wasn't ready to risk a relationship again. I feel as if I'll never be ready."

"But you were just a girl then. You're a woman now," he reassured her.

"That's what Dane said. But talk about damaged!" she said.

"You'd be surprised how many people survive things like this and go on to make better lives. People have survived so much worse—consider our ancestors."

"God, I felt like a princess, that he'd chosen me, though I had no idea how many he'd chosen before and after me. When I told him I was pregnant, he said it couldn't be his." She laughed hollowly. "As if I'd had lovers! He was the first and only! My grandfather loaded his rifle and my boyfriend ran for his life—but he'd already left me for at least a couple of girls. At only thirteen, my reputation was toast. That's when my grandpa decided we had to move, to start over. There were so many times growing up I felt that I'd lost everything— when I realized my mother left me when I was weeks old, when my grandmother died and was never coming back, when my grandfather took me away from home to try to save me from myself. And the boyfriend, denying he had any feelings for me and running from my grandfather's rifle..." She turned her head and looked up at him. "I just didn't think I could go through all that again. That's why it was so hard for me to trust."

"I'm going to find a way to show you that I'm the exception."

Tears began to roll down her cheeks. "I meant to be strong—I hate weakness. I didn't want to cry in front of you."

He wiped away the tears with the pad of his thumb. "I want you to cry *only* in front of me."

"I have been so afraid to love anyone..."

"Of course you have, but that part of your life is in

the past. And we have more important business. We have to move forward together now."

"What if love just isn't enough? What if we can't make it work?"

"Bull. We've made lots of things work," he said. "You know, one of the many reasons I couldn't be a successful husband to Isabel—she nurtured her pain. Silently. She never threw it out there and told me everything that happened to her and how she wanted to get past it—I was always fighting an invisible demon.

"So—we have our junk," he said to her. "I think one way to handle it—after we make love, when we're soft and vulnerable—we should talk. Hold each other and talk about things that bother us, worry us. I promise to be honest. I promise to be patient." He kissed her lips lightly, tenderly. Then he lifted her chin again so he could look into those haunting blue eyes. "Can you, Lilly? Can you try with me? Because I love you so much."

When she glanced away from him she saw that the Jensen Stables had come into view. She looked back. "I'm not sure," she said. "I'm still afraid."

"Of pain? Of unhappiness? Of finding your love not returned? Of being left all alone? What?"

Her mouth curved in a slight, painful smile. "Yes," she said.

He slowly closed in on her lips and covered them in a passionate kiss. Her arms found their way around him, pulling him close, her mouth moving under his. When their kiss broke, he smiled into her eyes.

"Well, my little sweetheart, be warned. I'm not giving up. I'm not letting you go. I love you, you love me and there's no way we can give up. Not now. In fact, I think we've been put through the hard times to get to this place—to find the good ones."

"I think you're probably just a fool," she told him. But she licked the taste of him off her lips and he laughed.

He nudged Streak into a nice, steady trot back to the clinic, holding her tight against him to keep her safe and warm.

Eighteen

Aiden Riordan had visited his brother, Colin, as promised, to assess his situation with the pain meds. To his enormous relief, everything seemed to be pretty manageable at the time. Oh, Colin was still quite uncomfortable and irritable, but as Aiden clearly witnessed he was doing fine with nonnarcotic pain meds, anti-inflammatory medication and lots of ice packs. His pals from his unit were available and helping him out; it all appeared to be under control. After a couple of days, Aiden left his brother in the care of his physical therapists.

A lot had happened in the three weeks since then— Virgin River and the surrounding area had been through an earthquake with damage. Luckily, no severe injuries, just a few bumps and cuts. As for Aiden, he'd been concentrating on getting himself a doctoring job in Chico, California, where he'd be making his home with his fiancée, Erin. He'd had quite a few interviews with that purpose in mind. Honestly? Although he talked to Colin at least three times a week, he'd forgotten there was anything to worry about besides the length of his recovery.

But then a call came from the Columbus, Georgia police department. Colin Riordan had given Aiden's name as his contact. According to the police, Colin had been caught in a DEA sting on a local physician who wrote willy-nilly prescriptions for narcotic drugs. Or, maybe not so willy-nilly; Dr. Feelgood was a known dealer of prescription drugs and the DEA had been staking him out for a long time with the complete cooperation and assistance of the local police. The arrest went down just as Colin was leaving the doctor's office with a prescription for OxyContin in his grip.

Apparently Colin was no longer able to get his drugs from the Army doctor and had taken his habit downtown. The Army wasn't going to like that.

Word traveled fast in the Riordan family; the brothers were thicker than thieves. On this occasion, however, Aiden decided to act independently. He even talked it over with Erin. "He's in trouble, he's in pain, he's not healed yet. Nothing about this is going to go well. He needs help. I'm going alone," he told Erin. "I'm going to find him the best possible help—physical therapy along with rehab. And if he's not completely cooperative, I'm turning the family loose on him."

"Wow," she said. "Remind me to never mess with the Riordan boys."

"You know what? I bet he was onto me the last visit. He knew Patrick called us all and complained about the pain meds. He toughed it out for a few days and the second I was gone, he cut loose. Well, there's no getting out of this one."

"Sounds like you could be gone awhile," she said.

"Long enough to be sure he's committed. There's a really good place in Arizona, close enough for me to check on him."

"You planning to keep this from your brothers?" she asked.

"Oh, hell, no! Once Colin is pretty much locked up and in a program I'll call everyone, even my mother and George. But a family reunion right now? Colin might not go for that—in fact, it might not be the best thing for him. I don't want to push him too far. I want him off the drugs."

"I don't really feel like I know Colin," Erin said. "Your other brothers have been so easy to know, but Colin…well, he's fun like the others, but holds back in a way. He's the different one."

"He's not much fun right now, that's for sure," Aiden said. But he'd been caught by the police and there was no way out. He was naked. Exposed. Fortunately for Colin, the judge had a son serving in Afghanistan. He released Colin to Aiden for treatment and suspended his sentence.

Aiden managed to get to Columbus quickly and without anyone else in the family knowing. He transported Colin to Tucson, but it wasn't easy. Aiden had the assistance of a little Valium to grease the skids; he wished he'd taken Patrick's panicked phone call several weeks ago more seriously. He wished he'd managed to see the real Colin during his own previous two-day visit. The guy was strung out on one of the most addictive prescription pain meds on the market. He'd been doubling up; his Army doc had given him something for sleep, completely unaware of the narcotic pain med. And Colin was still in pain—lots of things hurt.

Before they checked into the treatment center, Aiden confronted him one last time. "You want off this shit and a new start?" Aiden asked him.

"How? I can't sleep three hours in a row. My body hurts so bad it's unimaginable! You got any ideas that aren't going to kill me?"

"I know you aren't going to believe this for a good three weeks, but the answer is in getting off narcs and on the right meds. There will still be some pain, but most of what you've been feeling lately is your body's response to the absence of drugs. It's gonna get better, I promise."

"Have you told them all? Are they all on their way?"

"No. After you're settled in I'll call everyone and explain. That's the first they'll even know where you are. All you have to do is select who you want to take calls from while you're in treatment." Aiden shrugged. "You can say no one—you won't be punished. You'll have to talk to them eventually, but if you want to wait until you're better, that's reasonable."

"I don't want to do this," Colin said.

"Who would? It's gonna be a big step, a hard step. You won't believe this now, but you're lucky—you haven't been on drugs half your life. In a few weeks you'll feel like a new man—"

"A new man full of broken bones, titanium rods and screws?"

"I have you set up," Aiden said. "I know—you think you're the first guy to have a bad accident, take a lot of painkillers and wind up in treatment, but guess what? They've seen you before. You're going to treat the addiction and the rehab at the same time and you *are* going to get better. All you have to do is go with the program."

"The Army isn't covering it, so who is? You?"

"It's me today, but after I make a few phone calls…"

"I don't want to be into all of you for this!" he railed. "I'll pay you back! I don't want you guys doing this!"

"Whatever floats your boat," Aiden said. "How about we sort that out after you're discharged? Right now you have two choices—this place or jail. What's your pleasure?" And then he smiled.

"Arrggghhh," Colin growled.

"Just get in there, will you?" Aiden said. "I'm so ready for you to be someone else's problem!"

"And I'm so ready to be the hell away from you," Colin said, as though he'd completely forgotten who had the Valium that had made the trip bearable.

Aiden's first phone call was to Erin. "He's in," he said. "I hope they have really good locks on the doors. He's real unstable."

"You think he'll stay?" Erin asked.

"We're not going to know the end of that story till the end of that story," Aiden replied.

For the third time in as many months, a row of pickup trucks and a bunch of men gathered along the road into Virgin River. Clay Tahoma and Lilly Yazhi were riding horses from the Jensen Clinic along the road for several miles when they spotted the road construction site.

It had been a few weeks since the earthquake and what little damage it had done had been repaired. Also, the damage to Lilly's love affair with Clay. It turned out he was right—talking when they were soft, pliable, vulnerable and grateful seemed to work wonders for a relationship. In the time since that earthquake, they'd spent a lot of time with Nate and Annie—some of it mending their fences and some of it just enjoying couple time. Lilly was so relieved to be working at the clinic and spending what time she could spare with the horses and the most important people in her life.

There was a lot of noisy activity along the side of the road. Lilly was astride Blue but Clay rode one of the calmer Jensen horses. They approached the construction site slowly and cautiously, making sure their mounts weren't overwhelmed by the people, the noise, the confusion.

Clay was the first to dismount, leading his horse toward the men. Jack Sheridan was standing at the rear of the group of men. He turned and greeted Clay with a handshake. "Hey, haven't seen you around in a while. I hope that doesn't mean damage from the earthquake."

"No—everything was fine at the clinic. How about at the bar?"

"Some broken glass, but nothing too serious."

"What's going on here?" Lilly asked.

"Well," he said, rubbing a hand along the back of his neck. "This seems to be a weak spot in the road—not only weak, but on a curve with a drop-off. We've had more than one vehicle hit this soft shoulder and slide down the hill. Even had a school bus go down—fulla kids. Me and Preacher have written the county and highway department a bunch of times asking for some reinforcement and guardrails, but we always get denied." He shrugged. "We're a real small, unincorporated town without much traffic. We're pretty low on the priority list right now, during a recession."

Clay lifted his chin at all the action. "So what's this?" he asked.

"Well, remember that old woman who died—the one we had that estate sale for? She left a trust for the town. There's been a lot of disagreement about what to do with it, but she was always about taking care of the town. Seemed like it made sense for us to do it ourselves before someone gets killed on this curve." Jack Sheridan grinned. "We like 'em smiling when they come into our town."

"How'd you get all this heavy equipment?" Clay asked.

"Friends of friends made a lot of phone calls. We rented it. We're going to have ourselves a concrete and stone reinforced shoulder and a nice long guardrail. We could use a wider road all the way into town, but this spot is the worst. Hey, it's good to see you two riding together! Didn't I hear you'd had a falling-out of some kind?"

"Us?" Lilly asked. "Must've been some gossip."

"So—you're tight?" Jack asked.

"We're *dating,*" Lilly said. "In the Native community, you're not *tight* until the families sit down together. We have a lot of tradition to work through."

"And after you work through your tradition?" Jack asked.

"I don't know," Lilly answered with a shrug, looking to Clay for answers.

"Well…then we'll be engaged," Clay answered, smiling back at Lilly. "And married after that. She has to agree to have me. It could take some time, but I'm confident I can trick her into it."

"Good," Jack said. "Men who come to this town drop like flies. I'd hate to see one get away."

Clay reached up to one of Lilly's hands as she held the reins. "I never even struggled."

It was in the deep purple shadows of night, when Clay and Lilly lay entwined in each other's arms, that the fullness of what they had grown together became almost overwhelming to Lilly. As she ran her small hands over his beautiful bronze body, she whispered, "I love you. I find it so hard to remember why I was angry, why I feared trust so much."

He pulled her on top of him so he could look into those unforgettable blue eyes. "Have we put those old demons to rest?"

"I think so, yes."

"You realize that if we're together a long time, and that's what I want for us, there will be issues here and there? Things that have to be stared in the face, Lilly."

"What kind of issues? Do you plan to tell your ex-wife you'll always love her again?" She smiled at him so he'd know she was teasing.

But Clay didn't smile. "I won't make that mistake, but you can count on me to screw up along the way. I'm flawed."

"You're strong," she said, touching his beautiful face.

"I'm not strong enough to sleep alone again. I need you in my life. And I need your strength with mine. We have to make a promise, Lilly—when trouble comes, we'll face it together. Not alone and in silence."

"Promise," she said.

"I have wanted to talk to you about something—about letting me take you back to the reservation. I want you to meet my family."

She smiled at him. "I didn't think I'd ever go back. I take it there's a lot of family to meet?"

"There is, but that will have to wait for another event to pass. My sister tells me our parents are coming to Grace Valley for Thanksgiving."

"And will I meet them then?"

"They would like that, I'm sure. But first, if you agree, I'd like to ask Yaz if he'll sit down with my family."

She lifted an eyebrow. "What are you asking, Clay? You'd better be clear."

"If you agree, I want you to be my wife."

She shook her head. "You have a son. He'll have to give his consent."

"Oh, that's not going to be a problem. He congratulated me on having enough intelligence to work things out with you."

"You have to ask him, just the same," Lilly said.

"I'll do that. Now, what about Yaz?"

"I'm sure he'll be very agreeable. And relieved. He was afraid I'd be an old maid and he'd be stuck with me forever. But what of your family, Clay? They're very traditional. Will they find me acceptable?"

"They will—not that it matters. Lilly, you are the finest woman I've ever known and I want you for my wife if you'll have me. No matter how the families feel."

She gave him a short kiss. "I think if I say no, you'll be a terrible pest. But I would like to do something special for your parents. I'll think of what that can be."

"You're very sweet," he said. "Now that the important details are settled, why don't you go put the opera back on. Crank it up nice and loud." He grinned. "I *like* opera."

* * *

Lilly had been very young when she last participated in traditional Hopi ceremonies and since she was a child then, she had stayed on the sidelines. She had several long talks with Clay and with Ursula Toopeek about the old traditions. She didn't see her future as being enmeshed in the old ways, but she wanted her future in-laws to be clear that she respected them and their traditions.

She had to go to a great deal of trouble to find her props. When a Hopi maiden wanted to show respect for the traditions, she dressed in natural fibers, skins, feathers and beads. For a vegetarian like Lilly to wear the skins of animals was a huge compromise—she limited herself to the boots and wore a woven blanket around her shoulders. But when it came to the traditional cake she would present to the mother of the groom, rather than the ceremonial mush or wheat, she chose a pineapple upside-down cake, which made Clay laugh. "I think they'll begin to understand you, Lilly—you're not exactly going all the way."

"It's a brave new world, Clay," she said with a smile. "Will your mother understand?"

"I don't think she'll have any doubts."

On the morning of Thanksgiving there was a light snow, but the weather was agreeable. Yaz was told to be at the Toopeek home early in the day. Clay and Lilly took horses by trailer to Grace Valley, left the trailer in a wide space in the road at the bottom of the hill that led to the Toopeek home. While Lilly wore her traditional Hopi dress and blanket, Clay was clad in his usual jeans, boots and heavy suede jacket.

"Wish me luck," Lilly said to her intended.

"You don't need luck, baby. All you need today is good balance."

The Toopeek household was crammed full; their eldest, Tanya, was home from college to spend time with her family, and Yaz was present, as was Gabe. The older men were engaged in a serious game of chess while Tom Toopeek had been put in charge of setting the table. Cooking was in full swing and the women—Ursula, her daughter, her mother and mother-in-law were all in the kitchen, chattering and laughing as they crowded around the stove and worktable.

Ursula kept looking out the window.

"Relax, Ursula," her mother said. "They'll be here soon enough!"

"I know," Ursula said. "I'm so anxious for you to meet Lilly, that's all."

And then, finally, at about eleven in the morning, Ursula called her mother out of the kitchen. "Mother, come here! There's someone here to see you!"

Mrs. Tahoma went to the door, expecting her son and his intended, but nothing prepared her for what she saw. Coming up the road toward the house were two riders on horseback. She recognized Clay at once, but was stunned by the sight of a young Native American woman riding beside him, dressed in traditional ceremonial clothing, holding something in her hands in front of her, directing the horse with only her knees and one hand on the reins.

Mrs. Tahoma stepped outside and began to walk toward them.

At Ursula's direction, the rest of the family crowded behind her mother, all the men and children watching.

When Clay and Lilly were near, Clay dismounted first. He reached up to take the cake out of Lilly's hands while she dismounted. When she was on her feet, Clay gave her back the cake and held the reins of their horses while Lilly approached his mother. When Lilly stood in front of her in all her Hopi glory, she passed the cake into Clay's mother's hands. "Mrs. Tahoma, I've brought you a cake that I made myself and hope you'll accept it as a gesture of my respect and love for a new family." She smiled and said, "It's not the usual thing, but I hope you'll accept it, anyway."

Mrs. Tahoma took the betrothal cake, looking down at it.

Lilly caught sight of her grandfather standing behind Clay's mother with the men. There was a smile on his face and he seemed to stand a bit taller, proud of her for embracing even a small piece of their tradition.

All Mrs. Tahoma had to do to seal their engagement with her family's approval was to accept the cake. But she leaned forward and put a kiss on each of Lilly's cheeks. And she said,

"I am honored, daughter. Deeply honored."

* * * * *

Acknowledgments

I'm deeply grateful for the dedicated assistance given to me by Scott Lampert, all-around horse expert, farrier and creator of www.ONTRACKEQUINE.com, a sophisticated program used by horse professionals, owners and breeders to assure peak equine performance. This story could not have been told without your help.

Special thanks to Sean Vasquez, Native American musician and actor. Through your eyes I could better envision the Native American characters in this story.

For this story as for almost every story I write, special thanks to Michelle Mazzanti for early reading and research assistance. I just couldn't get to the end of a book without your input and help.

I am indebted to Kate Bandy and Sharon Lampert. Without your continual loyalty and support I would be lost.

My heartfelt gratitude to Ing Cruz for creating and managing Jack's Bar online, where hundreds of Virgin River readers exchange book news. (http://groups.yahoo.com/group/RobynCarr_Chatgroup/)

Thanks to Rebecca Keene for early readings of this and many manuscripts; her feedback is incredibly valuable.

Thanks to everyone at the Nancy Berland Public Relations Agency for the support and for always watching my back. Jeanne Devon of NBPR, thanks for the hours of reading and critiquing—your feedback is a tremendous help.

And as always, thank you to Liza Dawson of Liza Dawson Associates and to Valerie Gray, editorial director of MIRA Books, two of the toughest readers in publishing. Thank you both for being relentless, tireless, devoted perfectionists. Every push makes each book a little better and I owe you. This is always a team effort and I couldn't have a better team!